Barbara

a love story

✦ power
✦✦ passion
✦✦✦ regrets

Linda Carlino

VeritasPublishing
8 Vane Road Barnard Castle
County Durham DL12 8AQ
England

First published in 2008 titled A Matter of Pride

ISBN: 978-0-9555980-5-0

Also by Linda Carlino:
A Spanish Hapsburg Trilogy:
    "That Other Juana"
    "A Matter of Pride"
    "Wives & Other Women"

VeritasPublishing

Barbara

In 1557 a prematurely aged, ill, and very irritable Charles V (H.R.E.) retires to a small isolated monastery in western Spain. He is burdened by his failures and unresolved political, military and religious problems. His only comfort and solace are his memories and reveries of his much loved mistress Barbara.Blomberg who bore him a son who became Europe's celebrated and idolized, Don Juan of Austria. And his revelations of his lifelong relationship with Barbara are revealing and make a wonderful touching; and emotional love story.

Historical Background

In the early part of the sixteenth century the Holy Roman Emperor Maximilian died and Henry VIII of England, Francis I of France, and Carlos I of Spain (son of Queen Juana and King Philip) competed for the crown.

It was Carlos, the emperor's grandson who, with financial bribery, prevailed upon the German princes to elect him Charles V, Holy Roman Emperor. But it was a poisoned chalice he had bought; not only had he to deal with an often rebellious confederacy of German states there were many other more serious challenges.

Throughout his years as emperor the eastern countries of Europe were constantly menaced by the infidel intent on pushing the Ottoman Empire's borders as far west as possible, and he had to prevent France from extending her powers in Italy. Both threats required an armed response which needed money, far more money than even the bountiful New World could supply. Carlos had to borrow hugely from the German bankers, bankrupting Spain.

As the head of the family he also deemed it an unswerving duty to arrange international marriage contracts to ensure the enduring power of the Hapsburg dynasty and to increase its influence wherever possible.

This was also a period of religious unrest across the whole of Europe. Reformation movements, notably the one inspired by Martin Luther, were springing up everywhere threatening the Holy Mother Church and all good Christian souls.

It was little wonder then that Carlos abdicated, at the age of fifty-six, defeated both physically and mentally, choosing his brother Ferdinand to assume the role of emperor and handing the thrones of Spain and Naples to his son Felipe (Philip II).

Acknowledgements

Once again my thanks to all those in Madrid without whose help this book would not have been possible, in particular Antonio Machín García, Miguel Ruiz-Borrego y Arabal, and Josep M. Sanmartí.

My thanks also to the Biblioteca Nacional and the Casino of Madrid for the use of their wonderful libraries and archives, and the British Library and the Durham County Library especially the Barnard Castle branch, for all their help.

I am indebted as ever to my dear friend Lucía Alvarez de Toledo for her continuing advice and ideas.

A very special thank you goes to my friend Liz Angel for giving her time unselfishly and unreservedly to proof-reading (any remaining errors are mine) and to the lady members of B.C.G.C. for their encouragement and support.

And finally to my dear husband Charles, my boundless love and gratitude.

1557

February

Welcome to Yuste

I

A couple of sturdy stable lads, probably in their early forties, emerged from a gaggle of giggling village girls gathered on the far side of the gateway to the courtyard leaving them blushing, hands to their mouths unable to hide their embarrassment, their delight.

"What do you think, then? What's our chances?"

"I tell you, Alonso, we might just be lucky," Manuel the slightly taller lad clapped his friend on the shoulder.

"I hope so. It was a right washout in Jarandilla. Weeks of absolutely nowt."

"You're right, there was nothing doing there at all; a sour-faced lot they were. But now, well, this lot aren't half bad."

"Trouble is they stink."

"So would you if you had to live in the same room as your animals during the winter, you daft fool. We're the lucky ones, see, sleeping in sweet hay. They get to sleep on straw next to the cow shyte and them rank goats. Least that's what my nose tells me."

"Should be alright then so long as we stop outdoors, eh, Manuel?"

"My thinking exactly."

They tugged their coarse linen smocks down over their brown, ill-cut, but sturdy breeches, tightened their belts, readjusted their woollen coats, and pulled their caps over finger-combed hair. Finally they spat on the toes of their leather buskins and wiped them down the backs of their legs.

"How are we? Both presentable? Good, let's go," and Alonso led the way past the huge wooden gates, which had been thrown wide open in welcome, and across the cobbles to join other lads standing at the ready.

"Hell's fire, did you feel that, Alonso? Like somebody left a door open and an icy blast blew in."

"Nah, not me, mate. You sickenin' for somethin'? You'll soon warm up when you get yourself between a pair of soft thighs."

You must forgive our hot-blooded lads. It would appear they have so few pleasures. I hope our presence has not cooled their ardour.

Welcome to Yuste, to this splendid monastery of San Jerónimo. There could not be a more peaceful setting.

So, you are here to discover all you can about Carlos, the man who until recently wore the crowns of the Holy Roman Empire and Spain. As you so rightly said everybody seems to have heard of the emperor and king, but what do they actually know of the man himself?

I will do everything I can to help you. I will be your guide taking you, as an unseen observer, into the king's presence, seeing into the hearts and minds of all those we meet. I hope, too, to be a source of useful information.

You agree never to ask questions nor seek other avenues of enquiry, always accepting my judgement and discretion? Good! Then we can begin what I promise will be a most interesting experience.

But first, a word or two about Yuste. The Jerónimos order has been here for over a century and these days it is a wealthy

10

community, owning vast acres of good land in the valley and with orchards, olive groves and woodlands aplenty on the surrounding hills.

Not so long ago they built that beautiful second cloister on the left, and with these charming little apartments for the king, his little palace, so cunningly added to the right, the monastery has become a veritable jewel nestling in an emerald sea of evergreen oaks and chestnuts. And on our far left there is yet another equally necessary extension, the stables; you can just see into the yard through the archway.

Why Carlos should have chosen to retire here no one can really be sure but it certainly was not to become a monk that is for certain, much to the dismay of the prior. And when you consider the magnificent palaces Carlos has been accustomed to over the years, and the spectacular palace he built in Granada, this hardly seems an appropriate home either in size or location. It is nothing more than two floors, both identical, each having four rooms and a central corridor.

Its very remoteness may have been its attraction. And, come to think of it, now that Carlos has abdicated, this remoteness may well be a blessing to others; it will prevent his interfering in the affairs of state.

While we are still waiting, and it is not too cold a February day to be standing about, I will give you a little background information about this man, Emperor Carlos V. He is almost fifty-seven and has been a widower for seventeen years. He is a man prematurely old, plagued by illness, weighed down by defeat, who has come to spend the remainder of his days here in this quiet hilly corner of southwest Spain.

11

He was born in Flanders and by the time he was seventeen he was king of Spain and its vast dominions, had inherited Flanders and the Low Countries and the title of archduke of Austria. Shortly after becoming king of Spain he was elected to, or bought as some would say, myself included, the Crown of the Holy Roman Empire.

But listen. Yes. The bells. The bells are announcing his arrival. He is here. He has come to his place of peace and retirement at last. Did you ever hear such a merry ringing? Reaching out to the furthest parts of the valley, calling to everyone, *Rejoice, for your emperor and king is here amongst you!* Forgive me; the excitement of the moment caused me to lose my composure.

Now see, the chapel doors are opening and here come the friars in their habits, the white robes and brown scapulas of the Jerónimos. Let us move aside, over there towards the stables. Yes, this is an excellent vantage point; we can see and hear everything from here.

A cavalcade of about fifty horses ribboned its way up the wooded hill, curling itself around the final bends of the stony track, passing the local folk gathered to catch a glimpse of a person they had been told was their king. As it entered the courtyard its dignified shape fell into a tangle of shuffling indecision. After faltering and circling, a small group of riders guided the two-horse litter towards the entrance to the chapel.

The prior, with all the solemnity and dignity he had practised for weeks, adjusted his brown hooded cloak and approached the litter, a cleverly adapted wooden chest, which sheltered his most illustrious guest.

A gruff whisper from behind Alonso and Manuel urged them into action. "Right lads; set to it. Manuel, Alonso steady that horse at the back there. Get the halters."

"We're going. We're going! He doesn't have to tell us everything; think we didn't know our jobs! God knows we've been doin' it for years. Tries your patience, it does. Anyway, which of them lasses are you going for, Alonso?"

"By now I don't care. You know what them sailors was always sayin'; any port in a storm. Whoa there, me old beauty. I got you." He stroked the weary animal, calming it with a voice he reserved exclusively for his horses.

"Quija'a, Quija'a!" Growls of petulance, unintelligible splutterings, found their way out from deep within the darkness of the litter's protective wood and leather hood.

Quijada brought his horse close.

Ah, yes, when the king is speaking it demands all your concentration. Let me explain; his speech has never been very good, you will soon see why; the protruding jaw, the fact that he cannot close his mouth. He is also tongue-tied. Unfortunately matters are worse these days since losing most of his teeth. So he is almost impossible to understand without a lot of effort on the listener's part.

Quijada leaned down from his horse to speak to the monk. "His majesty needs a few moments to himself, good prior," he explained as Alonso and Manuel turned the horses to take the litter up the steep cobbled ramp that had been purposely designed to bring the infirm emperor directly to the first floor of his new home.

Quijada dismounted, handing the reins to waiting lads, then strode up the slope to the porch. Lean and still remarkably agile, it is only the pewter grey of his hair and short beard that remind those about him of his three score years.

Alonso and Manuel steadied the horses. Two attendants in their livery of dark green tunics and breeches hurriedly set about removing the litter's heavy wooden cover and hood.

"God da' it, watch the leg, you 'iserable cur." This and other curses filled the air as Carlos was lifted from his cocoon of velvet-covered eiderdowns and fur-lined rugs. Undaunted,

13

the two strong young men continued the process of transferring their master from the litter to his chair and swiftly wheeling him indoors, away from the icy winter air and into a room with furnace-like heat blasting forth from hearths and braziers.

Briefly, while we have a moment, Carlos's whole life has been one of continuous struggle: protecting all his inheritances, fighting the Turk, protecting his beloved Catholicism from the threat of the ever growing Protestantism, and trying to keep Germany united. And if this were not enough, there have been the perennial wars with France.

So here we are, almost forty years on and little, if anything, has been resolved. Indeed everything remains the same except that he has decided to abdicate. And, I might add, Spain is bankrupt. Spanish blood and Spanish treasure have both been squandered on ventures in which, in my opinion, there was never anything to be gained and in which so much has been lost. I repeat; Spain is bankrupt – in debt to the tune of seven million gold *ducados*.

Now, on that happy note, shall we follow the others?

II

As the little entourage entered the salon they were welcomed by a small and plump man bent with age and years of endless letter writing. This was Gaztelu, the king's secretary, sent on ahead to ensure all was in readiness. He shuffled to Quijada's side carefully keeping his back to the king, peering to right and left before deftly drawing a letter from the wide sleeves of his secretary's black gown, whispering, "This one is addressed to you; it was in with the others. There was no time to give it to you before I left; my apologies."

14

Gaztelu's permanently squinting eyes, the result of decades of laborious penmanship for royal letters and documents, looked up into Quijada's seeking some explanation. He knew already that there would be none, there never was. "Thank you. Do not concern yourself, my friend." Quijada glanced at the writing, recognising the firm hand of Barbara. He slipped it inside his jerkin; it could wait until later.

Carlos smiled up at him from his chair where he sat looking most unemperor-like; stooped and worn, his face long and crumpled with tired rheumy blue eyes and grizzled white hair and beard; an old man, almost as broad as he was tall, muffled from head to toe in quilted black velvets and dark brown furs.

He hunched his awkward bulk forward, his body a witness to years of gross overindulgence in food and drink.

"You may join me in a toast."

"Apart from the fact that your doctor has strongly advised against your drinking, you now invite us, or I should say, command us to join you in this wilful ignoring of the doctor's warnings," Quijada lectured.

I must tell you about Quijada. He had the misfortune to be the youngest son of an honourable family, receiving nothing more than the family name. He entered the army and distinguished himself throughout his military career, eventually becoming aide-de-camp to Carlos.

He was recently recalled to service leaving his luxurious days of retirement and his lovely wife Magdalena, who is quite beautiful and many years his junior, to arrange Carlos's journey here; no easy task I can tell you. The poor fellow first had to ride post for four days to get to the port to meet him; no mean feat at his age. He has ridden countless miles at the side of the king's litter, and walked almost as many guiding it over rough narrow mountain tracks, through wind, rain, and withering sun, forever vigilant for his

15

master's safety and wellbeing. And still he cannot return home, for now he is retained as the king's major-domo.

You may at first be shocked at Quijada's familiarity with the king, but as a brother-in-arms, close friend and companion of nearly forty years, he has been allowed to be absolutely frank about everything; and, you will find, he usually is.

Carlos wrapped his two swollen hands around his goblet, "One of the finer things of life, my friends, iced beer," he gulped down the golden liquid. "So, we have made it at last; my thanks to you Quijada. The journey would have been impossible without you; everything from start to finish; comfortable lodgings, getting help from here, there and everywhere. And what about getting us over that mountain pass? At one point I thought we would never make it. I admit it was my own fault, Quijada, no need to look so cross. I mistakenly thought it would be quicker. The blasted litter was useless too and the chair. Damn it, Gaztelu, I ended up being carried on some evil-smelling backs." He tugged at his secretary's sleeve, "There I was, strapped into somebody's old farmhouse chair, tied to some fellow's back, being humped and bumped with no idea where in hell I was going. Last pass I ever go over, except for the one into Heaven, eh?" Carlos laughed.

Gaztelu smiled and nodded, he had heard it all before; so many times.

Carlos tilted his head back and poured the rest of his drink into his mouth, much of it spilling down the beard adorning his large Hapsburg chin.

"Quijada; that was a damn good job you did at Jarandilla. More beer," he demanded, wiping the dribbles from his beard with his quilted sleeve.

"My lord, may I remind you that it is most unwise for you to drink …" Quijada began.

"Of course you may, but I shall reply that in the first place I have had a trying day which has given me a great thirst."

16

"What an exaggeration! You have only travelled six miles, and you all the while in your bed of downy cushions!"

"That is beside the point. In the second place, I feel it right and proper to toast our safe arrival at our new home. In the third place, I am the king therefore I decide what, when, and wherefore. So no more arguments! More beer, I said."

It was no sooner poured than downed. "Now, having satisfied that need the second of my priorities will be dealt with. Lads, where are you? Take me to the lavatory. Quijada you may inform the good prior that I am almost ready to attend his service of welcome."

It was pleasing to hear Carlos give due recognition of Quijada's worth. What a wretched time he had at Jarandilla. It is only a small village and to have had over a hundred people descend on it, well you can imagine the pandemonium that caused. He had to find accommodation for everyone, often against fierce opposition from the locals. The poor man spent most of his time ploughing to and fro through ankle-deep mud, dealing with the quarrelsome retainers and villagers; an endless nightmare. Then would you believe it, the king sent him chasing off to his home in Villagarcia to dismantle a stove to have it brought here, where it now resides in the royal lavatory to provide extra warmth. One must have one's creature comforts.

You are already finding it easier to understand Carlos? Good; it will make everything so much easier for us.

But let us go into the chapel and wait there. I hope you will not find it too chilly after this heat.

III

The chapel sparkled with a hundred flickering candles. Carlos was brought in and seated beneath a canopy bearing his coat of arms. He gazed up at the painting over the altar at the top of a steep flight of fourteen steps; *La Gloria* which had been specially commissioned. There he was alongside his beloved wife Isabel, both in their white shrouds, and just to their right was their son Felipe. All three were in the company of angels in the Heavens reaching up in prayer and adoration to the Holy Trinity. It was perfect, quite perfect.

Listen to the choir. That is the very Te Deum composed and sung for one of his forebears in Flanders many, many years ago. Which reminds me, I wonder how the new choristers are settling in; not everyone was happy about this 'invasion' of outsiders. But it had to be, Carlos is determined to have the best voices around him.

But this is everything it should be. Such peace and tranquillity; the king should be content here.

When the service had ended the friars would not suffer Carlos to leave before each and every one had been introduced to him and they were determined that they would not be denied this favour by any of his retinue. Carlos, still in obvious good humour, allowed them all to kiss his hand.

Quijada scowled his impatience, "I pray to Heaven that his majesty may tolerate these friars as well in the future as he seems to now. For my part I find them importunate," he shook his head, "but then ignorant people often are."

"You were never one to suffer fools gladly," smiled Gaztelu patting the major-domo's arm in a gesture of sentiments mutually shared. "I also know that you do not hold these monks in very high esteem."

"You are right. You know as well as I that these men of God did not want the king to live here. It was not him they wanted, it was his *money*! They did everything in their power to delay progress on the building, desperately hoping there would be a change of mind, and that instead of royal apartments there would be new and more comfortable accommodation for themselves."

"I do remember some controversy. Well, well. But we have got him here despite all the setbacks. And the last of the retiring servants have now gone?"

"Yes, there were men weeping with sheer joy at finally receiving their wages and able, at last, to return to their homeland. And I can tell you there were a few tears amongst those chosen to continue to serve Carlos, without the immediate prospect of seeing any money at all."

"Quijada, you are a hard man."

"Hard? Maybe so, but an honest one. I love my master better than a brother but I refuse to pretend to be blind or deaf. The continuing embarrassment of it! The king has to go a-begging week after week for the wherewithal to settle the months of unpaid staff wages. I thank God that the regent, his daughter Juana, has finally managed to persuade someone to take yet more promissory notes."

He felt the bulge of the still unread letter and the thought occurred that while some were made to wait for months there was one, a certain lady, who had to ask but once.

Reminiscing

I

Good morning, and welcome to the king's bedchamber. You are shocked to find Carlos sitting here still in his nightshirt and night cap and not yet dressed? That comes later in his daily routine.

Carlos has had his chicken and milk pottage, heavily laced with spices and sugar, and well washed down with beer. A novel breakfast would you say? It is of his own inventing and so far as I know he is the only one ever to have sampled or enjoyed such a gastronomic treat.

The elderly priest you see at his side is Brother Regla his confessor. He has just finished leading him through his prayers. He is a Jerónimo like the friars here, but is not one of their company. I find him an interesting man, a strange mixture of humility and self-righteousness; it is so easy for someone to be misled by those compassionate eyes. I apologise, it is not for me to pass judgement.

He is the son of a poor Aragonese peasant. He spent much of his childhood outside a convent gate, not begging for food, no, he went begging for books. For books! Now is that not fascinating? To cut a long story short the monks educated him then found him a position with a rich family to accompany the son to university. Perhaps you are familiar with this not uncommon practice? Naturally Regla did more studying than his student master, and that does not come as a surprise I am sure, and was soon reading Greek and Hebrew.

Later on he joined the order of San Jerónimo and recently was commanded to come here to Yuste. He protested that he was unworthy. So many of these priests make the same protestations; even the famous Cisneros in his day insisted on his own unworthiness to Queen Isabel. Carlos, however, was as determined as his grandmother Isabel before him, and in each case the men of God had to yield to those with the greater earthly power. And I can tell you that the brethren here, not least the prior, are not best pleased with his presence.

And now to add to the poor chap's feelings of unworthiness and general discomfort he is made to sit the whole time whenever he is in the presence of the king. This is something quite unacceptable for it flies in the face of all protocol. Naturally he finds it excruciatingly embarrassing every time someone enters the room. Carlos, for his part, finds all this most amusing. He has such a novel sense of humour!

But the room fascinates you I see. Not the style of decoration that most would choose. Perhaps words like gloomy, sombre, even macabre spring to mind? The choice of black velvet for wall and bed hangings and window curtains is not to everyone's liking, certainly not to mine, but the king chose black because he says he is in mourning for his mother, Queen Juana, who died two years ago; may God rest her soul and keep her in His Glory.

If you ask me, Carlos is simply trying to salve his conscience. Incredible, but believe me when I tell you that not only was there no state funeral for her royal highness but for the small ceremony she was accorded not even her granddaughter showed up and she was living but a few miles away in Valladolid.

Ha! It makes me laugh! I hope I do not offend you, but this display of apparent love for his mother does not impress me for one moment; a veritable mockery of the word. Oh that he could have shown her but an ounce of compassion while yet she lived, rather than to have had her held prisoner for nigh on half a century.

You find it difficult to believe? Sadly it is only too true.

Many reasons, and excuses, have been expounded over the years. But let me put this to you. Let us suppose that you are the king but the law of the land says you may only rule alongside your mother the queen. In addition it has been made manifest that the majority of the people have a great deal of affection for your mother and harbour not a little resentment against you and those you have brought with you from a foreign country. So, you are in an awkward situation I grant you but those are the conditions; you and your mother must reign jointly.

Now for the good news; your mother has no desire to rule! Indeed she wishes to continue her life retired from the world, something she had begun when her husband died, but which then unfortunately changed to a life of confinement imposed on her by her father. But we will ignore that for the moment. To continue, your mother, the queen, says she is more than content for you to rule. What do you do then? What anyone would do for their mother? You would ensure that the palace she lives in meets the necessary requirements of a queen, a home offering all the comforts you would want for your mother. Of course you would!

But Carlos did not. Instead his lady mother had to endure over forty years of indignity and cruelty; suffering alone, friendless, a victim of scandalous inhumanity. Carlos, her son, the child of her womb was guilty of … of … I beg your pardon.

There you have it then; this very man you see before you who has just finished his prayers and has furnished his bedroom in a show of mourning is responsible for those forty and more years of torment.

Some said that the queen was mad. I tell you, if you only knew the entire story your response could be no other than who would not be mad? I will say no more for the moment.

Ah! Here comes Giovanni Torriano the mathematician, clockmaker, and inventor extraordinary. He is here for his regular morning meeting with Carlos. That is fortunate. It will give me some time to compose myself. I really must try harder to control my emotions.

II

There was a gentle knocking at the door.

Carlos sat up straight in his chair, his face brightening. "Come."

A middle-aged gentleman entered, bowed then with ponderous steps crossed the room. He straightened his heavy surcoat at his neck and shoulders then returned his right hand to support something concealed in his left sleeve.

Torriano was of medium stature and build, quite ordinary in fact; it was his face that set him apart. He was always deep in thought, his brows knitted as if constantly plagued by problems, his dark and beady eyes darting here and there as if seeking the solutions. His narrow lips, more used to being

23

pulled and chewed as answers to teasing questions were grappled with, had stretched themselves into something akin to a smile.

"Good morning Torriano, and how are you? I trust you slept well? Good, good," Carlos did not wait for a reply. "Before we discuss anything else you must take a look at these small pocket clocks. I wonder if simply, like me, they are the victims of all this travelling, or have they always been bloody useless."

"My lord?" Torriano was taken aback at having his workmanship questioned.

"Well, take a look at them man," Carlos tapped his puffy fingers on the table making the four small clocks jump. "See how each one has a damned different time, and I am sure I had them all set the same last night. These blasted fingers do little to help," he glared accusingly at his swollen, misshapen hands.

"The rough journey could be a reason, my lord." His voice was quiet and sympathetic like that of a patient teacher, "Another could be that you take these delicate mechanisms apart and reassemble them so often you may be exacerbating any problem; in fact you may be the very cause of it."

Torriano bent over the table, without removing his supporting hand from his left arm, and studied his four tiny 'babies' as they merrily ticked away oblivious to the various times they proudly displayed. "I would like to suggest that we observe them for a few days. By that time we may have a better indication … and also your hands may be less swollen by then?"

"Very well, leave them, leave them." Carlos pushed them aside, still irritated. "You are probably right. In any case I have decided I am not of a mind to fiddle today. Here I am," he growled, "the greatest emperor since Charlemagne, having ruled the largest empire the world has ever known, controlling the lives of hundreds of thousands, now reduced to being completely incapable of getting a few timepieces to do my bidding. Too damned annoying. Tell me what you have been up to."

"Your majesty will be glad to know that your favourite clock, the Metzger, is safe and working well. I have checked it most thoroughly and have put it in the audience room awaiting your inspection."

"Good, good. Now there is an exquisite piece of workmanship in gold. As good a match for any of yours my friend," he was still pouting. "Anything else?"

Unaware of any lingering criticisms Torriano was quick to reply, "If I may, I would like you to take a look at this little mill I am working on."

"Spectacles!" Carlos bellowed. "Where are my spectacles? Is there no one to get my spectacles? Blast it; can I not have some damned organisation here? I am surrounded by bloody inept servants."

Regla stood up to offer his services, "Perhaps, with your permission?"

"You still here? Pardon my language Father. They should be in the drawer of that table by the window. Come along then, Torriano, you have me intrigued, where is it?"

"Not until you have your spectacles. I do not want to spoil the effect."

"Quick then Regla, do not keep us waiting, what the devil is keeping you?"

"Your majesty there are so many here I do not know ..." Regla was shuffling and rattling the contents of the drawer.

"Then close your blasted ... excuse me, close your eyes and grab any, just do not exasperate me. Good." He snatched the spectacles from Regla's hands and pushed them on his nose; the dark horn rims, two thick and heavy black circles, looking so incongruous on his pallid face. "At last, now show me."

Torriano rested his left arm on the table, his right hand now free to loosen the ribbons of his chemise at the wrist, and there, hidden amongst the folds, was a small brass mill.

"Now what do you say to that?" Torriano, despite himself, was quite proud.

"A toy mill for pepper? What is so remarkable about it; not the little chute at the base? But wait; the top neither twists or turns, and where is the handle? How does it work?" He picked up the tiny object.

"Gently, my lord." Torriano reached protectively towards his fragile newcomer to the world.

"Ah, it opens at the back."

"Yes; and with your permission ..." Torriano carefully retrieved his new creation, left the room for a moment to return with a small leather pouch. He took out a small white cloth and spread it on the table then placed the mill on a stand. Next to emerge from the pouch was a tiny key on its chain. The back of the mill was opened revealing springs and cogs. Finally the top was removed.

"Are you ready, my lord?" Torriano wound up his small machine then his hand disappeared into the pouch and reappeared bearing a fistful of wheat grains. A small switch was moved and there was a whirring and clicking and ticking. The grains were fed in through the open top.

There was a moment of hesitation, the mill faltered, seemed about to fail; but it was just for a moment before it suddenly rushed into action and down the chute slid the flour. As swiftly as the grains were fed in so the small hill of powdery flour grew on the cloth.

Carlos was wide-eyed with astonishment; he pinched the flour between finger and thumb, "Bravo, my inventor friend!"

Torriano stopped the operation. The mill was still in its early stages of development and he didn't want any unnecessary damage.

"Amazing. It looks no more than a toy, and yet see what it can do. I wish I could see more of its innards, see exactly how it works. It is nothing short of a wonder of the world. Is that not so, Regla?"

"I do not know that I approve. It goes against the natural order of things. I am sure that God in his wisdom would not look too favourably on something so ... in fact ... the Inquisition ..."

"Poppycock!" Carlos threw down his spectacles. "And will the Inquisition, will God, be concerned about my clever chair, the clocks with their remarkable moving figures, and the fountains, all masterminded by Torriano? Now do not be so tiresome, Regla. You concentrate on heresy; there is nothing evil in the world of science. You simply do not understand it, that is all; and that, sadly, is your loss! Let us leave it at that. For my part, I am mightily impressed. You say you are still

26

working on it; there is still work to be done? Then you must bring it again when you are satisfied it is finished."

A brief word here; in a few years time Torriano will indeed be called before the Inquisition accused of necromancy – but do not alarm yourself because common sense and science for once will prevail, allowing his scientific talents to be used for the benefit of many a town and community.

Carlos glanced at his little clocks with their confusion of times. "Now you must go, I have enjoyed your visit, but whatever blasted time it is I know it must be time for me to dress and prepare for Mass. On your way out tell the servants I am ready for them."

The king's clothes had been chosen and laid out in readiness the night before in the 'stove room'; the lavatory. The master of the wardrobe, the master of the king's jewels, and the barber, headed the line of servants making their way down the corridor. Some carried gold ewers of steaming water; others had basins with piles of snow-white towels.

The two chair boys helped Carlos into his wheeled chair and pushed him the few yards to his lavatory, luxuriously warmed by Quijada's stove, and the process of washing and dressing was carried out speedily and carefully so that he suffered no more than the minimum of discomfort.

He was returned to his chamber dressed in black velvet, his doublet showing to fine advantage the gold chain with its pendent lamb, The Golden Fleece, the highest and most noble honour of Flanders. A velvet eiderdown was tucked about his legs. One of the chair boys opened a door across the corner of the room, climbed a few steps to swing open what appeared to be the shutter to a window, while the other found the best position for the chair.

This, you will find, is most ingenious. Come closer, further into the room, and you will see something quite surprising. Stand there, just behind the king, and what do you see? Yes;

27

at the top of the steps is a door, not a window, and beyond that, lo and behold, we are at the same level and have a perfect view of the altar and the officiating priest. We can attend the services without ever having to leave the bedchamber as the altar is so much higher than the nave of the chapel. Ingenious; the architect de Vega must have been inspired by feelings of the most sensitive kind, realising that there would be days when Carlos would be unable or unwilling to be trundled along corridors and down ramps to the chapel.

"Did someone leave the damned door open when they left? There's a hell of a draught down the back of my neck!" Carlos pulled at his collar.

I am afraid I have that affect on people.

III

The friars could be heard gathering in the chapel below. Carlos had ordered that four prayers for the dead should be said every day: for his mother, his father, his wife and for himself. He did not participate in the prayers, however, until they were for his own soul.

The introit began, *Requiem aeternam dona eis, Domine …*

"Some *hijo de puta*, son of a whore, is off-key! Do you hear that cacophony, Quijada?" He screamed at his major-domo who had quietly slipped into the room to be by his side for what was becoming a daily routine. "You will tell the prior I will hear every damned one of them to discover the bastard who cannot sing and who is ruining the music. There is no point in my bringing good singers from all parts of Spain if somebody here is going to make sounds like a hen being strangled!"

"You have a keen ear, your majesty, and know better than the rest of us. This music sounds quite perfect to me. I thought someone was simply throwing in a few extra notes to add a little flourish here and there."

"You are right; you are ignorant when it comes to these matters," Carlos dismissed Quijada's pathetic observation. "Unfortunately, it is a great weakness on many folk's parts, not just yours. Nonetheless, I will have the matter sorted. But shush, they have mentioned my father."

Carlos listened for a while, "Sadly I have only the vaguest recollection of him ..."

"But you intend to reminisce now, I take it?"

"I do, and I warn you no more interruptions. Sit if you wish."

"Thank you, my lord." Quijada made himself comfortable in a leather-seated chair, arranged his short gown over his knees, rested his elbows on the chair arms, interlaced his long, bony fingers, then leaned forward ready to interrupt when necessary. It was an old, well-established routine. "You were about to speak of your father, my lord?"

"It is really quite a sad tale. I was only six years old when he died. I saw him once or twice when I was barely four. I remember him as being very tall, very fair. He had fine hands with long slender fingers. He was athletic, virtually unbeatable at *pelota*, real tennis, in spite of his cartilage problems. Did you know he could put his knee joint back in place in next to no time at all?"

"You have no recollections of this. You are simply describing his portraits and repeating stories you have heard."

"Quijada, do not be so bloody awkward. By God, but he was good at another sport, too. A regular devil with the fairer sex, never had enough of them. Drove my mother to distraction. Jealousy. She should have turned a blind eye and closed her ears as wives should, but no, she had to have screaming storms of rage ..."

Quijada coughed.

"Alright. So, I have only heard these things too. The Terror the courtiers called her. Did I tell you about the time she found out that my father was having a really serious affair with a lady, a noblewoman. She was quite a beauty, with exquisite golden locks and ..."

29

"And your mother sought out the lady in question and hacked off her yellow curls with her scissors and in the struggle managed to cut the beauty's face. Your father was told and he was furious with your mother and had her locked in her room ..."

"Interrupting again! You are exasperating!"

Quijada threw up his arms declaring his innocence, "Only to let you know that I am listening to your every word this morning, just as I always have in the past."

"You win! I may even forgive you. You know, I often wonder what would have happened had he lived. From the stories I have heard my mother gave him some very difficult times from the very moment they arrived in Spain to be crowned. She was determined never to allow him to rule alone as he demanded. Ridiculous; she had no interest, incompetent, just bloody awkward. His every ploy to have the half-crazed woman locked away was thwarted; somehow or other she managed to outwit him. Such incredible guile, you know, for someone who was crazy." He stopped and half-turned to Quijada, his major-domo and friend, raised his eyebrows, his rheumy eyes challenging. "I am waiting. What is this; have you no comment to make about my mother's madness?"

"On that subject, no. Those events took place fifty years ago and all we are left with is rumour and gossip about a lady who, after all, was Queen Juana of Spain."

"Humph! At all events, my father died. In his prime. Poisoned some say. A chill or a fever say others. So fit and healthy yet dead within a week of his feeling unwell after a game of *pelota*. I have always suspected it being the work of some bastard disgruntled Spaniard."

Quijada idly flicked at a small white downy feather that had escaped from the king's quilt and found its way onto his gown. "You may recall, my lord, that the Dauphin Francois, heir to the French throne died in exactly the same circumstances. Perhaps it is a complaint common among princes? Among princes who play *pelota* I should add."

"No mocking! God, but you can be infuriating. But I tell you this; I could never defend my father's wayward exploits, hopping into bed with other women. You know only too well how I have indulged myself with the ladies, but unlike my

30

father I was never ever once unfaithful to my dearest wife throughout our married life. I was devoted and loyal to my Empress Isabel. God rest her soul."

"Not even the slightest hint of dalliances, my lord, not the merest suggestion of temptation. That is the truth as God is our witness. Your exploits all took place either before you were married, or later after the death of the Empress, may God rest her soul."

Carlos began to smile, a wheezy giggle following, "Do you remember the Germaine de Foix story? I shall tell you anyway. It was just before you worked for me and years before my marriage. Quite a tale. The dear lady had been married to Ferdinand, my Spanish grandfather, she being his second wife and something of a child bride. He married her in his dotage, desperate to give Arag∴n an heir to deny my father and our family that part of our Spanish inheritance. Apparently the old stag did his utmost, even taking elixirs to strengthen his efforts. But either the love potions or the constant strivings killed off the poor fool. Can you picture him dragging his withered hocks to the bridal bed time after time?" He laughed and wheezed.

"Not a pretty picture."

"Bless me; he stated in his will that I was charged to look after Germaine, as there was no other, save God, to offer her comfort and help. Well, I met her a year or so after he died. Not a bad looking woman, but tending towards plumpness. Anyway we met. I decided it was my duty to carry out Ferdinand's wishes and she was just as eager for me to comfort and help her. We spent some excellent days, and nights, comforting and helping. I organised banquets and tournaments and afterwards we had the more intimate sports in bed where I comforted her two or three times a night. Good lord! I have just remembered the cleverest thing of all; we had a little bridge built between her house and mine so that we kept our feet dry during all the comings and goings. Aye, some good times."

Carlos fell quiet for a while. Quijada watched and waited patiently for the story to resume.

"The result was a little girl. Called her Isabel." He shook his head. "Of course I had to get Germaine married off. But then, just when I thought that everything was settled, damn it, her husband died."

"But she came to see you, to ask for another husband?"

"Yes, by God, she did. I got her settled again. She was the size of an elephant by then!" His laughter became an uncontrollable cough, his face turning purple.

Quijada rushed to find him a drink, "Only warm beer, my lord."

"Fine," he gasped. He choked, coughed, gulped at the drink then dried his beard with the back of his hand. "Where was I? Yes, I found a husband for this huge mountain of flesh. The fellow was not the happiest of men, to be sure, but he had debts, terrible debts that could not be met. I kindly came along with the perfect solution. He got a wife and the debts disappeared."

Quijada thought this was the ideal opportunity to break away from the Germaine story. "Speaking of debts, a letter arrived yesterday, from Barbara."

"She cannot still be in want nor need anything, can she?"

"Not this time, my lord. The letter was to let us know that, sadly, her mother has passed away."

"Good lord, not old … what was her name?"

"Katherine."

"Katherine. God rest her soul. But what a character!" He began to chuckle and Quijada joined him. "Are you thinking what I am thinking? That night?"

"Probably, my lord. That was some of the best, or worst, acting I have ever witnessed."

"I can see it as if it were only yesterday. The Lord only knows how she came by a letter of introduction to my court."

"Where there is a will, there is always a way."

"True, Quijada, and by God she made the most of it. The penniless widow's sob story, but she did it so well, it was a well-rehearsed performance."

"And not just by Katherine; it seemed the whole of your court had practised their parts too. It was like watching the parting of the waves."

Carlos slapped the arms of his chair, "They fell back opening a pathway, like the Red Sea for Moses, and she emerged, arms reaching out towards me, sobbing, 'Your majesty, help me!'"

Quijada took up the tale, "And she sank to her knees, most gracefully as I recall, and then began recounting her tale of woe, that she was the widow of a gentleman; left with a son and two daughters to support. She clutched at her breast and hung her head sorrowing because of her deep shame, distraught that she could not afford the final payment to buy her son a commission in your Imperial Army. She had promised her dying husband on his very deathbed that his son would become an officer; but she had failed, and now she and her son faced dishonour."

"I remember, I remember it all. Not a sound was to be heard from, what, a hundred courtiers? Everyone's attention was focussed on the woman. Handkerchiefs were held to mouths to hide smiles, such was the melodrama."

"She was excellent, my lord."

"Excellent, dreadful, embarrassing? Tragic or comic?"

"All of that. And it worked. You gave the boy his commission."

"I had to, Quijada. It was unbearable, impossible to keep my face straight any longer. Dear, oh dear, so Katherine Blomberg is no more. Send my condolences to Barbara and her family. She is well, I take it?"

"She and her boys are all well."

"Good. But enough; I must not miss the prayers for my soul. You may leave now. Have Gaztelu write to my daughter again to arrange the payments for the household. I shall join you later. And do remind him to insist on twenty thousand gold *ducados* each year, in quarterly payments. And there must be a further thirty thousand set aside for my own personal use. He must emphasise that nothing less is acceptable. Go."

Barbara you will discover is very like her mother; certainly could never be accused of being shy and retiring. But I think we should go now. We will leave the king to his private prayers.

Celebrations

I

"We should really be gettin' back," Maria sat up and retied the knots of the kerchief covering her hair, pulled her shawl tightly about her shoulders but showed little if any inclination to leave this hidden world. Instead she lay back idly watching the clouds change their shapes, as they moved from the bare-branch tracery to billow, spread, or break up before disappearing behind a tangle of leaves on the mighty evergreen oaks.

On the other hand, she would like to show off Alonso to her friends. Yet that wasn't the truth; what she really wanted to do was to bask in their envy. Not only had this man picked her out from her friends; he was far from being your ordinary man. He didn't come from any of the local villages, but from a very distant part of Spain. Her Alonso was big and strong, he smelled different, a wonderful mixture of sweat, horses and leather. Even more extraordinary, this man worked for the king of Spain. And ... and ... it was almost too scary to think of, he might be able to find her a job in the king's household!

"I said we should be going, really."

There was no answer from the man lying on his back at her side, who continued to chew on a twig, eyes closed, head cushioned on his arms. He was thoroughly enjoying being master of his own time, being at liberty to lie just like this amongst the trees, freed from the labours of the stables, released from the bellowed orders of others. And, there was a couple of hours or more still to come.

Maria snatched the twig and poked it at his chest to help him remember his promise, "And so you'll get me that job as scullery maid then, Alonso?"

He turned towards her, resting on his elbow, looking down on her bonny face. She had sparkling dark eyes, lovely rosy cheeks. Her mouth was a bit on the big side, perhaps, but was given to ready smiles and laughter; and that, after all, was what a fellow needed, as much fun and good cheer as he could get.

"I said as 'ow I'd do me best for you. Should be able to manage it. Don't you fret yourself; if I says I'm going to do something then I'm going to do it."

"Because you're a man of your word, right?"

"Exactly."

"There's one good thing about having a king live right close. I mean, this is the second time we've been told to leave our work and come up here, and him not in these parts long at that. And it isn't just not having to work, we gets to feast with meat and drink and all the rest."

"The rest being a bit o' this, eh?" he chuckled, hauling up her skirts.

"Not again, that's wicked, that is! You're greedy, you are," she rolled over to face him. "What did you say today is?"

"His birthday."

"Fancy knowing when you was born."

Maria knew when to go to and when to return from the fields because the bell in the church steeple told her; she was aware of the yearly pattern of seasons, and church festivals; but birthdays? She plucked pieces of soil and grass from Alonso's coat spread on the ground beneath her, wondering about the lives of the rich who knew things like dates of birth or saints' days without having to be told when or what for, and she sighed. "This coat's going to be a mucky mess if we're not careful."

"You let me worry about that." He pushed her onto her back, "Anyways, I feels it's my birthday and it's time for a bit more of the rest like what we were talking about."

"You won't forget about that job, will you? It would be easier for us to be together, and we could be indoors all warm and ..."

"No time for talking. The old dagger is desperate to get back into its sheath."

"You cheeky devil! It's easy to tell you've been a-soldiering."

"Sh." Alonso pushed up her skirts, parted her welcoming thighs, found his way into her and thrust his weapon home, grunting and groaning as his mission was finally accomplished.

"Ooh! Did you feel that, then, Alonso?"

"Feel what? I was busy."

"Well all of a sudden it went all cold. Made me all shivery, it did."

"Aye, it seems to be going around. Manuel mentioned it the other day. It don't bother me none."

II

Good day to you. I never would have supposed there were so many people living in this area. Just look at them all. At times it was impossible for me to make my way through the crowds and at one point I had no option but to make a small diversion and walk up the hill amongst the trees. Even so I had to take great care not to tread on those who thought they had discovered their own little islands of privacy.

It stands to reason that if you offer folk a free day with feasting and drinking they appear from anywhere and everywhere.

Have you noticed the pulpit erected under the trees? That is for the benefit of these villagers, the farmers, and the peasants, that they might all participate in the religious services of thanksgiving and celebration. The message was sent out days ago announcing today's events and inviting all to come, and it would appear that the whole of Estremadura decided to accept. I have a sneaking suspicion that not all will be attending the mass. Many have already found their way to the woods, hoping their absence will not be noticed, and will probably only return in time for the feast. I suppose one cannot blame them. Such days of leisure are virtually unknown. Yet we all know what the devil can do with idle hands!

36

What are we celebrating? I shall tell you. Today, being February 24th, is the birthday of Carlos and he has now reached the grand age of fifty-seven. He came into the world in a desperate hurry while his mother was attending a ball; why, she barely had time to find a small retiring room before he made his sudden appearance. Fortunately, neither mother nor child was any the worse for the unusual circumstances.

We are also celebrating this day because it is the anniversary of his glorious victory at Pavia in Italy; or rather the Imperial Army's victory for Carlos was not there. It was nevertheless a resounding defeat of the archenemy France. That, incredibly, was on this very same day. Coincidence or divine intervention?

The third reason for rejoicing is that on this day, Carlos was crowned emperor; the ruler and master of the largest empire the world had ever known.

He was first crowned with the Iron Crown of Lombardy, and then with the Imperial Crown. Such a glittering affair, my friend. It cost him at least ninety thousand *ducados*, the amount which he apparently raised on his wife's jewels. His cape and crown were made of gold and precious stones in such quantities that it would be impossible to estimate either their weight or value. The hands of His Holiness Pope Clement VII placed the Imperial Crown on the head of Carlos witnessed by hundreds of noblemen, many of them travelling from Spain to Bologna for the occasion. All wore robes of velvet heavily encrusted with jewels. Afterwards, as if money was no more than the rains that fall from the Heavens, gold and silver coins were thrown to the crowds.

Now does that seem reasonable to you, that Carlos should squander his wife's dowry in such a way?

And what about this for further satisfying his ego; he had purposefully delayed the ceremony to have it coincide with his birthday! The months of waiting annoyed many a lord eager to return to his home. But, goodness me, if an emperor cannot determine the time and place, who can?

By sheer coincidence today is also the birthday of someone who I think you will find is rather special, someone you will eventually meet, but who, for the moment, will remain my little secret.

Couples began reappearing from the woods summoned by the monastery bell, and they swelled the numbers of those already waiting near the pulpit. Giggles and laughter died away replaced by hurried last-minute conversations. Those who had never wandered away greeted some of those returning with a shake of the head and a knowing "Aye".

A hush settled over the crowd as the priest climbed up into the pulpit. Their thoughts turned to the waiting meal and the things still to talk about after the service, which they earnestly hoped would not take too long. It went without saying that a good gossip would go down well with all that food that had been set out for them.

They are almost ready to start. I think we should view the indoor service from the king's vantage point, for the chapel will be too crowded to see anything. So, if you are ready, we had best make our way now to the king's bedchamber.

Now, through the door to the chapel. You remember it from the other day? Up these few stairs. Perfect; an uninterrupted view of the entire nave.

There is Carlos. How magnificently he is dressed today, perhaps looking with nostalgia to long-lost days by adding crimson satin and gold cloth to his everyday black; a touch here and there on his cap and in the slashes to his sleeves. Some jewelled pins too and of course his gold chain with The Golden Fleece. These are similar to the colours he wore for his triumphant entry into Castile when he was but a youth, only seventeen years old.

On that day, he was handsomely dressed in yellow, white and red. Some said at the time, and I am convinced they were all Flemish, that Castile had never had a king so noble and triumphant enter Valladolid. He rode under a canopy of cloth of gold carried on four silver poles. The precious stones he wore were worth a king's ransom, I can tell you. His horse was caparisoned in crimson, gold and silver. Carlos has never been conservative or cautious about spending money, whether his own or someone else's! Though not wanting to sound churlish, I would point out that the same Flems who sang his praises carefully forgot to mention that he always looked tired and debilitated, was stubborn and morose; but that would detract somewhat from the picture of the noble and triumphant king.

I see you shake your head, is that a mild rebuke? I apologise for the criticisms. As usual, I digress.

It appears that all are present, and everyone turned out in their best. And see, his friends are all here for the celebration. Quickly, watch Carlos. You see the purse he is handing to the priest? Inside are

39

fifty-seven gold coins; one for every year of his life. They will be blessed and then handed out after the service. I wonder how many squabbles there will be over who should receive one; but when your master is often late with salaries and is generally parsimonious any handout would be greedily sought.

When the service is concluded we shall make our way down the corridor to the grand salon, the audience room, which today is being prepared for a feast that befits the occasion.

III

How glad I am to find you here. I wondered what had become of you. What made you leave? Perhaps the obsequiousness was too much? If there had been a levy on all praises after the first half dozen a small fortune would have been raised for the Treasury today. And it is all so hypocritical. There is not one of those priests wants him here.

Do you like this Grand Salon? The arched recesses mirroring the arches of the windows offer it some character, do you think? Even so it remains a rectangular box. I say thank goodness for those tapestries with the Christian armies felling the Turk. Some lively scenes there to dwell on. In fairness I do think the room has two redeeming features: its southerly aspect, and the delightful view overlooking the garden with its fish pond.

Ah, I see the portraits have caught your attention. The artist is Titian, a great favourite of the emperor. They often spent more time talking than actually getting the portraits painted. We will never have the opportunity to meet the master himself, alas, but at least we can enjoy the one or two works Carlos brought with him.

Yes indeed, that one, the study of the late Empress Isabel. Such a beautiful lady, and yet Titian, a master craftsman, reveals more than superficial beauty. Her whole personality positively speaks to us. It is little wonder that Carlos was always faithful to her; he must have thanked God every night for his good fortune in finding such a wife.

Actually, he was betrothed to Mary Tudor his six-year-old cousin on the English side of the family. But such a marriage would not have been to Carlos's advantage. Some years would have to pass before Mary was of a suitable age and he was already so deeply in debt to the king of England that she would have come to him a penniless bride, her dowry being gobbled up in the cancellation of his debts. Now what use would that be when an emperor needs all the money he can lay his hands on? Meanwhile Carlos's sister Leonor initiated negotiations for this marriage with Isabel. And lo and behold the prospective wife was not only beautiful but came with a dowry of nine hundred thousand Portuguese *doblas* – all promptly spent on his journey to Italy for his coronation!

Oh, those eyes are so wistful, tender, patient, understanding, and yes, they are proud. That face says so much to me of years spent without her husband, years of painful separation. Those around her said she was often low in spirits and wept easily. As for the royal garments, what other brush could show the contrast between the heavy velvets, the stiff brocades and the ruched fine Holland at her throat and wrists, or the small sparkling gems and the heavy and bold

41

ruby and pearl brooch with its looped chain
of enormous pearls?
    Footsteps. You hear them? It is time for
us to make way for the arrival of the feast. I
warrant you have never seen so much food at
one time.

Servants brought in gold-plated dishes of olives, asparagus, and truffles and set them down on the awaiting tables.

"Here we go again lads; he's finished with the God bit now here comes the gorging. He never changes," one of them whispered from the side of his mouth as he crossed the path of yet more bearers of laden dishes and tureens. These held pies: pork, mutton, and eel.

"At least there'll be leftovers for us lot," someone else whispered heartily.

Yet another table was being covered with silver platters of fish: trout, flounders, lamprey. More gold dishes were delivered filled with eels, frogs, pickled herrings, sardines, anchovies, and oysters. Last to arrive at the tables were partridges, wild boar, venison, cured beef, bears' legs, chickens, and sausages.

Gold and silver wine pitchers, goblets, and large beer jugs stood marshalled on other side tables.

Carlos stopped in the doorway to survey the scene. He was followed by Zuñiga, a specially invited military friend then Quijada and Gaztelu.

"Magnificent! Now for one of my favourite pastimes," cried a jubilant Carlos rubbing his hands and beaming at his companions as he studied the tables and sideboards. "Everything I asked for is here. Where shall I start?"

Zuñiga nodded his head in approval at the variety and richness of the spread.

Quijada viewed the scene with despair knowing full well the results of today's feasting.

Gaztelu peered between the two and the corners of his mouth twitched with pleasure at the prospect of sinking his teeth into one of those savoury pies, preferably the venison; after Carlos had had his fill, naturally.

The king's dining chair was turned from the wall to face the table, and he was carefully manoeuvred into it.

"Enough, no more fussing. Now, perhaps a few olives then the pies. Not bad, not bad. Someone remind me to have my cook get a decent recipe to prepare the sad little olives that grow here, they need something to give them some vigour. Beer for the thirst," he spluttered.

Quijada and Gaztelu made their way to the far side of the room to join Regla and the doctor.

I suggest we follow the example of these gentlemen and direct our attention elsewhere for a little while. I would not recommend watching the king eat, it is offensive both to the eye and stomach. Let me remind you that he cannot close his mouth so his food is sloshed and squashed about in his mouth for a moment or two before being sluiced down his throat with a good swilling of beer or wine. The spittle, flotsam and jetsam scattered over his beard, the debris about his person, not to mention the belching is, to speak plainly, disgusting.

Although embarrassing for all concerned throughout his entire life he has had no alternative but to take some of his meals in public; one of those inescapable duties of a monarch. As you can imagine he prefers to dine alone and his companions are more than happy when he does.

His guests today will partake of a small repast from the dishes he sets aside as he abandons one savoury delight for another.

But, how remiss of me, you have yet to meet Zuñiga. He was the Commander of the Imperial Cavalry; saw action in Africa, France, and Germany; quite a historian too. I think he still looks every bit the soldier and, although the hair is white, the shoulders no longer pulled back and perhaps he has grown

somewhat rounder, the traces of the dashing
officer linger on.

IV

"Pavia was a damn fine victory then, ZuZiga?" Carlos
spluttered across the table in the direction of his old comrade in
arms. "Remind us all, marquƌs, why we are celebrating Pavia.
You always enjoy telling a good war story, and you do it so
well. Entertain me while I eat."

ZuZiga moved closer to the table, taking care to adopt a
defensive position a little to the rear and to one side of the king.

"As your majesty wishes. I shall begin the tale with the
siege. Pavia is a strategic hilltop town in Italy, gentlemen, for
those of you among us who may not know. Our General de
Leyva, God rest his soul, had prevented the French from taking
the town for almost four months. Those had been four cruel
months of a severe Italian winter, with relentless cold and bitter
blizzard-filled winds racing up the hillside from the plains
below. The French army had completely surrounded the town,
holding positions all around the several miles of its perimeter.
Inside the walls the food had run out long ago and they had
resorted to eating the horses and mules. Firewood had become
so scarce that once all the furniture, doors, carts, and whatever
else they could find had been used up it was then the turn of
building timbers to provide the fuel, and that included the
church beams. You are shocked, you men of the cloth? It was a
question of survival. And they did survive. De Leyva saw to
that by ensuring everyone was treated alike, that all should
suffer the same privations, whatever their rank. But, for all that,
our fine fighting forces were quickly becoming shambling
wrecks of men."

He paused for effect giving his listeners time to appreciate
the desperate situation. Then he fired angrily, "And what was
happening outside the walls? That was quite a different story!
As well as abbeys and castles offering shelter to the French
there was a huge area, a hunting park I suppose is the best way
for you to visualise it, and this was where the main French
encampment was situated. They had set up a huge market with
stalls groaning with all kinds of food and wines. At one point it

44

even took on a carnival atmosphere with peddlers, vagabonds, and of course plenty of girls. So all needs were catered for, so to speak. It was a city really, albeit more of canvas than of stone, a city of thousands. You can be sure that no one there lacked a fire or suffered an empty belly! King Francis of course had a table overflowing with meats and wines, and his bed kept warm by his mistress."

All this talk of food reminded the listeners that they were still waiting to eat and although they were not starving they were growing hungry and would enjoy the tale much more if their own bellies were full.

ZuZiga sensed he was losing his audience; that was always a danger when talking to non-military men. "But as they say, all good things must come to an end. Time was running out for the French because fortune began to smile on us. Some of Francis's troops had to be sent home to deal with internal strife. Our General Pescara finally made it to Pavia to assist in raising the siege. Now for the battle. The French were in battle formation. Our Imperial Army then advanced. The French artillery fired, round after round, all sadly finding their target. Bodies were blown to bits, limbs and torsos slung into the air like huge clods of earth …"

"No further details, thank you," Carlos sent a hail of pastry bullets across the table.

"Your pardon, my lord. To continue, the survivors retreated to a point of safety. Then came King Francis's big mistake, misreading the situation and playing right into our hands."

"You are not going to suggest that it had nothing to do with our brilliant strategy, surely, ZuZiga?" Carlos butted in spitting out his annoyance alongside chunks of meat, "Our commanders were well versed in military tactics."

"Far be it from me to belittle our glorious armies; neither their expertise nor their enthusiasm. Nor would I forget that our men had not been paid for months and yet continued to have the stomach for the fight. Nor would I ignore the pride of our generals and their zeal to represent your majesty on the field of battle. But to continue; King Francis, seeing the devastation he had inflicted on our troops, gave orders to advance. A mighty error, for in doing so he put his cavalry in front of his own guns, neatly placing them to form a Heaven-sent shield for our men. Now it was the turn of our soldiers to move up, and putting our faith in God and yes, the inspired strategy of mixing cavalry with pikemen, lances and arquebuses, we pushed into their lines. One of their wings was quick to collapse. Then others began to fall back. Before long our men were in amongst them causing complete disarray. Francis's horse was felled from under him. Within moments he was surrounded by those seeking him and his magnificent armour for booty. One of our chaps fiercely fought them off until our Viceroy of Naples, Lannoy, arrived. He had the French king at his feet, helpless, blood streaming from the wounds on his face, his jewelled and plumed helmet lying useless on the frozen earth. All his military commanders were either dead or dying around him. There had been three hours of fighting and ten thousand had fallen …"

"Listen everybody, I like the next part! Pure chivalry!" Carlos rapped a dish with his knife. "Carry on, ZuZiga."

"The defeated King Francis took off his sword and presented it to his captor, Lannoy. Lannoy then kissed the king's hand and gave him his sword in return saying that it did not become a monarch to remain disarmed in the presence of one of the emperor's subjects."

"A moment," Carlos fumbled with the strings of his purse. "Damned fingers."

Quijada whispered down into Gaztelu's ear, "I know of someone else who can recite the whole battle almost as well as Zuñiga; and not even there, not even born then."

"Ah the young chap you have in your home? Perhaps his father was a military man, though I have no reason to suppose …"

Quijada didn't answer.

"Infernal nuisances," the king's purse was at last open. "Brought this with me; here, read this Zuñiga. Everyone must hear the whole story."

ZuZiga unfolded the paper, "Of course; the letter from Lannoy. It says,

Sire, we gave battle yesterday, and praise be to God, He gave you victory and handed you the king of France. Now we have him prisoner. The

46

victory that God gave you was on the day of San Matias, your birth date." "

"And what a gift for my birthday, eh? What a happy birthday. Now you can tell them about the bullet."

"One of our soldiers approached the French king and presented him with a small gold bullet saying that it was the very bullet with which he had intended to shoot him."

"Very good. Very good. Now it is my turn to tell you something about this King Francis. After we got him safely from Italy to Spain he wrote to his mother saying how everything had been lost save 'honour'. That infuriated me. I tell you he never knew the meaning of the word. There is plenty I could say about his so-called 'honour'. Next he wrote to me bleating about, what was it Gaztelu? We were looking at it just this morning. You tell them!"

"You will correct me if I am wrong," his secretary wearily replied, knowing full well that he was word perfect for he had read the letter so many times. "It went something like this; *I beg you to decide in your own heart what you must do with me, but I am sure that whatever you do decide it will be honourable and magnanimous. If it pleases you to offer such security as befits the king of France, it will make me a friend instead of a desperate man, a good brother instead of a prisoner. If you treat me honourably I shall be your slave forever.*"

"Precisely. So what did he do the moment I did set him free? Reneged on his oaths. He even refused to hand over Burgundy. And what is more, gentlemen, Pope Clement exonerated him of these broken vows, and then welcomed him as an ally. Just goes to show you cannot trust anybody – not even a pope!" He thumped the table venting his self-righteous spleen. "And another thing; some of you might recall Francis's sister. She came to Madrid to see him and to beg for his release. She tried to bribe me into giving Francis his freedom by offering to return Burgundy to us as part of a marriage settlement between her brother and my sister Leonor; but I make my own decisions and do not allow any woman to persuade me one way or the other and certainly not a damn French woman! What else was I going to say?"

"Did you wish to tell your guests about the dog?" Gaztelu offered.

"Of course, Gaztelu. I allowed this sister to visit Francis in his rooms in the palace; magnanimous of me I thought, and when she left she said he could keep her little black dog. Thought it would be good company for him in his confinement," he laughed, wheezed and choked.

A swift half goblet of wine and he was ready to continue. He waved away the alarm he had caused, "The best part is, someone else came forward with an even better idea for providing a little diversion. Good Lord I had forgotten all about it."

Gaztelu was embarrassed, "Perhaps, my lord, there are some who might not want to hear this?"

"Nonsense! Francis was offered a black slave girl. Now that, my friends, truly would be a deliverance from solitude! We had many a laugh reading Francis's letters to his dear sister telling her about how he spent at least an hour every morning playing in his bed with the 'little black one'. The devil."

Carlos slapped the chair arms with both hands and roared with laughter, and then drained his wine goblet signalling to have it refilled. There were several shocked faces but most were quietly enjoying images of the prisoner and his early morning pleasures.

"You may think it sounds no better than many another one of the army tales soldiers tell but I swear I have not spoken one word of a lie, gentlemen. Playing with the 'little black one'; the old fornicator."

ZuZiga's coughs reminded him of the presence of clergy, "Perhaps, my lord, if you were to tell the story of the charcoal?"

"Ah yes. One day the silly fool decides to black himself up with charcoal, borrow the evil smelling rags of a slave and try to pass himself off as a blackamoor so he could just walk out of the palace. All good entertainment for the guards. They had all known of the plan but it pleased them to let it run its course so they could greet him with, 'Morning, your majesty. Going somewhere?'" Carlos tipped more wine into his mouth. "But enough. You told your tale well, ZuZiga, even if you did cut it short today. I brought your book of our campaigns with me; have it in my library. Damned exciting those Commentaries, all of them. But how much better to hear them from the master himself."

"Your majesty I have something even better in my home to recall our prowess in the field. Our very last battle, my lord, you remember around Renty, when we had his son Henry's Frenchies scurrying away from the field in disorder and completely humiliated? I have had the scene painted on a wall; a dramatic mural for all my visitors to admire."

"My friend," tut-tutted Carlos, "we all know you are prone to exaggeration and while I have been known to bask in it, we must surely draw the line here." He pulled ZuZiga close then lowered his voice. "You know as well as I there was no sensible reason for the French to prolong that war and King Henry, a man with at least a modicum of intelligence unlike his father, decided to leave the field and retain his dignity. Dear ZuZiga you must ask your artist to repaint the retreat giving it at least some semblance of the truth. A pity though, the idea is a good one, and I wager it does make a damn fine picture." He belched then sighed, "It is too damned bad that all I can do to celebrate is to have church services and banquets, eh, Quijada?"

Quijada, who had watched in dismay if not alarm at the vast quantities of food and drink that were being rapidly despatched, shook his head. "It is indeed, and you show no inclination to push yourself away from the table."

"I meant, Quijada, the loss of my dancing days."

"Precisely, if only you had always done more dancing and less eating and drinking."

"Never danced that night at my birthday ball in Germany."

"You mean you were unable to dance at your birthday ball, you were too sated with food and drink. You could do no other than sit and watch. What a way to celebrate your birthday!"

"I shall ignore that. But that woman was there, and ..." an explosive belch put an end to his story. He had eaten too much, had drunk far more than usual. His chin sank onto his chest and he drifted into a strange world of dreams and memories.

49

He was in Germany at one of those glittering occasions befitting the birthday celebrations of a Holy Roman Emperor. Everybody who was anybody was there in their best velvets and satins and sparkling with jewels from head to toe. The banquet had been everything he could have asked for, and he had asked for a great many things and in huge quantities.

Now everyone had gathered in an enormous hall lit by hundreds of candles and, should Carlos be affected by the February cold, two enormous fires blazed their comfort. There was dancing, cards, chess, and gossiping, lots of gossiping.

At the far end of the hall Carlos sat on his throne on a dais, near his musicians; at least he could enjoy the music.

A stately pavan followed by a galliard had just ended and the dancers were slowly drifting towards the outer edges of the room.

"Good God, Quijada!" Carlos leaned towards his aide. "Look; the widow-woman Blomberg is here again. What, in God's name, is she here for this time; and how did she get an invitation? This is the second time."

"I have no idea, my lord; her name was most definitely not on the list."

Katherine Blomberg approached Carlos, making three deep reverences, and making the young maiden at her side follow her example.

Four guards with their halberds hurriedly barred their way.

"Have no fear, good sirs," she chided, "I intend going no further. I am quite content to say what I have to say right here."

Carlos motioned the guards to stand aside.

Katherine curtsied once more to Carlos then turned to address the astonished gathering. "My lords, ladies, you are in the presence of the most Christian monarch ever known to mankind. Some time ago I begged a favour; that my son be given a commission in the Imperial Army. I was penniless, a widow unable to afford to buy one. Knowing nothing of me the emperor granted my request. I am here to publicly thank him. It is because of his most generous spirit that my family is able to maintain its dignity and pride."

Carlos tugged at Quijada's sleeve, "What do you suppose the old woman wants this time, a husband for the damsel she has dragged along with her? Go ask the widow what she wants; be kind, but firm and say no. Mind you, that is a very pretty young wench at her side."

In fact, throughout Katherine's speech his eyes had never left the young lady. She was tall with hair the colour of gold framing the most beautiful face he had ever seen since that of his beloved Isabel. He was angry with himself for comparing the looks of a nobody, she was not even a noblewoman, with the exquisite and most royal Isabel.

But he was no different from any other man, he told himself, and he was taken by the girl's wonderful figure, her milk-white breasts modestly revealed by the cut of her satin gown, a satin gown as blue as the skies in summer; and her golden hair the shimmering sun.

He was beginning to drown in feelings unknown for years. The room was growing too hot; there were too many people, too many candles, and there was suddenly no need for those two huge fires.

Quijada returned, smiling. "Frau Blomberg wishes nothing more than to be given the honour of kissing your hand in gratitude."

"Are you sure she wants nothing more?"

"That is what she said."

"She may approach."

Katherine came forward, the young lady in tow. She knelt at her emperor's feet and kissed the proffered hand.

Carlos nodded, smiled; pleased to have been of service. He raised a hand towards the musicians, the ball could now continue.

The next thing he heard was not music but the voice of Katherine Blomberg announcing that, by special request, her daughter Barbara was going to sing.

Carlos managed to remain seated by grasping the chair arms, Quijada visibly rocked on his feet as if having been dealt an enormous blow.

"Quijada, this is embarrassing."

"Only for the two ladies. I suggest you let them have their moment then the audience's reaction will be sufficient to speed them on their way."

"Get me a handkerchief. I would hate to be seen as ungallant; must have something to bury my face in."

A golden dish with a snowy pile of linen squares was offered.

Katherine hugged her daughter then joined the onlookers and proudly waited.

Then Barbara sang. Her voice was perfection. Carlos had never heard a voice with such colour and velvety richness.

"Oh, Barbara."

          CS   **BO**

"Oh, Barbara." Carlos raised his head with a jerk. "Quijada, are you there? Have I been saying anything?"

"Nothing, my lord. You dozed off and snored a little; not surprisingly, considering."

"Wine," Carlos demanded.

"My lord, a word of advice," whispered Quijada, "think of tomorrow and the likely repercussions of today's intemperance."

"Quijada, if I have another attack of gout my doctor will have the remedies."

"You possess the best remedy, my lord, in keeping your mouth shut and refraining from eating and drinking to excess. But as usual ..."

"You are an incredible killjoy. I said I want wine!"

My friend, it goes without saying that Quijada is right; the morning will bring great pain and suffering for the king. We shall postpone our next meeting until his health and the accompanying ill temper improve. Some very stormy, disagreeable days lie ahead.

I noticed you were intrigued with Carlos muttering the name Barbara. More of that another time.

March

Still in Command?

I

You were most wise to stay away. I promise you we will not remain long in this dreary bedchamber. Life has centred round the bed of Carlos day and night for weeks. You may recall from your last visit his friends and advisers, including his doctor, all warning him of the consequences of his gluttony. But years ago it was already too late to make Carlos see reason, and he is certainly not of a mind to heed advice now; he is like a man driven.

Following his day of intemperance he was forced to take to his bed suffering from an extremely painful attack of gout afflicting his feet, legs, hands and arms. He has also been tormented by agonisingly painful haemorrhoids, another ailment he has had to endure for years. Then there is the unpleasant business of syphilis, but perhaps it would be indelicate to go further on that; forgive me. Carlos has been dosing himself daily with barley water, egg yolks, and senna wine in the hope that these would flush and cleanse his system.

The people you see about his bed, young Dr. Mathys and his assistants, have never been far from his bedside, while potions and ointments have been prepared daily by the pharmacist. They could all probably do their work blindfold, after goodness knows how many years practice of mixing and applying; no doubt they would prefer to. At the moment a thick paste of chicken grease and barley flour mixed with wallflowers and parsley is being applied to the inflamed piles, the royal rectum will then be cosseted in a napkin. You know, people often complain about the money doctors make. They mock them, mouthing unkind sentiments such as, 'You can tell he is a doctor, pisspot in one hand a money bag in the other'. I tell you I do not envy them their task not for one moment, nor the money in their purses.

"How does that feel, your majesty?" Doctor Mathys enquired as Carlos was gently rolled onto his back.

"Good; for now; but we shall see when I am dressed and sitting in my chair."

"And do you require fresh plasters for your arms and legs?"

"No, I certainly do not want fresh plasters! How would I dress with arms and legs bound in windings of linen? In any case I have no desire to go about the place reeking of vinegar."

"I had thought perhaps comfrey root plasters?"

"Are you trying to annoy me? I said; no plasters!"

Carlos was manoeuvred to the side of his bed so that his hose could be inched slowly over swollen feet and ankles then distended knees; toes were guided into wrapover shoes of the softest suede. Next, the night shirt was removed and his arms carefully fed through the sleeves of a fresh chemise. He was lifted and propped up by strong arms under his shoulders as the linen was tucked deep into his hose to cover the protective napkin. That done, a bowl was held beneath his chin as first he had his face refreshed with a sponge of welcoming warm water, then his beard tidied by his barber. Warm towels patted dry the wrinkled cheeks. After his hair was combed, a wool skull cap was pulled into place. Finally, his doublet and jerkin were on and fastened and his bonnet positioned over his skull cap.

"God, but it feels good to be dressed again. I feel like a new man." He beckoned his chair boys José and Samuel, "Right, lads, lift me over to my table and chair. I am going to have breakfast. Van Male, let the cook know I am ready." He beamed from ear to ear, already savouring the treat to come.

Van Male, a man in his late forties, all in black except for the elegant silver buckles on his shoes, a gift from his previous employer the Duque de Alba, and the broad red sash of the Companion of the Bedchamber across his breast, forced his weary feet forward carrying him towards the door, his head determinedly held high despite his exhaustion.

Ah, Male. Poor fellow, such a quiet and placid man; he is far too amenable, too self-effacing. Those who decide not to overlook him take advantage of him. He served in the army for a while in the service of the Duque de Alba. A friend then succeeded in finding him a position in the king's household about five years ago. It is Male's privilege to read aloud far into the night when pain keeps Carlos from his sleep, stopping at times to change the cloths about his temples or sprinkling them now and then with a mixture of opium, henbane and mandragora. Have you tried it? Very soothing I assure you. He has permission to rest on a truckle bed nearby when and if Carlos does fall asleep.

Let me share an amusing anecdote with you. When Male married recently, instead of the more usual gift of a piece of leather for shoes, or a bolt of cloth, or even a piece of jewellery; the king gave him what? I ought not to ask; if you had a thousand attempts you would never guess. He offered him his wise

55

counsel upon entering into the matrimonial state! And that was it, nothing more!
But here comes breakfast.

The cook led in his small team: one bearing a gold dish with fitted dome, followed by another with a basket of bread, the next carried gold bowls, yet another held a gold jug, the last a gold salver and goblet. Male stood at the ready with table napkins.

Carlos looked merrily about him; this was his first venture into the land of real food after weeks of an enforced punishing diet.

The domed lid was raised; Carlos beamed and tore into the bread then dipped it into the greasy sardine omelette.

Doctor Mathys, with a heavy heart, ushered his assistants from the scene that heralded the beginnings of the next attack. His only course of action was to study further in an attempt to discover other cures.

"This is excellent." Carlos wiped his oily chin. "What could be better? Well, perhaps another one. No, there is no time for such a luxury, I must meet someone – but there is time for another beer."

This is an important meeting and will be held in private. We will make our way now to the king's private salon.

II

This is by far the best room in the palace, a haven. One could easily spend the rest of one's life here.

Look at all the book shelves holding but a small selection of the king's vast library built up over the years; every one of them gems, the sacred and the profane: Psalters, Bibles, art, music, science – all so inviting. Over there on the large table, the maps and charts are all waiting, demanding investigation. Immediately above, more shelves with

Torriano's timepieces and mechanical toys. See the little trumpeter, the chickens, and the charming dancer holding her skirts, all frozen for the moment, merely waiting for someone to bring them to life. And there are even more treasures tucked away in those drawers and cupboards. Lastly there stands Carlos's small clavichord, the lid tightly closed, but surely begging to be played.

Light and sunshine can both enter this room, from the east and from the south, and there is a splendid view of the garden.

Then, of course, the chairs and stools including Carlos's gout chair all grouped intimately around the fire; who could ask for more?

It is, nonetheless, like all the rest, too damnably hot. May God forgive me for such an outburst!

A tall gentleman in a black velvet jerkin, a ruff of crisp undulating waves of the finest Brussels lace, padded trunk hose with green panes, a green bonnet trimmed with silver cord, was deep in conversation with Quijada and Gaztelu. Gaztelu stood facing the two, squinting up at them through his spectacles, a sheaf of papers still awaiting attention held snug against his breast.

Our visitor is quite a handsome man, perfectly proportioned. And note the face, too, with such a deep forehead, large hazel eyes keen and intelligent, a rich dark beard framing sensual lips. He could have his choice of the ladies without doubt.

This is Ruy Gomez; recently promoted to Chief Accountant of the Treasury, and close friend of King Felipe, Carlos's son.

Carlos has known Gomez since he came to this country from Portugal with his mother, a lady in waiting to the Empress Isabel. In his early youth he was transferred to Felipe's court; first as pageboy, then later as his chamberlain and trusted confidant. As a reward for his continued services to his king a young lady has been selected from one of the most influential Spanish families to be his bride. The bride-to-be as I said is young; in fact she is just seventeen while Gomez is already forty. She is said to have an astonishingly beautiful face but is never seen without a black eye patch. Now, an incurable romantic like me insists that the reason for this is because she lost an eye while practising duelling with one of her pages; others tending more to the prosaic declare she has the misfortune to have a terrible cast in that eye.

But let us hear what they have to say.

"Yes, thank you Quijada, I am most fortunate with my accommodation in Brussels. I am staying at your former residence and enjoying the attentive services of your former staff. They were eager, by the way, to hear of the child who was so briefly in their midst before being fostered by one of the emperor's musicians. I said I would ask." He smiled what might be considered a mischievous smile.

"They were, were they?" Quijada was offhand.

Gaztelu put down his clutch of papers, rubbed his spectacles on his sleeve and perched them once more on his nose as if to hear all the better.

"They said he was the most beautiful baby boy they had ever seen."

"Did they, now? And did they have anything else to say?"

"As a matter of fact they did." Gomez toyed first with the silver buttons on his jerkin then adjusted the lace at his wrists, "All gossip, of course, but when the child's existence is shrouded in such mystery it is not to be wondered at."

"I am all ears; and if I can be of any help ..." Quijada's tone was non committal as he folded his arms and leaned forward to study the toes of his shoes.

58

Gaztelu was all ears too. This was all news to him, even if it was just gossip; and it made such a welcome change to a life of endless letters of state, financial reports or requests. '

"They told me that ten or so years ago you and the emperor's head groom, in the middle of winter, brought this tiny babe to Brussels from Ratisbon."

"That is true. But the child was accompanied by a nursemaid and a wet nurse, and they travelled in a carriage; so he was not exposed quite so brutally to the elements as perhaps you supposed."

"I never doubted it. They intimated that the reason for the child's removal had to do with his mother. I gathered from this that he is an illegitimate child, and someone on the emperor's staff decided he should have a Spanish upbringing."

"Both are correct assumptions."

"I hope you will not be offended when I say that although it was their general opinion that the father was the head groom, I also heard whisperings that it might be you."

Gaztelu's spectacles slid off the end of his nose in astonishment and only his plump cheeks saved them from disaster.

"I suppose they could not resist that thought; that is natural enough." Quijada's smile was aggravatingly inscrutable, his eyes betraying nothing. "What I will tell you is that a musician about to retire and return to Spain signed a paper taking responsibility for the boy and giving the assurance that no one would know the identity of the father. The groom signed for the wife, who is illiterate, before countersigning the agreement."

"So, the groom is the father?"

"I never said that."

"Princess Juana told me that the child is now in your charge."

Gaztelu's spectacles were pushed all the way up to the bridge of his nose, as he smiled his delight with all this information.

"He is. The musician died; and to be perfectly frank I had been dissatisfied for some time with the inadequacies of both parents. My wife and I are childless, and, since I could think of no better mother in the world to care for the lad, and not

59

wanting to risk another poor placing, I decided to take him into our home."

Gomez stroked at the dark curls of his beard. "There is little wonder, you must admit, that there should be gossip about a bastard child when such efforts have been made right from the beginning, from the moment of his birth, putting two hundred miles, an ocean included, between him and his mother. What of his mother, by the way?"

"Married. Yes, the mother is married, and the child has an excellent home. So everyone is happy."

"And who is the father?" Gomez tried once more.

Gaztelu settled his spectacles firmly on his nose in readiness for the revelation.

Quijada smiled. "What would be the point in knowing? It would serve no purpose; it cannot change anything. If, one day, the father should choose to reveal his identity, then that will be the appropriate time."

Gomez eyed him quizzically; would Quijada go to all that trouble for a groom's child? But, then again, surely he would not bring a former mistress's child into his own home expecting his wife to be its mother. It happened all the time; but Quijada? Never!

Gaztelu shuffled his way round his desk, sat down and arranged his papers.

Gaztelu will be disappointed not to hear more of the young lad in Quijada's care, but there was enough there to whet the appetite and stir the imagination.

III

The wheels of Carlos's chair trundled noisily across the tiled floor. José and Samuel transferred their charge into his gout chair; one of Torriano's inventions with a splendid system of ratchets to raise and lower the leg rests independent of each other, and to allow the back to recline. Once Carlos was installed and comfortable the wheelchair was set to one side and the two servants took up their positions by the door, feet slightly apart, hands behind their backs.

Carlos quickly appraised his son Felipe's aide and once again congratulated himself on the excellent decision he had made all those years ago in transferring him to Felipe's court.

"Welcome, welcome dear Gomez." Carlos smiled and raised a hand from the arm rest. "I trust you slept well in your apartment. Faithful Quijada here arranged everything for you."

"Your majesty," Gomez made three reverences before kneeling to kiss the royal hand. "How it pleases me to see you once more; and to see you fully recovered from your recent illnesses. My thanks to you Quijada for having the room in readiness for my arrival; after such a journey I cannot begin to describe how much I appreciate such comforts. I am deeply grateful."

"It is as well that this place has something to commend itself to you, it does nothing for me. For my part I would rather be miles away."

Gomez laughed, "In Villagarcía, no doubt, with your arms about your lovely wife DoZa Magdalena?"

"At the very least, Gomez; and away from this rain. I tell you there is more damned water falls on this place in an hour than falls on Valladolid in a whole year."

Carlos wagged a twisted, swollen finger at him, "I must point out that my secretary Gaztelu has never been known to utter a word of complaint. You are beginning to sound like an old man, Quijada, nay worse, an old woman. Come, gather around the fire, draw up some stools, so we may talk in comfort."

Quijada bowed, "Comfort for some is Hell for others, my lord. Indeed some may feel they are in the fiery furnaces at this very moment. I beg your forbearance if I sit a little apart."

"You are in a crotchety mood this morning! Can you believe your ears, Gomez? What am I to do with the man? He would deny me my little comforts for his own when he knows how I suffer intensely from the merest hint of cold. It gets right into my bones. Shame on you, Quijada, for being so selfish. But to more serious matters; how is Felipe, my dear son? Is he still in the Low Countries? He is not as constant with his letters as a good son should be."

"Your majesty, he is well, and if he does not write to you in person it is because he has many duties to attend to. The winter has been exceedingly bitter with more snow and ice than I care to remember; but your son, like a true Christian has arranged relief for those most affected. He has distributed straw, firewood, bread, and beer where needed. We have witnessed some desperate cases, my lord. However, there have been occasions of respite from the cares and woes of a very sorry situation. Many of the company have enjoyed winter fun and games including skating on the pond in the park."

"Did Felipe join in the activities?"

"No, my lord, but he enjoyed many a laugh at their antics."

"Well that, at least, is something. I feel he is often far too serious for a young man, not knowing how to relax. All work and no play makes for a very dull person."

"I am sure he has his own ways, my lord, to escape the weight of ever present responsibilities."

Carlos spluttered furiously, "Aye; and those are a damned sight far removed from skating and snowballing! Oh, yes, I have heard tales that he goes out alone at night and in disguise to seek diversion and amusement with women at a certain house."

Then just as the sudden outburst had shocked Gomez, he was equally taken aback by its disappearance. Carlos grinned, "I am sure you know all and I am equally sure that as his faithful friend you will not tell me. We understand that sort of loyalty do we not my friend Quijada? But I am his father and should know if he has decided to ignore my sound advice on such things. More importantly I am concerned whether he is being unfaithful to his queen, the Lady Mary. My advice, by the way, is good advice for any man, you included, Gomez," he leaned towards him. "Squandering good seed is harmful to the body. Moderation is called for. Good God my uncle killed himself with too much sexual sport."

Quijada coughed.

"I know." Carlos was peeved. "It is only hearsay, and perhaps not necessarily true. Nevertheless, I do know that overindulgence in that sort of thing weakens a man's seed. And lastly, I would remind you of the teachings of the church."

Ruy Gomez cleared his throat, recovering from the shock of the mood changes, the embarrassment of the lecture. "I thank you for your wise counsel, my lord. Regarding the rumours about King Felipe; there will always be those who exaggerate, and those who are only too ready to spread calumny, especially against the good and the great and even more so against the innocent."

Carlos narrowed his eyes, "You leave me with no answer to that, for you are so right. Then I shall remain in ignorance. But we will set that aside for the while."

Just a quick word; Felipe, I am afraid, has transgressed at least twice. One of the young ladies now finds herself in an 'interesting' condition. There are also stories circulating about him and his cousin, Princess Christina of Denmark, his erstwhile ambassador to England newly returned to Brussels. She is a young woman, most intelligent and more than qualified; but far too pretty.

"My lord, with permission, let me turn to urgent matters. Felipe is on his way to England to seek military support against the French. It beggars belief, my lord, to think it is just months since we signed a peace treaty with the French, yet they are on the move once more, and His Holiness the Pope is in league with them. If one cannot trust the pope who is there to trust! The situation is critical. France, at the bequest of the pope has invaded Italy, while at the same time attacking Flanders. Unfortunately we are in a perilous financial position. King Felipe has had to suspend all loan repayments to the banks. We are in desperate need of money for the wars, and to repay our debts. Things are in a sorry state."

He stopped, alarmed at Carlos's reaction; the face livid, eyes ablaze; he looked to Quijada for reassurance. Quijada encouraged him to continue.

"Your majesty, King Felipe has sent me to seek your advice and support to get us out of this impasse."

The anger was quite gone, disappeared. Carlos closed his eyes. "The sure signs of a dutiful son; to turn to his father is in itself most gratifying. It is good to know that my many years of experience have been noted, and noted well. Of course we will do all in our power. Nothing is beyond our capabilities; is that not so, Quijada?"

"Quite so, my lord; goodness me, we have been in this situation so often before and fought our way through it," he was well practised in sounding positive, he had had years of it. "We need to know everything. How bad is the debt?"

I did say a few moments ago that Gomez is the Chief Accountant of the Treasury. Well in truth there is no Treasury, or at best it is a great misnomer.

I hate to sound pedantic but a treasury is responsible for monies deposited and dispersed, requiring organisation, a system of accounting for revenues and expenditures; correct?

For years this country's finances have been conducted on an ad hoc basis; the Treasury waiting for, hoping for, income to arrive from someone or somewhere while trying to meet the demands of creditors and at the same time seeking funds for foreign campaigns.

I tell you the only system in operation is one of limping from crisis to deepening crisis.

But back to Gomez.

"I am afraid to have to report that Spain is so seriously in debt to the foreign bankers that at this point not one, no, not one of them will exchange gold for our promissory notes; and if this were not all ..."

Carlos exploded, "Those blasted Germans! Oh, they are only too ready to have someone protect them; but by God, when it suits them they can be too damned reluctant to part with the wherewithal to pay for that protection! God knows I have always given them their damned money in the end; and with a pretty hefty interest too. Yes, they have always got their pound of flesh. They have never been the ones mortgaged up to the hilt. For how many years have I poured Spanish gold back into their coffers? Paying over forty per cent interest, I would have you know! Humph! Bankers: the Fuggers, et al. I suspect the poisonous talk of some of those damned German princes behind this. Downright insulting. But I shall not lose my temper. I need time to think."

"Have you been to Valladolid to speak with the Princess Juana?" Quijada enquired. He knew full well he had, hadn't he just said that the princess had spoken of the child, but he had to ask.

"I have. But more grave news awaited me there. Something is sorely amiss in Seville. Let me explain. When the princess, acting on behalf of Felipe, sought loans for the Spanish troops, the response from Seville was that there was no gold. I mean, I ask you, no gold? My lord, I do not seek to cause your majesty any alarm ..."

Carlos's face had turned purple; strangled gurglings of rage forced their way from between lips rigid with anger. "I do not believe this! How dare they!" He held his hand to his throat.

Gomez rose to his feet, alarmed. Quijada leapt up, sending his stool clattering to the floor. Gaztelu rushed for a goblet of barley water.

"Sire, shall I send for Mathys? For some medication perhaps?" Quijada was concerned.

"No, dammit!" Carlos fumed, "I shall soon recover. This is anger, not an illness you fools!" He threw the contents of the goblet into his mouth before furiously spitting the whole lot back. "Get rid of that horse piss, Gaztelu, and bring me a beer. Gentlemen help yourselves to some refreshment. We must think."

IV

"This sounds a most worrying affair," whispered Quijada to Gomez as he poured a small quantity of beer into a goblet for the king.

"Very. Wait until you hear the whole story. I hope his majesty is strong enough."

"No whisperings over there," Carlos threw at them, "my ears are about the only part of my body not to fail me these days and I heard every word." He took the offered goblet, peering down into its meagre contents. "It is as well for you, Quijada, that I owe you so much for your years of friendship, or I swear to God I would have you ... do you call this a drink?"

"It is, albeit a small one."

They sat and drank in silence until Carlos showed his readiness to hear more.

"You may continue. Do not spare me the details," he growled.

Ruy Gomez began hesitantly, "The vaults in Seville, my lord, normally full with bullion brought home in the fleets from the New World have been emptied. Felipe on hearing this wrote to the merchants stating his fury in no uncertain terms, but it was not until my arrival at Valadolid that I discovered the whole truth."

"I take it we are not speaking of the gold that belongs to the merchants who finance the shipments?" Carlos measured out the words slowly, quietly.

"No, my lord, not entirely; although as you are aware that while much of the gold is in truth theirs it has always been made available to the crown; but not so now. Normally there is other gold too; brought back in payments for goods delivered, and in the past this also was at our disposal, but again, not so now. And what of the Royal Fifth of all bullion plus the Royal Taxes, equalling approximately forty per cent of all the gold shipped into this country, which also belongs to the Crown? I am afraid there is even very little of that left. Apparently most has been taken because of unpaid royal debts. What little remains in the vaults is woefully inadequate for our needs."

Carlos continued his valiant effort to remain calm, "Presumably the rest of this gold still exists somewhere? It cannot just have disappeared."

"Indeed it does my lord. It has been removed by the merchants themselves and taken to their own private vaults to prevent us having access to it."

"Jesus Christ! God in Heaven!" he bellowed. "Did you hear that, Quijada? What kind of treason do we have here? To prevent us having access; unable to touch Spanish gold! That the king, that the country may not have it when the need is so great!"

"Disgraceful, unacceptable. Yet there is every reason to expect its return, my lord. I remain optimistic." Quijada certainly sounded positive. "They have yet to hear from you, and I honestly believe that the merchants will sing a different song as soon as they do."

Gomez's spirits were lifted hearing this optimism, "You have echoed my hopes exactly. This is why I am here, to beg not only your wisdom and experience but the power of your voice. I am only concerned that I had at first to be the cause of your displeasure in order to obtain your help."

"Gomez, not only have you come to the right place but by God you have come to the right man! You have rekindled the fight in me. You will see that this old man can do more from his sick bed than many an able bodied ruler. And rest assured I feel no ill will to you the messenger."

Quijada's words had stirred up an almost forgotten strength and resolve in him. "Gaztelu prepare to write some letters. The princess regent shall be informed of our intent. You will state at the outset that were it not for my infirmities I would go to Seville myself. I would personally sort out the lot of those bastard merchants. Tell her that I intend, nevertheless, to have them all brought to justice. I order their immediate arrest; they are to be clapped in irons, thrown into the dungeons … I want them tortured to within an inch of their lives, whilst I contemplate with pleasure every imagined scream. You can use any other expression of this sort provided it is blood curdling and terrifying. Follow it up with an apology to her for my intemperate language. Secondly, you will tell the princess that when the next fleet is expected to return with a shipment of bullion she is to order a ship to set out with explicit orders to intercept it. All, and I mean all, the gold will be brought into the safekeeping of the Royal Treasury. That will teach the bastards a lesson! Give my apologies for my not writing this in my own hand but because of the gout …"

He thought for a moment. "When that is done you will write to the various bishops, convents, etc. etc., and tell them I want gold advanced immediately for the war in Italy. A copy of that letter is also to go the princess."

Carlos turned to Gomez, "As soon as that money comes in you can despatch it to Alba. We must not keep him from important duties, must we? Damn fine general, Alba, probably the best, a bit too much on the cautious side, but he is successful for all that. Just so long as he is kept out of government, too powerful a man, but I have warned Felipe about that side of him. I know you and Alba do not always see eye to eye ..."

"Two different schools of thought, my lord, different approaches, nothing more."

"Ever the diplomat, eh? No matter. So, what do you think of our strategies?" Carlos sat back immensely impressed with himself.

"My lord, how can we ever thank you enough. But there is just one more request. Spain needs you. Sire, will you not consider returning to the helm of our gallant ship?"

"You make a pretty speech and I may yet be swayed."

Quijada gave Carlos one of his fierce stares. "Not while I am here, no matter who comes a-calling and a-wooing. There are no captains of ships here. Let that be understood."

"You see how he treats me Gomez? I suppose I must do as I am bid. So, having sorted out Felipe's problems let us move on then to happier subjects. I shall treat myself to some of that delicious Serrano ham and more beer while Gomez tells me of his betrothed."

Quijada challenged, "Would there be any point in my suggesting you refrain from this constant eating and drinking?"

"None whatsoever; especially not today, Quijada. You cannot have your way in everything. Ham and beer!"

V

"Hey, José, he didn't half get his dander up about them men with the gold, didn't he?" Samuel whispered from between lips that barely moved, his head bent, staring down intently at the toes of his boots. "Fair scared the living daylights out of me, shouting like that."

"He can't stand them merchant fellas, or bankers. Can't blame him, they all sound like bastards to me. Have you noticed how he's always 'aving to beg, and after everything he's done for everybody. A bleedin' shame, it is."

"Doesn't seem right a king being made to ask. He should just be given what he wants. I mean, he's more important than anybody. How come they have more money than him anyway?"

"'Cause they keep theirs or spend it on themselves while he spends it on looking after everybody, Sam. Got his own back on one of them, at any rate," he smiled. "Yes he showed him alright."

Samuel was curious. "When was that then?"

"You remember nowt; you. Just after we left Valladolid on our way here. Do you really not remember stoppin' at that house in Medina del Campo?"

Samuel screwed up his eyes and nose. "Oh Gawd, that place. Like walkin' into Heaven it was."

José sneaked a glance at him full of incomprehension, "What you mean by that, you daft beggar?"

"Well it was all gold and shiny, like, beautiful cloths on the walls, and a smashing smell. That's how Heaven is, seems to me."

"I suppose. Anyway the king got so bloody mad about the feller showing off with his gold this, and gold that, even gold braziers and all the rest of the posh stuff, includin' burnin' cinnamon in the braziers, that 'e says, 'Right mate, I'll get my own back on you'. Well, when I says he said that, he didn't actually say it; but he might 'ave done cos he gives him this great purse and it's full of money, bursting it was. Come on, you must remember that."

"I do, José, but what had that to do with anything? What has that to do with getting 'is own back?"

"Gawd, are you thick, or are you thick, Sam? When the king gave him the purse of money it was like telling the bloke he was no better than a regular innkeeper."

Samuel thought hard about it for a moment. "Aw, right!"

69

Carlos wiped his hands on a napkin, "Gomez, tell me of Ana de Mendoza."

"My lord as yet there is not much to tell. I have been betrothed now for four years or more. But I fear it will be some time yet before we marry. There is still much to be done before King Felipe may return to Spain. Perhaps within two years? All I have to cheer my heart is a picture of my intended spouse." Gomez offered Carlos his treasured miniature.

"By God, Gomez, you are a lucky man to have found such a young beauty, perfection itself, and at your age too. Look at this Quijada. What would you say, about nineteen, or twenty?"

"Perhaps, my lord."

"She is seventeen."

"Only seventeen? Just a child then when you were betrothed. But why the eye patch?"

"An unfortunate accident, I believe, when very young; fencing."

"Makes her look damn mysterious; yes fetching and alluring. I beg your pardon; how ungallant to talk about a lady, your lady, like that. But man, I am taken with this face, the seductive smile on those full, moist lips; wicked I tell you. Dammit, looking and imagining are all that are left in this old frame of mine, sadly, so you are in no danger from me. But had I been younger ..."

Carlos will never sample the delights of the alluring Ana de Mendoza y de la Cerda but his son Felipe most certainly will.

"You had best help Felipe settle his foreign affairs quickly that you may come home before it is too late for you to enjoy the raptures of the wedding bed. Is that not so, Quijada? God knows you had to wait long enough to have a young wife to warm your sheets!"

For an instant he saw another young woman, the beautiful Barbara, and, dear God, hadn't he himself been almost too old by then?

Quijada sighed, "As you say, my lord, and even now, after only a few years of marriage I have little opportunity ..."

70

"Then bring your wife here, for God's sake! Get her a house in Cuacos, it is only a couple of miles down the road. It might help cheer you up, too." His eyes returned to the miniature. "But this pretty young thing puts me in mind of Ursolina. Did I ever tell you about her, Quijada? She came to my court in Brussels; had a husband at the time, but he died suddenly. I was twenty-one or twenty-two? I forget. But she was just the sort of maiden I liked; if you know what I mean," he wheezed an ancient's lecherous giggle. "She was beautiful, gay, enchanting, and she needed consoling and comforting. I was damned good at that kind of thing. Unfortunately she became pregnant and that put an end to it all. Then the little madam had the effrontery to go ahead and marry without my permission; without my choosing her husband..."

"Excuse me, but I thought we were talking about the betrothal of Gomez and not about your beautiful Ursolina and your incontrollable jealousy when she married." Quijada's interruption was icy.

Gomez looked from Quijada to the king, uncomfortable at such boldness, waiting for the ensuing explosion of fury.

Instead Carlos laughed, "You are right again, Quijada. Gomez, you know, this man is always right, and honest. Speaks his mind readily. I appreciate that, would never have it any other way. Probably the best friend I have ever had. Now let me just tell you about ..."

Let us leave them to enjoy each other's company while they can. They have some weighty problems to face over the next few weeks.

"The king's a right devil for the women, isn't he?"

"Strikes me they all are, Sam, and I bet we don't know the 'alf of it. Struth, there's one 'ell of a draught coming from somewhere. Can you feel it?"

"Yeah. It's like someone is walkin' over me grave, least that's what me mother would say. Maybe the door wasn't shut proper." He adjusted his collar. "Or maybe we's getting as soft as the king."

71

June

An Important Visitor

I

Good morning, good morning, how lovely to see you again. I have missed your company. Why, it must be two months or so since we last met. It must be. Yes, it was March and here we are in June; time goes by so quickly. But here you are, and early too; good, for we need a lot of time. There is so much for me to tell you before you meet an important visitor who is staying here at the moment. I also think it would be helpful if you were to have some background information on him.

As it is such a beautiful day, shall we take a stroll in the gardens? We can take this path with the myrtle hedge and the lime bushes. How delicious the limes look; and over here, these splashes of colour, such magnificent carnations; Carlos has had most of these blooms imported. Of course, he has always been a keen gardener. This is his special garden. When he arrived it wasn't ready for him. Brother Ortega had promised that everything would be in place but when Quijada came to inspect he found it far from finished, and he was furious beyond words. Be that as it may, you can see the king has worked wonders – directing and instructing

72

from his chair, obviously. The days are long gone when he would have been down on his knees, soil deep under his fingernails.

Right then; let me bring you up to date with events following the visit of Ruy Gomez. So much has been accomplished in so remarkably short a time. It is absolutely incredible; would you believe that huge sums of money have been found by enforcing the advanced payments of church tithes and taxes on church rents? Of course the workers on the land will inevitably be the ones who pay for all this.

Now this is quite ingenious; someone has had the clever idea of increasing the sales of Papal Bulls of Indulgence, under a new and novel title Crusades. I tell you, the emotional appeal rarely fails! It was an added inspiration to suggest that these indulgences must be renewed every three years. That will provide a good steady flow of revenue into the coffers.

One simply has to marvel at the industry and ingenuity involved throughout all this. By the way, Carlos was asked if he too would accept a promissory note for some of his own gold, but he is far too wise an old owl to fall for that one!

And more positive news! The eagerly awaited bullion fleet will be in port within days. All told, the money chests will soon be full, and Spain's new found fortune will soon be on its way to our armies in France and Italy. Of course this is nothing more than a temporary solution to an ever worsening situation.

And then there is the useless, wanton waste of life! I beg your pardon I was only intending to refer to the positives.

The king's health has not been affected by any of this. Oh no. In fact he is so well these days you would barely recognise him, or rather you would be amazed at the change in him. A few days ago he almost leapt out of his chair with delight when he received a letter from his daughter Juana saying that several of the merchants of Seville had been arrested and imprisoned. His joy seemed boundless when he read that some had even perished on the rack. I must add however, he showed exactly the same emotion over an accompanying package of melon seeds. I find it all very odd.

I should also mention that as much as his health improves, that of the people about him deteriorates. I have never known of so many ailments, none of them serious. The fact is many of his entourage are downright unhappy living here, and therein lies the problem.

Here we are; this is the king's fish pond. A goodly size, but I would have preferred a more natural shape instead of this uninspiring rectangle; all too Roman. Some of the kitchen lads make sure it is always well stocked with trout, and he manages to while away an hour or so, cane in hand. The chair lads are always at the ready should there be a tug on the line. However, it is my opinion that it is unwise to spend any length of time here, in fact I beg you not to linger for the water attracts the mosquitoes in their millions; and they cause such fevers and sweats! Several of the household have already been made quite ill by the little beasts. Of course there are always the lucky ones who go unscathed.

There above us are the windows to the king's audience chamber and to the right his private salon. On the left at the end of the gallery are the ramps to these gardens and the pond. Such imaginative designing, it makes it so much easier for the chair lads to get Carlos down here.

The ground floor apartments echo those of the king's. They may look attractive from here, but I assure you they are cold, dark, and damp throughout the winter months, disgustingly humid in the summer, and another paradise for those winged brutes I just mentioned.

Shall we leave and make our way up that hill towards the trees and the little chapel? The views are exquisite and I assure you we will find some welcoming shade there. This way, if you please.

Ah, yes, every day is washing day. I do feel there is a wholesomeness about washing hanging out to dry. But it is amazing how much dirty linen is created by so few people. Row upon row of white linens of every shape and size, assembled like a vast fleet.

The young girl, Maria, worked her way along rows of white laundry searching for spaces for yet more wet linens. She set her basket down on the grass put her hands on her hips and rested.

"Maria! This sheet, she is not clean. Do again," announced a harsh female voice from behind a line of gently wafting squares and rectangles.

Maria, her moment's peace shattered, ducked under some pillow cases to be confronted by a crumpled white bundle looking as pure as the driven snow. Holding it between disdainful fingers was her mistress, a formidable woman in her fifties. Madame Male was tall, thin, grey, and unbending, with ice blue eyes at once searching, critical, and accusing.

"Maria," mimicked the girl to herself, taking the bundle from her mistress. "This sheet she is not clean."

75

"This also, she is not clean," her mistress called from another row.

Maria dropped the first offending article into her basket then ran to gather the second piece of unacceptable linen into her arms, muttering, "This also ..."

She waited until Madame Male had moved some distance away before giving vent to her anger, "Just what does she expect? Gawd knows I do my best. What's she think I was doing all morning since break of dawn? I'll tell her what I was doing. I was scrubbing and rubbing; I was standing sweating over boiling water forever, stirring and stirring." Scalding tears of hurt ran down her cheeks, she smudged them with the backs of her hands. "But did she say, 'Maria see how that sheet, so stained when she came, she is now so clean! How that chemise with its bloody marks, she is so clean! How that towel she is clean! How that pillow cover with its dried yellow spittle she is clean!' Did she? Did she say, 'These things they are looking like new'? No, she bleeding-well didn't; and them looking exactly like they'd never been used."

She moved about inspecting these, the finer examples of her work, her lower lip quivering, before stamping her foot at the unfairness of it all. She picked up her basket and hoisted it onto her head.

"What you doing, Maria?"

A woman somewhat older than Maria, and very much thinner, hurried from the laundry room, finishing tying a bow to her white apron.

"Taking this lot back, Ana, that's what."

"What for?"

"Her ladyship says they're not good enough."

"What for?"

"'Cause I 'aven't got all the marks off. You know why? It's that greasy stuff they paint on the king's arse." She dropped her basket breaking into helpless laughter her hurt and anger forgotten, "Oh my Gawd! Fancy kings 'aving arses just like us ordinary folk!"

"You're terrible, you are, thinking of things like that," Ana spluttered into her apron. "It's true though, it's not something you expect. You don't think of them being real people, really, do you; having bodies under them fancy clothes?"

"And not only 'as this one got an arse, he 'as one that needs fixing."

"You get worse, you do."

Maria remembered she was furious, "Anyways I tried hard enough. Look at these hands with that hot water and powder stuff. If they was any redder you would swear they was bleeding." She showed Ana her sore hands; angry red, chapped and stinging. "What you doing out 'ere then?"

"Seeing if anything is dry enough to press."

"What I wouldn't do, Ana, for a job like yours, making everything so neat and being able to wear a lovely white pinafore."

"Just so long as there's no creases in my work, Maria. And I tell you Madame Male has eyes like a lynx, and if there's the slightest wrinkle it's all to do again. As if anybody'd notice. Don't you be in such a rush, anyway; Alonso did good by you, getting you this job. You should be more patient if you ask me."

"I know. I keep on pinching meself and reminding meself I should be grateful. It's nowhere near as 'ard as farm life, really. I don't have to worry about where the next meal's coming from. And more important than anything, I can sleep peaceful at night; no stinking animals or forever being pestered by people."

"What's that? Don't tell me you had to sleep with animals; you couldn't. It doesn't seem right."

"Nothing right nor wrong about it, it's what you 'ave to do, especially in winter. Animals are the family's fortune; you got to bring them in nights. Believe me they are more important than people; not that that makes them stink any less."

"You poor thing. Sleeping amongst us women must be lovely."

"And I can sleep easy at night knowing I'm not going to be wakened with somebody trying to get up my shift to do you know what."

"Why, that's terrible! I can't believe my ears. Who would do that?"

"All of them, Ana. They all pester you: fathers, brothers, sisters' husbands, the lot of them. No one else bats an eyelid, but I hated it, and it was hard work fighting to shove them off,

77

and them trying to hold me down telling me to lie still and shut up."

"Then all the more reason you should be grateful to Alonso, and no mistake. I never knew things like that went on. I guess I was very lucky living with just my widowed mother."

"Too right, cos I tell you everybody does it. You don't know the half! I am grateful to Alonso, honest; I'm just feeling so damned angry with the old cow for not saying something nice about my work and me doing my best."

"Oh, Lord, here she comes. I bet her husband feels the sharp end of her tongue often enough, and him such a quiet chap. Can't see him forcing his way up her shift!"

They swallowed their giggles.

Madame Male planted herself before them, arms folded, glowering, "Is this the way the laundry of the king she is done? This talk and talk and talk, this laugh and laugh, this is how? You do not talk, you do not laugh, you do not get the payment to do so. Ah, good, at last a cool breeze, this makes better. Ah, but now she is gone."

"I've noticed that quite a bit around 'ere, Madame Male."

"I do not think I ask you about this, thank you … to work."

You are shocked and offended by Maria's revelations of family life amongst the common folk? What she says is perfectly true. I can assure you it is more of a surprise that she should be objecting. It is quite acceptable for men to take their pleasure with any of the females in the family.

II

Returning to our visitor. He is a priest, Francisco de Borja. But first I must tell you a little more about Queen Juana, Carlos's mother.

The setting is Tordesillas, a small hilltown standing high above a river not far from Valladolid. You nod your head, you know it? Of course you do, you saw the

78

delightful sketch Carlos has in his salon. Could you hope for a more idyllic setting than that to retire to? You have simply to cross the bridge and up the little rise to reach peace and tranquillity. It was in a little used palace in that town where the widowed Queen Juana was hidden away from the public eye by her father. It proved as secure as any prison could ever be. Yes, he had her locked up then settled himself down to rule as Regent of Castile.

It would take too long to tell of the indignities and torture she suffered at his hands but suffer she did and for several years. Juana's only solace throughout this time was her youngest daughter Catalina.

Well, her father died a few years later and Carlos was summoned from Flanders. Juana, freed at last from her father's tyranny, had transformed her prison into a palace once more. It was splendid: exquisite furnishings had been rediscovered; the walls were hung with luxurious tapestries; silver and gold plate made welcome reappearances to be displayed on chests and sideboards.

The family was reunited. Happiness and joy abounding? Oh, if only ... But Carlos set about organising the palace in Tordesillas to his liking, not his mother's; and it is at this point that Francisco enters the story.

Shall we sit a while in the shade of this oak? Allow me to spread my cloak over this fallen bough. These trees are colossal, such height and strength. How many centuries have they stood here witnessing events? If trees and buildings could only speak, such tales might they tell!

Where was I? Yes, this Francisco was a member of an elite little circle of boys and girls chosen to accompany Catalina in her studies, her dancing classes, her sport, and her riding. Juana, however, was not to enjoy any of the court activities. Nor was she was ever allowed outside the palace. She was granted no favours; in fact she was removed to more isolated apartments, and these were situated in a rear yard overlooking the kitchens and sculleries and the rotting heaps of rubbish hurled from their doors!

Francisco remained in Catalina's court for about eight years, until she left for Portugal to marry King John III. Not long afterwards Carlos married Isabel and he entered their household. Yes, he became a part of the court of the beautiful Isabel, the Isabel everybody loved. Do you know, it was even rumoured that Francisco was greatly enamoured of her. I shall say no more about that except that a ballad was distributed which told of his heart's affliction and his inconsolable days of mourning when she died.

Now, before you fall into the trap of believing that Isabel was all virtue (and I must confess to that probably being my fault) I should point out that she, as well as others in Juana's family, was not averse to a little thieving. Perhaps you would prefer calling it unauthorized borrowing without any intention of returning.

In bygone days Juana had found great pleasure in beautiful jewellery, and had brought a considerable number of very fine pieces with her to Tordesillas. These were all packed away in caskets as she wore very little in the way of adornments at this time. Carlos, from his very first visit to the palace had helped himself liberally to many a handful. Isabel considered herself equally free to take whatever caught her fancy, and believe me she did fancy quite a few items; never a by your leave or may I.

Sorry; back to my story. Both Carlos and Isabel thought so highly of Francisco that he was found a Portuguese wife. She brought a most generous dowry with her; I would remind you that the nobility of Portugal as well as its royal house are very rich. Francisco was created a marqués, a move to make him equal in status with his rich bride.

Sadly, Isabel's thirteen years of marriage came to a sudden and tragic end. Shortly after her seventh pregnancy, which ended in a miscarriage, she died of puerperal fever. Carlos was inconsolable and retired to a monastery with his confessor for a month while his son Felipe and Francisco were given the task, in the searing heat of summer, to accompany the funeral cortege to Granada, where Isabel's mortal remains were to be laid to rest.

The body had to be identified prior to the committal ceremony. The lead-lined coffin was opened and Francisco fell to the ground mumbling almost incoherently that he could not swear other than that this must be the body which he had seen robed in the Franciscan habit and placed in this coffin in Toledo, but as for what he now actually saw? Alas, the beautiful face of his beloved queen had become a heaving, worm-ridden, fetid mass of stinking putrefaction. It was then that he expressed a desire for a life of reflection and piety; aware, painfully aware, that human flesh is nothing, the human soul everything.

When his wife died he renounced his wealth and title in favour of his son and retired from the pomp and splendours of court life to join the Jesuits.

This, then, is the person we are to meet a little later today, the Jesuit priest Father Francisco.

Doubts

I

The June sun flooded in across the furnishings and floor of the private salon to be stopped short by the chill about Carlos as he sat hunched forward in his chair his face set in a grim mask. He peered through his glasses first at one then another of the sheets of paper handed to him in glum silence by Gaztelu and Quijada.

"Yes. Yes. Do you have to bore me with such trivia, for God's sake? I am having a very bad day and there is no need to make it worse. Have the chair boys gone?"

"They are at the door."

"Not good enough. I want them out."

Quijada turned to José and Samuel, "Wait outside lads."

They bowed and left, José mumbling, "That's a bleedin' disappointment. Bet we're going to miss some gossip."

Carlos sighed, "Do you not have some news from home, Quijada, to cheer us? How is Doña Magdalena?"

"Lonely. If it were not for the boy ..."

"Bring her here to Cuacos! How often do I have to say it?"

"That will be far from easy."

"Well, thank you for sounding so positive! Is that what you consider cheerful news? What about the boy?"

Quijada gazed out through the window, into the distance, his thoughts crossing the miles between Yuste and Villagarcía, smiling. "Doña Magdalena tells me he has completely charmed all the village womenfolk. At the bull fight last week a bull escaped from the ring in the village square. Admittedly it was very young and quite small but, nevertheless, a bull, and it was on the wrong side of the barricade. There was screaming, people fleeing or climbing to safety. The lad simply stepped out in front of the animal, holding his cloak before him like a shield. The bull stopped dead in its tracks, pawed at the ground, lifted its head, and looked him square in the eye."

"And?" Carlos leaned forward anxiously.

"And the bull turned and allowed itself to be ushered back to the ring, with a few slaps across its hindquarters to encourage it. Delighted ladies threw down flowers from upper windows, men cheered and waved their neckerchiefs and, I believe, a few of the other young lads there were just a tiny bit envious."

Carlos relaxed and shook his head, "By God, but you have a fearless one there. Must be your influence, Quijada, you were never one to shy away from danger. Just so long as the boy is careful, sensible and not being foolhardy or headstrong."

"My squire is his guide and mentor; I have no concerns. He is also instructing him in horsemanship for hunting and jousting. Juan is an excellent pupil; it is as if he were born in the saddle."

"I was damned good myself once."

"Would that he might prove to be half the horseman you were."

"And his studies?"

"He applies himself well, but not for long, his thoughts soon drift to the outdoor pursuits."

Carlos chuckled, "I hated the schoolroom. I was always being censured by my tutors for being inattentive. Books were of little significance to me as a youth. Let the lad beware, got to get his priorities right. What of his music?"

"Quite good; improving. At least the musician did us a favour there. Also, according to my wife, the lad appears to have some natural talent. You will understand that it would not be for me to comment, you know my limitations when it comes to music."

"Too true. Has there been a letter from Barbara?"

Gaztelu, who had listened, pleasantly diverted, to the progress report of this child snatched from the arms of its mother somewhere in Germany, hoping to hear something to really excite, now pricked up his ears. Barbara; this was a new name.

"A request for money."

"Again? Her husband had a decent enough pension as a commissary, surely?"

Gaztelu blinked over his spectacles; this could prove interesting. That lady's hand on all those letters, he now assumed, belonged to someone called Barbara, and she was apparently often asking for money in those letters. Moreover, it was not a secret that Quijada withheld from the king as he had suspected.

"She requests a one-off payment, a pension for her chaperone."

Carlos tugged first at his grizzled beard then at his lower lip revealing the few yellow, broken teeth, randomly scattered along the gums of his protruding lower jaw. "Everything to do with that family is on a 'just this once' basis, have you noticed?"

"Indeed I have; all the same, perhaps a gesture would be in order. As a chaperone she did perform a sterling service as I recall."

"It took no effort; good God, she was such a fearsome woman. There was only Barbara who would ever dare say anything to her without dreading a counterblast. Yes, I suppose you could give what you think is appropriate, but insist that there will be no further allowances of any sort. How long am I to be made to pay for that voice?"

"You do surprise me. I might remind you that it was Barbara's voice that calmed you, rid you of all pains and concerns."

"All of ten years ago or more!"

So the question was finally answered and it was so disappointing. This Barbara, the writer of all those letters, the letters Quijada often hid in his jerkin, used to sing for Carlos. There was no real mystery after all; although Gaztelu still found it a little strange that he had never heard of her until now. He removed his spectacles, placed them on his papers, then, without a hint of guile, offered, "May I venture, my lord, that given your very high standards the lady must have had a remarkable voice to be remembered for so long and with such affection."

Carlos and Quijada, shocked to discover that Gaztelu had been sitting there all this time and listening to their conversation, could only stare at him.

Ah, the timely arrival of Francisco de Borja, our visiting priest. Shall we stand as close as

85

we can to the open window? We can enjoy the occasional breeze carrying the precious mountain air perfumed by summer flowers from the garden below.

II

Carlos cheerily called across the room, "The Old Duque himself, come to visit!"

His joy immediately changed to irritation, "For goodness sake get up off your knees. You know quite well I am a nobody these days. And in any case I have known you too long for such formalities. We shall be as cousins, and we are more or less, thanks to Grandfather Ferdinand straying from the straight and narrow. Sit down, sit down, you make me damn nervous hovering over me in those dreary robes."

Francisco was saddened by the bitterness and disappointment etched on Carlos's face and in his voice, in the droop of his shoulders. The man looked weary of this world. This was the Emperor Carlos who had ruled most of Europe with an iron will and fist. He had also hoped for a warmer welcome. "My lord, black is the colour chosen by the Jesuits, the Company of Jesus, which it pleases God to allow me to be a member."

Carlos grumbled, "I see no need for this kind of innovation. There were plenty of well-respected orders already. But I am not going to argue with you."

"With respect, my lord, I would like to tell you about the Company; why we are so different."

"We cannot wait to hear, is that not right Quijada?" Carlos made no effort to disguise his sarcasm.

"Our General, Loyola ..."

"Must butt in. Your general? Makes your lot sound like a regular army to me. Is that not so, Quijada?"

"Perhaps God's army, my lord, fighting in a different manner to those of the Empire, but with the same aim?"

"Exactly," Francisco turned to this most receptive of his three listeners. "We are employed in the service of God working as the army of the pope doing whatever he commands, going wherever he says there is the greatest need in this world.

Apart from taking the True Faith to countries far afield the Church here in Europe is in crisis and needs help. Look no further than Germany infected with growing Protestantism, cast your eyes to England with hundreds of monasteries destroyed, Sweden is lost; and as for France and its internal struggles ... God needs an army such as ours. We are the fighters for the Catholic Faith."

Carlos fumed, "Well, there is not one person can say that I have not always done my damnedest to protect the Faith with my armies! I can think of no one who could have done more. No, there is not a single soul who could criticise me on that account. So where does this 'army' of yours base itself? I suppose you have camps for your troops as you go about your various campaigns. You have some tents just down the road, no doubt?"

Quijada chided, "My lord, you are intent on mocking whatever Francisco says. You know well enough that he is in this area to oversee the building of one of their new colleges, and out of courtesy he came to visit you. Why not ask him about the college's progress?"

"Jesus Christ in His wisdom, is there only me with a sense of humour this morning?" Carlos growled, "Can you people not see I am trying to bring a little levity into our conversation? God knows, the Old Duque here sounds like he is giving a lecture. Go on, go on then, tell me about your colleges. And try to make it sound interesting."

"Our colleges are among the best; we teach using the most modern methods. And yes, we do have a new one nearing completion near Plasencia."

"Surely a university would be preferable. Sounds much more impressive. No need to answer. So, what makes you all so special, then?"

"My lord, there is not one order committed to a life serving God that can ever approximate the Jesuits. Loyola insists that as well as being educated men we must continue our studies throughout the whole of our lives. We must also preach, perform acts of charity, teach the catechism, hear confessions. To ensure we are all dedicated to carrying out all our General's rules no one is accepted into our Company if they come from another order."

"Ah, now then, what is this? Criticism? Pride? Superiority?" Carlos raised his eyebrows, a triumphant smile lighting up his face. He congratulated himself for he had surely nettled this priest who, so far as he was concerned, had joined a group of fanatics; and furthermore, for some inexplicable reason, had been chosen as confessor by his daughter Juana.

Francisco would not be drawn into a discussion of the shortcomings of other orders, even though they were glaringly self-evident to anyone prepared to believe their eyes and ears. "My lord?" he replied diplomatically, "You must have some information about other orders of which I am ignorant." He shook his head, "I was making no judgements. There was no criticism ever intended. It is simply that it is so much easier to instruct those who come to us without preconceived ideas or opinions on how to hold to the ancient and tried ways. And this is of the utmost importance in a world where it is unsafe to do otherwise."

"Well, thank you, thank you. This is all becoming far too serious so I do not wish to hear any more. But this business of following the orders of the pope, that worries me. I do not trust him, not one iota. I could tell you a thing or two about that evil ... Never mind, we will yet see victory over his villainy. Enough, I have weightier matters on my mind today."

"Forgive me, I would not have presumed to indulge myself in ... I had no idea ..."

"I have received some bad news. My sister Catalina's husband, King John of Portugal, has died. Long live the new king, his grandson, Sebastian."

Francisco bowed his head thinking that this must be the explanation for the king's churlish and miserable behaviour. "Amen to that. You will allow me a few moments of private meditation? My condolences, my lord."

God rest King John's soul. I was speaking only this morning of Catalina's departure from Tordesillas to marry the Portuguese king. Married for thirty-two years, and by all accounts it was a happy marriage.

Her sister Leonor arranged it when she was married to John's father, Emanuel. Poor

Leonor, she had been furious about Carlos marrying her off to the old king, because she was in fact originally betrothed to John. Unfortunately for John, and even more so for Leonor, the father promptly fell in love with her portrait and decided he would have her for himself. Carlos jumped at the opportunity to have his sister marry the king and not the prince, even if he was sixty and she only nineteen. And, would you believe it, with this new contract he would benefit from an immediate loan of fifty thousand Portuguese *doblas*! Not a bad bargain, fifty thousand *doblas* for a sister!

So she was married off to an old man about whom the best compliment that could be paid referred to his wearing fresh clothes every day. What was not divulged was that he was an ancient cripple dribbling and senile.

By the way, Carlos was most magnanimous, allowing Leonor to 'borrow' a few items of their mother's jewels; possibly to sugar the pill, or to salve his conscience, and of course providing her with a few necessary gems befitting a bride-to-be.

The marriage with Emanuel lasted three years and there was one surviving child, a little girl. As soon as she was widowed Carlos required her services again; another marriage. So she returned to Spain, leaving the infant behind.

And then John and Catalina were married.

III

"Aye, Francisco, Catalina was most fortunate. Had a happy marriage. Lasted more than thirty years. I was going through

89

some of her letters this morning. All of them speak of her contentment. And now she, like me, is left all alone."

"My lord, it is a great blessing to find harmony in one's marriage. I too was fortunate. The grief and loneliness will be difficult to bear, but God will be a great support to her in these days of sorrow. I know this from personal experience."

"Amen to that."

Francisco continued, "I remember Catalina so well when she was but a child, how she changed from that little country girl in unadorned plain woollens into an elegant young lady sparkling as wonderfully as the jewels that decorated her satins and velvets. And I recall her affection for her pet dogs. Why, she even had a collar studded with diamonds for one of them," he smiled, shaking his head. "The silly things one does when one is a child. Ah, but those were happy days when I was her page, playing my part in that little court. There were dancing lessons, riding, excursions, as well as our studies. The joys of youth, a lifetime away; nay, a different life. Whenever I reminisce I find it almost impossible now to think that that carefree young man was me." He sighed, "Then one day it was all over. We watched her dazzling cortege leave the town, cross the bridge, then grow ever smaller and fainter until disappearing from sight. She would never be seen again. Gloom and despondency fell like a leaden cloud on the palace and on everyone. Queen Juana, God rest her soul, was thrown into the blackest despair. It took days to persuade her to leave her vigil at the window, to convince her that Catalina would never return. All very sad, very sad. Then of course, I left shortly thereafter to come to your court, and many years passed before I found myself once more in Tordesillas. I was shocked that Queen Juana was so … had become …"

Carlos had been brutally wrenched from his fond memories of his sweet young sister Catalina to face unwelcome images of his mother. He interrupted Francisco, rather too loudly, "My dear sister has turned out to be an excellent monarch and true friend to me and to Spain. Had me worried, you know, back then at the time of the revolutionaries, when I was out of the country. Those damned Comuneros. How much had she and our mother collaborated with them, how far dared I trust her? I know there were many defending the pair of them, and

Catalina put forward a good case to prove that her actions had never been less than loyal. But, for me, there was always that nagging doubt. The information that Denia, the governor of the palace, gave me was very disturbing."

Quijada made a great show of folding his arms by first stretching them out in front of him, groaning, "Denia; that ogre of a man."

Carlos pointedly ignored him and continued, "However, it emerged eventually that all my doubts and suspicions were unfounded, and she was and always has been a loyal and loving sister." He wiped a tear from his eyes, covered his nose with his handkerchief and snorted into it.

"Exactly so," Francisco was eager to voice his long held views. "I would prefer not to speak ill of any man, and especially a dead man, but I feel I must come to the defence of Queen Juana and Princess Catalina. In my opinion the two ladies were greatly wronged. The real root of the problem all along was Denia himself because of the many lies he told. Everyone knew that your sister and Queen Juana never said – nor indeed did they permit anyone else to say – a word against you. Her highness's only desire was to put an end to the injustices suffered by the people of Castile. That was the sole purpose of her involvement in any discussion with the rebels. And then, my goodness, the vigour with which the governor Denia renewed his authority once the revolt was put down! Stories were running wild, in the palace where he was feared and in the town where he was hated, about his being rewarded for his supposed services to you throughout the rebellion while Queen Juana and Princess Catalina were being punished, and for no good reason. There was gossip, too, of him and his wife treating Catalina badly, of their stealing gold and jewels from the Queen, of his locking ..."

"Now just one moment! You stop right there!" Carlos shouted and jabbed a gnarled finger at him, "You were too bloody young to understand, far too young to be gossiping about things that had nothing to do with insolent young pups. By God, you had no idea how damned difficult it was for me at that time. I was out of the country. Yes, I knew the rebellion was quickly crushed and order restored, but family affairs remained to be dealt with. I had to trust Denia's judgement.

This I did and I was more than content I can tell you. I was left free to concentrate on other matters. I needed a man of iron discipline; there was no room for foolish sentimentality."

"But then, when you did come back to Tordesillas, was there nothing about the conditions there to make you …?"

"Youthful exaggerations, you were no different than the rest. In any case I was far too busy for petty grievances," he shuffled uneasily in his chair determined to shrug off guilt. "There was so much to attend to, and all vitally important. There were the marriages of my sisters, and you know quite well what I was faced with when my mother discovered that Catalina was to wed. But what you were probably not aware of was my concern about my mother's refusal to attend to her religious devotions. Compared with this everything else was trivial. I certainly do not need to remind you that heresy is a serious business. There is only the one True Faith, the Christian Faith, the Catholic Church and its teaching, which must be adhered to without question. To depart in any way from this true path is heresy and must be rooted out; Protestants, Reformers; heretics all!" He ranted, his words getting lost in a strangled, high-pitched scream. "I'll have no truck with them anywhere, and certainly not in my own family!"

"My lord, I beseech you, calm yourself," Quijada urged. "You do yourself no good going over this same old ground time and time again."

Carlos waved him aside. "Of course Catalina made excuses, said that there had been no problems until the removal of my mother's confessor, Brother Juan. After his dismissal, on my orders and with good reason, she simply refused to confess or attend Mass. Now, whatever anyone might say, you do not fail in your religious duties simply because you are not allowed your favourite priest, do you? So, as I was saying, I did not know how far I could trust my sister; did she speak the truth or was it dissimulation to protect my mother? I decided she was being a silly child blinded by filial loyalty, unaware that by protecting my mother she was putting all our souls in jeopardy. You see what difficulties children are capable of causing? Still as things turned out, once Catalina was removed from Tordesillas and placed on the throne of Portugal we discovered her true worth to us all. And all the past was forgotten." He wiped his eyes again. "So there we are. We can do no more until we have more news from Portugal."

IV

Francisco, who had been quietly studying Carlos all the while, decided that he should repeat that he had visited Queen Juana shortly before her death.

"I was in Tordesillas two years ago. King Felipe sent me there to determine whether or not your mother was a heretic."

There, the words were out in the open filling every corner of the room. Gaztelu blinked at him. Quijada stood tall and took a deep breath, relieved that at last here, from the lips of Francisco, an honest and intelligent priest (there were so precious few of them) Carlos was about to hear a carefully reasoned opinion instead of so much abstruse pontificating that said nothing.

Carlos, alarmed that Francisco was determined to pursue the subject that he had been so unwise to introduce simply to divert attention from Denia's questionable behaviour, prepared himself for the worst.

"It was King Felipe's earnest wish to resolve the conflicting rumours pouring from Tordesillas linking Queen Juana with, as you say, heresy or madness," Francisco paused to smile, remembering that ancient lady, in her seventies, frail yet with an undaunted spirit. "As soon as I entered the room she took my hands clasping them in hers in the warmest of welcomes, tilted her head to one side, smiled at me saying, 'I remember you. You were a page in my daughter's court all those years ago. You are Francisco.' I was speechless, over thirty years had passed."

"Yes, yes, quite. And you could actually bring yourself to touch her? I found it was bad enough just being anywhere near her. Oh, my God!" Carlos shuddered, remembering the filth and her disgusting smell. "But then you priests can do that sort of thing. So tell me, after all your investigations, do you honestly believe that my mother died a good Catholic?"

"She was reluctant to talk about it at first, insisting that people were only just beginning to show any concern for her, and that even so they only worried about her spiritual health

93

and not her physical comfort. She said that no one had cared or given her a moment's thought for nigh on fifty years."

"Humph!" Carlos shrugged his shoulders dismissing any criticism.

Francisco rose to walk about the room, deep in thought. He stood for a moment looking out at the trees, watching the leaves shimmer and tremble in the faint breeze, before turning back to the stuffy room, "Sometimes I was sure she was intent on provoking me, repeating the outrageous statements she had made to Denia; for I am convinced I detected a mischievous glint in her eye as she awaited my reactions."

"Were they Lutheran, the things she said?" As ever in these discussions about his mother anxiety gripped Carlos.

"No. Not at all. No; she was teasing. She said I had to excuse her nonattendance at Mass in the palace because, she maintained, when she did attend the ladies turned her prayer book upside down. Even worse, they spat in the Holy water."

"Dear God in Heaven." Carlos wrung his hands.

"As I said, she was teasing; looking to see if I would respond in the same horrified way as others had done before me. When I did not she made the excuses ever more bizarre, until, realising I was not one to be tricked, she ceased trying. But, you see, by that time I had got behind the facade and had begun to understand the true reasons for her behaviour. I recognised them all as acts of defiance; ways of retaliating against injustices, against those who she felt had wronged her."

"I have no interest in what other people were supposed to have done," Carlos snapped. "What about her being a … a … heretic?"

"Never once throughout our many conversations had her highness expressed any doubts about the Catholic Faith nor said anything that would suggest she was not a dutiful daughter of the Church. So why did she not attend Mass? I shall give you what I see as the reasons for her rebellion. She had had her trusted friend and confessor taken from her. He was replaced by someone not of her choosing, someone she regarded as an enemy. She was denied the small private altar in her apartment, Denia deciding to have it removed. For many years she had been prevented from attending Mass at the convent of Santa Clara. She was escorted directly to and from the chapel in the corridor, but was never allowed to linger there. There was always someone standing over her; watching when and how she genuflected, staring at her lips when she prayed. She was under constant hostile scrutiny. And, yes, there were those about her only too ready to ridicule. How difficult, if not impossible, to commune with God. So she gave vent to her anger, like a wilful child, and as such reaped the ensuing punishments."

"Someone who dares," Carlos lowered his voice to a whisper, "who dares to raise an arm and sweep everything from the altar and then attempt to tear off the altar cloth must be either a heretic or a crazy fool, and not a wilful child. And it will bring down the wrath of God ..."

"Her behaviour certainly could not be condoned. Yet neither could it be entirely condemned if one takes into account the suffering and provocation leading up to it. Who knows, perhaps it was a cry to God, begging for His help? And of course God in His infinite wisdom did forgive her and led her once again to the paths of righteousness. She accepted that she had sinned grievously in seeking to worship in her own way, and promised she would never do so again, accepting that she was bound by the doctrines which the Apostles had received from Christ. From then on Queen Juana confessed all her misdemeanours regularly, seeking God's forgiveness. She constantly sought my guidance and support as her confessor, and those dark days of the past began to fade, leaving her heart and mind tranquil and at ease. At the end she died a contrite daughter of the Church. It was not heresy that drove your mother to disgrace and shame; it was humiliation. There was no heresy, my lord."

"Just so long as there was no heresy; I do not give a damn about anything else. Anyway it probably all goes to prove what I always said. She was crazy."

"My lord, the sanity of the queen was my next priority. It was of grave importance for us to know the state of her mind."

Quijada and Gaztelu were still coming to terms with Francisco's revelations when after the briefest of pauses the priest decided to take his arguments further.

"Choosing the correct course in assisting her soul on its way to Heaven when the time came was all important. An expert on diseases of the mind spent some time with her majesty before bringing me his findings. These reinforced my own. However, it was our opinion that although Queen Juana was sane she was so gravely ill that our only option was to administer Extreme Unction and not give Viaticum. But ever since her passing I have been plagued by this recurring problem; since she was sane, and we were certain she was, why was she locked away?"

Carlos snapped at him, "You never saw enough of my mother to get a full picture of all her ways. And another thing; it would have been dangerous had she not been isolated. Good God, have you forgotten, she very nearly assumed the throne during the rebellion? We would never have been free of civil strife if I had allowed her to live as a dowager queen; she would have had too many rallying to support her. And for that very same reason I decided not to abdicate until after she died; the thought of passing on such a burden to Felipe was intolerable. A father would not do such a thing to his son!" He brushed angrily at the spittle on his jerkin, irritated with himself for admitting some of the truths, for laying bare some of his fears. "In any case, Francisco, you were not the one who had to make the decisions about how my mother should be looked after, so your conscience need not bother you if that is your worry!" There was now no restraint to his fury and frustration, he bellowed, "Nor will I be preached at. And I shall remind you once more I had, and still have, every faith in my judgement and I trusted Denia!"

Francisco knelt before the king and bowed his head, "I meant no disrespect, my lord. I only seek the truth. Forgive me. Let us rejoice that your mother died a good Catholic, a true daughter of the Church. Perhaps it would be best for me to retire. With your permission I would like to spend some time in the chapel in private prayer and contemplation. I shall pray for King John and all our dear departed."

"Yes, yes, go. I have had enough of the whole damned subject."

Certainties

"Quijada, bring me my box of letters; should be on the table near the door. I want to show you some. Then, by God, you will see which of the two is right; a simpering priest or a strong king."

"I am surprised that you remain unconvinced after listening to Father Francisco."

"It would take more than what I heard this morning. Gaztelu, you may go, you have letters to attend to. Did they remember to bring my spectacles?" Carlos called across the room. "No? That is the blasted disadvantage of living here, the damn servants lack the sense of the dumbest animals."

"Oh, if that were the only disadvantage."

"I shall ignore that. You will have to read them to me. Damnation take it, priests are so aggravating! They can be so damned self-righteous."

Quijada muttered to himself bringing the precious casket, "If only that were all. But Francisco is certainly not in that category." At any other time he would have liked to enlarge on his views on priests but not now, not with the delightful prospect of discovering the contents of these inviting letters. "The letters, where do we start?"

"Read the one written by Catalina, sent to me after the revolution. It should be on the top. The Old Duque Francisco has set my mind to wondering. God, why did he not remain as the Duque de Gandía instead of becoming a convert to the Jesuits? Converts are always the worst. Yes, that one," Carlos pointed at the letter in Quijada's hands. "You may find it a bit of a difficult scribble at times."

The writing was that of a fourteen-year-old still seeking to find a finished form; dainty curls and loops which were a charming mixture of child and emerging lady.

"Could this be the one? It says,

I know that letters have been written from here telling of my disloyalty to you when the rebels were in Tordesillas. Your majesty wrote to me more severely than I deserved."

"Obviously that is the one, Quijada, do not play games with me."

"Oh! We are in a fine mood! To continue then, she writes, I did speak to them, how could anyone do otherwise, they were in command. And it is true, I did write to them, not because I wanted to but because Denia and his wife forced me to, fearing for their jobs, begging not to be dismissed. Until now I have been unable to let you know what is happening here because I may only write what governor Denia dictates. If I speak to the queen's servants or try to send notes out to my friends his wife searches me then sets guards on me. I do not want my confessor to be replaced by another. My mother is restricted to her small apartment; she is denied the freedom of the palace. Everything I have written is the truth, please demand a change as quickly as possible, Catalina."

Quijada tapped the edge of the letter against his chin, "Well, it seems to reinforce everything Father Francisco said."

"A spoiled little madam, more like. Whimpering, I tell you, because she was never allowed to have all her own way. For three years I had seen to it that she had everything she wished: jewels, silks, satins, velvets. And how was I repaid? With behaviour nearing treachery; fraternising with rebels. She needed humbling and Denia was the man to do it. Good God, man, she was only fourteen years old."

"No doubt Denia enjoyed his role. It all sounds rather harsh to me." Quijada took another letter from the box.

Carlos shook his head, "Exaggerations, no more. Yes, I was right. She had to be put in her place. What do you have there?"

"Something from the admiral, the queen's uncle."

"Dear God, another relative to plague me. My mother and sister had him completely hoodwinked. He refused to recognise the truth. Go on then, we will hear what the interfering old beggar had to say."

"We are not forgetting, of course, that the admiral was the one who put down the revolt in 'twenty-two and brought order to Castile for you, the man who proved himself an excellent regent during your absence in Flanders. However, here we go, he says,

When we were in Tordesillas J observed Catalina very closely and certainly she appears to be a most sensible young lady. She is concerned about her mother, especially her accommodation. This does not suit the governor and he ignores her pleas; J include detailed notes on this."

Quijada shuffled through the contents of the box but was disappointed. "Nothing here, unfortunately."

"Would not be in the least surprised if they no longer exist. The man should have minded his own business and allowed others to mind theirs. Anyway, forget that letter; he was a dithering incompetent by then. I want you to bear that in mind."

"Another time I would take issue with you on that. I wish I could have found those notes, they would have been most enlightening."

"And I tell you they are not important, Quijada. What you continue to fail to realise is that the admiral was old and therefore easily manipulated by Catalina. In any case I was not prepared to listen to anything he said."

"My lord you surprise me for I thought you were very much in his debt; and old or not, let me reiterate it was he who put an end to the uprising, who raised a huge army at his own expense, who persuaded other Grandees to join your cause. Yes, by Jove, once they saw his colours tied to the mast they soon followed, quelling civil strife, ensuring peace in Spain. So what on earth could he have done or said to be so out of favour?"

"Do not lecture me Quijada! Listen and learn instead. He had my mother sign a letter telling the rebels to lay down their arms."

"An excellent move. He would naturally believe that they would respond speedily to the queen's command."

"Do not play the idiot with me! There it was in a nutshell. The queen. It was a command from the queen. God, you must be naçve if not an idiot. A command from a queen who must have been of sound mind, able to rule; Queen Juana of Spain! Where would that have left me? Reduced to a nobody, and with some scheming grandee waiting for such an opportunity to seize power for himself. Thank God the admiral was shown the folly of his ways and the letter was destroyed."

"And she was of sound mind?" Quijada enquired with an air of innocence.

"Not you too! Dear God in Heaven!" he screamed. "What is this obsession that is infecting everybody? Why is everyone so preoccupied with this? You should all attend to your own affairs. I will not be judged by any of you. I know better than any. I shall say no more. The subject is closed. No; it is not closed, not yet," he grinned his satisfaction. "I have the best card still waiting to be played in this game. Read me the one from Denia. That might help you understand better, give you the other side of the coin – or it would were you not so damned biased."

"I have found one here. This was also written shortly after the rebellion was put down,

> Most Sacred, Jmperial and Catholic Majesty,
> Our Lord be praised that your majesty enjoys the
> health your vassals desire and may it ever be so.

Goodness me just listen to the man as he grovels. Obsequiousness thy name is Denia.

> The illness of the queen is as usual but at present
> she is paying more attention to her personal
> cleanliness and to the care of her clothes.

Strange. Whatever can the man be talking about, were there not enough servants to attend to her majesty? The rest of this is in code. It must have been sensitive material for the man to be so secretive."

"Do not play coy with me."

Carlos was busy congratulating himself for decisions made more than thirty years ago when Quijada cried out, "Dear God in Heaven, I cannot believe my eyes, he writes

> ...... allow me to apply torture, it would be a
> good thing."

He watched as Carlos squirmed for a second before regaining control.

100

"Quijada, explanations would take too long, and you have come to your unshakable conclusions already, so there would be little point."

"Here it says that the queen walked out of Matins, taking Catalina with her."

"Exactly! Now, that is what I wanted you to see. That was the other great worry! Surely you can understand why. It is all very well Francisco excusing her behaviour as that of a wilful child, but supposing it became common knowledge! The shame would have been too much. And what of the threat of the Inquisition, and the damnation of our souls? By God, Denia took care of everything. Kept the whole of the situation under control; never a slip-up. He had to be firm."

"It all makes me uneasy, here where it says **using the necessary force** and here, **torture** and here, **her obstinacy** or here, **taking the most suitable action**. No, no more letters. I cannot be convinced that the man was anything other than a despicable brute, enjoying his power over Queen Juana."

"Damn it, Quijada, I had hoped for a moment that you might understand. Desperate circumstances call for desperate measures."

"Ah, so the end justifies the means."

Carlos straightened his hunched shoulders in defiance, and wagged a warning finger, "I will have you know I will answer to God and to Him alone about anything I have done or that was done in my name. So let that be an end to it. I tell you I will not go shamefaced before my Maker. A king has to do what he is called upon to do."

He interlaced his fingers across his chest, rested his elbows on the chair arms and looked smug. "Now then, my self-righteous friend; we both know that you, too, have taken unilateral decisions without any concern for other people's feelings, is that not so?"

Quijada looked at him puzzled. Carlos enjoyed a moment of total satisfaction.

"Shall I remind you how you ran roughshod over the poor musician's widow? There was no explanation, no apologies, no compensation. You rode up to her house, unannounced, followed by a thundering carriage. That, I would imagine, was threatening enough. Then you demanded the boy be brought to you telling her you intended taking him away. It broke the woman's heart. She loved him, had loved him for nearly seven years. You then proceeded to berate her for her slovenly home, the boy's unkempt appearance, his singular lack of education; you would not allow her to utter one word in her own defence. She got on her knees to you, holding the child to her breast. Without further ado you simply pulled him free and bundled him into the carriage." Carlos leaned forward, exhausted yet exhilarated by his speech. He rubbed his hands, *"Touché,* I believe, Quijada?"

"Nothing of the sort; you know you exaggerate to suit your argument! My actions were all justifiable; and you make them sound far worse than they were. To put not too fine a point on it, the child did and does deserve better than to be allowed to run about wild, a raggedy-arsed urchin. The couple had had seven years to follow my instructions; and what had I discovered? The priest who was supposed to be in charge of his education had delegated the job to an illiterate sacristan while he pocketed the money! When, and if, I might add, the lad went to school; he had to walk miles to get there. Most of the time he was not in school; he was fighting with other ruffians, stealing from orchards, wantonly killing birds and animals with his sling. Was that what fifty *ducados* a year was supposed to ensure? No, the couple had had their chance, and I could not in good conscience allow the situation to continue. I insist that my decision was taken solely for the good of the child and to ease the heart and mind of a friend."

"A friend? Are you sure?"

"I earnestly hope so."

"Well, so be it, perhaps. Then suppose we forget that argument and move on to your letter to your wife. Was that not high-handed and insensitive?"

"Not if she loves me; and I know she does. She has complete trust in me and when I said I could not disclose the father's name, she knew it was for a very good reason and she has never pressed the issue. And the letter had to be short, terse even; the more one tries to explain the more complicated and dangerous it becomes. My wife appreciates that everything I have done was in a good cause."

"Exactly, my friend! And so you see your reasoning is echoing mine when I maintain that a king has to do what he is called upon to do. I say again, *touché*."

"And will it make you feel even better if I concede victory?"

"Oh, yes!" Carlos was positively jubilant. "I now feel so good I am of a mind to send to Tordesillas for the recipe for my mother's famous sausages. Have Gaztelu write a letter. Now I think I shall go to the chapel with my confessor to pray for King John."

"Then, my lord, if my services are no longer required, I shall go down to Cuacos. The ride in the comforting evening sunshine will lighten my wretched spirits."

The letters were returned to the casket, the lid firmly shut and locked.

Quijada mumbled down at his hat and gloves as he took them from the table by the door. "Gracious me, the man now talks of sausages as if we had been merely concerning ourselves with a provisions list: deceit, intrigue, incarceration, torture, a boy's abduction – sausages!"

He turned and bowed in the doorway. "Adieu, my lord, I shall tell the chair boys to come in, and send for Regla."

"Do that. Do not be late tomorrow morning. I shall need you to be here very early."

Those letters tell a disturbing story. And what of Quijada's reactions? At least you now see that I do not stand alone in my opinions and judgements. And how cunning of Carlos to turn the tables on Quijada! They make a fine pair.

A Family Business

I

I am sorry to rush you but we must hurry for they are on their way; and I might add that some are not in a good humour this morning. That, along with such an early start, will sorely try tempers. Ah, here they come.

Quijada was accompanying Brother Francisco to the private salon where he had been summoned to await the king's presence. They walked swiftly along the outer gallery leading from the new cloister. Additional rooms had been constructed on the exterior of the cloister's south side to accommodate palace officials and the occasional visitors; the gallery linked these rooms directly to the king's apartments. The two gentlemen passed through doors hurriedly opened to them, the major-domo scurrying along beside the priest.

Eventually they stepped into the central corridor, the last door closing behind them.

"And then; the sheer audacity, the arrogance of that man, Brother Francisco. Simply outrageous behaviour," Quijada continued. "I could not rid my mind of it yesterday. But you were actually in Tordesillas; you must have witnessed what was going on."

Quijada had barely paused for breath since they met. He had been almost running at times to keep pace with his companion, tugging at his sleeve; to slow him down, to command his attention, to emphasise the extent of his anger.

Francisco stopped. He placed his hand gently on Quijada's shoulder, "I cannot say anything which might be considered controversial when the king is not present. Nor will I speak of matters which may be nothing more than pure conjecture. What I will tell you is that there were two distinct periods during my stay there in my youth, and there were also two quite separate households, one for Princess Catalina the other for Queen

104

Juana. Repeating what I said yesterday, there were those first joyous years in Catalina's newly established court. We, her courtiers, were all young with no responsibilities other than those to our princess. We were free to enjoy all the good things of life. That was our philosophy if you wish. The second phase followed the rebellion, when, it is true, Denia ruled like a mythical despot. However, we youngsters still had our dancing, riding, hunting, excursions, and when youth has so many diversions it is relatively easy to forget those things which at first are all-consuming subjects for gossip."

They took several steps before halting again, the priest lost in thought, Quijada impatient for him to continue.

"The other household, and nothing to do with our lives, was that of the queen." Francisco paused, his thoughts staying in the past leaving Quijada isolated and frustrated.

"Her apartments; what were they like?"

"To be honest, I had no idea at the time. They were, naturally, some distance from the public rooms and the smaller salons too, all of which were solely for our use. It was only recently that I discovered they were to the rear of the palace and overlooking a small courtyard. Queen Juana, being unwell more often than not, rarely, if ever, left her apartments; but enough, I did say I would not discuss ..."

Quijada, aggravated by Francisco's determined diplomacy then urged, "Tell me what are your opinions on the Denia dynasty?"

They entered the private salon making their way towards the windows to stand there silently; the priest in quiet thought, Quijada in restrained exasperation.

"Come along, Francisco, we all know how the king felt and continues to feel about that family. We have also all heard the rumours that have issued from the palace year in and year out about their despicable behaviour. What I want to know is what did you honestly think of them and the callous way they treated Queen Juana?"

Francisco responded gently, as if to appease a fractious child without yielding to its demands, "As for the older Denia, we could not fail to notice his fawning over the king when he visited. Also, Denia and the truth were total strangers. He was pompous, obnoxious, and we made him the butt of many a private joke. The son living there now is very like his father. But I will say no more."

"I shall tell you what I discovered yesterday. Did you know that when Queen Juana was in her forties he actually wrote to Carlos about the need to use force against her, to torture her, and that she should be imprisoned in the fortress at Arévalo? Did Denia actually carry out any of his recommendations?"

"No more. I said I would not involve myself further," Francisco raised his hand to close the subject. "Fortunately for us both I think I hear the arrival of the king."

Carlos was wheeled across to the fire and transferred to his gout chair. Gaztelu followed close behind, a sheaf of blank paper tucked under his arm and clutching several freshly prepared quills to his chest.

"Good morning your majesty," Francisco bowed deeply. "Hopefully you have slept well."

"Stop this bowing nonsense, for God's sake! And no, I did not sleep well. Too many damned things on my mind, including a special errand for you." Carlos beckoned him close to whisper. "But first I must know, once and for all, about my mother's sanity and faith at the time of her death. I tell you I am still concerned that my own soul is at risk."

"My lord," Francisco also kept his voice low, "all is well with the soul of the queen, have no fears. If it will give you comfort and reassurance I will tell you of her passing into glory."

Carlos rubbed his hands together then beckoned to the others, "Gentlemen, we shall all listen to what Francisco has to say." He snapped impatiently at the chair boys, "I want to be nearer the miserable remnants of a so-called fire. This room is always damned cold in the morning. Does no one listen to my orders? I insisted on fires in every room, every day. Is that supposed to be a fire? Put more wood on it, right now."

Samuel picked up a couple of logs and added them to the smouldering remains sending ash and a few angry sparks across the hearth and a curling plume of grey smoke up the chimney.

"Now fix my chair; raise my legs. Why are you so damned slow this morning?"

There was a clanking and grating of ratchets as the leg supports were adjusted. "Now lower the back a little more." More metal rasped against metal and the king was at last comfortable.

Their tasks completed the young lads retired to wait at the doorway. They took up their positions, hands behind their backs as they had been instructed, and began to whisper as they had taught themselves, never taking their eyes from their boots, heads as if made of stone, never moving.

"With a bit of luck Sam, they'll forget we're here. Bet we did miss some good stuff yesterday, eh?"

"Yeh, but never mind that, what's all this he's talking about, José? What does he mean about the queen's sanity?"

"You mean you never heard of Crazy Juana? Well whether you heard it or not, Crazy Juana is what everybody was calling his mother; the one who lived in Tordesillas."

"I know about her; she had an affair with a bloke, her palace governor. He was a really 'andsome feller. Like love birds they were, never apart, her playing the vihuela and him the lute, and them both singing. Then they'd read love poems to each other. But I guess he had to be sent packing in case he married her."

"Strange; no, I never heard that one, so it can't be true. What I do know was she had bats in the belfry. When she really got her blood boiling she wouldn't eat, nor sleep, nor wash, nor change her clothes."

"Doesn't sound a whole lot different to most folks as I know who can be like that without getting their mad up."

"You're being awkward. Anyway she threw pots at people."

"You been near any of our cooks on a bad day?"

"Do you want me to tell you or not?"

"Course I do, go on."

"What they did was leave her some bread and cheese in pots outside her door, 'cause if she saw anybody, she threw the whole lot at them. Then they say as how she wouldn't go to church, and kept rabbiting on about bloody great big cats eating up all her family …"

"Bloody 'ell now that does sound crackers."

"What did I tell you! Anyway let's listen then we'll have a good tale to tell the lads tonight. Could be worth a few extra drinks, eh?"

II

Quijada, Francisco and Gaztelu gathered at the king's side.

"Let me have you all closer; no excuses about the heat, Quijada. Gaztelu, sit yourself down and for God's sake no fussing. Francisco, I want you beside me. Now, we are ready. Francisco is going to tell us of the final hours of my dear departed mother. Slowly now, I want every word loud and clear."

"It was late in the evening of Holy Thursday. Her highness had confessed, begging God's forgiveness. Let me stress, my lord, that the queen was of sound mind and able to confess her sins. After Extreme Unction was administered she fell into a deep slumber. There were many who stayed to keep vigil as she slept. The dawn arrived and as the world awoke so Queen Juana opened her eyes. All the lines of pain had disappeared. Her face was younger, happier. There was an aura of peace emanating from her. We were all conscious of it, all enfolded within it. In the faintest of whispers she asked for the crucifix that I had been holding over her throughout the night. Then God guided my hand to choose what I thought was a trinket from a box by her bedside. I put it into her hand. She smiled and barely audible she told us that this medallion with its image of the Holy Virgin, the Mother of God, was one of her most treasured possessions. Her mother had given her it for her fifteenth birthday, the day she had been told of her forthcoming marriage to Philip of Austria. She kissed the Holy Virgin's likeness then laid it on her breast. I brought the crucifix close to her and with her lips she gently caressed the blessed feet of our Lord. After a few moments, as if summoned, she raised her arms towards Heaven. Then it was as if our Saviour was reaching down to gather her up, for she called to Him, 'Sweet Jesus who was crucified, help me …'"

Quijada's tears fell onto his black velvet jerkin. He watched the diamond droplets gather before changing to damp smudges. He drew his short gown about him to conceal them,

"Free at last, may your soul have eternal peace, you poor, dear lady," he wept silently.

A long silence followed, everyone held prisoner by images, until the mood was broken by the harsh throat clearing of Carlos. He made the sign of the cross on his breast, "Good, good. That leaves not the smallest doubt then. Confession, Extreme Unction, the Crucifix, calling on God."

Francisco nodded, "Queen Juana's soul is at peace, and your soul and those of your family are safe."

"Dear God, but that's an enormous weight off my mind I can tell you. You have no idea how worrying this whole damned business has been."

Then he turned to snap at Quijada, for the tears had not gone unnoticed, tears which he himself found impossible to shed, "Sitting there snivelling. You grow more like an old lady every day and you are beginning to exasperate me. I want you to make plans to go to Villagarcía, get your wife and bring her to Cuacos. You should find a place decent enough there for certain. Do it immediately. No arguments, you will do as I say. At this rate you are going to have us all as miserable as yourself. One of the monks will attend to things in your absence. We can discuss details later. If those lads are still there I want them out of the room."

Quijada motioned to Samuel and José. They bowed and turned to go.

"So what was all that then? Where was the crazy bit?" Samuel whispered.

"What the 'ell do I know? I was only telling you what I'd heard."

"Just shows you can't believe everything what you 'ear then. Nice little story about her dying though, wasn't it?"

III

Carlos turned partway towards the door, "Are they gone? Good. Now to pressing business; Francisco, I have an important matter for you to deal with. You will have to forget your plans for your new college for a while. I want you to leave early tomorrow morning for Portugal, to visit Catalina. The letter you are to carry will be ready by the end of the day."

109

"If I can be of any service, my lord; and I must admit I half expected you would call on me."

"You have to ask Catalina if she still has all the necessary documents for the dispensations for several marriages; first that of our Aunt Maria. It was a long time ago but Maria's sister had been married to Emanuel and after her death Maria became his second wife. Catalina must also be sure she has those for my daughter Juana to her son John Emanuel, and of my son Felipe to her daughter Maria."

"My lord?"

"Nothing of significance, first cousins, nothing more; this is simply a precaution should the Portuguese court require them. I hope to God she does have them because this damned pope might decide to be awkward if we had to ask for copies."

"My lord, you misjudge his holiness."

"The hell I do! He is hand in glove with the French and would take great delight in prevaricating, putting us to great inconvenience and causing us embarrassment."

"And do you envisage a problem with the Portuguese?" Francisco asked, careful to avoid further discussion about the pope.

"No; but it is best to be prepared for all eventualities. This is the situation; Sebastian, my daughter's son, has inherited the Portuguese throne from his grandfather. But Sebastian not being very robust may well follow his father to an early grave."

Francisco thought of the many times Princess Juana had spoken to him of her tragically short marriage and her beloved child. "The princess often speaks of Sebastian, she misses the little fellow, and he is always in her prayers. Heaven forefend that anything should befall him."

"Yes, yes, quite; but in the event that something does, then Felipe's son Prince Carlos is next in line."

"Because he is the child of Felipe and Catalina's daughter Maria."

"Precisely, so you see the need for the evidence of dispensation for that marriage."

You see all the burdens a king must carry when he has the interests of his family at heart! I suppose Carlos is no different than

110

most. Kings carry many weighty problems they create themselves, just like this one. First you bend the rules on consanguinity then later you find yourself worrying about the consequences.

"And these next matters are of great importance; I cannot emphasise just how important. Remind Catalina how it broke my heart that despite all my earnest efforts to bring about the reconciliation between Maria and Felipe I was unsuccessful, and how I still grieve her passing at such a tender age. Say how delighted we all are that it is she who will assume the regency during the child's minority, that there is no one more suited to the task. Lastly I want you to put forward the idea of the exchange of marriage contracts between Sebastian and my granddaughter in Bohemia. Tell Catalina that the proposition would be for the girl to be taken to Portugal, immediately, to be raised as a Portuguese princess. I think that covers everything. Gaztelu, have I missed anything out?"

"Indeed not, my lord."

"Speed is essential for there is always someone else hovering, ready to negotiate alternatives. The damned French are bound to be the first in the queue. You will have my letter, naturally, but my sister knows you well so will have every trust in you ... What the blazes! What is all that commotion out there? What the devil is going on?"

There was a thundering of boots and a jangling of spurs coming from the corridor. Alarm struck them all. They suddenly felt vulnerable in this peaceful little retreat. The three gentlemen around Carlos rose as one and rushed to the door, Quijada's hand ready on the hilt of his sword. Gaztelu pulled the door open and Quijada stepped out into the corridor, sword unsheathed, Samuel and José moved swiftly to his side.

Two guards had by now halted the progress of the intruders.

Carlos called from his chair, "Quijada, who is it? Quickly, tell me, man!"

Quijada returned to the room, "The princess regent's ambassador."

111

"Damn and blast! Organise their welcome. Think of something to detain them awhile, refreshments and the like, until I get the details of this letter sorted out with Gaztelu. This must be attended to first before we get involved in anything else, this is too important; unless, of course it is of some greater urgency, in which case ... oh, you deal with it!"

Francisco bowed, "With permission then, I shall take this opportunity to have lunch then make arrangements for my departure."

"Yes, yes. Go then. Go."

Has his majesty's urgency surprised you? He is still driven by the same tireless determination to have the Hapsburgs rule in as many countries as possible.

Until he knows for certain that upon the death of the ailing three-year-old Sebastian it will be Prince Carlos who inherits the Portuguese throne he will have no peace.

And then France is such a worry too. What if Portugal were to accept the offer of a French princess for Sebastian? That would never do; it would be risking outside influences, importing foreign weaknesses. Only the Hapsburgs can assure the protection of the True Faith in Europe! And here is another serious consideration; a Portuguese-French alliance would mean the French on Spain's western border as well as on the north.

A Blushing Bride

Carlos, relieved to know that he did not need to see the ambassador until later in the day, called for his usual 'light' refreshment.

Quijada, after a stern look of warning, which was promptly ignored, left him chomping on slices of ham liberally spread with a compote of pomegranate, believed to ward off gout, and swilling it down with copious amounts of beer.

Francisco and the visitors had waited for him in the corridor and they now made their way out to the gallery.

"Samuel, José; take these gentlemen to Madame Male and say my orders are that rooms are to be prepared for them." Quijada then turned to the priest, "I think a short turn about the garden before lunch would be an excellent idea, Francisco, what do you say?"

"Provided I am not required to fend off further questions about Denia."

"I promise."

"Good, because I would like some information myself."

They walked down the stairs and stepped out into the arcade that ran along two sides of a formal garden and was completely in the shade hiding behind its stone pillars and the jasmine branches cascading from the gallery above. Garden paths led them between walnut trees and orange trees offering some shelter from the summer sun. Close by a fountain splashed its refreshing music.

"Quite a choice of places to stroll; this is all very pleasant, Quijada. Now then, to business. I have the suspicion that my role as emissary may require more diplomacy than at first would appear, and to be forewarned is to be forearmed. So, to my query; Princess Juana often speaks of her cold reception in Portugal, she was obviously quite hurt by it. Could you enlighten me?"

"It is because there was a decided rift between Carlos and Catalina regarding that business of the unhappiness of her daughter Maria, and although it was more than ten years ago you will have noted that Carlos is still unsure as to whether or not he has been entirely forgiven."

"It must have been very serious."

"All very tragic, really; from the moment Maria set foot in Spain her happiness was drained from her. By all accounts she was a pretty young thing, with blond curly hair; and, of course, very rich. Felipe was everything a young maid could ask for; a youth with a handsome figure, good looking, fair hair, blue eyes. So, there were two fifteen-year-old hearts all a-flutter! They married in Salamanca. The Duque de Alba performed a miracle in providing reasonable accommodation – you see Carlos was paying for this and as we seem to be forever living in straightened circumstances economies were called for."

"Even for his son's wedding? The wars, I assume?"

"Be that as it may, although the accommodation was almost commonplace the bride, bridegroom and guests made it a glittering success. The room was one huge jewellery box, ablaze with sparkling diamonds, sapphires, rubies, emeralds, pearls, as the dancers traced their steps to all the popular dances. But that was virtually the last joy the girl knew."

They stopped by the fountain to watch the leaping and tumbling of iridescent droplets performing dances of their own in the sunlight.

"I know you to be a sensitive man, Quijada, so perhaps this is an exaggeration?"

"Wait until you hear more then I shall let you be the judge. Carlos was in Austria at the time. Because of this he felt it necessary to send his written advice on the comportment of the young married couple; in effect telling them how often they should share the same bed. Unfortunately he gave the Commander of Castile the responsibility of ensuring that his advice was followed."

"You make it sound serious."

"I tell you the man took to the task with extraordinary zeal. It started on the wedding night! After the young couple had been in their bridal bed for only a short while, he strode into the bedchamber, threw back the curtains revealing the amorous newly weds and ordered Felipe off to his own room; and all this in the presence of courtiers!"

"In the name of God, why?"

"As a military man I would suggest he felt that the engagement was accomplished, time to retire the troops."

"Embarrassing!"

"From then on it got worse; they were never allowed to be together except for public appearances, never permitted private conversations. They were allowed some time together for the purpose of providing an heir, but those occasions were kept to a minimum; Felipe's seed had to be kept strong! Felipe, being a young man decided to find satisfaction elsewhere, and he did so with increasing regularity. When he was with Maria she spent most of the time weeping about her loneliness, her disappointments; not much company for a lusty youth. Any affection he may have felt for her was soon gone. There was no one for her to talk to – except her mother – so she poured her heart out to her in her letters telling of her distress at her husband's coldness and infidelity, his open philandering."

Francisco smiled wryly, "How much of this is gossip?"

"It is the truth, I only speak the truth. For instance, Felipe's affair with a lady in waiting was an open secret, had been for some time before his marriage. I also saw the letters from Catalina to Carlos, and very angry letters they were, too. She was not prepared to stand by and see her daughter the victim of such cruelties. She demanded Carlos take immediate action to protect Maria. Carlos, however, decided not to interfere, believing resolutely in his philosophy of the management of visits to the matrimonial bed. He also dismissed Maria's complaints about Felipe as nothing more than a young girl's exaggerations. And then came the news that convinced him he was justified in allowing events to run their course; Maria was with child."

"So at least the girl would have something to fill her empty days, looking towards the joys of motherhood, the pride in providing an heir."

"Not a bit of it, it was a nightmare. After nine months of illness and bloodletting she was finally brought, in a very frail state, to her childbed. The birth was difficult, several days of labour before she was delivered, forcibly, of a baby boy, our Prince Carlos. Yes, it took terrible intrusive intervention."

"No need to say more."

115

"Maria became seriously ill. Her Portuguese doctor was forbidden to give salt water baths to treat her infections, and then he was dismissed. That was something else to infuriate Catalina. The Spanish doctors began further bloodletting, and within days Maria was dead. She had lived in this country for two years; years of loneliness, disdain, pain and illness before her life was snuffed out; aided and abetted by incompetent quack doctors – according to Catalina."

"Little wonder that Princess Juana found her mother-in-law icy when she arrived in Portugal to marry John. She has told me that she felt as if she was being called to account for actions taken by others about which she knew nothing, being but a child at that time. So, just as I thought, there will be more of a demand for me to be the diplomat rather than merely appearing as a trusted old friend. There are some insecure bridges to be crossed. I see now why the king sounded conciliatory, using honeyed words; quite out of character for him. Well, you have given me plenty to think about; shall we go to lunch?"

One House, One Master

I

Carlos handed back the letter to Gaztelu, "Perfect. You may tell the others we are ready for them now. I am impatient to know what my daughter Juana is up to."

"Perhaps this is a courtesy call on their way to Portugal? I expect that she is sending her condolences to her mother-in-law," Gaztelu suggested crossing to the door to summon Quijada, Father Francisco, and Juana's ambassador.

"I hope you are right, but I have my doubts. For some reason she and her sister have always plagued me with problems. Damned nuisances the pair of them, always something not to their liking, or hoping to have their own way, instead of doing as they are told and no questions asked. Well we shall soon see what it is we have today."

He nodded his head towards the ambassador to welcome him. "Ah, ambassador; good to see you. And such a splash of colour; gladdens the eye, like a rare bird in these parts, what say you all?" Carlos turned to whisper to Gaztelu, "I might go so far as to say a regular popinjay."

The ambassador removed his black velvet bonnet with its dark purple rosette before making three low reverent bows and kneeling to kiss the hand of Carlos. His black jerkin, the sleeves slashed with the same dark purple satin to match that of his bonnet, was complemented by black breeches and hose. He felt ill at ease, "Your majesty, I thought it only fitting to come before you wearing my ..."

"Of course you did, of course. It is we folk who are the dowdy ones. But what have you brought?"

"Your majesty, I bear two letters from the Regent, Princess Juana. One is for the queen of Portugal, and this one is for you my lord."

"Open it, Gaztelu, my fingers are too stiff. Quickly man, break the seal. Give it here. Spectacles, Quijada." He thrust

117

them onto the bridge of his nose, Quijada assisting with the more complex business of settling them securely over his ears.

They waited.

Then came the explosion, "Good God in Heaven! How dare she presume! And she expects me to support her? The stupid, arrogant bitch!" The letter was thrown towards Gaztelu, "Take it, read it, read it!"

Carlos glared at the ambassador. "Give me the other letter."

"My lord? I am the regent's ambassador. I am to deliver this to Queen Catalina. It would be an offence to my lady ..."

Carlos bellowed, "Give it here, goddamn it! Never mind what the regent might feel, it would be an even greater offence to me not to hand it over." He snatched at the letter as the ambassador drew it from his pouch. "I can tell you what I am going to do, I am going to read this, then destroy it. As from this moment you will travel to Portugal as my ambassador carrying my letter. What does the stupid ... what does she think she is about? You know the contents? Of course you do. It is no fault of yours, you had to follow her orders. But not any more. I am the ruler of this family and I will not tolerate ignorant meddling. Gaztelu, this one, here, open it."

"As you command, my lord."

"You are damned right, I do command."

Juana's letter was opened and returned to Carlos. He read it then angrily crumpled it before erupting, "Take it, tear it up and burn the damn thing! No one else may see what I have just read. Gaztelu, you will write a letter to Catalina stating the mission of the ambassador. It will say that he bears Juana's unreserved support for her. You know how to word it, something following along the lines of my earlier letter, a repetition of my sentiments only more so."

Gaztelu sat down at a nearby table, put on his spectacles and took up his pen. Faint scratchings of pen on paper told of his progress. Francisco and Quijada guessed that the sentiments in Juana's letter had been somewhat different to those of Carlos.

Carlos turned to Francisco, "What was I just saying about my daughters? Nothing but headaches, the pair of them, and Juana the worst. How old did we say Sebastian is?"

"Not yet four years old."

"Four years!" Carlos growled and spluttered, "And the sickly father had to die a few weeks after he was born. By God but my daughter was quick enough to abandon the child in its cradle when Felipe went to England to wed Mary and Spain needed a regent. God was she quick; I tell you there was not a moment's hesitation when she was told; left in indecent haste, thrusting her child into the arms of his grandmother."

Quijada tried to be the voice of reason, "To be fair, she had no choice. She returned because you commanded it; she returned because she was surplus to requirements in Portugal being nothing but a widow."

"Nobody asked for your opinion," Carlos snarled. "And now after four years of not giving a damn she thinks she can just return to Lisbon to be regent there until her son comes of age. I tell you it is outrageous for her to even contemplate such an idea. Who does she think she is to presume to be in a position to bargain with the queen of Portugal, my dear sister, about any rights she may have to the regency? My sister Catalina, should you need reminding, is not only beloved by me but by all Portugal; and King John on his death bed willed that she should be regent during Sebastian's minority. And yet this daughter of mine intends to contest this. How dare she! The impudence! The arrogance!"

Spittle and spume sprayed his beard, his face was livid, his eyes blazed and his swollen hands beat out his fury on the arms of his chair. "Get me up. I have to stand. Bring that chair over here."

Francisco and Quijada helped him to his feet, placing the chair that he might lean his weight on its tall back. "You know what it is? You know what it is? I shall tell you what it is!" His rage reached a new level, "She has enjoyed playing regent here for the last couple of years, and, incidentally, causing me one or two problems along the way that I could well have done without, but she knows that Felipe will probably be back in Spain quite soon. So, she sees this regency not lasting much longer, whereas that of Portugal is just starting and will have years to run. That is what she is after; and she dares to seek my support. Well she is in for a rude awakening. Far from getting any help from me she is going to discover exactly what I think

119

of her plans. The idiot cannot see past the end of her nose. She lacks the sense to see that by this one stupid step she would put the unity of the Peninsula in jeopardy. Holy Jesus, this is the only area where we have peace, the stupid, ignorant, bitch! Gaztelu, we will write to the young madam as soon as you have finished that letter. She will get a flea in her ear, by God she will."

Father Francisco and the ambassador had kept their heads bowed low, eyes downcast throughout the tirade. They were embarrassed that Carlos had spoken so harshly of his daughter in their presence. It was unseemly, too, that the ambassador should witness such lack of respect for his mistress, the regent of Spain; and what of his predicament when he met Catalina, carrying only letters from Carlos?

Quijada's cough attracted the attention of Father Francisco; then a slight movement of a finger suggested they move to the far end of the room to engage the ambassador in conversation to save him and themselves further discomfort while Carlos was occupied dictating his letter to Juana.

Francisco whispered a quick aside to Quijada, "This is going to complicate matters."

"Your majesty the letter you require for the ambassador is ready for your signature." Gaztelu kept his voice low; afraid that even his words might further offend.

"Good, now you will sit down and write something to this effect. Daughter, in reply to your letters, let me just say that your ambassador has arrived and I know of your instructions as to what he should do in Portugal. However I have directed him as to what he must say and what he is definitely not allowed to say regarding the Kingdom of Portugal and its government during the minority of King Sebastian, your son."

He paused, waiting for Gaztelu to show he was ready to continue. "It is not for you to hold or express any opinion on the setting up of Sebastian's household and the people he must have about him. This sort of interference would create a multitude of problems and I simply will not allow it. In fact the substitute letter I am sending via your ambassador – enclose a copy for her – contains nothing more than your wholehearted support and prayers for Sebastian and Queen Catalina. You should have accepted the fact without my having to tell you.

Catalina and I, not you, will deal with everything. We are the ones who know best how to further the other's cause."

He stopped again as if rallying his strength for the final onslaught. "It also appears that I must remind you of your position and that you behave accordingly. You wrote using such disrespectful language to my sister, who is after all your aunt and mother-in-law, that I am deeply shamed for you. That should do it, Gaztelu. Over here you others. Come quickly, no dawdling, I have to sit. Dear God the pains in my legs."

"A word, my lord?" Gaztelu hesitated.

"What is it now?" Carlos winced in discomfort as his bulk was lowered into his chair.

"If I may be so bold? Perhaps a postscript to your daughter? An apology for its not being a very personal and private letter? She may well feel distressed that other eyes know of its contents. You could use the excuse that the gout in your hands prohibits you from writing yourself."

"At this moment I am damned if I care how she feels. She is setting out to destroy the peace between Portugal and Spain, and making it damned awkward for my grandson Carlos's prospects into the bargain. And you talk of my apologising?"

Quijada broke in, "You do surprise me, my lord, by sending such a letter at all! Here you are, the one with all those years of experience in diplomacy, with supposedly political astuteness that many a monarch would give a fortune for; and yet you are about to fall at this the smallest, simplest of hurdles by allowing your temper to get the better of you. You are going make the princess regent's position untenable, and all because of your clouded judgement. No, you do not surprise me – you disappoint me."

"Good God in His Heaven, Quijada, but you are right. I was blinded by my anger. What would I do without you? Indeed you must write the postscript, Gaztelu. Then she will think that you are the only other person to know. There now, how is that for a concession?" he smiled his magnanimity.

Quijada shook his head, Carlos had completely missed his point.

"Will you stay awhile, Quijada, I need a word or two in private."

They waited a moment until they were alone.

II

"Sit down, sit down. Has there been any news from Ghent?"

"My lord, there is a reply to the letter of condolence we sent on the death of Barbara's mother. It is too soon for a response to the pension you sent to the chaperone. Barbara thanks you for the warm and tender words of sympathy and wishes to be remembered to you."

"No need for that, she is never far from my thoughts these days. Is that wrong of me? Is it stupid for an old man to look forward to, to hope for letters from someone?"

"Not at all; and certainly not from Barbara, she was after all very important to you at one time, my lord, playing a significant role in your life."

Carlos laughed, "Barbara played more than one, and all to perfection. Do you remember her singing that night?"

"Oh yes, and how we were all set to cringe at the weak warbling of Katherine's nervous and reluctant daughter."

"Instead we were treated to something divine. She could teach some of this lot in the choir quite a bit I can tell you. A natural gift, Quijada, no training."

"And despite having vowed there would be no more charity you gave her the job as your private musician."

"Well, could you imagine a more perfect end to the day? To have your ears flooded with such sounds, your eyes dazzled with such beauty, your senses intoxicated with such loveliness."

"She was indeed your beautiful blond and blue-eyed Barbara."

"Some men can only dream of such blessings, and there was I, well past my prime, with the unexpected good fortune of having her all to myself."

"My lord, many would say it was the other way about, that she was the lucky one. Fortune had smiled on her more than once."

"Either way, there we were, just the two of us, with the insufferable, ever-present chaperone standing on guard at the door."

"Old and toothless she may have been, but she had more fight in her than many an infantryman; and I have known many," laughed Quijada.

"It was wonderful, and I thank God I have so many memories to fall back on, and just as well, especially when life gets so bloody aggravating, like today."

Carlos started to hum, then sang,

"Good wine makes us gay, let's sing,
Forget our troubles, let's sing,
While eating a fat ham
Let's make war on this jug ..."

Quijada tapped out the rhythm of the music on his knees, remembering Carlos and Barbara laughing and singing.

Carlos slapped the arm rests of his chair, "You know; that is a damned good idea. I think I shall do that right now. Refreshments are called for!"

"You are incorrigible, my lord!"

Poor Juana, only seeking what, after all, are her rights as the mother of the new king. Poor Carlos, only wanting the best for the Hapsburgs. Happily, Barbara appears to have come to the rescue just as in those days long ago.

123

An English Marriage

I

"Ah, Father Francisco, you have excellent weather this morning for the start to your journey, it could not be bettered," Quijada called across the yard. "My ride to Cuacos and back was most pleasant. I do enjoy the early hours, the more so if I am alone with my thoughts. I wish you a safe, swift, and successful mission. Aye, dear me," a groan escaped from him as he lowered himself from his horse. He handed the reins to Manuel then crossed the yard to join the priest who was watching a group of stable lads saddling up the horses and securing the baggage.

"Amen to that, Quijada, for the sooner this is over the quicker I can return to my more favoured mission. I have little stomach for the world of politics." He sighed, "I suppose it is as well that Carlos did discover the contents of Princess Juana's letter or the situation would be worse than it is. Still, it is going to be very awkward. I just pray that everything goes smoothly. On my way I shall be stopping at the college to exchange greetings with the brothers who will be disappointed that I am to be further delayed and still unable to join them. The king's will, in this instance, must supersede all other demands."

"Looking on the bright side at the end of your journey you will have the pleasure of seeing Queen Catalina. I suppose you never thought to see her again. But my goodness, she will have changed considerably from that beautiful young lady you watched riding across the bridge and away from Tordesillas."

Francisco is in for a rude surprise without question; the beautiful young girl has become an exceedingly plump, elderly lady.

124

"You need not remind me of the ravages of time, nor of the frightening speed of its passing when there is so much still to be done."

"Nor do I need remind myself Father Francisco. Why, it seems but yesterday that I married, yet years have flown by."

"And I suspect you will not have had many opportunities to go home?"

"You are so right. When you spoke just now of the king's demands, you never spoke a truer word. I have been absent from my home for months."

"Meanwhile your wife remains alone, without you at …?"

"Villagarcía. You may know of it, it is not far from Arévalo. The village is charming and with such warm and friendly folk. And my home? My wonderful wife DoZa Magdalena de Ulloa has turned the castle into the most perfect of homes. Yes, I consider myself the most fortunate man walking this earth. It was an arranged marriage, but I am one of the lucky ones who finds himself blessed with a bride who although many years his junior shows such understanding and wisdom and who showers her love on an old man such as I. I confess that when my eyes first beheld her, I thought it all a dream, that I was unworthy of such providence. So perhaps you can appreciate my frustration?"

"I do indeed, for I have known the joys of a contented marriage, the love of a good wife, the happiness that children bring to the hearth. But surely, you are not old Quijada?"

"If sixty-one is not old, then what is?"

"You have the bearing of a much younger man."

"You flatter me."

"That is not one of my weaknesses. But I do sympathise with you; you are here while she is there." He found himself thinking of the regent, the beautiful Princess Juana, of her kneeling before him making her confession, speaking of her child Sebastian lost to her when she was commanded to return to Spain; widowed at eighteen and within months taken from her child. He saw again her eyes flooded with the tears of a distraught mother, and it wakened within him tender emotions far beyond those of a priest. He had to blame Carlos for that; it was his fault with those brutal words. He pushed the image aside.

125

"But, praise be to God, Francisco, this is all to change. As you heard I have finally been granted permission to visit my wife and home. To be quite frank, I would not care if I were never to return to this place. I know I will feel this even more strongly once I am in Villagarcía. Yes, if I allow myself to think of Yuste I will quickly remind myself of the dreadful weather here; nine months of mire and three months of fire, and I will say to myself, please let there be plenty of good souls about my lord the king that I need not return."

"But you are not a man who would disappoint his master. In Villagarcía you will continue to be concerned that those around the king are indeed performing their duties to your satisfaction, and I know that you would rather be here to ensure it."

"You are right. I have to admit to a continuing brotherly concern for him, but these days I find myself torn between my love for my wife and home and my loyalty to my king." Quijada altered his tone to one of resolve, "So, this morning I have been touring the village hoping to find a suitable home for Magdalena that I may have her near when Carlos does need me. There is nothing, of course, in this godforsaken part of the world. But, and it is a large but, with some imagination and effort I think something of a reasonable size could be developed by adapting three vacant houses. A poor substitute for our castle, but I shall have it made as much like a small palace as is possible."

"I shall pray for a speedy completion of the project. And meanwhile does your wife have the comfort of children at her knee?"

"Not of our own, it seems that God does not will it." His face brightened, "But we do have a foster child whom my wife loves dearly, as dearly as she would if he were her own. He is a good boy and he helps dispel the loneliness caused by my enforced absences. You have known the joys of a family. Until comparatively recently I have not. Mine has been the life of a soldier in close service to the king, which I would not have missed for the world, but now, since this little chap came into our home, it grieves me to be away."

"So tell me more. How old is he? His name?"

"He is eleven years old." He smiled. "Originally he was called Jerome, but my wife changed his name to Juan. She said that the name Jerome was more suited to someone who would become a priest whereas this little lad was cut out for an adventurous life. He has a courageous spirit, loves horse riding, fencing, and she says the name of Juan reflects this."

"And his parents?"

"Juan is the son of a very dear friend of mine. A friend, who, for many reasons, wishes to keep his name secret; I respect his wishes and on pain of death would not reveal it. Ah here is Gaztelu. Good morning."

"Good morning to you both. An early start for you Father Francisco; a good day for travelling," his eyes squinted up at and found confirmation in the almost cloudless skies. "I will wish you success; although there is no doubting the outcome. Catalina will do as her brother bids, and after all he is not asking the impossible. By the way, Princess Juana's ambassador will remain here for a further two days which will give you ample opportunity to deal with the king's private business."

"I do not care for the implication that I might be doing something underhand." Again his thoughts returned to Juana, the young woman on her knees seeking absolution, weeping.

"No. No. It is, rather, that after dealing first with the matters of state you will have sufficient time to smooth the way for the ambassador. It is going to be a difficult situation for him, presenting as Juana's ambassador but only carrying papers from his majesty."

"Just so; I shall do my very best to ensure there is as little embarrassment as possible for the man and to dismiss any misunderstandings caused by the lack of personally written condolences. I shall certainly find it easy enough to support the Princess Juana; I know her better than any and am convinced she is being misjudged." He pictured the innocent Juana with those large, honest, hazel eyes.

The horses and mules were now ready, hooves shuffling in anticipation. Packs and rolls had been securely tied, all final adjustments made, riders only awaiting the order to mount.

127

Alonso and Manuel stood apart from the rest sketching arcs in the stony earth with the toes of their boots.

"Who's a lucky son-of-a-bitch, then?"

"It's not luck, Manuel, it's 'cause me talents is recognised. They needed someone special, like, someone who'd know better than anybody how to look after the horses."

"Yeah, but how come you and not me?"

"I had me ear to the ground, mate. I heard very quick from Maria about this lot getting pulled together, so-to-speak, to go to Portugal with that priest over there. Right out of the blue comes this decision to send him there, something to do with the king of Portugal dying. Maria says that the widow is our king's sister. So I 'specks he wants to send the priest to let her know just how cut up he is. Anyway, Maria hotfoots it to let me know what's up, so I goes to boss Pepe and volunteers, like."

Manuel kicked out in frustration destroying the pattern that he had been so diligently forming, "Did they not want more than you, Alonso? I mean, I'm your mate."

"Do you really think I didn't try to have you to come along with me? Course you're me mate, and course I asked, but it was no go."

"Some folk get all the luck, all the same. Least that's the way I sees it. I mean, just look at your Maria, not here any time at all and there she is doing the pressing of the clothes, no less."

"Now you're right there mate. That is good luck; well it was bad luck for the other lass. She ups and dies of some horrible fever and Maria steps right into her shoes."

"Ooh, don't you talk about dead men's shoes, gives me the creeps. I could just feel a cold shiver go up me back right then I could, exactly that moment when you said that. Anyway, just you wait and see; she'll be after something better afore long, I know her sort."

"You're right there an' all, Manuel. She's told me, says she wants to make something of herself. Cleaning and polishing is what she's after next."

"Who's she hoping will die this time? Hey up, though, you know she might just be heading for a nasty fall."

Alonso was taken aback, "How do you reckon that, then, Manuel; you know something I don't?"

128

Manuel laughed, "Didn't mean to scare you mate, it's only the old story about the farm girl on her way to market. You don't know it? Sounds just like your Maria she does. Well, see, there's this young lass on her way to market carrying a basket of eggs on her head, like they do. And going through her mind is what she's going to do with the money she gets. She says to herself, *I'll buy more chickens, they'll lay more eggs to sell so I can buy more so's I can start to raise chickens to sell as well as eggs. Then I'll buy some land. I'll get richer and richer.* Then as she's going along she decides she'll need a husband and she imagines herself telling her father. He says, *How about a farmer? What? You must be joking,* she says. *A gentleman, then? No, not good enough,* she says. *I know, you wants a nobleman,* he says. *That I do not!,* she says, stamping her foot. *I know, me girl, you wants nothing less than a prince, I'm right, aren't I?* And she nods her head. Get it? She nods her head. The daft beggar nods her head for real, and down comes the basket, eggs and all. Well your Maria and her fanciful ideas put me in mind of that story, that's all."

"She says you and me is just two simple stick-in-the-mud fellers. Leastwise that's the way she sees it."

"She can keep her opinions to herself, who does she think she is and her not here five minutes." He sought revenge, "So how's the hayloft romps? Going to miss them for the next few weeks?"

"Nah," Alonso sniffed, rubbing his nose on the back of his hand and wiping his hand down the side of his breeches, "not really; cooled off a bit it has."

"Who? You or her?" He knew the answer and felt he had evened the score somewhat with Alonso.

Alonso sniffed again.

Father Francisco was up on his horse and calling, "Time to be on our way."

Those who were accompanying him swung up into their saddles. With a hesitant start they were off, while those who remained in the courtyard watched them follow the stony track along to the cluster of trees at the corner, saw them as they turned left to disappear down the hill one by one until all that remained was the dying sounds of hooves and the occasional voice.

Manuel returned to the stables, with a firmly engraved image of Alonso's triumphant grin as he turned to him from the saddle, settling his wide-brimmed hat on his head.

"Lucky sod. I still says as there's some gets all the luck."

II

"An auspicious day to embark on such an undertaking," Gaztelu turned to Quijada.

"Auspicious day? Indeed you are right. I had forgotten, what with one thing and another. Yes, the day of Santiago el Mayor, Spain's patron saint. I tell you, Gaztelu, I sometimes wonder if I am not growing too old for this job. I am becoming ever more forgetful. Fortunately I keep catching myself out before others do. But you caught me out today. Ah well."

"Have you ever visited the shrine of the saint at Santiago de Compostela? No? What an experience, my friend. The cathedral is quite magnificent. The doorway with its apostles, prophets, and angels playing their musical instruments; all of them looking so real you could swear they were moving. And then there is this enormous censer, half the size of a grown man, hanging from the dome where the transept crosses the knave. When it is required for the solemn ceremonies it hurtles the full length of the transept like some celestial being, like a comet perhaps or some enormous magical projectile leaving a trail of fire and perfumed smoke. Someone told me that it is swung not so much as a part of the church ritual but to sweeten the air. I can believe that; the stink from the hundreds of dirty, sweaty pilgrims from all over Europe crowded into every available inch of the nave is indescribable."

"It would certainly alter the odour of Christian virtue from the physical to the mystical." Quijada chuckled, "I like that, very clever, must remember to tell it again. I wonder if it would amuse the king? Changing the odour from physical to ..."

"You are light of heart today, Quijada. Is it because of your intended visit home, returning to your young bride? You have been better blessed with your marriage than our King Felipe to be sure."

130

"Aye, poor Felipe. A second disastrous match. And today is the anniversary of his wedding. Now, you see, I have remembered that. July the twenty-fifth; some wedding day that must have been! Sad, old Mary Tudor. Well when I say old, I realise she is only forty or so, but to become a bride at the age of thirty-eight and to someone eleven years her junior ... well, what can one say? Have you seen the portrait? It has just arrived, a gift for Carlos. I think she might well have been pretty once, but she looks far more like she should be Felipe's mother and not his wife."

"I believe this match is far worse than the first, Quijada. Doomed from the beginning, both parties knowing in their hearts it would be a failure both for themselves and for their countries."

"I had heard gossip of Felipe's opinions, in reply to Carlos's command for this marriage, but as I was then absent from the court for some time and happily going about other business I never got to know of Mary's feelings."

They strolled from the courtyard to the ramp leading up to the king's apartments.

"I can tell you exactly; she went through months of torment before finally deciding to marry, and since then has suffered a different torment."

"The English, of course, were not too happy about the marriage."

"Not too happy, Quijada? Good Lord, they were fanatically opposed to it. They would rather have had an outbreak of the plague. This union signalled a return to the Mass, monasteries, the pope. They feared we Spanish would force England into some kind of bondage; in fact for many the return to the Catholic Faith as it was before her father broke with Rome would be a better fate than subordination by the Spanish. You know there were uprisings? Carlos's ambassador along with his retinue had to flee England, to save themselves from the rebels' swords. Mary was brave, though, she never ran away; she faced those people, and she told them that she was not marrying for her own satisfaction. In fact, she vowed that if her Parliament said it would be inadvisable then she would not marry at all."

131

"Brave lady. Obviously that silenced them. But it would still be a hornet's nest that awaited Felipe. He and his entourage would have crossed the Bay of Biscay, a sea that is friend to no man, with storms that have ended many a venture, to find himself facing even greater storms. Gaztelu, tell me honestly, did Carlos realise the dangers his son might confront?"

"He did," Gaztelu admitted. "And you might also ask why Mary continued to insist on the marriage. She was convinced, or someone had convinced her, that only the Spanish Catholics could rid England of its heretics, that only Spain could protect England from the French and the Scots. Last and not least she was deluded into believing that this marriage would provide an heir for England and the Netherlands."

Quijada shook his head, "Ridiculously optimistic on all counts, Gaztelu. It stands to reason that if she, the monarch, cannot rid her country of heretics, what chance would a foreigner have? If she cannot protect her realm from neighbouring enemies how could she expect any useful support from so distant a country? And as for producing an heir, although we hear so many rumours that Mary is with child, I fear like you that this is asking for a miracle."

"And let us not forget that the young Protestant Princess Elizabeth, Mary's half-sister, is ready and waiting and, who knows, possibly threatening. And France is forever plotting. Aye, the troubles continue."

"And yet, Gaztelu," Quijada stopped, knitted his brow and stroked his trim beard before continuing, "Mary chose, as did Carlos for that matter, to go ahead with the marriage plans. Surely that was a gross misjudgement?"

"Perhaps, but she promised her parliament that Felipe would never be more than her consort."

"And they swallowed it?"

"Indeed they did."

"The whole thing beggars belief, Felipe would never be content as a mere consort."

They paused once they were on the covered terrace. Gaztelu sat on the low wall giving his knees a comforting rub. Quijada sat nearby leaning against a pillar placing his gloves by his side. They watched a small group of monks making their way to the fields and the smaller kitchen gardens.

"Oh for the simple life, eh, Gaztelu?"

"Just so. Getting back to Mary," Gaztelu was eager to continue the gossip enjoying the rare occasion of being the source of information. "Did you know that it was Carlos who did all the wooing, and not Felipe, including sending the engagement ring?"

"So what did Felipe do? He has such a reputation for the ladies, he must have thought of sending some little token of his affection."

Gaztelu arched his eyebrows, "Felipe? He wrote nothing, sent nothing; in effect, did nothing."

"I suppose we should not be overly surprised. That damned fiasco with Portugal was embarrassing. Now that King John is dead we can hopefully put that behind us. To think the marriage contract with John's half-sister was virtually finalised when Carlos announced, thank you but I have had a change of mind. The king of England is dead, Mary has inherited the throne, she needs a husband; England must be helped to return to the Catholic Faith, therefore we no longer require the Portuguese princess. Such an insult," Quijada flicked at fallen rose petals that had settled by his side. "And to think that Felipe did no more than go along with his father's decision, saying he must, as a dutiful son ought; arguing that the Portuguese dowry had been insufficient as a basis for a realistic contract. He was prepared to marry an old woman living on a cold island knowing that there was a young, or at least a younger lady in Portugal who would be deeply wounded. Such a heartache for her; to be spurned so publicly. I imagine Catalina would not have taken kindly to that either; the princess is, after all, her niece. Perhaps another reason for our king to be so conciliatory at present?"

"Carlos had no option but to push Felipe's suit for he had heard that King John was all for having his brother wed Mary."

Quijada jumped up angrily, "And would that have made such a difference to us? I thought Spain and Portugal were at peace, have been for years, for goodness' sake!"

Gaztelu's myopic eyes twinkled mischievously. "It would have been at the very least a blow to the Hapsburg pride.

Carlos was determined to have a Hapsburg on the throne of England. Why, at one stage, he even pestered his brother Ferdinand to put forward one of his sons as a possible suitor. Nor should we forget that a Hapsburg on the throne of England would ensure more power against France."

"So our fair prince won the prize. Much good will it do him."

"But he was no longer a prince. Remember that Carlos thought it preferable for Felipe to go to England as the King of Naples instead of a cap in hand Prince of Spain." He slapped his thigh, "You will enjoy this, Quijada. A Papal Dispensation was required, and for granting it the pope named his price as two mules. To my mind that smacks of pure contempt for the two royal houses."

"Who knows? I grow weary of it all, Gaztelu, for the world has become nothing more than a market place. Everyone is seeking for the best bargain; everyone is haggling so as not to be the loser."

"The happy pair was wed, a bishop blessed the bridal bed, end of story. Ruy Gomez wrote saying she was even older than they had been led to believe, that she dressed like an old lady, and was short-sighted into the bargain. He said she had to screw up her eyes to see anything." He smiled, cleared his throat, "Come to think of it that sounds like me, so I suppose I am not in a position to criticise. Moving on, evidently she laughs and giggles like a young maiden in love. Apparently Felipe finds all this quite nauseating."

"I cannot say I have much sympathy for him, to be honest."

"Well, he is free of her for now, Quijada; gone to fight the French. Poor Mary was left brokenhearted, wept pitifully as he sailed away, so I was told."

Quijada walked up and down before admitting, "Partings are very painful, I know only too well. But speaking of partings and adieus, I have a titbit of gossip I came across very recently; then we really must go indoors. Do you know anything of an Isabel Osorio?"

"No, but then I am usually the last to hear any gossip or rumours." He gave Quijada what he hoped was a meaningful look regarding his lack of information about that singer Barbara.

"She was a lady-in-waiting for Princess Juana before transferring to Felipe's court. She remained there until he left for England, spending many an evening in his bed. Well I know for a fact he is deeply in love with her, has been for some time. What I heard was," he looked all about him then whispered, "he evidently gave the lady a document declaring that she is his wife. I am also reliably informed that he commissioned Titian to portray their love in the guise of a mythological scene, *Venus and Adonis*. Apparently it takes but little imagination to recognise the young fully clothed departing god, whilst the blushes of the naked lady are spared for we see only her bare backside as she reaches towards her lover for one final embrace. I believe the painting travelled to England with Felipe that he might enjoy warm memories on cold English evenings."

"Never," whispered Gaztelu also peering about him for possible eavesdroppers, "surely none of this can be true."

"Got it from a reliable source, I assure you. And there is more. She has retired from the court. Felipe has set her up in her own home, a good sized property at that. Some people of an unkind disposition have named it The House of the Whore. The presence of children has been mentioned too."

"What would the king say if he were to find out?" Gaztelu tut-tutted.

"Who knows? And who knows what he would say if he knew of Felipe's present philanderings in Brussels. You know his opinions on infidelity."

For no reason at all an unsummoned image of Barbara suddenly flashed before Quijada. It lasted no longer than a second; he was opening the door to Carlos's bed chamber, she was slipping past him, he was closing the door.

"Enough for now, Gaztelu. Shall we go in?"

So Carlos was prepared to send his son to a hostile country. He was content to marry him off to a woman whose only hope of having a child would be by some miracle. For what reason; Hapsburg pride, personal triumph? I would question if any of his plans for Mary and England could possibly be

135

regarded as realistic. Did he not stop to consider that this marriage might cause deeper hatred and resentment for the Catholic Faith and the Spanish throne? I ask you, was this the action of the great statesman, the great Caesar? Or was it the rash, insensitive behaviour of a man besotted with power?

Forgive me, I have allowed myself, first, to become angry and, second, to try to draw an opinion from you. Let us follow the two gentlemen indoors to await the king.

July

A Suitable Monarch

"Good morning, my lord," chorused Quijada and Gaztelu, bowing to Carlos as his chair boys wheeled him into his private salon.

"There is nothing good about it," he growled at them over his shoulder.

"But it is a glorious day, and so perfect for the feast of Santiago el Mayor."

"You heard me say that there is nothing good about it so far as I am concerned; and that is exactly how I feel."

"Oh, my, to what do we attribute such good humour today?" Quijada gibed.

"I am not of a mood to play games, Quijada. I have had not one wink of sleep. Not the gout chair, fools, the other chair! God Almighty," he snarled at Samuel and José as they lifted him. "And what do you think you are carrying? Think I am nothing more than a sack of corn? Watch out or you will be out on your arses, the pair of you."

The lads set him down in his chair then fell on their knees before him, muttering a stream of apologies.

"Get out of my sight! Impossible to rely on anyone these days."

They had backed their way to the door and taken up their regular stance.

"What the bloody 'ell did we do wrong, José?"

"Beats me. Nowt, if you wants to know the truth. It's just him this mornin', he's like a bear with a sore head."

137

"Bleedin' scary, talking about bootin' us out though, José?"

"Nah, it'll all be forgotten by the time he wants us again, just you see."

"Gawd, I hopes so. I mean, where'd we go? What'd we do?"

Quijada made sure that the footstool was in the best position for the comfort of the king's legs and feet. He fussed with the cushions hoping that this would give Carlos time to compose himself, "Should I dismiss the boys, my lord?"

"Yes, yes. I told them already to get out of my sight."

"I think they were so frightened by your anger, they did not fully understand, my lord."

"No bloody use in the army, the pair of them!"

Quijada told Samuel and José to leave then turned to Carlos, "And you did not sleep?"

"I said I had not one wink of sleep."

"Not even one wink?"

"Are you determined to annoy me this morning, Quijada?"

"No. Are you unwell?"

"I am not unwell. I am deeply troubled."

Gaztelu stepped closer, "Is there anything I can do to help, my lord?"

"Dear God in Heaven, if only someone could."

"Have you received some bad news since our meeting yesterday?"

"No, Gaztelu, nothing new. My brain is in a torment about my grandson, Prince Carlos."

Quijada asked, "And what was it about the young prince that kept you from your sleep?"

"Everything. The boy worries me, worries me deeply. Good God, you just have to look at him."

Quijada put his hands on his hips, looked questioningly first at Carlos then at the secretary, tilted his head and laughed, "If we are to speak of looks, not one of us in this room is what you would call an oil painting."

"Speak for yourself. I was a good looking chap when I was young, I can tell you. Had women falling for me wherever I went," Carlos wagged an angry finger at him, "I even had someone desperate to be at my side not so many years ago. You know who I mean."

"Ah, you mean the singer Barbara."

"Damned right, Barbara. You cannot deny it can you?"

Gaztelu hastily reached for his spectacles expecting to hear more, at last. Then Quijada changed the subject.

"Nor can I deny that you are a crosspatch today. Come then, if you must, tell us all about it. Hopefully that will rid you of your temper and we can begin to enjoy the day of Santiago el Mayor. I am almost tempted to offer you an early luncheon if I knew that would help cheer you. However let us speak of Prince Carlos. The boy, as you say is not handsome. We are all aware of that."

"His head is too damned big for his body. That is bad, no denying it. It shows that his brain might be ... and one leg is longer than the other, his back is crooked ... and he seems to have to drag one side of his body."

Gaztelu set his spectacles down and leaned towards him, "My lord, the birthing if you recall? It was very difficult. A delicate matter to discuss, but, well, did not the midwife have to, how shall I put it? The child would never have come into this world without a lot of help to release him from his mother's womb. The instruments, the pulling and twisting; these surely are the reasons for his physical imperfections: the size and shape of his head, his twisted legs and spine." He pressed the palms of his hands flat against his chest, "But these are nothing. Many a time nature has seen fit to impede the start of a child's life, and as a consequence some children have to carry the scars of the midwife's actions. Yet I would venture far rather this than the alternative of the child not given the chance to live? We must surely thank God that He granted him the precious gift of life."

"Gaztelu you look and sound like a blasted priest, except that your words, unlike the priest's, are of little comfort. In any case you know as well as I that these are the least of his problems." Carlos stared down at his misshapen fingers as if to find some answers there.

No one spoke, no one stirred. The two companions occasionally exchanged glances until Quijada could bear the silence no longer, "My lord," he said gently, "if you are

139

referring to the reports of the doctors, there are many who try to disguise their own ignorance and who seek to confuse us with a pompous manner and arcane language …"

"Another blasted priest with us!" Carlos thundered "I have a monastery full of them next door, I do not need any more thank you," he slapped at the arms of his chair. "So how do you excuse his biting the breasts of three of his wet nurses?"

"Ah, quite easily," Gaztelu spoke with a greater confidence than he actually felt, "the child was still suckling at an age when most, but by no means all I hasten to add, are content with a bowl and spoon. There is no doubting that this would cause some discomfort for the nurses. And then you know how women exaggerate." He smiled nervously, "Goodness me, here we are, three men talking women's talk. I beg you, sire, let us leave this sort of nonsense to the ladies as they gossip over their needlework."

"And how are you going to explain away his speech?" Carlos demanded of them.

Gaztelu shook his head, "We can do no more than repeat what you already know. It is true that he was late in learning to speak, but that was no fault of his. Poor mite; everyone thought he was dumb until he was more than three years old, when all the while he was tongue-tied and needed surgery to set it free. Perhaps somewhat remiss of the doctors? I have great sympathy for the young prince; he has had much to contend with. Might I venture to suggest you are too hard on him? Quijada, would you not agree with me?"

"I would indeed. I wonder, my lord, if you set too high a standard for the boy, and because he does not match your expectations, you …"

"My standards too high?" Carlos bellowed, "Unable to match expectations? If only that were true. His tutors are very disappointed in him too. They say that he finds reading and writing too difficult. Dear God, he is eleven years old. They have been trying to teach him Latin; Latin, when he cannot even master Spanish, for God's sake. He cannot, or refuses to, take any of his studies seriously no matter how his tutors beat him. He has told them they can beat him as much as they like but they will only get work from him if they pay him first."

The other two laughed.

"That is priceless. I like it. Clever thinking on his part," said Quijada.

"I wish that I had tried that when I was young," commented Gaztelu.

"Stop trying to make light of a very serious situation," Carlos would not be humoured.

"How many of us, if we are to be honest, were willing students?" Quijada suggested. "Look on the positive side, the prince is fit and well. He is strong."

"Strong enough to throttle hares," snarled Carlos. "Strong enough to hold live, struggling rabbits over flames; strong enough to go amongst the horses in the stables to slit their throats and wallow in their blood as they kicked and screamed."

Gaztelu interjected swiftly for even he had heard this gruesome gossip, "My lord, have we not all been guilty of some cruelty or other when we were boys? I remember once ..."

"I know none of us ever bit off the head of a pet tortoise to teach it a lesson for nipping our finger!"

Quijada tried to assuage his master's despair with platitudes, "I am certain that many of his problems will be rectified given time and patience. Be fair to the boy, he has had a most unhappy childhood. For a start he has never known a mother, God calling her to Him only days after he was born. Throughout his infancy and early youth he has rarely seen his father who is out of the country much of the time. The final blow for the child must have been when his dear Aunt Juana, whom we know he loves so dearly, and is the only one ever to show him affection, abandoned him to go to Portugal."

"Speaking of which," Carlos broke in, "the boy blubbered, *And what will that little prince do when his aunt has gone away and left him, when he is left all on his own?* That is how a baby talks!"

"Perhaps it was his method of emphasising his distress?" Gaztelu hoped he sounded philosophical.

Carlos lowered his head into his hands and screamed, "Shut up! Shut up, the pair of you! You make me sick with your unending sermonising. Say nothing. Do you hear? Just say nothing, not one word," he mopped at his face with his

141

handkerchief. "I blame Juana. She is the one at fault. It is not love she shows him, it is indulgence. She panders to him in every way. She still treats him as though he were an infant. God, she has yet to teach him that I am not his father and Felipe is not his brother. How dare she allow this to continue? And discipline? No such thing exists. When I was with him in Valladolid, he made me feel damned uncomfortable I can tell you. Would not suffer to be corrected; damned infuriating; I have commanded thousands of men, and not one of them insubordinate like him; refusing to obey any of my orders. Two days I spent with him. Two days too many." He glowered at Quijada when he saw him about to interrupt, "Not one word from you, I said. And temper! Juana ought to have dealt with that long ago, as well, but no, she lets him do or say what he likes. This is the very lady who wants to return to Portugal to be regent, to be responsible for the education of her son. God help us should that ever come to pass. Do you know what happened one day? Prince Carlos wanted my portable stove, nay, demanded it. I explained – imagine my having to explain anything to anyone – that he could not have it, told him I needed it for my aches and pains and that I took it everywhere with me. The scene that followed was unbelievable. He clenched his fists, started stamping his feet. He turned purple, screaming that he wanted it, must have it, would have it. The only way I got him to calm down was by promising it would be his after my death. An eleven-year-old having tantrums like that. I ask you, is that right? A three-year-old might, but surely to God not an eleven-year-old?"

Gaztelu and Quijada said nothing, as ordered.

"And what about this then – and not another soul must hear this – I thought I would tell him a war story, just a very short one, thinking to entertain him for a few moments. I expected him to find it exciting; that I, the famous conquering hero, should have found myself in such a precarious situation. Well, I was wrong, because when I started to tell of my retreat from Innsbruck he interrupted screaming that he would never commit such a cowardly act; refused to listen as I tried to continue, to explain that I only had my personal guard with me; refused to accept that we would be no match for an opposing army. He refused to see that the daring escape of our tiny group at night in a violent snowstorm, me in my litter, and every horse slipping and sliding over the snow-clad mountain pass, was our only possible means of survival. *No, by God,* he lunged at me, screeching, *You lily-livered excuse for a man. You disgust me. I shall be forever ashamed of you!* I have never known such a thing, never seen anyone carry on like that. My Isabel would never have tolerated it. She gave Felipe many a clip around the ear for far less. That is what he should have had, that is what has been lacking!"

He was quiet for a long time. "And how about this? I heard that a pageboy had upset him, doing something trivial no doubt, but Prince Carlos said he would never eat another bite until he had seen him hanged. The servants had to hang an effigy of the pageboy in his stead to appease him. Dear God, where will it all end? Now you may speak. Now show me your wisdom, your vast experience in such matters."

Silence. Complete silence.

"So, you have finally run out of excuses. Now do you see why I had no sleep last night? The boy has a sick mind, should be seen by that doctor from Salamanca, that fellow that Francisco was speaking of, the one who went to see my mother."

He rubbed at his eyes, dragging his hands down over his cheeks, revealing the angry redness inside the lower lids, the livid tracery of his veined eyeballs, then he shook his head, shaking off his temper and frustration.

He sighed, and the beginnings of a smile twitched at the corners of his mouth. "Cheer me up, Quijada. Tell me of your young charge as I call him. How is he progressing?"

"Are you sure you wish to hear? There is such a contrast. It seems inappropriate at this moment. It is sad that two youths almost of an age should be so different. No, this is not the best time to sing Juan's praises; and you have heard it all before."

"It will rid me of my dark thoughts. Juana was most impressed when she saw him, she spoke highly of him, not that that means such a lot I suppose coming from her."

Gaztelu's spectacles were retrieved and put on in readiness.

"It was embarrassing for both of us. Her first impression of him was as a village lad; that was after all what he had been for several years. I had to explain that I had never suspected that a retired musician from your court would allow himself or the lad to live in such conditions. Massy's pension was more than adequate to maintain a small staff, to provide a comfortable home, and then there was the additional allowance from the child's father. Had the situation been drawn to my attention earlier I would have acted sooner. However, the princess, without any fuss, gave him clothes far better suited to a child about to meet his new foster mother. When Juan arrived at our home he looked every inch a little gentleman."

Carlos nodded, "And you say he is a clever boy; intelligent and learns easily."

"DoZa Magdalena is more than pleased with his progress. But he is no bookworm, so although a life of contemplation may have been the original intention, I think a military career is favoured instead. But, these are still early days."

"How old is this Juan of yours?"

"He is eleven years old."

"Good God, eleven years old already. How the time has flown. About the same age as Carlos, a coincidence that. And what of his behaviour?"

"DoZa Magdalena has no complaints. He is a boy, however, and boys do sometimes get into mischief; the usual high spirits. He is certainly not a little saint."

"Describe him," Carlos rested his head on the back of his chair and closed his eyes.

"He is a tall, handsome youth, and strong, my lord. His forehead is a goodly size, denoting his intelligence or so my wife insists. His hair is like the golden sun and it curls about his temples. His eyes are blue and, according to my wife, they are warm and honest. You must forgive a mother's bias. For myself, speaking as his father, I beg your pardon, his foster father; I must tell you he has a noble bearing."

"Noble bearing, eh? I want to see this lad of yours. I expect his true father must surely wonder ... would surely want to know ... Before you go to Villagarcía see to it that you find a home here. Yes, I insist you bring both DoZa Magdalena and Juan to live in Cuacos."

"I am ahead of you already, my lord. Work will commence on a home for my wife and child within days."

"Nothing suitable available? That is disappointing; could take some time."

"It is only a small village with small houses. However, two have fallen vacant and I persuaded the tenant of the third to move into other accommodation. I have found workmen and given instructions to make a decent sized home. There will be several rooms as well as three goodly sized bedchambers and an upper corridor or gallery where Magdalena may walk on inclement days; and the Lord knows there will be plenty of those."

"I shall ignore that."

"Another consideration is that I am uprooting Magdalena from her home, her beloved duties and responsibilities to the local church, the convent, and the poor of the village."

Carlos brushed aside any possible difficulties. "Oh, you will see that everything will work out for the best, for all of us. But what a man, eh, Gaztelu? He has thought it all through already, and it cannot be too long before we see this lad. Excellent news, eh?"

"Why yes," he replied, "I suppose so. Why, I should say most definitely."

Gaztelu had almost cried aloud *yes* at the prospect of meeting two people he had heard so much of recently, and who, whenever mentioned, were showered with superlatives: this boy, Juan, of humble beginnings, who was now apparently handsome, intelligent, strong and of noble bearing; Quijada's beautiful, young, but childless wife, a lady of fine breeding, deciding to take on the daunting challenge of raising this particular humble child (when the church orphanages were filled with unwanted bastard children from many a noble family). Seeing Juan and Magdalena would make a wonderful change to the interminable days so often filled with routine letter writing, his master's ill temper, tolerating the enforced isolation of this small community in the middle of nowhere. Was this excellent news? It was indeed, and he earnestly prayed it would become a reality; but it was best not to get too excited.

"Now I do feel cheered, I have something to look forward to. An aspiring soldier to chat with. We can get out all my campaign maps and charts, go over battles. I can barely wait.

145

Now, how about the celebrations for our patron saint's day? We have tarried far too long. To the grand salon, it is time to eat and drink and of course to be merry. Summon those chair lads."

"Indeed, my lord," Quijada bowed. "And then I must tell you my joke about the enormous censer in Santiago Cathedral."

You must find it truly amazing that only yesterday Carlos was promoting the young prince's claim to the Portuguese throne should Sebastian die, but today is bedevilled by doubts about, to put not too fine a point on it, his sanity; such a change of attitude. A sovereign having to be of sound mind must be of little consequence after all! There are obviously rules for some and not others. I was put in mind of Carlos's mother. But I am not here to pass judgement, and I digress. Forgive me.

August

Pen or Sword?

I

An elderly visitor had just arrived in the courtyard. As he dismounted he stopped, turning at the sound of other hoof falls.

A broad smile of surprise spread across his face. "My lord, this is indeed a sight that gladdens my heart. I never thought to see it. Up and about and riding, no less."

He handed the reins to a stable lad, straightened his cape about his shoulders as he waited for Carlos.

"ZuZiga! Here in Yuste at last and after so long an absence. I thank God you came to my call. I need a friend desperately. No one to talk to you see. Quijada has gone home."

Alonso and Manuel helped the king out of his saddle. José and Samuel stood by his chair ready to receive him.

Carlos steadied himself, leaning heavily on Alonso, "You. What is your name again?"

"Alonso, your majesty," he bowed.

Carlos let go of him to ease his stiff back with his hands. Alonso returned to patting and stroking the king's one-eyed mule; a longtime favourite.

"Alonso. Well, you did a grand job out there today Alonso. You led her well. She did everything you asked. A good ride, a damn good ride. But I will have to get more practice if I am to accompany a young visitor who is coming soon; the old back, you know. Yes, you are good with horses. Worked with them long?"

147

"Pleasing your majesty, I've been workin' with horses for years. I was with you at Mühlberg and Metz an' all. Both me and me mate got to looking after your horses at Metz ..."

"Yes. Yes. Well, there you are then," Carlos looked away, he was not about to allow this day to be marred by memories of that disastrous military campaign at Metz. "Tell your mate as you call him," he nodded towards Manuel who was handing over an eiderdown to the chair boys, it having fulfilled its task of protecting the royal backside and its haemorrhoids from the discomforts of too firm a saddle, "tell him he was most helpful too."

The master of the wardrobe almost ran down the cobbled ramp, "My lord, do you wish me to get warm water, towels? Are you requiring fresh ...?"

"Not now. Later. Do not fuss me man! Right now I am going to talk to my friend ZuZiga. Go and tell them we expect refreshments out here. Immediately." He beckoned José and Samuel, "Right lads, we can dispense with the chair, today I am going to walk. Let us see if I can make it up the ramp and after that the gallery."

The three set off together, Carlos leaning heavily on the lads' shoulders. ZuZiga followed accommodating his pace to theirs. The master of the wardrobe scuttled off to seek out the servants.

Alonso and Manuel led the mule and ZuZiga's horse to the stables.

Alonso couldn't hold back a moment longer bursting out with, "Did you notice? He didn't want to talk about Metz, did he? Sharp changed the subject he did."

Manuel agreed, "Would you want to talk about it, if you'd been in charge of that bleedin' mess? Middle of winter, bleedin' snow and rain. All of us up to our bloody necks in mud, blood, and guts we were; noses filled with the stench of vomit and shit, making you want to retch something terrible. And everybody moaning, complaining, and arguing; all of us wanting to get away from death what was looming on all quarters. Scared stiff I was. Jesus we was lucky. When you think how many thousands died. Yeh, the only good thing about that whole stinkin' business was that we came out of it alive and all in one piece."

"You're right. Trouble was the poor old boy was past it; had no bloody idea what was going on. He was sick, he was, with his headaches and what have yer. And having trouble with his private parts, front and back. Aye, and I heard plenty enough folk saying as how he couldn't make the right decision if it came up, stared 'im in the face and grabbed him by the throat. Some great leader, eh?"

"Yeh, he was already gettin' too old by then. Somebody told me as 'ow all he wanted to do was play with his clocks. Folk dying right, left, and centre and he's playing at clock repairs; I ask you! Mind you he's had his successes."

Alonso snorted, "Maybees that was when he should've stopped, when he still knew what he was doing."

Yes indeed, Metz was miserable for everyone, not least his aides. Day after day the Duque de Alba and other generals had to contend with the king's outbursts of rage, or weeping and puking like a child, and at times his total inability to comprehend what was happening around him, refusing their advice. Yes, the campaign at Metz was, well, words are inadequate to describe the horror of it all. Thirty thousand dead and the pitiful spectacle of the remnants of his army in retreat.

But enough of that. Carlos is looking decidedly better than he has in a long while. And obviously he is feeling well enough to take a short ride through the olive groves and vineyards. A few weeks ago I would have thought the only possible way of his travelling anywhere would be by horse litter. On this occasion I am more than happy to be proven wrong. Shall we join them to discover to what he attributes this new vigour, this new lease of life? Thanks be to God that Carlos

149

has opted for the shade of the gallery rather than the delights of the fly-infested garden.

"My old comrade, Zuñiga. Sit down, do sit down. I have been so impatient to see you, to tell you all the news. It is just unfortunate that Quijada cannot be here to share these wonderful times."

They sat at a table facing out over the garden and fish pond.

"I am delighted to see you enjoying such good health, my lord."

"I tell you, ZuZiga, I feel years younger. And here comes Gaztelu to join us. You brought the letter?"

Gaztelu's feet propelled him at double his normal shuffle along the gallery and he was looking positively jubilant. "Yes, my lord, when I was told of the arrival of your guest I knew you would want to show him. It is so good to see you, ZuZiga."

"I see you have a certain lightness in your step, Gaztelu. Something extraordinary is going on here for sure. Do tell."

"ZuZiga," beamed Carlos, "we have received such heartening reports from France, but I will leave it to my secretary; he can read you the letter. Felipe's handwriting is almost indecipherable; God knows what his tutor was about."

Gaztelu unfolded a letter, "It comes from Brussels and says,

It has been decided, finally, to take Saint-Quentin. It will prevent the French advancing beyond her territory, and it will provide us with a route to Paris. I have sent orders for the Italian and German troops to rendezvous near the town with those from the Netherlands. Meanwhile I have organised the supply of munitions and food. I hope to be in Saint-Quentin within a few days. I cannot leave here sooner because I am still waiting for the English forces. It really is very annoying but after all the difficulties in getting the English to finally declare war on France it would be churlish for me to leave without them. Munchausen and his regiment have not arrived

150

either. J told Savoy not to enter into battle until J arrive, unless it cannot be avoided. Naturally he is eager for action, seeing this as a prelude to his return to his homeland. Jf we win, J should say when we win, we should net some fine fish. J hope that this letter will bring some joy to your heart. """ ...."

"Now then, ZuZiga, what do you have to say? We shall have those damned Frenchies by the scruff of their necks. That should put them in their place. And my son Felipe at last is a soldier king, just like his father!" Carlos chuckled and rubbed his hands with childlike glee.

"The French certainly need to be brought to heel," ZuZiga concurred, "and Savoy will see this as a grand opportunity to open his campaign to regain his lands. And how gratifying for you after so long a wait to have Felipe win his spurs. Of course he was given a good grounding in all the military skills."

"Damned right, I saw to that," Carlos glowed with pride. "Even if I could not be present I insisted he was raised a soldier." His face clouded suddenly, "But I am bothered by so many delays. I just hope to God that Felipe will get to Saint-Quentin in time."

"No worries should he not," ZuZiga shook his head, "for the Duke of Savoy will surely have plenty of men under his command to continue without him. And I remember you often saying how skilled he is in the art of warfare; second to none you said; told me that you had immediately recognised his potential, his abilities. You even nicknamed him Philibert the Ironhead."

Gaztelu's laughter was chilled by Carlos's stony look. Those high spirits were disappearing fast.

"I am not talking about how bloody wonderful Savoy is nor about how many men he has. Goddammit, I am talking about my son being there! My son must be there to lead the troops ..."

"With permission," Gaztelu interrupted, "Savoy is there, a man with an outstanding military record. I am certain you, as well as King Felipe, can trust him to make the right decisions. King Felipe's responsibilities go far beyond being present at the scene of action."

"You refuse to get the point! I could not give a damn about how good Savoy is; I want Felipe to be in command!"

"Well it is not for us from this great distance to judge the situation, my lord," proposed ZuZiga. "Ah, perhaps I see your problem. You are frustrated because you are not there to take over Felipe's role so that he could then be deployed alongside Savoy and the others. I hate to disappoint you but I think Felipe seems to have everything perfectly under control, from tactics to supplies. This will inspire everyone with confidence. But I am interested to know how Felipe managed to persuade Queen Mary to send English troops."

"You tell him Gaztelu, obviously nobody wants to listen to me," a sour, surly, and very disgruntled Carlos mumbled.

"Queen Mary of course is always ready to support King Felipe. It was her council who were loath to get involved. Anyway the French themselves finally settled the issue. They played right into Mary's hands. Let me explain; for years they have plundered English ships, and have continued to secretly support English rebels."

"Makes it all the more bloody remarkable that it has taken the English so long to come to their senses," Carlos grumbled into his beard.

"Yes, indeed, sire. Well it came about like this. In April a spy handed the English a plan of one of their ports. It was recognised as a place called Scarborough, on the North East coast of the country. At first it was thought it must be where the French had chosen to invade. But no, it was forty or so Englishmen who landed; and every one of them a French spy. They seized the town proclaiming that all kinds of evil would befall the country at the hands of the dreaded Spanish. They said Queen Mary was Spanish at heart. Fortunately they were all captured and hanged. However this was the catalyst we so desperately needed. The climate of opinion changed immediately; the English were now afraid of the French, so they provided us with an army."

Carlos clapped his hands and laughed, all frustration forgotten, "Aha! So there you are ZuZiga. Another victory. We have at long last got England off her arse, to come out openly against France. What an achievement! I knew all along that marrying Felipe to Mary would turn out to be a brilliant move on my part. It takes intelligent planning, you see; one has to have the wit to foresee these things. And there is yet more good news. Tell him about Portugal."

"The king is referring to the succession to the Portuguese throne."

"He knows what we are referring to, Gaztelu."

"Father Francisco has been an excellent diplomat and ambassador. His majesty sent him to Portugal regarding legal rights to the throne, concerned that there might have been some doubts about the wording of various Papal Dispensations. He has reported back that everything is correct in every detail, and has been approved by the Portuguese. Juana's son Sebastian inherits the crown." Gaztelu became serious, "Incidentally, Father Francisco almost died. He is sometimes too hard on himself. He is not a young man, and yet he felt that God would prefer it, and indeed would lend strength to his endeavours, if he were to walk to Portugal instead of travelling on horseback."

"ZuZiga doesn't want to hear all that twaddle! Get on with the story. This is the best part."

"In the event of Sebastian dying without issue, Prince Carlos will become king of Portugal."

"Am I not a genius? I have sorted out the English and the Portuguese! Now I only await news from Bohemia. I must have one of my granddaughters marry Sebastian. Before you say this is all premature because he is very young, allow me to tell you the damned French are already making overtures."

"His majesty rightly suspected this from the beginning," Gaztelu announced with pride.

Carlos positively glowed at this further evidence of his continuing astuteness.

"It seems that you have everything going to plan. It is little wonder you are in such high spirits. I congratulate you," Zuñiga bowed.

"But I do miss Quijada. I can tell you it has been a damned nuisance without him. The priests are useless, and to tell the truth they get on my nerves. They are only good for priests' business and nothing more. This place has become a bloody nightmare; and Cuacos too with no one to keep control. Everything everywhere is in total chaos. Anyway, Gaztelu has written to Villagarcía demanding his return. But not only will we have him here again, oh no, he will be bringing his wife and foster-child with him."

"Ah, the young Jerome, destined for the priesthood."

Carlos leaned towards ZuZiga, slapping him jovially on the knee, "Wrong on both counts. You see, you have been away too long. DoZa Magdalena has changed his name to Juan, and, would you believe, he has decided to be a military man! We are to have a little soldier in our midst, only too eager to hear my tales of the battlefields."

"And you intend to ride with him, judging by what I witnessed this morning?"

"Precisely."

Faint sounds of a horse galloping at some speed put an end to the subject. ZuZiga rose, "It sounds like even more excitement on its way."

All attention was focused on the gateway to the courtyard, waiting for the sounds of clattering hooves to grow louder, to take shape and form. Then suddenly the horse and rider were there – it was a courier.

II

Carlos pushed himself up from his seat, gabbling, "A messenger from Valladolid, Portugal, France? Must I go myself? Damn it get him here. All this waiting."

Gaztelu placed a restraining hand on his arm, "Why so impatient, my lord? Is good news not well worth the wait? And we cannot doubt that it is good news."

ZuZiga smiled, "Why, do you know, it is quite like old times. Do you remember? The anticipation, nerves all a-tingle, waiting for the latest despatches? Ah; and here he is."

A man of about thirty years, his ruggedly handsome face burnt by wind and sun, strode along the gallery, the jingling of his spurs accompanying his heavy steps. He removed his hat mopping his forehead with his sleeve as he did so. With dark eyes reddened with fatigue he sought out the king and fell to his knees before him.

"Welcome, welcome. Stop all this bowing nonsense. Hand over the letters. Quickly man."

"Your majesty I mean no disrespect coming before you in this befouled state, but I thought it important to come straight to you." He looked down at himself, inspecting his lamentable appearance. He was hot, dusty and exhausted, his brown jerkin flecked with horse spume, the band of his hat and his armpits stained black with sweat, his dark hair glistening with wet, dripping curls. He took his satchel from his shoulder and fumbled with the buckle.

"Good God, man, do you have to be so damn clumsy," Carlos reached to wrest the leather bag from him.

The courier held out a letter; the awaited letter. "I have the honour to bring this letter from His Majesty, King Felipe."

"Here, Gaztelu, read it. Must sit down."

Gaztelu, spectacles perched on the tip of his nose, broke the seal. "This is from Beaurevoire, near Saint-Quentin and dated August 10,

I kiss your Majesty's hands. Savoy has informed me that our armies have been victorious. Montmorency has been captured. Savoy and Egmont have completely routed his troops, and Savoy lost only five hundred men whereas Montmorency lost five thousand ......

oh, such news, your majesty!"

"Yes! Yes! We have beaten the goddamned French," Carlos punched at the air. "Go on."

"I am to visit the field tomorrow and will forward more information."

"With permission, there is a second letter," the courier handed it to Gaztelu.

"What have we here?

Today I visited Saint-Quentin to congratulate the troops. I also inspected the lines of prisoners and I am pleased to report that there were some illustrious names amongst them including Montmorency who is quite seriously wounded. The captured colours, more than eighty, made an impressive sight. Savoy thought to kiss my hand, but I hugged him instead saying I should be the one to kiss his hands for he was the one who had gained such a great and glorious

155

victory. And that we should have won such an important battle on San Lorenzo's day! J am determined to build a church to commemorate the occasion."

"Well, this is certainly worthy of a celebration." Carlos, overcome, dabbed at tear-smeared cheeks. "Such a damn fine victory, ZuZiga. Get this man a drink to rid his mouth of dust so he can give us details. A victory against the French on San Lorenzo's day." He stopped then spluttered, "But why was Felipe not there? Where in God's name was he, what was he doing?"

"There will be reason enough," said ZuZiga offering the messenger a goblet of cool beer.

"So tell us about the battle for Saint-Quentin, Don whoever-you-are?"

"Don Fernando, your majesty. Your health," he drank deeply, draining the goblet, wiping his mouth across the back of his hand. "Initially the Duke of Savoy deliberately confused the French. He had marched his men to and fro along the border of France so that the French had no idea where he was going to make the breakthrough. It worked! They thought he had decided to attack Champagne and moved all their troops there to defend it, and that is when Saint-Quentin was attacked. Frenchmen were hurriedly brought to defend it. We cut off half of them but the rest managed to get into the town ..."

"Good God! Savoy slipped up a bit there I would say." Carlos sought agreement from his friend. ZuZiga merely shrugged his shoulders.

Don Fernando continued, "The Duke of Savoy and Lord Pembroke then commenced the siege. Somehow or other the French managed to despatch a messenger urgently requesting further reinforcements from Montmorency; and they arrived, thousands of them. Next thing we knew they were trying to force an entry into the town, while Montmorency diverted our attention. Thank God we killed most of them before they could ..."

"You mean some did get into the town?"

"A few, my lord."

"How many is a few? A dozen, fifty, a hundred?" Carlos demanded.

"About five hundred or thereabouts."

"Jesus wept! That is more than a few, man!" He looked again at ZuZiga. "A reinforcement of five hundred got by them, for God's sake! Some commander Savoy turned out to be!"

ZuZiga shook his head still saying nothing.

"Sire, Montmorency then advanced, but he got trapped. You see he had moved too deep into our lines. Before long there was absolute chaos and confusion amongst his men. They turned tail, falling over each other; routed they were. Montmorency surrendered."

"How many were taken prisoner?"

"We took about four thousand. And five thousand dead."

Carlos was ecstatic, "Yes. Oh yes! Now that does sound like a victory, eh, ZuZiga? An army routed, thousands killed, thousands taken prisoner? And on our side, what were the casualties?"

"No more than five or six hundred dead, my lord."

"Good. Very good. Better than good; excellent!"

"A wonderful start to your son's reign, my lord," suggested Gaztelu.

"Yes.Yes. So, Fernando, if there is nothing else you may go. Get yourself some more beer, some food, some rest. Gaztelu, show him where to go. Send for the prior. I want him here immediately, we have to discuss prayers, processions, a Victory Mass."

III

No sooner were Carlos and ZuZiga left on their own Carlos gave vent to his anger. Starting with the mildest observation that Felipe should now be well on his way to Paris, he changed abruptly to screams of rage. "And Felipe not at Saint-Quentin! Where was he? He was in a blasted village writing damn letters, for God's sake! How are we going to live with the shame of it all? Why did he not use his power as king of Spain to insist they wait for him to lead the charge? How could I have sired someone so pathetically weak? What is he made of? A pen in his hand instead of a sword. Ink in his blasted veins instead of fighting blood. Damn well afraid to fight."

157

ZuZiga sought to calm him, reminding him of the events leading up to the action: the delayed English, the delayed Germans, Felipe's role as commander in chief, then Savoy having no choice but to move against Montmorency. His words were no match for the barrage of oaths exploding over him like canon fire.

He capitulated, threw his arms in the air in despair and walked away. He looked down from the balcony to the tranquil garden below; his ears, his whole being, bombarded with the ranting and raging behind him. It was that dreadful debacle at Metz all over again with Carlos screaming and shouting blaming everyone but himself.

Oh dear, Felipe does not appear to have fulfilled the role of soldier as well as had been expected and desired. But, who knows, another day's news may yet prove more favourable. I wonder what we do now. To celebrate or not to celebrate. If only Quijada were here, he would know exactly how to deal with Carlos and this unwarranted tantrum. He simply would not tolerate it.

Ah, here is Gaztelu with the prior. And the master of the wardrobe, too, probably anticipating orders for a particular outfit for Carlos suitable for the occasion.

Would you believe it? This is incredible. Look at Carlos; the purple-faced, spluttering-jowled rage has gone. The invective, the execrations, the maledictions, quite disappeared. It is as though they had never occurred. Amazing.

Carlos greeted the prior, smiling, "Excellent news. King Felipe has vanquished the French at Saint-Quentin. Paris is ours for the taking. I want a Victory Mass, tomorrow, with full processionals, et cetera, and it has to bear special reference to San Lorenzo, for that was the day God guided us to our victory. Following the Mass we shall have a celebratory feast."

"Your majesty it will be an honour and a privilege for our community to play our part in so momentous a period of our country's history. May I take this opportunity to congratulate you, the King Felipe, and the glorious Spanish forces."

"You may indeed," Carlos beamed with pride. "Yes, we can feel justly proud of all our gallant Spanish heroes, from the highest to the lowliest, from my son to the humble foot soldier."

I hate to nitpick, but it is only fair to point out that only an eighth of those gallant heroes were Spanish, equal in number to the English. For the rest: about a quarter came from the Netherlands; the bulk of the army was therefore German.

"So, good prior, you know what is required of you; you will want to get started," Carlos waved him away. "Now, I want my casket of chains. Oh, and my purse as well. I want the courier back here too."

Gaztelu and the master of the wardrobe set off along the gallery, Gaztelu muttering, "I feel no better than a courier myself today; bring the letters, take Don Fernando to the refectory, find the prior, bring Don Fernando back here."

"Well at least I have saved you the task of bringing the master of the king's jewels with the casket and purse. Why do you suppose he wants those?"

Carlos looked about him, "ZuZiga? Ah yes, still here. Come here. You are about to witness the actions of a very happy and magnanimous man." Carlos couldn't contain his delight. "You are about to be astonished."

After witnessing the pendulum swings of Carlos's emotions Zuñiga knew that nothing could possibly astonish him. "Today is certainly a day for surprises, my lord."

"What surprises? The news was hardly a surprise, we expected it man!"

"I only mean it has been a most eventful day, one way and another."

159

"Well, I say it is an excellent day. Here they come with our messenger." Carlos beckoned the young man towards him, "It was remiss of me to send you away without some token of our gratitude. I will not detain you longer than is necessary. Now let me see what I should give."

The casket was opened. Carlos studied its contents carefully before withdrawing a broad solid gold chain. "Here, my fine fellow; let me place this on your shoulders. There we are. And now the purse. Count out sixty gold *ducados*, for that is fitting for someone who has been the bearer of such welcome tidings."

All were stunned, dumbfounded, by this display of sheer madness. The king had just given away an exceptionally valuable gold chain and a fortune in gold coins – to a messenger!

Don Fernando's travel-stained face turned an ever-deepening red of confusion and embarrassment.

Carlos beamed at each one in his audience. He was well pleased with his demonstration of royal generosity, and remembered for a moment how he had rewarded another soldier, years ago, a certain Trooper Blomberg. It was only natural, as well as fitting, to show gratitude when the heart and soul are wonderfully warmed and gladdened.

The Best Leader

I

The two chair lads are still waiting, unoccupied, outside the king's bedchamber; it has been this way for days, and it appears that yet another day will go by with Carlos remaining confined.

He will never learn. You would think that at his age and having suffered so many distressing and painful attacks he would have some sense; show some restraint.

We should stand aside for a moment to allow Madame Male and the soiled sheets and nightshirts to pass. Here come those whose role it is to bear the washbowls and the covered pots and bowls of waste. I always think it such a shame for damask and lace to be relegated to the lowly task of shielding the eyes from unsightly matters. And lastly here comes another servant with a salver and its mountain of crumpled and stained bandages.

I must say I have never known it to be so quiet. Have you noticed that there is no laughter, no banter to be heard from the kitchen or stables; in fact anywhere? The place is like a tomb. Hopefully that will all change very soon; Quijada arrived in Cuacos last night and should be here this morning.

And speak of the devil, I beg his pardon, an unfortunate choice of expression, here is the man himself.

"Cheer up lads. No work for you today?" Quijada greeted the glum chair boys.

"No sir."

"And no work yesterday, nor the day before?"

"Not for many a day, sir. Couldn't begin to count, sir."

"Meanwhile you wait here to be summoned for nothing more than perhaps the occasional trip to the lavatory? And to make matters worse, there is nothing for you to eavesdrop on, am I right?"

José and Samuel shuffled their feet, swallowed hard, straightened their tunics, determined to look innocent of any such crime.

"Never worry lads. My lips are sealed. Your job needs some perks, even if it is but a jug of beer as a reward for your idle gossip. But why so miserable? Not just you, all the others too. Even Manuel and Alonso are down in the mouth. I had hoped to receive a happier welcome, but they had little to say."

José could barely wait to answer, "With permission sir, we's all as 'appy as can be to see you back. You can't know how 'appy, truly. It's been bleedin' miserable for us all for weeks, it 'as ..."

Samuel cut him short, "You shouldn't talk to your betters like that. The way things is these days, that could be just enough to get us kicked out."

Quijada shook his head, "No, no, you do right to let me know of any discontent, otherwise how will I be able to set things to rights. I must have a happy, orderly household for his majesty. So, please, tell me the cause of all these long faces."

"Sir, it starts with the king hisself. He's in a real foul mood with everything and everybody."

"Shut up, José. I tell you, you're doing your bleedin' best to get us slung out."

"Well, maybes you're right. What you 'as to understand, sir, is all the villagers is in uproar. They's arguing with us, chucking stones at us if we's anywhere near them. An' we do have to go near the bastards to chase them out of the king's orchards, away from our streams."

Quijada was shocked, "Are you telling me that the villagers are stealing?"

"Stealin'? Thieving something rotten they are. Plunderin' more like. The king'll be lucky to have a apple, a orange, or a fish left for hisself. And they've done worse than that an' all," José was well into his stride now. "Do you know they's had the bleedin' cheek to stop the mules what brings the king's food from Valladolid. Yeh, they have, and they takes what they wants."

"But lads, something must have gone sorely wrong. There must be some serious discontent at the root of this."

"The thing we heard was that they 'adn't taken kindly to the king's cows wandering on what they calls their land; that set them going, like. Anyways, what they did was they just kept the cows, said they wouldn't never give them back until they was paid for all the damage, like. Then 'cause they 'ad to give them back and didn't get paid they got madder than mad. That's about the size of it, really."

"Thank you, José, for telling me. Do not upset yourselves further, I will find a way to get this sorted out. Is there anything else I should know?"

Samuel, emboldened by the reception of José's information now felt he could speak, "Well you might as well know, sir, there's a really bad problem here too, worse than anything in the village." He looked at José.

"Go on, you might as well," José shrugged.

"Shockin' it is. In fact, some money 'as gone missing."

They were interrupted by a voice from the bedchamber; it was Carlos, "Is that Quijada out there? Has Quijada come back to us? If that is you Quijada, what are you skulking about out there for? Come in, come in! God but we are all desperate to see you."

Quijada reached for the door handle but wanting to stay to hear more, "Lads, I appreciate your telling me these things. Additional eyes and ears are most useful, but see to it you are never taken unawares with your ear tight pressed against any keyholes," he tapped his temple with his forefinger then pushed open the door. His already low spirits caused by his enforced early return had dipped even lower with Samuel's disturbing news. Could there really be a thief in the palace?

163

Not a happy reception. Shall we follow him in? I am never comfortable in this room. It chills my whole being. As black and claustrophobic as a family vault. Now if we position ourselves here close to the door into the church, which mercifully someone has left open, we will know for certain that we have not been interred.

Incense has such a soothing perfume, although I fear it will soon be overpowered by the king's vinegar dressings. He looks most unwell. I do not remember having ever seen his face so pallid, or his eyes so bloodshot and red rimmed. Nor does his sagging jaw help, leaving his mouth gaping like that – a dark cavern with those ugly yellow stumps of teeth. How shockingly, tragically old he looks.

Quijada was welcomed by a small group of men: Dr. Mathys, Male, Torriano, the masters of the king's wardrobe and jewels, and the cook. The king was slumped uncomfortably on a commode over a steaming pot of a brew of mallow, trefoil, parsley and other herbs. His nightshift had been drawn up and a quilt placed across his knees. His arms and legs were swathed in fresh vinegar bandages. The top part of his head was encased in a thick linen skull cap. A second quilt of black velvet thrown about his shoulders completed the sorry picture.

Quijada's spirits sank lower still.

Carlos pointed at him, "I will not have you look at me like that, I know what you are thinking, Quijada. Can see it in your eyes. You think me a pitiful sight."

"My lord, I can only say that I am shocked. I am equally saddened that I was not here at a time when you needed me. Dr. Mathys, has the patient been behaving himself? Has he been taking the prescribed medicines without argument? Has he adhered to a beneficial diet?"

"Oh, that he would! I sometimes think the only reason he chose me as his doctor was because he knew I was not in a position to give orders, apparently being too young, too inexperienced."

Carlos hushed him. "Never mind asking him, Quijada, ask me. Think I cannot speak for myself? Yes I have done exactly as I was bid, unless of course I knew better, which was often the case. I have been treated with potions and pastes from every kind of flower and plant. We have had carnations, marigolds, buglass, lily-of-the-valley, plantain. Got more of them inside me and spread on me than you could find in the whole damn garden. I still say you cannot beat these vinegar and rose water bandages. A young lady taught me that years ago. And we are not going to discuss food. Nothing but pap, slops. Disgusting. How can anyone expect me to survive on that filth?"

The cook bowed. "Don Luis Quijada, his majesty has just this minute complained again about the meals I have prepared today for him. It's all so very difficult; goodness knows I have done my best, preparing what the doctor says is necessary. But because there are no spices allowed, and washing food down with beer or wine is strictly forbidden, whatever I have cooked does not suit the royal palate. Everything I have suggested this morning has met with a swift refusal." He wrung his hands in despair, "I am completely at a loss. Perhaps if I were to offer him a fricassee of clocks; that might be acceptable."

Torriano almost laughed, he certainly smiled, "The very thing. It may just keep him ticking over better than the other recipes."

Carlos glowered, "Was that supposed to be humorous?"

"Actually we have tried to humour his majesty as well as keep him on the straight and narrow," Doctor Mathys continued. "And it has been no easy task I can assure you. We are heartily pleased to see you. The king needs you, yes, but we probably need you more."

All echoed his words except Male, who simply nodded from where he stood, almost asleep, leaning heavily against a table.

"Male how tired you look. I take it that the king had a wakeful night, one of several?" Quijada touched his shoulder sympathetically.

"I am always glad to be of service."

165

Carlos feigned surprise at Male's presence, "Good God man, you still here? You should be in your bed. Get you gone this minute."

Quijada wasn't fooled. "You need not pretend with me. How often have you put upon Male in my absence? I know your ways; you keep him standing by your bedside reading to you until some unearthly hour and then expect him to be here in the morning ready to be of further service. You ask too much of the man. If it is for no other reason than Male's comfort I can say that I am pleased to be back."

Carlos pouted, "How was I supposed to remember details such as when his rest times are? And before you accuse me of further thoughtlessness, I want you to know that I am doing him a great favour; giving him a reward, if you prefer. You know that poem he has been helping me translate, *The Determined Knight*? Well, I have given him permission to go ahead and have it printed. All the profits will be his. That is true is it not, Male?"

"Correct, my lord."

"So, what have you to say to that, Quijada?"

"Most kind; and I take it your majesty, that your name will also appear on the book and that you will share the cost of the printing?"

"Certainly not."

"But it must have occurred to you that Male might not sell many copies without your name; shame on you."

"Good God, Quijada I have made a generous enough offer in giving him the blasted book. Off you go Male, get you to bed."

The book will never be printed. King Felipe, a few years hence, will demand the manuscript be destroyed. Poor Male, he is such an unlucky sort of fellow.

II

Gaztelu shuffled into the room, his face suddenly brightening on seeing Quijada. "My friend, how good it is to see you," he hugged him warmly before turning to Carlos. "And how are you this morning, your majesty?"

"Feeling much better for the presence of this man. We might get my house back into some semblance of order now that he is here. Quijada you would not believe what has happened in your absence. The blasted villagers have turned into a bunch of thieving, rebellious bastards. I cannot understand it. All because some of my cattle strayed into their fields or gardens or whatever. Good God, they have started stealing my fruit and fishing my streams, and even daring to rob my shipments from Valladolid. Damned infuriating. And after all I have done for them. Come on, Gaztelu, remind us all how good I have been to the ignorant *hijos de putas*."

"You have always been most liberal, my lord. You have set money aside for debtors to be released from prison, you have provided money for young maidens wishing to marry, and you have shown charity to many a household. It is my humble opinion that once you start giving to these people their wants increase. And they expect even more from you now because their crops are failing." He appealed to Quijada, "Yet there has to be a limit to handouts. I realise how strong the temptation must be for the poor and needy when their bellies are gnawing their painful emptiness, and their eyes tell those same bellies that there is food to be found in gardens and streams nearby, that there are supplies on their way from Valladolid." He turned once more to Carlos, "Do not misunderstand me, your majesty, I do not condone ..."

Carlos screamed at him, "I never asked you for a bloody lecture or to make excuses for them! God, were it not for these useless arms and legs I would have been down to Cuacos to let them know who is master."

"Calm yourself. I am sure everything will be amicably resolved," Quijada spoke with his customary reassurance. "I shall attend to it personally. I have never had any trouble with the villagers, we always see eye to eye. It helps, of course, my sending extra income their way for them to provide accommodation and prepare meals for the many visitors who come here to see you."

167

"Most of whom I have no desire to meet, and most of whom I refuse to meet. Anyway, whatever you may have done for them is no match for my generosity," Carlos added.

"You are right. Does anything else trouble you?"

"Yes, something else damn well does trouble me. You others go now. I only want Quijada and Gaztelu with me." He waited until the door closed. "I am only going to mention this because you are not aware of what has happened, Quijada, but once I have told you we will forget the whole terrible business. It is too distressing to contemplate." He took a deep breath, "Some money has gone missing. A casket of money. It grieves me to have to admit to you that someone in this house has robbed me."

"How much?"

"Eight hundred gold *ducados*."

"Dear God, I cannot believe it! Eight hundred? That is outrageous. Surely a mistake? Perhaps it was put somewhere for safekeeping and the place then forgotten? Has there been a thorough search?"

"Yes we have been thorough," Gaztelu replied. "Every conceivable place has been searched, and there is no sign."

"Then there must be a search of the belongings of all who work here."

"Everything has been done that could be done, Quijada."

"The last resort then is physical persuasion, that never fails to provide ..."

Carlos raised one hand, wincing with pain at even this simple movement, "I refuse to allow that. In any case the whole affair sickens me so much I would prefer to remain ignorant of the identity of someone who would do such a thing against me, their lord and benefactor."

"But to have the villain continue to live under your roof?"

"I said I only wished to inform you and nothing more. The subject is closed."

"The servants will remain suspicious of one another."

"I will leave it to you to come up with some explanation. I am tired of it all," Carlos eased his position, groaning, his face distorted, tears of pain and self pity flowing freely.

"As you wish, my lord."

168

Gaztelu, having heard nothing but misery and moans since he came in clapped his hands. "But we must bring Quijada up to date with the news from France. How much do you know?"

"Only what you said in your letter telling of Savoy's success at Saint-Quentin. And I presume his majesty's indisposition is the result of the ensuing celebrations?"

"Yes. Yes." Carlos grumbled, "But I had to celebrate. I would hate the world to think I had not been impressed with the valour of our soldiers, the glory of it all. But it seems we can never have good news without bad news hanging on its skirts."

Quijada glanced at Gaztelu, "Nothing has gone wrong, I hope. King Felipe is not wounded?"

Gaztelu shook his head, "Have no fear, he is safe and well and has personally led his men to victory."

"Then what is this about bad news?"

Carlos grunted, "Felipe led his men to victory, humph! Some victory. He led his men to take the town of Saint-Quentin alright, but only after the major battle had already been won. Then on he went to capture two pathetically small towns nearby. My God, boys' stuff, humph! Why did he not decide to advance his troops to take Paris?"

Quijada did not disguise his impatience, "Come now; be fair. You know full well that Saint-Quentin is the gateway to Paris; a staging post for movements from France into other parts of Europe. It was also vitally important to take out any other towns in the area lest they reinforce their garrisons. Anyone could see that."

"No guts, the lot of them; should have marched on Paris!" bellowed Carlos.

"I repeat, my lord, you are unjust."

"I will silence you yet Quijada. You listen and you shall see what is fair, what is just. Get those letters, Gaztelu. Good Lord, if only Felipe would have spent more time with a sword instead of a blasted pen, how different it all could have been."

"Each commander has his own individual style."

"Quijada, I hope that when you meet your Maker you will find Him to be as ready to absolve you of your failings as you are for others, and that He will forgive you for the many excuses you have put forward for them. God knows, I

169

sometimes find it hard enough to forgive you; you can be so damned exasperating at times. Listen to the letter from Ruy Gomez."

"He writes,

The victory was all of God's making, for it was gained without experience, without troops, without money."

"You see what I mean? A hollow victory; a victory won by God's grace or sheer damned luck. What sort of men are we talking of here, bumbling idiots led by those with barely more than an ounce of wit?" Carlos fumed.

"For a start Gomez is no soldier. You surprise me by taking any heed of his words," Quijada argued.

"More excuses? Carry on Gaztelu."

"It was decided that after taking Saint-Quentin we would retire the troops to our winter quarters, money being in short supply for a further campaign. We agreed that a withdrawal following such a glorious victory would be viewed as being entirely honourable."

"Exactly. An intelligent course of action." Quijada reasoned, "Had Felipe marched his troops towards Paris, as you would have preferred, and assuming that the men would have obeyed orders and not mutinied when they discovered, as Gomez says, that there was neither pay nor food, he would have marched his men to their deaths. Let me have the letter, Gaztelu. Ah, yes, it says that the French king was already calling up thousands of reserves. We know how quickly and easily that can be done, it takes practically no time to recall all the retired soldiers, to impose levies on towns and villages."

"I know, I know. But supposing they had set off immediately instead of sitting on their backsides around a table talking, talking; all that interminable talking; God if they are not talking they are writing goddamn letters. What if they had set off straight away, they may well have ..."

"You shock me with your 'may well have'! That is all you can say; and what kind of basis is that on which to build any kind of military strategy?"

Carlos grunted, "Well, I will wait to see what you dare say about Felipe's letter."

Gaztelu unfolded a second piece of paper, this one bearing the royal seal. "Right, here you are."

Quijada scanned Felipe's scrawl,

"Tomorrow we head for the Netherlands. I know you will be disappointed that we have turned our backs on Paris, but I was not prepared to have our valiant men be a subject of French ridicule. You will recall how they mocked your soldiers for entering France dining on the best of meats, but leaving France scratching the earth for roots to gnaw upon. No, I was not going to allow strong, healthy men who had fought gallantly to become starving wrecks dragging their bones through foreign fields and along alien roads only to die."

He returned the letter.

"The insolent young pup, daring to throw that in my face!" Carlos choked on his anger: a strangled coughing, spluttering, howling, purple-faced temper.

"Sadly it is all so devastatingly true. One cannot change facts," Quijada reminded him as he brought a calming drink. The cries of fury had become a wheezing, gasping fight for breath.

Do not concern yourself; Carlos will recover in a moment or two.

His campaign in France in 'thirty-six to which Felipe was referring was a most embarrassing fiasco. More than twenty thousand died of disease or starvation. The roads were littered with the dead and the dying; corpses lay in piles by the wayside rotting and stinking alongside the remains of their once proud chargers. Perhaps now you can understand Felipe's reservations about being drawn deeply into enemy territory. So which is the great leader? I ask you!

Carlos whimpered, "That failure in France, was it all my fault, Quijada?"

171

"Of course not, far from it. There is very little anyone can do when faced with a scorched earth policy, poisoned wells, and then dysentery decimating the troops. You had to retreat. But that was the past; far better to dwell on King Felipe's victory. Unfortunate, all the same, that you had to celebrate the victory to excess."

A movement on the king's bed caught Quijada's eye.

"Ah, that!" exclaimed Gaztelu. "It came while you were away."

A ball of gingery brown fur became a horseshoe arch with a head that was mostly yawn.

"How did that damn cat get here?"

"Arrived with the bird," Carlos beamed, pointing to a rather large covered cage. "The last two of my loyal old troopers who had managed to get themselves unavoidably detained or lost on the way. But now they are here and my army is complete. Thank God I had them for company while you were away."

"Loyal old troopers indeed! Damned cats and birds; just so long as they keep out of my sight; you know how I feel about them. There is nothing wrong with a dog for companionship," Quijada snapped.

Old Grievances Run Deep

I

Following an obviously unsatisfactory lunch of slops and a disastrously painful visit to the lavatory Carlos summoned Quijada and Gaztelu to listen to further rantings and ravings about Felipe's failings as a military leader. We have missed nothing, I assure you, except further repetitions of everything you have already heard.

Quijada was annoyed. "It was bad enough that I returned to a complete breakdown in relations between the village and the palace and the suspicion of a thief amongst us without having to go over the battle for Saint-Quentin and its aftermath yet again. It is quite unacceptable. I am sorry, my lord, but I will hear no more of it. And you know fine well that Felipe must be given credit for his decision not to commit his men to a campaign with all the hallmarks of disaster. Let that be the end of the story; oh, unless, of course, you wanted to be generous and commend him for saving the Treasury a considerable amount of money. I think congratulations are also in order for the capture of Montmorency. Savoy must find it a sweet revenge for the devastation of his homeland. No doubt he is eagerly anticipating its return from French hands."

Gaztelu's little eyes twinkled with delight at Quijada's daring.

Quijada was not quite finished, "You are like a pup with an old slipper, not letting it go, tugging it this way and that, tearing at it because it continues to offend, growling at its very presence. At least the pup can be entertaining."

"Anyone would think you were my tutor the way you lecture and bully me. You are fortunate I allow you such liberties," pouted Carlos. His face suddenly lit up and he

173

chuckled, "The other day, Quijada, I was put in mind of Trooper Blomberg. Do you remember?"

Quijada was completely taken aback not by the change of topic, there was nothing new in that, but by the subject. He shot a swift glance at Carlos. What had he told Gaztelu while he was away? "What exactly made you think of Trooper Blomberg?"

"It was because everyone got themselves all upset. They felt I had been over generous when rewarding the messenger who brought us the news of the victory at Saint-Quentin."

"And were you?"

"Mere trifles, about sixty gold *ducados* and a gold chain."

"Good God, trifles indeed, and no one to prevent such madness?"

"No one but you would dare. But it put me in mind of that night when Trooper Blomberg came to my tent," he smiled, his lips collapsing into his mouth.

Quijada was quick to mouth to Gaztelu, "Perhaps if you were to go."

Gaztelu was peeved. He could sense a good story was in the offing about this Blomberg chap, knowing it couldn't possibly have been the same soldier he'd heard mentioned somewhere before, because Carlos had bought that one a commission; no ordinary trooper he. But perhaps he had been demoted, relegated to the ranks for some grave misdemeanour. That could well be the story and he had no wish to miss it. He virtually bleated, "My lord, do you wish me to leave?"

"No, no need, just thinking of due rewards for lightening the heart and raising the spirits. It cheered me up for a moment."

Gaztelu was more intrigued than ever; rewards for what? From an officer turned trooper? Why?

"No, enough of that, what I want to do now is to look at that blasted business in Italy. If you considered Felipe's strategies in France to have been successful, Quijada, you will more than likely make the mess in Italy sound like a glorious victory."

Quijada addressed the ceiling stroking his bearded chin. "You refuse to leave the subject alone; you are worse than a pup, worse than a dog with a bone; worrying it to death. So, whose mess or disaster might this be? Are we discussing a defeat of Alba in Italy? I think not. Are you referring to some woeful orders of King Felipe despatched from France? Again, I think not. Or are you speaking of a disaster according to the perceptions of King Carlos? Let me consider a moment knowing, as I do, King Felipe, Alba, and you ..."

"You are no better than a sarcastic knave to treat me so. What are we to do with the man, Gaztelu?"

The mystery of the Blomberg chap was sadly not to be revealed but at least Carlos's mood had lightened which was a blessing of sorts.

"If I were you, my lord, I would take care to guard him well, as you would a priceless treasure." Gaztelu allowed himself a little chuckle, the day had definitely brightened; this was much more like old times.

"True. Quijada you have been a sorry miss over the last few weeks," Carlos sighed. "I await your gems of wisdom. So then, let us begin with the facts. I leave it to you Gaztelu and mind you tell them the way I see them."

"Pope Paul sent his ambassador to the French Court demanding that King Henry help rid him of the Spanish. The Duke of Guise was despatched immediately with an army of twenty thousand. And there was many a French nobleman tagging along thinking it an honour, as they had at Metz, to accompany their hero; desperate to distinguish themselves in the field."

"Naturally," observed Quijada, "he is an outstanding example of excellent leadership: an intelligent military strategist, a man who leads by example, a man of great compassion towards the enemy's sick and wounded. Why, even our soldiers sang his praises. They had been left for dead and he saved them, commanding his own men to care for them."

Carlos screamed, bursting into tears, "Enough of that! There will be no talk of Metz!"

Quijada offered him a fresh handkerchief, "Weeping will not wash away those facts."

Gaztelu gave them both a mock disapproving look, enjoying every moment. "Back to my story; you are also aware that his progress through Italy met with no resistance as all our forces were deployed in the defence of Naples."

"Yes, and Guise was given a tumultuous welcome by the citizens of Rome," continued Quijada.

Carlos spluttered, "I am sick to death of hearing about Guise, the blasted saintly knight in his blasted shining armour! More to the point; what about the pope? May the devil take his bones and grind them into … The pope, at the same time as he was welcoming this hero, this god of war, was refusing to pray for my soul. Ha! Some Christian he is."

"But we know why; he has never forgiven you for violating the sanctity of Rome those many years ago. Nor did Felipe improve matters when he ordered Alba to march his troops into Vatican territory after the pope's refusal to talk peace. So you see all three of you are guilty of spilling the blood of holy men and of profaning holy places. Nor would Pope Paul be best pleased that disgruntled exiles from Rome had decided to join Alba, hoping to regain the land which the pope had stolen from them."

"The pope is a two-faced swine, Quijada. He pretended to agree to a truce with Alba and all the while the devious bastard was buying time until the arrival of the hero of heroes, Guise. He dares call himself pope!"

A squawking, "Pope Paul's a bastard, Pope Paul's a bastard," came from under the cover of the bird cage.

"Gentlemen, if I might proceed!" Gaztelu exclaimed, feeling rather like a parrot himself always being called upon to repeat words everyone had heard countless times. "Guise was soon to discover that although it had been an easy matter for Rome to drum up crowds for his triumphal entry into the Holy City, it was a far different story when it came to forming an army. The pope had actually promised to furnish a contingent to equal the French. But all he had to offer was a pathetic gathering of pretty poor specimens."

"I have always told you that you cannot trust this pope! He got the French to fight his battles for him by promising support. He is a liar; he had no support to offer!"

"Yes, my lord," Gaztelu sighed, "but Guise was not deterred, he had every confidence in himself and his soldiers.

He advanced on Naples. Unfortunately for him that turned out to be a complete disaster. He had to retire."

"Dishonourably, in my opinion," Carlos interjected.

"You will insist on giving your opinions at every turn," Quijada retorted, "I thought you were seeking mine?"

"Please, the pair of you, no further interruptions." Gaztelu shook his head in despair. "Guise still hoped to engage Alba's troops. But Alba would not take up the fight, no matter how much his men tried to persuade him. He said he was not prepared to wager the Kingdom of Naples against nothing more than an embroidered surcoat, which was about all Guise had to lose by then. In any case by that time Guise had far greater enemies to contend with. His army was bogged down by incessant rains, the gunpowder was ruined, food was spoiled, rampant disease and death decimated his troops. So he set about a hasty retreat; he had to. Then, would you believe it, King Henry chose that very moment to recall him to France, because he needed every available soldier following the disastrous defeat at Saint-Quentin."

Carlos grunted, "And thereby allowing Guise to avoid ignominy by a hair's breadth. I would dearly have liked to have seen the pope's face when he was told that King Henry was withdrawing the French soldiers. Worth a few thousand *ducados* to witness that, eh?"

"Alba just let them go, nudging them in the rear, a little harassing here and there to make sure they were leaving Italy. And now it was Alba who had the satisfaction of being welcomed into all the towns on his way. He next turned his attention to the Papal States."

"And then by God, the pope was in a damned hurry to settle for peace!" Carlos pointed a bandaged hand at Quijada.

"Please, no more interruptions," insisted Gaztelu. "Alba's troops threatened the city. The Romans panicked and begged the pope to start peace negotiations. The treaty demanded the pope revoke his alliance with France and henceforth remain neutral. King Felipe must surrender all the towns within the papal territory, and Spain must seek forgiveness for having taken up arms against God's Vicar on earth."

Quijada shrugged his shoulders, "Sounds like a victory to me."

"Then just wait till you hear this part," Carlos was jubilant with I-told-you-so satisfaction.

"The Duque de Alba went to Rome for an audience with Pope Paul and prostrated himself before His Eminence and kissed his feet."

"Aha! And there you have it!" Carlos beamed. "Who won this blasted war then? Tell me, who was the victor? And as for Alba, demeaning himself, belittling our nation ..."

Gaztelu spoke to Quijada, "ZuZiga was here the other day and he had a letter from Alba. It sought permission to come to kiss the king's hand on his return to Spain. It also mentioned his distaste at having had to prostrate himself at the papal feet. He felt it should have been quite the other way about, with Pope Paul seeking forgiveness from King Felipe. But when ZuZiga read the letter our royal master feigned deafness, pretended not to hear a word."

"The royal prerogative of bad manners? Shame on you, sire."

"Quijada, I do not want him here, do not want to hear anything more of the whole disgraceful affair. Anyway, your opinion?"

"I see no problem with the peace treaty if that is what you mean."

"What do you mean no problem?" Carlos spluttered. "Have you gone soft in the head?"

"Think about it. King Felipe sees himself as a champion of the Catholic Church, and as such would never wish to be at war with the pope. I am of the opinion that it must have pained him greatly when he issued the order for Alba to harass the Papal States. Now, with this treaty, he has found a way of finally extricating Spain and the pope from all those years of bitter antagonism. He may also have provided an opportunity to unite and strengthen the Church in these difficult days of reform. My lord, Felipe has lost nothing, indeed he will have gained much by this diplomatic move. You must admit it is most unseemly for a Christian king to conduct a war against the Holy Father."

"But why did Alba kneel to him? It would make the pope feel he was the victor. I hope Felipe gives him a flea in his ear."

Gaztelu turned once more to Quijada, "Alba did say in his letter that he was following Felipe's instructions and that it grieved him to ..."

"I refuse to listen to that!" Carlos shut him up. "But imagine what sweet music it would have been to my ears to hear from Alba's lips that that eighty-year-old bastard of a pope was dead. But sadly ..."

"Shame on you to hang onto those old grievances; it is time to forgive and forget," Quijada butted in. "But let me remind you yet again that you have retired from public life, handing the reins of government to Felipe. Let go of those reins! You must recognise your son as king and respect his authority. Everything he does is for Spain and, more importantly, for God. I will tell you something more; something I witnessed on my journey here. All Spain is jubilant; bonfires of celebration are ablaze throughout the land. What better indication of a country's thanksgiving for its leader's decision to make peace with the Holy Father! Finally, I would suggest that by going over events beyond your control and influence you are wearying yourself and others, and to no good purpose."

Carlos snorted, "Anyway I have had enough for today. Gaztelu, go for Doctor Mathys. These bandages need to be changed; and my backside is getting sore. Quijada stay until Mathys arrives."

Gaztelu bowed and left the room, his face a picture of disappointment, certain that the Trooper Blomberg story was about to unfold.

There are times when others speak so eloquently for me. I think that Quijada is quite splendid. He voices all the right arguments. As ever, Carlos is loath to hear opinions which differ from his own.

II

"My lord; that was very nearly a most embarrassing situation, you mentioning Trooper Blomberg; what does Gaztelu know?"

"Nothing at all; never mentioned the name until today."

179

"With respect, you must be more guarded. I could so easily have fallen into the trap of believing you had allowed Gaztelu into your confidence."

"You worry too much. Anyway you are the one at fault for not being here when I needed you; I could have got it all off my chest there and then, the day the courier came, so I will not have you placing any blame on me! But Barbara was bold alright, just like her mother. I had her nicely set up in Ratisbon so she could wait for me there until the battle had been won. But that was unacceptable, remember?"

"Impossible to forget; we were holding a conference in your tent at the time."

"And word came that a trooper had arrived with a message for me. I had no idea what to think because a courier had only recently arrived with the latest despatches." Lines of pain and age softened about Carlos's eyes and mouth.

"And I went out to discover what it could be that could not wait until morning," Quijada added. It was as though it had happened only yesterday.

Carlos closed his eyes.

ജ   ഇ

Two guards stood either side of the brazier, red and yellow flame patterns danced on their armour and halberds. Four other soldiers were nearby, their glinting swords drawn against a young soldier. Torches in their iron sconces burned in angry twisted yellow flames, their black smoked edges curling and chasing in the bitter wind.

Quijada allowed the tent flap to fall closed behind him and pulled his fur-lined cloak tight across his chest.

"What is it trooper that cannot wait until morning? His majesty is not to have his precious time wasted."

The trooper, on his knees, directed some mumbled words towards the ice-hard ground.

"Speak up man," Quijada ordered.

"… important information, must not wait."

"Give it to me."

"No, I must deliver …"

"Stand up. Come here. Give me …"

The trooper stood up, rubbing agitatedly at his forehead before pulling his hat further down over his ears.

"I must see the king," the trooper pleaded, the words almost lost in his cloak.

Something told Quijada that although it might be irresponsible he had to let this lad in to see the king. He also knew that if need be he could deal with the young lightweight whipper snapper. "This is quite in order," he told the guard, "the lad will come with me."

Once inside the tent Quijada addressed the huge hat on the lowered head. "What message do you bring trooper?"

"A private message." The voice seemed to struggle.

"Wait here."

Within minutes, generals, chiefs of staff, and their aides emerged from behind a brocade curtain. Helmets and maps were thrust under arms; fur cloaks slung over shoulders.

"You may go in. His majesty will see you now."

The trooper strode by him and into the royal presence. Quijada watched just long enough to see the trooper go down on one knee before letting the curtain fall back into place.

The young man pulled off his hat, and long golden curls tumbled free, the bluest of blue eyes looked up at Carlos and burned into his heart.

"Your majesty, Trooper Blomberg at your service."

For a moment Carlos was unable to speak. He was still recovering from the shock of Quijada's urgent whispering about a soldier Blomberg being here with some important news. Assuming the soldier to be Barbara's officer brother he hurriedly dismissed his military chiefs of staff. And now here he was face to face with his beloved, his dear heart. Could he trust his eyes and ears? He leaned forward to cup her face in his hands.

"What in God's name are you doing here? I left you safe with your chaperone. Dear God, did she come with you? Tell Quijada to take her somewhere, deal with her. We have no room here. In any case she scares the life out of me."

Barbara put her hands over his and laughed a melody of silver notes, "You are safe, there was no soldier's uniform large enough, or a horse strong enough to carry her."

181

"And you have ridden here alone? My dear that was foolhardy, dangerous."

"Who would dare to stop a soldier on a mission for his emperor? And danger doesn't exist for me when I want to be by your side."

He stroked her silken hair. "Some wine to warm you." Carlos pushed himself from his chair drawing his Barbara to his breast to hold her tight, his eyes flooding.

"To the invincible soldier." He offered her a silver goblet, shaking his head at this vision in the leather jerkin and thigh boots, the thick woollen breeches. He raised his goblet in homage.

"And to her warrior king," she responded.

Of one accord they began to undress, Barbara joking about the ease with which men's clothing can be unfastened and removed.

The bed was small, little better than a truckle bed, but surprisingly big enough for the two of them.

"I can only stay until dawn when I must leave to return the horse."

Carlos chuckled, "Then Quijada is in for a long night! Oh, sing to me, Barbara."

*"A thousand times I regret to leave you
And go far from your loving face …"*

ೞ   ೲ

"How could I have been so fortunate, Quijada, to have had someone like Barbara to love me; someone half my age, beautiful, courageous."

"Tender, devoted …"

"Was I stupid? Was she using her charms only to seduce me, to use me?"

"Never allow such thoughts to take shape or form themselves into words. You know it to be untrue. She was always there for you whenever you needed her to bring comfort."

"And to rekindle … I had feelings for her that I had never felt before. That night I held her face, stroked her hair, and before long there was life in this old dog again!"

"It is all very much the stuff of ballads; a beautiful stranger, a lonely knight, a tent, flickering candlelight, wine, fur rugs."

"And she slipped away before dawn, saying she had promised faithfully to return the horse before sun-up."

"And she would, my lord, she was always a woman of her word."

"God, how good it is to have you back, Quijada."

Surprisingly, sometimes I make no comment whatsoever.

November

Errors of Judgement

I

The tranquil swishing of brushes and cloths, the squeaking of leather and the jingling of metal came to an abrupt halt.

"Quick, lads, let's be 'aving you out here now, double quick." It was Pepe, the stable master, out of breath and nervous.

Manuel threw down some reins along with his waxing cloth onto an already cluttered worktable. He rubbed his hands on the rag hanging from a nail giving them a final wipe down the front of his tunic then threw on his wool coat and ran out into a veil of cold grey mizzle. "What's goin' on sir? You made it sound bad."

"It's the king's sister Maria, that's what," the stable master groaned. "She's here. Just caught sight of her coming up the hill. Gawd, and me not understanding a bleeding word she says. And then I go and get all flustered." He turned to shout back into the tack room, "I said you had to be double quick, didn't I? You want to keep your job don't you? Alonso, where the hell are you? Come on you other lot. Let's be having you. Now!" He scurried across the yard muttering, "I'd better warn them over at the house."

"Who did he say was coming?" Alonso shouted from the corner where he leaned across a water barrel washing his hands. "Bloody murder getting them brasses clean. It'll be good to get away from it for a bit. So, who'd he say?"

"The king's sister, Queen Maria."

"Oh, him." Alonso was unimpressed.

184

"Jesus, you shouldn't say things like that," Manuel nervously hissed back noticing two or three other stable lads coming to join them. If they heard, they might just report them; it was one way to get their jobs, sure enough.

"Everybody else does. She's a man in ladies' skirts is what they all say. You just listen when she opens her mouth. You just watch the way she walks. And if that's not enough, what the 'ell does a lady want to be riding over here in this kind of weather for? I mean, it's not right, is it? There's some things as men do and some things women do. Now this tells me she falls into the category of blokes."

"That's a bit strong, that is," Manuel threw at him. He then whispered, "So she's big and has a deep voice ..."

"And walks like a feller." Alonso clapped him on the shoulder. "Just makes you wonder what's under them skirts, don't it?"

"Can't keep your mind far off them thoughts, can you?"

Pepe raced back to them, gasping, "Right, line up over here you lot. I'll go over to the mounting steps for her highness." He paced nervously backwards and forwards over the glistening cobbles, fine watery beads gathering on his leather jerkin.

"Think he's got ants in his pants?"

"Worried sick he is, Alonso. She scares him. I think it's 'cause she speaks French and he can't understand her."

"So, if she was a feller what spoke Spanish, he'd be 'appy?" He put on a mock female voice and fluttered his eyelashes, "Parley voo Fransay, mon ami Pepe?"

"No comprendey, mate," Manuel hissed back, hoping Pepe hadn't seen or heard Alonso's antics.

As this is not the weather for standing about in courtyards I suggest we move indoors as soon as possible.

Maria, Dowager Queen of Hungary and retired governor of the Netherlands, rode into the courtyard with an escort of four gentlemen. The stable lads ran to grab at bridles and reins while Pepe met Maria's horse at the steps. He steadied it as she slipped easily and nimbly from the saddle despite carrying more than fifty years and rather too much weight.

185

"Bonjour les garçons." A voice disconcertingly deep and loud filled the air, "Le wezzer makes not good, c'est vrais?"

The lads all kept their heads down stammering a jumble of 'Good day' and 'your highness', choking on guffaws.

Maria hurried down the steps booming instructions in halting Spanish to her riding companions, "Now you go. I will send when I go to leave." Then she turned to give orders to the stable master, "Les chevaux sont ..." but he hadn't waited. Pepe had eagerly grasped the opportunity to hurry away with the queen's horse while she was occupied with others, arguing why should he wait only to be told what he knew already, how to deal with wet, steaming horses on a chilly day. In any case he wouldn't understand a word she said.

Alonso called to Manuel from under his horse's neck, "What did I tell you? She's a feller. That voice is still a bleedin' shock though, every time. But it isn't 'alf nice to see our Pepe in one hell of a panic instead of being so bloody cocksure all the time."

This warmth is distinctly welcoming. It feels so good to shut out that damp air, it can get right through to the old bones.

Now I can give you some background information on Carlos's sister Maria who until only a few months ago was a total stranger to this country, and its language. She decided she would retire to Spain with Carlos and their sister Leonor. I find it most odd that after being born and raised in Flanders then spending much of her adult life there, apart from a few years in Hungary, she should choose now to live in this country. But you see you have here an example of sisterly love; desiring that the three of them should spend their twilight years together, with at long last the opportunity to enjoy each other's company and to be at hand to support and comfort one another. The king, however, did not share his sisters' enthusiasm, preferring to live here alone while they, at least for the moment, are staying at Jarandilla. Poor old Oropesa has to play host again.

It would be impossible not to notice that Maria is quite a robust lady, quite unlike the other sister, Leonor, who is rather frail these days and succumbs easily to illness.

About twenty-five years ago Carlos made his sister Maria governor of Flanders and the Low Countries. There were many eminently suitable people worthy of the position, but Carlos thought a dowager queen would enhance its status somewhat. And, of course, it kept the control of the area in family hands. I hasten to add that not for one moment was I suggesting that Maria was not equal to the demands of governor; she is a very clever woman. She most certainly is; far more intelligent than Carlos and much wiser too, someone to whom he has readily turned for advice over the years, not that he usually heeded it.

But here comes Quijada.

"Votre Altesse," Quijada came rushing to greet Maria. "Cela fait plaisir a vous voir. Mais, aujourd'hui …?"

"You know well enough the weather never bothers me."

He helped her remove the hooded waterproof cloak and untie the soggy ribbons of her travelling hat, motioning to a waiting servant to take away the dripping garments. "A hot drink of some kind, perhaps?"

"Good Lord no, Quijada. I am not the least bit cold; damp perhaps but not cold. I say but it is damnably hot in here."

"I think we may have all grown accustomed to it, ma'am. The large salon, however, will perhaps be more comfortable; with the option of course that should you feel a slight chill there is the choice of a roaring fire or a hot stove. This way ma'am. I have informed his majesty of your presence."

"Good, good, but why so formal today? No need for it at all."

She stepped into the large salon taking mental notes, not wishing to omit the smallest detail when she reported back to her sister: the long dark oak dining table; the chairs with either red leather or red velvet cushioned seats; the tall clocks, two with gold faces; halberds standing to attention with their silver points and blades emerging from ruffs of red, yellow and black ribbons; next to them the shields with their protective two-headed eagles; the side tables one of which was being hurriedly covered with red velvet and the gold and silver plate set back in their places; the portraits and finally the tapestries, her gift to her brother to celebrate his victory at Tunis.

Quijada beckoned the busy young girl, "You may go now. Tell your mistress that the Dowager Queen Maria will be in this room for some time and is not to be disturbed. You will have to finish your work later."

The maidservant bobbed a curtsey and snatched a swift look at her namesake as she left. What she saw was a plump lady old enough to be her mother, perhaps grandmother; it was hard to tell, for hers were both long dead. The lady was, she reckoned, the same age or older than Madame Male. The rather ample lady was dressed in black velvet. Running all around the hem of the skirt were two rows of what looked like very fine silver chains. Black satin bows tipped with silver aglets went all the way up the front of the skirt and the sleeves. Her hair and neck were entirely covered with a widow's barb of the finest Holland.

As she closed the door behind her young Maria called down the corridor in a loud whisper to Samuel and José who stood waiting for the king, "Do you know it's like she just stepped down from one of them pictures on the walls in there. Gawd, them clothes must've cost a fortune. If only she lived here, her hand-me-downs would still be in pretty good nick by the time it was my turn to get them."

"If they didn't get sold first," José teased.

"Enjoy your dreams, Maria," Samuel sniggered.

"And to think we even have the same name. Fancy that, eh, her and me, both called Maria. Ooh, heck, there's that cold draught again, I wish folk would make sure them doors is closed."

José nudged Samuel before advising her, "Better get one of your servants to check, DoZa Maria."

"Cheeky devil!"

Our little village girl is gradually climbing up her social ladder. I am happy to inform you that this time it wasn't a case of dead men's shoes or should I say women's shoes; the last person simply left; an offer of marriage.

II

The portrait of Mary Tudor looked down at the Dowager Queen Maria and Quijada with an icy stare full of mistrust; almost ready to accuse.

"And she is Felipe's bride?" Maria wrinkled her nose studying the portrait. "Good Lord! Might have been a fair lass once upon a time, but not for a young man to marry now. Difficult, very difficult. I doubt if it was such a wise decision to promote this marriage. By all accounts it is not very successful."

"The Lady Mary has not had a very easy life almost from the beginning. Perhaps that is what we see written on her face; the fears and anguish of those earlier years."

"It might have been better had she chosen more attractive colours for her clothes; the dowdy browns and flat greys and beige do little to help." Maria turned to Quijada, "Let us hope that God in His mercy brings her pregnancy to term and she is delivered safely of a child."

"I would like to say amen to that, but as you know there are grave doubts in fact about there actually being a pregnancy."

Carlos's sister was now giving the portrait of Isabel her full attention. She spoke without ever moving her gaze from the painting, "Aye, dear Lord, she was beautiful. Carlos was lucky there. I wish I could have met her. I remember ... it was not long after her death; I received a letter from Carlos asking if I could find a likeness of her in our aunt's palace in Mechelin. He said that he seemed to remember seeing one there. Astonishing, really, to think he did not possess even one

189

portrait of his beloved wife. So I went looking, and sure enough I found a small portrait, supposedly of Isabel. I sent it along with a note excusing it for being so poor and really not worth the bother. Now that I see this masterpiece I am embarrassed. I expect Carlos destroyed it."

"This is a masterpiece indeed. I was fortunate to see her highness, and believe me if this portrait could be given breath, I swear it would be … So tragic she died so young." Quijada cleared his throat.

"My brother is right, you are an emotional chap; a leader in battle, strong and resilient, but sentimental when it comes to the ladies. Not a bad fault. Of course you are in a position where you can allow yourself that luxury."

"Meaning, ma'am?"

"I was musing on the luxury of emotions, Quijada. When I was sent to Brussels to become governor, I implored Carlos to appoint our brother Ferdinand instead. Of course I realised later that it would have placed too much power in his hands and that would never do. But at the time I was unwell and I was afraid of going there on my own. By God, but he gave me short shrift. Told me to consider how lucky I was, that he, himself, would be only too happy to be there but that his duties took him elsewhere. But I was a young widow you understand, only twenty-five years old, and still needing sympathy. My pleading went unheeded. Apparently royalty must always sacrifice their own feelings for the greater good of their people. 'Responsibility, not sentimentality'; how often have I heard that?"

Quijada was surprised at her speaking so openly about private family affairs and moved the conversation on. "You never sought a second husband, someone to be at your side, to …?"

"God, no, Quijada. I even made that a condition of accepting the position. No, I had had a wonderful marriage. Sadly it had lasted only five years. No one on this earth could possibly have taken the place of my Luis."

"But Carlos did eventually relent and gave you a special, a close, adviser."

"Yes, but only when he was forced into recognising just how ill I was. No one can fully appreciate the despair of a young widow when she has lost someone so dear, so wonderful." Maria's voice became surprisingly mellow and soft, like the velvet of her skirts. She moved to the window and looked out at the greyness of the day, at the wet shrouds enveloping the garden and its ghostly trees, the ditchwater dullness of the fishpond. "I am not such a fool as to think that his actions were entirely fraternal, regarding either my health or happiness. He was desperate to have me well again in order to govern. Later on I discovered that he was also worried that I was suffering an illness similar to our mother's and he was determined to lift me from the depths of my melancholy."

Quijada raised his eyebrows.

While Maria lost herself to the remembered devotion and attentiveness of her treasured companion Quijada was thinking if only Carlos had offered the same support to his mother. Ah, but there was the difference, he needed Maria to rule, whereas he had been afraid that his mother might decide to do just that or even be persuaded to. He smiled at Maria, "So you did, in effect, have someone at your side. That was good."

"Yes, a companion without equal. A firm but gentle master. He made me follow the doctors' orders, take their medicines. We walked and talked, and he kept me free of all duties until I was strong enough. Good Lord, Quijada, he sounds like a duplicate of you! No wonder my brother holds you in such high regard and will not let you go."

"I thank you ma'am."

Maria recovered. I am tempted to say that she recovered purely and simply because of the aid and support of her companion and that all other medications were unnecessary. He was with her almost day and night. There were those, of course, who suggested that their relationship went far beyond the bounds of friendship. Well, twenty-five is young to be a widow and as long as she was returned to full health who are we that we should judge? Queen Juana at one stage had found such an attentive companion but

191

only briefly. Carlos found him unsuitable for his plans and had him replaced.

"If I may change the subject, are you planning to stay overnight? It will take some degree of organising; for it does mean there are five extra to feed no matter at which table they sit."

"I know, Quijada, food is scarce enough as it is without us imposing on you. Do not look so worried. I intend to ride home today. It has been dreadful these past few months, there is no denying it; poor weather, bad harvests."

"I can tell you we would not have survived without the caravans of provisions arriving regularly from Valladolid. I was beginning to wonder what we could offer you other than iced water, of which we have an abundance." He smiled.

"You jest of course. I tell you one thing, Quijada, a scarcity of food would do my brother the power of good. I am sure you do your best to curtail him, but he got into the habit of surrendering to his passions at the table and, by God, in ladies' bedchambers at a very early age."

Quijada was rescued from the need to reply by the timely appearance of Gaztelu to say that Carlos was in his private salon and ready to see his sister. He and Quijada stood aside to allow Maria to pass.

"Gaztelu, I tell you, the dowager queen is still outrageously outspoken. No shrinking violet by Jove. I thank God you arrived when you did." Quijada tut-tutted his way down the corridor.

III

"Mon cher frère, comment vas-tu?" Maria curtsied and gently took one of her brother's hands in hers.

"Tres bien, et toi aussi j'espère."

"Never felt better."

"What brought you here, then? It is such a dreadful day. You had best not stay long."

"Well thank you so much for the hearty welcome! But I will not be dismissed so easily. I am here for my own diversion

192

not yours. To tell the truth I could not bear to remain indoors at Jarandilla a moment longer."

Carlos turned to Quijada, "My sisters ought not to be at Jarandilla, find them lodging in Cuacos. I cannot have my sister riding such a distance to visit me."

"Sire I will do what I can, but I am afraid you are asking the impossible."

Maria shook her head. "Do not begin to trouble yourself. My sister and I are quite comfortable. And I might add that I have seen enough of Cuacos to know that I have no desire to move there; a dreary collection of cottages, nothing more, and not worthy of consideration."

"And this from a sister at one time ready to move Heaven and earth that we might live together as one happy family under one roof."

"Did I go that far? Ah, well, enough of that good brother. See, I have brought you this gift from Valladolid. Your daughter had them made especially for you to convey her joy and congratulations on the success of the Italian campaign. Both Leonor and I are greatly impressed with the workmanship."

Carlos grappled with the package which refused to be opened, "Someone has tied this too tight; I give up, you do it."

Maria untied the yellow, black and red ribbons, "A thoughtful touch of Juana's to use your colours, brother," she unfolded the protective linen cover to reveal a pair of gloves exquisitely embroidered with gold thread and studded with precious stones.

"Jesus! The stupid woman; whose hands are these supposed to fit? Just look at them; look at my hands."

He studied his balloon-shaped hands with their misshapen fingers that would never fit inside the gloves.

"Ah, well, Juana did her best. It is the thought that counts, after all," Quijada shrugged. "And who knows but that with determined effort on your part, they may fit one day."

"No lectures, thank you. Put the damned things away," Carlos tossed them aside. "So you came alone? No Leonor?"

"Leonor is not fully well. She is still determined to make the journey to Badajoz to see her daughter so we felt it wiser for her to remain indoors on a day such as this."

193

Carlos nodded, "Sensible. Gaztelu is everything arranged for my sisters?"

"Everything, my lord. Ma'am may you both have a safe and pleasant journey and a happy reunion with the Princess Maria."

Carlos invited his sister to sit beside him. Quijada and Gaztelu moved some distance away.

"So, tell me the truth, why are you here?" Carlos curtly demanded of his sister.

"Come, come. I have brought you Juana's congratulations and a gift. I also came because I wanted to see you. And then I thought too that you might want to wish me a belated happy birthday."

Carlos grunted something resembling birthday wishes.

"I also came because I was tired of being cooped up indoors with a sickly sister. Mostly, I suppose, I came because of late I have been given to reminiscing – and thinking about my eventful but lonely life."

"I have told you often enough that royals cannot choose a life for themselves."

"If they hold sufficient power they can! But I was more than happy once, with Luis. We loved each other so much; and he had such plans for us. Yes, those were five blissful years. The Turk ended it all for me. Brother, if you could have seen my handsome Christian Knight setting out to defeat the infidel; the Cross marching out against the Crescent." Her voice cracked and wavered as she tried to sing;

"Oh unfortunate Luis, Luis you darling
Where are you young king
So full of life, and so charming."

"Humph; sickening sentimentality. At your age it is unbecoming. He had no chance, anyway, the young fool, not a clue about military tactics. His head was too full of romances, tales of valour. Infantile; naçve."

"Of course he was. He was young, only twenty years old, and inexperienced. His army was pathetically lacking in numbers and experience. But he believed that with God on our side ..."

"Come here, Quijada," Carlos beckoned, "you remember the battle. Remind Maria of the facts."

194

"No need Quijada," Maria stopped him, "God knows they are engraved on my heart. We had less than thirty thousand men, while Solyman had ten times as many. What good would any tactics have been facing that horde? My darling husband, the dear, sweet, innocent man, thought that riding out onto the plain following a bishop wearing the habit of a Franciscan friar would be enough to ensure victory. Oh, brother, what a senseless waste of a beautiful life. My husband and most of his men slaughtered. Hungary was lost; the crown gone."

Carlos's harsh voice broke the silence, startling everyone, "You know, of course, that King Francis lied when he said it was my fault that you got no support. I tried. As God is my witness, I tried to get support as soon as I heard the news. It would have been short-sighted not to. Good Heavens, Christianity was in danger, the damned Turk not so very far from Austria, our family home was under threat."

At the time Carlos had only recently married and, in fact, the news of this appalling defeat at the hands of the Turk was received when Carlos and Isabel were on their honeymoon in Granada.

Carlos continued, "There was no support though. Oh, the nobles said they would fight, provided I paid them. They refused to come up with their own money, complaining they were always emptying their purses for one cause or another. The clergy decided not to help either because they were put out about my disagreements with the pope. God, what a petty minded lot. So there I was, unable to do anything."

"But years later when you finally did march against Solyman and sent him packing from Austria, why did you not continue the fight? That would have helped our brother to regain Hungary."

"Dear sister, you may have the wisdom of an excellent governor but you do not possess the practical brain of a soldier. As you say we advanced on Vienna and Solyman withdrew. Victory was ours. The kudos was ours. How stupid it would have been to have thrown all that away pursuing a cause that may have brought devastating consequences." He fought off an uncomfortable twinge of guilt remembering his campaign in France when he had forged ahead ignoring all the danger signals; remembering the dead and the dying he had had to leave behind. "One has to consider these things. Anyway I did leave Ferdinand my Italian recruits."

"And a fine lot they turned out to be! They lost no time in deserting." She paused. "And come to think of it exactly the same thing happened in Tunis. Once again you stopped short of total victory."

Carlos sat rigid in his chair, glowering, "What is all this? Have you come here to set yourself up as my superior? You dare to criticize my judgements?"

"I simply enjoy putting my mind to subjects beyond sewing and embroidery, nothing more. So to continue, you had won the most glorious battle at Tunis, but then you ..."

"The tapestries you had made for me are incredible, Maria. Have you seen them in the salon? The galleons; the galleys; the flags of Spain, Italy, Portugal all reaching out impatient for action."

"I will not suffer to be put off. Why after Tunis did you not finish the Turk off there and then instead of waiting years to then suffer that dreadful disaster of, where was it? Where was it, Quijada?"

Quijada, who, along with Gaztelu was thoroughly enjoying Maria's daring, as bold as any a man, offered the dreaded name; Algiers.

"I did not finish off the enemy, sister, because I did not need to take the battle further at that time. You do not risk men unnecessarily!" he snapped at her remembering once again the decimation of his troops in France. "And I would like to remind you that it was not the Turk who defeated us at Algiers, it was the weather."

"Exactly, it was the ill-timing of the enterprise. I warned you at the time."

"Maria, in Brussels you coped admirably with diplomats, with all the intricacies and intrigues of government, but it is as well that you were never a military commander."

"If you say so brother. I did not come to argue. I shall yield to your judgement."

196

Carlos sighed and beamed a benevolent smile on his sister, happy to be released from his conscience, relieved, too, that they would not, after all, be discussing his disastrous North African campaign and the subsequent loss of Menorca. "Well, there we are then! What else do you want to talk about?"

"I want to praise you for the way you dealt with the rebels in Ghent."

"Hear that, you two?" At last he was on safe ground. "Come over here and listen to my sister praise me."

IV

Maria beamed first at Carlos then at Quijada and Gaztelu. "Gentlemen, you will remember full well the uprising after the imposition of additional taxes to pay for our defence against the invading French."

Carlos grumbled, "Always were a suspect lot those Ghents, even ready to side with the blasted French given the opportunity."

"Brother, please. Well, after the rising was suppressed, Carlos and I were on a dais in the patio at the Prinzhof Palace, and the Ghents came en masse to beg his pardon. Many wore black and were bareheaded. Others had a hangman's rope round their neck. Some had even crawled all the way on their knees. The place was filled with their chanting of the Misericordia. Then I stood up to intercede for them. I played the part so well. Was I not impressive pleading their case, Carlos? Then you spoke to them."

"Not I, you have got that all wrong!" growled Carlos, "I would not waste my breath on them."

"Let me finish. I grant you, you spoke to them via your chancellor. They were told they were forgiven, but that if they ever attempted such a thing again you would show such wrath and vengeance." She turned again to her listeners, "He was so powerful, so magnificent."

"I showed them who was master. I had all the houses torn down in the centre of the city and ordered a castle to be built there. I was determined to show them who ruled."

197

"Oh, gentlemen, he was marvellous. An emperor through and through; imperious! How fortunate I am to have such a brother," Maria looked at her brother, and glowed with pride.

"And I am fortunate to be blessed with such a sister." He reached for her hands, "Maria you have always been so level-headed, shown such wisdom and diplomacy; I would ask a favour of you. Maria, I only ask because of my implicit trust in you and your thinking – I want you to be the regent of Spain."

Gaztelu looked at Quijada, shocked. Quijada was more than shocked, he was furious and for the moment speechless.

"Oh! But I am too old. I am not Spanish. And yet, if you need me? What does my niece say? Does Juana no longer wish to be regent?"

"My daughter Juana is a damn nuisance! She has been a thorn in my flesh for long enough," Carlos fumed.

Quijada had to put an end to this nonsense. "Sire, with respect, let me remind you that these days it is not you but your son that makes appointments."

Gaztelu quickly added, "Your majesty, all this reminiscing has caused us all to forget that we are, all of us, supposedly retired from the world of politics. Surely none of us wishes to return?"

Maria rose and crossed to Gaztelu to give him a resounding clap on the back. "How right you are Gaztelu. Our heads were turned by triumphs of the past. It was too stupid of me to contemplate such a responsibility. And yes, Quijada, it is for Felipe to decide. But I thank my dear brother for showing such confidence in me. Those are warm thoughts to carry back to Jarandilla. Now, I will bid you farewell. I shall see you soon."

She turned to go then stopped. "There now; such heady thoughts made me almost forget. I received a letter the other day from Brussels, from the Governor Marguerite de Parma."

"Did she mention her son Alessandro by any chance?" The nervous words were out before Carlos had time to prevent them. He fervently hoped not, he couldn't face the prospect of another difference of opinion with his sister and this time about his efforts to arrange a marriage between Marguerite's son and Leonor's daughter. This had been his latest foray into arranging marriage contracts. Marguerite had not been best pleased, but that was because she, like so many, couldn't see the greater picture. One should always try to keep power within the family. He had endeavoured to explain this to this obstinate love child of his, reminding her of how and why she had been chosen governor of the Low Countries. He had repeatedly emphasised that this marriage with Portugal would help maintain and strengthen the family's power. Of what importance was it that Alessandro was only twelve and Princess Maria of Portugal well into her thirties? Yet Marguerite was stubbornly refusing to allow her son to be pushed into a marriage in which the bride was older than his own mother.

"No, nothing about her son, but she mentioned a Barbara Kegel's son."

"Barbara Kegel, Barbara Kegel?" Carlos sighed with relief, there was to be no fuss about Alessandro. "Do I know a Barbara Kegel, Quijada?"

"If I may remind you, sire, many years ago as a favour to the widow Katherine Blomberg, you gave her son a commission in the Imperial Army and then found a husband for her daughter Barbara. She married Jerome Kegel, a commissary in the Imperial Court."

At the mention of Barbara Blomberg Gaztelu was moved to take his spectacles out of his pouch. He rubbed the lenses eagerly on his wide black sleeves, preparing himself for some gossip. The dowager's sport with Carlos had been entertaining to a degree, but this should be better by far.

Carlos thought a moment or two. "Ah, that Barbara. Yes, the mother had fallen on hard times. The daughter Barbara was a tavern singer, am I right?

Quijada was completely at a loss as to why Carlos had adopted this line, "I have no recollection of that but I know she did sing most charmingly at your birthday celebrations on one occasion in Ratisbon."

"Well, it is of little importance where she was singing," Carlos snapped. "But what of this son?" He desperately wanted, but was more than a little anxious, to hear Marguerite's news. He forced himself to sound only vaguely interested.

199

"In her letter, Marguerite said she was sure you would remember the family, but if she is mistaken ..."

Gaztelu beseeched both her and Quijada with his pleading bespectacled eyes. Quijada came to his rescue, "Oh, but we do remember the family; I assure you. Your majesty, if you recall this lady, this Barbara, got married and had two sons."

"You are right, of course, how stupid of me to forget. Go on, Maria."

"There has been an appalling tragedy; the youngest child. Evidently the little fellow was playing in the courtyard, exploring, I suppose, and being overly inquisitive or daring, he clambered up the side of a barrel and tumbled in head first. Poor little chap was drowned. It must be dreadful for the mother. Her heart must be breaking. Life can be so very cruel. Sorry to have been the bearer of bad news. Now I really must go."

"Allow me to escort you," Quijada accompanied the dowager queen from the room.

My heart goes out to Barbara. How does a parent cope with the death of a child, especially when that child was happy and healthy. Imagine; he was playing merrily outdoors one moment, then dead the next. Think of the pain.

Quijada returned bringing a hint of cheer with him, "Your sister will have a more pleasant ride home. The rain has cleared and the sun is making every effort to show itself."

"Good, good." Carlos shook his head, "You see how easily, so damned easily, these accidents can happen. I hope that the Kegel fellow can give her the comfort she deserves."

"Sadly not, your majesty, he died. He was much older than Barbara."

"Her mother dead, her husband dead; dear God, then she has no one! What can we do for her, Quijada? We must think of something."

Gaztelu removed his spectacles and squinted at Carlos. Two minutes ago in the presence of Maria the king had pretended not to know his favourite musician, now he was all

200

concern for her. That business of her possibly being a tavern singer might be the very clue. Carlos must not want his sister to know he had been involved with a common woman, someone from the lower classes.

Quijada was quick to reassure him. "There is no need to upset yourself, sire, I am sure everything will turn out well. The chaperone will probably decide not to retire after all; we both know she loved Barbara as if she were her dearest child."

"Of course, Quijada, that is the obvious answer! Good, that is a good point at which to put an end to all my dark thoughts." Carlos wanted only to think of the good times with Barbara and remain ignorant of any misfortune befalling her. "We will turn our minds to something far less serious, in fact not serious at all; something to brighten our spirits. But first we must have some ham and some beer."

Quijada covered his eyes, "Dear Lord!"

Carlos pouted, "Just this once you win, I shall deny myself; satisfied? Maria mentioned Algiers, and that reminded me of Hernan Cortes, you remember, the one who did all the soldiering in the New World? By God, but he told us some tales about the Indians there. Come here, the pair of you. Sit down, I am about to tell you a story."

V

The companions drew two chairs close to Carlos.

"Hernan Cortes must surely have been quite old by the time he was in Algiers?" asked Gaztelu, wearily resigned to hearing another far-fetched soldier's tale while trying to equate a tavern singer with someone who could afford a chaperone which didn't make any sense whatsoever.

"He was only in his late fifties. Just a slip of a lad like me," quipped Quijada.

Carlos thumped his hand against his chair, "Be quiet, I want to tell you something. He told us about how the Aztec priests had boy prostitutes dressed up as girls, and how they ravaged them after having gorged themselves on roasted human arms and legs. Think about it."

"No thank you," Gaztelu turned away, he would far rather be preoccupied with the mysterious Barbara.

"Then there was the tale of some of the Indians bringing him gifts but he knew the men were really spies so he cut their hands off before sending them back to their chief."

"Yes, we have heard that one, too, is that not so Gaztelu?" Quijada shook his head, surrendering to the inevitable, yet another of Hernan's tales of the New World.

"You have not heard this one. You can blame my sister for reminding me of Algiers and how we sat steaming in our wet clothes in the heat and fug of our tents listening to his stories. You will like this, it is hilarious. Ready? There was this young warrior prince whose tribe was starving; they had suffered a terrible drought. He was sent to a neighbouring tribe that had been clever enough to devise excellent irrigation systems giving bounteous harvests. So there he is in this other land disguised as a seller of chilli peppers. He sat in the market naked as the day he was born," he began to chuckle.

"I doubt that he was entirely naked." Quijada looked up from the ring on his finger, a gift from Magdalena, which he had been idly twisting this way and that. "I find that difficult to believe."

"Yes he was, entirely naked, goddamn it! And he was showing all his, you know, his endowments; and by God they were big. A princess came along and took one look at him and was overwhelmed by the size of his, his ..."

"Chillies, my lord?" Quijada chipped in dryly, making Gaztelu snort and splutter in spite of himself.

"You know very well what overwhelmed her. She was so filled with desire for his, and don't say chilli, for his ... well she became so ill with longing she took to her bed. The doctors could do nothing. She told her father that she must have the chilli seller. They brought him to the palace, but he refused to go to the princess. The king insisted. He was put under guard and forcibly bathed. His body was then painted; they do that sort of thing there. Then he was escorted into her chamber. And would you believe she got better in next to no time. Shows what a good ..." he started to laugh then wheezed before a paroxysm of coughing overwhelmed him.

"Obviously an excellent cure," Quijada commented bringing him a drink. "Then they got married and lived happily ever after and had lots and lots of little chillies. My goodness what a good story, my lord. After a few beers I expect it had you all roaring and rolling with laughter."

"You can be an insufferable killjoy, Quijada. The number of times you spoil everything …" Carlos protested.

"I never was one for that sort of humour; it is usually either stupid or offensive, but never funny."

"Well we are being self-righteous today Quijada. You are not that bloody perfect, you know! If you are not going to listen properly to my stories, I shall have my ham and beer."

Gaztelu rubbed at his forehead. "Did the point of the story get lost among the chillies? What happened to the starving tribe?"

Carlos glared at him, "Dear God preserve me! I shall have my ham and beer now."

We should have left the room before the tone of the conversation was lowered to such depths. The problem is, once a soldier always a soldier.

December

Chattels

I

It was a clear, bright December morning. The November rains had finally ceased and the grey blankets of mist had rolled away, disappearing over the hills. It was, however, much too cold for Carlos to venture out. He had to content himself with a short stroll in Felipe's room, the room he had planned for his son when the very first drafts were drawn up for this quiet little palace. All other visitors would be offered accommodation in one of the rooms built onto the exterior of the second cloister or given lodging in Cuacos; only Felipe would be allowed this intimacy.

He looked about him; over there was Felipe's bed with its red velvet covers and curtains, his coat of arms on the canopy. A chair standing by the fire was where his son would sit while his servant helped him pull on his hose and his boots. Not far away was the desk where, no doubt, Felipe would spend interminable hours writing those endless letters of his.

"Right, let us try for the window, José," he leaned heavily on the young lad's shoulder as he urged his reluctant legs forward, planting a shaking stick a few tentative inches ahead of each shuffled step. Samuel walked alongside should he be needed. Having negotiated the few feet successfully Carlos tried releasing his hold of José to rest against the wooden frame of the window. "Damn and blast it lads. The old legs are useless. And it is too damned cold, God what a draught. A man could catch a chill. Need to get out of here."

Carlos was installed in his chair and neatly tucked about with furs in next to no time. "Now that is decidedly better; nothing like creature comforts I say."

Quijada entered cheerily rubbing away the winter's cold from his hands, "The news is that they are almost here."

"Good. The sooner we get it over with, the better. I hope to God they will not be here for long."

"Sire," Quijada tut-tutted. "These are your sisters."

"They will be in a cantankerous mood, and well you know it."

"Misunderstandings that can easily be dealt with, and as soon as Leonor is with her daughter, I am convinced ..."

"Humph. Just you wait and see. I blame Maria. She will not let things be; forever questioning, putting doubts in her sister's mind. Leonor on her own would be easy to deal with but with Maria beside her with her constant demands for answers, for explanations; I tell you I smell trouble"

"Here they are, my lord."

The grinding of wheels over the cobbles in the courtyard below announced the arrival of the king's visitors.

Samuel craned his neck to look down, "Holy Moses," he gasped, "take a look at that José."

Quijada was touched by their amazement, "Not seen a carriage before, lads? My son Juan found it beyond belief the first time he saw one. I tell you his eyes grew as big and as round as the wheels themselves." He turned his head towards Carlos, "His bewilderment was precious, my lord."

Samuel pointed excitedly at the huge, lumbering box, "Sir, it's a house on wheels. I mean, look, it has a roof, a door, and windows."

"Gawd," continued José, "what a clever idea. It's marvellous isn't it the things what people can think of? I like them windows, all fancy like, with that wooden lattice stuff. Blow me it has curtains as well."

Quijada stared down at the carriage, remembering that it was the wonder at a carriage so similar to this that had so readily persuaded the seven-year-old Juan to allow himself to be lifted up to sit alongside him and opposite a dumpling shaped nurse. Never once did he look back at the little village, his home, and the elderly lady who had had to care for him on her own after her husband died. But then again perhaps he hadn't realised, didn't know that he was being lifted up and away from it all never to return.

What a day that had been.

CR   SO

"Look here! See over there," the excited young Juan called from the other side of the curtains drawn against the dust kicked up by the horses. All that was visible of the child were dirty grey breeches reaching down to his knees, a pair of sturdy tanned legs and filthy feet in badly worn sandals standing tiptoe on the richly carpeted floor.

Tiring of the view or afraid of missing something he scrambled between the knees of Quijada and the nurse's abundant brown skirts, clambered onto the cushioned bench seat and lifted the curtain on the other side of the carriage. He watched the vineyards and olive groves come and go; his eyes followed goats, whose bells accompanied their dainty skipping and scrambling over stones and rocks. The rumble from the rutted road beneath them changed from time to time to a splashing and clattering over the stones as they passed through fords.

"It just goes on for ever," Juan emerged once more this time to sit cross-legged, hugging his sandaled feet, inspecting the cushioned seats, the silk covered interior, the curtains at the windows, the rich carpet. He saw Quijada's eyes fixed on him and chuckled, "It's like a make believe house that somebody's put on wheels." But now was surely the time for more adventure. "Where is your horse?"

"Travelling behind; hitched to our make believe house on wheels."

"Let's ride on it. I've never been on a horse."

"Not today."

"I could sit in front of you. I'd sit very still."

"Another day, I promise."

Disappointed, Juan returned to his window to continue his sightseeing.

The countryside eventually gave way to the streets of Valladolid, the coach wheels now rattling their way over cobbles. The nurse pulled Juan to her side. She straightened his tunic about his shoulders, re-threaded and tied the lacing at the neck, then with the hem of her skirts rubbed at the shabby sandals, dismayed at the state of his feet.

Horseshoes and iron clad wheels clattered through a gate and across flagstones then came to a halt in the arcaded patio of a convent. Quijada stepped down then turned to lift the boy, but Juan avoided his arms to leap down and scamper to the stone wall of the arcade. He pulled open the front of his breeches and with boyish delight aimed his pee here and there, making a series of dark, glistening rivulets.

Quijada looked Heavenward in full agreement with the nurse as she nervously made several signs of the cross on her anxious chest, hoping that none of the nuns had witnessed such behaviour.

"Now then, young man, a most important lady has asked to see you before I take you to your new home." Quijada patted him on the shoulder, "All I ask is that you remain still and quiet."

"What new home? What about Mama Ana? Is she coming?"

"No. That has all changed. But you will be happy in your new home; have no fears about that little fellow. My wife will love you like no other mother ever could. Believe me everything will turn out perfectly; why, you will even have a little horse of your own!"

"But Mama Ana has to come, she'll be lonely. That's why she was crying, because I'm not going back," tears began to well up. "I want to live with Mama Ana. I want to go home."

"Ana is too old and too ill. My wife and I will care for you now, and, listen to this, I am sending someone to care for Ana; she will not be alone. So, come now, dry those tears; show me you are a brave little soldier."

This oddly assorted three; the gentleman in his finery, the old, waddling nurse in her workaday woollens, and the tear-smudged dishevelled peasant boy, made their way up the steps and along a corridor. They were ushered into a large salon of Princess Juana's apartments.

Juan's eyes darted from huge windows to grand tables and chairs, the enormous fireplace, the tapestries, the candelabra, the beautiful woman in a magnificent gown before he was drawn down to kneel beside Quijada.

"Your highness."

"Welcome Don Luis Quijada."

Quijada kissed the hand of the Regent Princess Juana. He was then invited to stand.

Princess Juana inspected the child at Quijada's side, the child who had so aroused her curiosity, the child that had brought Quijada across half of Spain to rescue. Who was he? What was he? He was nothing but a street urchin, or a peasant child, a little ragamuffin.

"I suspected as much, Don Luis, but my imagination had not gone quite this far. I cannot possibly allow your good lady wife to see him like this. What has he been doing, how did he get into such a state?"

"Anything and everything he has ever wanted to. There has been no control."

A door opened and a voice boomed, "His Royal Highness Prince Carlos."

For an instant Juan saw a boy, probably about his own age, start to cross the room to bow to the lady who curtsied to him before Quijada already on bended knee pulled Juan down beside him greeting the prince, "Your royal highness."

When they stood up Juan stared open-mouthed at this boy's clothes. He was dressed so strangely, in a doublet with bright red slashes in its sleeves and padded and paned trunk hose that looked for the world like some sort of stuffed fancy cushion with his legs sticking out from the bottom. There was a short cloak over one shoulder, which was definitely higher than the other, and he was wearing a small bonnet with a rather grand feather. And, marvel of marvels, he had a boy-sized sword.

"Is this the one who is to have some of my old clothes?" squeaked this person called Prince Carlos.

Princess Juana smiled and spoke gently, "Yes, your highness, this is the boy we have spoken of."

Prince Carlos limped towards him. "So, is Quijada your real father or your pretend father come to look after you? You should consider yourself fortunate either way; fathers are difficult to come by."

"I don't know," Juan answered before throwing in a swift, "your highness", since everybody seemed to be called that. He looked up at Quijada through a tangle of wayward blond curls, "Are you my father?"

Quijada tousled the boy's hair, "As of today I am your father."

Juana turned to a small group of servants hovering in the doorway, "Is everything ready?"

"Yes, your highness."

"Then follow them good nurse."

The round nurse, all bosom and hips took a reluctant Juan by the hand to follow a small group of servants to an awaiting much-needed bath and change of clothes.

"You must tell me why you have gone to such lengths, Don Luis, for a ... for a ... words fail me."

Quijada bowed, "In due course, your highness, I am sure all will be revealed; but until that time I am honour bound to say nothing."

"And your wife, is she a party to this secret?"

"No, nor can I travel to Villagarcía to explain the boy's presence. My squire Galarza will give her my letter of brief explanation and that must suffice. I pray she has faith in me."

"Amen to that. Let us turn to business; so much time has been lost because of the child."

Quijada's return to Flanders was imminent and they had to discuss several problems at home and abroad. Princess Juana handed him despatches for her father, the Emperor Carlos. These contained the Cortes' decisions on proposed actions to be taken.

And then there he was, the new Juan, standing before them. The transformation was complete and astonishing. Here was another little prince.

"Quijada, when your squire delivers this young man to your home Doña Magdalena will not be disappointed."

☓♲   ♳

Aye, it had been such a day for all of them.

Samuel's voice ended his reveries. "And now, look, they's got some lovely little steps in front of the door, so's you can get down alright. Oh, it's their 'ighnesses."

They watched as the two dowager queens were helped down from the carriage while Gaztelu, his old legs doing their best to speed him, crossed the open space to greet them, and to escort them indoors.

"No time to be standing about lads," Quijada clapped his hands, "Take his majesty to his private salon."

"Did you see the size of them great 'orses; and four of them at that?" marvelled José.

"Yeah, well, just them wheels on their own must weigh a hell of a lot, and then there's the, what did Don Quijada call it, a carriage? I mean that must be 'eavier than at least two farm carts."

"Probably more. I bet they only use it when the weather's good."

"Don't talk daft, how are they going to know if it's going to be good or not?" Samuel changed his voice to a whisper, "And I'll bet it's a bugger to get out of the mud. I've had my fair share of that kind of thing, I can tell you."

The little cortege of king in his wheelchair, the two lads pushing, and Quijada following behind made its rumbling journey through the apartments to the welcoming fireside of the smaller salon.

Carlos sat apprehensively awaiting the inescapable confrontation with his sisters whose approaching voices were sounding a warning message. Discontent was in the air.

"I told you, Quijada, this is not going to be easy," Carlos scratched at his temple and scowled.

The king is justifiably concerned. Leonor and Maria ought to be all a-quiver with anticipation (insofar as older and more mature ladies find themselves a-quiver at anything) for at last they are on their way to meet Leonor's daughter. Thirty years have passed since she was abandoned. Call me over-sensitive, but I find it distinctly disturbing that deserting one's child should

210

be so readily accepted, almost as a matter of course. It happens all the time with royalty. Carlos, Leonor, Maria and their sister Isabel were all left in Flanders to be raised by their aunt then a few years later their brother Ferdinand was left in Spain. Most recently you heard of the infant Sebastian left in Portugal when his mother Princess Juana came home to be Spain's regent.

Leonor had to leave her daughter in Portugal when Carlos had her marry the French king. I dare say there will be many who would cite all the political reasons for such decisions but I could never be persuaded; to my mind all these little ones I have just mentioned were abandoned by their parents. Yes, the little princess was deserted by her mother Leonor at a tender age. But that was not all; there was worse to come. Carlos might well feel some discomfort for his part in it. But here come the ladies.

II

Maria and Leonor brought with them a waft of winter air clinging to the folds of their velvets and furs. They were two old ladies dressed in black, two dowager queens, two sisters, and yet so unlike: Maria with determined step, Leonor treading with caution; Maria's stance at once receptive and challenging, Leonor simply quiescent and accommodating; Maria's round face with large eyes speaking of wisdom, gravity, intelligence, Leonor gaunt, her pale blue eyes with barely a trace of their former beauty and sparkle; Maria's mouth always firm but today perhaps more tightly drawn, Leonor's once inviting laughing rosebud lips now colourless and curved downwards; Maria's wrinkles drawn on her skin to emphasise she is still a force to be reckoned with, Leonor's lines the haphazard cracks of an old parchment worn and weary.

Leonor stopped to set down a small wooden box on a nearby table while Maria strode towards her brother and the

211

fire, "I would much rather be on horseback any day, brother; a carriage can be damnably cold. Greetings, I hope we find you well," she kissed his hand.

"Good day to you brother," Leonor bobbed a curtsy, then she too kissed his hand.

"But you look a miserable pair of old crows; a fine sight for my niece to set her eyes on. Top to toe in black and if that is not bad enough, those heavy black veils streaming out behind the pair of you; you look like crows descending on carrion or ghosts come to haunt. Would improve matters, you know, if you wore some gold chains, a few jewels here and there."

Carlos knew from the moment he opened his mouth in criticism he had committed a dreadful mistake. He was inviting retaliation from Maria, but their dreary appearance had aggravated him. It was too late now; the hornet's nest had been disturbed.

"Brother, I have much of my jewellery carefully packed to take to my daughter," Leonor turned slightly towards the carved box standing proudly on the table.

"Why would you wish to give away your jewels at this time? Best to hold onto them, I would have thought. Never know when they may come in useful."

"I shall tell you why she is taking the jewels." Maria was angry. "She is taking them in order to apologise for former errors committed, to try to soften her daughter's hardened heart."

"Sister," pleaded Leonor raising her handkerchief to her mouth, "do not be so unkind."

"I am not being unkind. I only try to get you to face reality. Ha! You speak of us as old crows, Carlos? I can tell you that our niece Maria caused quite a few of our feathers to be ruffled when she decided never to set foot in this country until her marriage demands were met. And you, my poor sister, you tragically still hope that a few baubles will set everything to rights."

"You are being too cruel to me today. I only hope to convince my child that I am not the cause of her hurt. Her pain is a heavy burden on my heart. This gift may offer her a little compensation perhaps."

Carlos raised his hand to quieten her. "This whole problem has arisen quite simply because your daughter has dared to presume she has some say in any arrangements for her future. Why are the women in my family all alike? Why are none of them able to see anything beyond their own pathetic little heart with its whims and fancies? Why do they continue to be governed by their emotions instead of being ruled by duty and yielding to the greater cause? God, but you test my patience!" He glowered at Leonor. "In the first place your child was in no different a situation than we three, left in Flanders when our parents came to Spain. Did it do us any harm? Has it damaged her, for God's sake? Good Lord, imagine it; she has been brought up in the wealthiest of royal families and in the care of our sister Catalina, one of the sweetest, dearest, most sensitive ladies on this earth. If your daughter feels she must continue to dwell on where she spent her childhood I would say she should consider herself damned lucky and leave it at that!"

"Brother, her grievances have more to do with later events rather than those years of abandonment. There was that first occasion when instead of being the one chosen as Felipe's betrothed she was passed over in favour of her younger cousin." Leonor plucked at her handkerchief.

"Why should she have been expecting to be chosen, for God's sake? I determine what is to be. In that particular instance a marriage to strengthen the bonds between Portugal and Spain was vitally important, but not with your daughter! No, it had to be with her cousin, because she was the child of the reigning monarchs and not the ..."

"Not the little leftover orphan," Leonor whimpered. "If, from the very beginning, I had been allowed to choose for myself none of this would have happened."

Carlos threw his hands in the air in despair, "We are surely not going to go through this again? I am head of the family. I decide. End of story!"

"You allowed our sister Maria to make her own decisions. Yes, you permitted her to refuse all suggestions of marriage."

Carlos pointed at Maria, "I knew it. You are at the root of all this nonsense."

"Not guilty, brother," was the stern reply. "My only crime, if crime it be, is in being so different from my sister. It appears that she always bent, apparently willingly, before strength whereas I always met force with force." She turned to Leonor, "You never had the spirit for the fight and now you regret it. Is that not so?"

"Oh, but I did. I tried. Oh, how I tried. Brother, had you allowed me to marry Count Frederik everything would have been so very different. My life would have taken such a happier course. Maria, how often have I told you how I glowed in the warmth of his love? I was impatient to be in his company; longed to have him touch my hand, to set my heart and head afire."

"All this again! God give me patience! The man was only a count and you were a princess. I would accept nothing less than a king or a prince for you," Carlos tried to brush away the subject with a dismissive wafting of his hands as if to rid himself of a bothersome fly.

Leonor would not let go, "You will never understand. I never wished for a king or a prince. All I ever wanted was Frederik. How often did I plead? But you forbade him to ever look at me again. And who did you chose for me while flames of passion burned in my breast? You chose an ugly old hunch-backed cripple, dragging himself through his remaining days dribbling as he went. He was the one I had to receive in my bridal bed."

"You refuse to accept that the negotiations failed through no fault of mine. I had intended you to wed his son. You cannot blame me for the father deciding to have you for himself," Carlos blustered.

"Oh yes she can. And I certainly do!" Maria boomed. "If only I had been with you sister. Carlos you know well enough you could have insisted that my sister marry Prince John of Portugal. Be honest, it suited you to have her wed a king rather than a prince."

"Your tongue has had too much liberty for too long. You speak too freely. However, madam, as you say it suited me to have my sister marry the king; political expediency."

Maria shook her head, "Such impatience, you would not have had to wait long for the prince to become king. There was nothing to be gained except, of course, an immediate loan."

"I refuse to discuss this further."

214

"So my sister did as she was told, married the old man, and even provided him with a child."

"Children," Leonor interrupted. "I provided Emanuel with two children, the first, a boy, was dead within months, sad little mite, and then my Maria was born." A long pause then she raised her eyes from the handkerchief she had been tugging at nervously on her lap. They twinkled, and a mischievous smile started to play on her lips, "But I did find a lover, someone to bring warmth and joy to my day and passion to my bed at night."

Only the ticking of a clock broke through the shocked silence.

Samuel and José at their post by the door glanced quickly at each other thinking how many extra drinks this piece of gossip would bring their way.

Gaztelu and Quijada pursed their lips and stroked their chins also exchanging glances at this quite sensational revelation.

Maria gave her sister a congratulatory look then turned a challenging eye on her brother.

Carlos shattered the quiet, "Good God in His Heaven! I refuse to believe my ears. My sister, the daughter of a queen, the sister of an emperor, a queen herself ... that, that, that she would dare to cuckold her husband! This is dishonour, madam! We are speaking of lascivious behaviour; lechery! You, my sister, are no more than a whore!"

"Now that does amuse me, brother," Maria did not disguise her contempt. "When a man seeks consolation in welcoming arms between warm sheets, no one turns a hair. If a woman chooses the same avenue for comfort she is immediately condemned as a whore." She admonished him further, "Now listen to me. You got what you wanted when Leonor was crowned Queen of Portugal; you received a massive loan. The fact that she had a lover should be of no consequence whatsoever."

"This is monstrous," Carlos's words spluttered from a face purple with rage. "To be discussing whoring, with no sense of guilt, no shame. You are no better than soldiers round the beer table boasting of deeds in brothels. Tell me, who was the bastard who dared ..."

"The one who dared, brother, was none other than myself. I was the one to reach out to grasp some moments of love and laughter, of tenderness. And, yes, I allowed my burning desire full freedom during those three years. No one until today has ever known I had a lover. So far as I know, no one knows his name, and it shall never escape my lips. And before you use any more insulting words about an affair which I refuse to have sullied, I will remind you it would not have come to pass had I been allowed to marry Frederik."

"Do not try to offer lame excuses for such sinful behaviour. May God forgive you. I never thought I would live to see the day when I could be so shamed by the actions of anyone in my family. Disgusting ..."

Maria stopped him, "I do not think there are many in this room that have the right to cast stones. Anyway you put an end to it all when you recalled Leonor to Spain."

"It was as well I did from what we have just heard; or God knows what mischief she would have got into. Emanuel; poor devil; cuckolded!"

"She came to your summons leaving her child behind."

"Fortunate for the child not to have such a whoring mother nearby to corrupt her innocence."

Leonor ignored him, "I came as a dutiful sister to be offered in wedlock a second time. And remember Frederik at that time was widowed and free to marry me. But once again you refused."

"And did you make that an excuse for further whoring?"

"No, brother," she flinched at his words. "If you remember you had decided I was to be the wife of the Duke of Bourbon."

"At least a handsome suitor," Maria smiled.

"But I was swiftly denied him ..."

"Enough is enough! For the life of me I cannot see why we should pursue this. Political decisions must be made. At that time it was in Spain's interest that you wed King Francis."

"Naturally, as part of the peace treaty with France," asserted Maria.

"I do not need your observations but," he added sarcastically, "if my sister was in search of passion, like some common wench, did Francis not fit the role of gallant suitor admirably?"

216

"Oh, how right you are, brother," sighed Leonor. "A handsome man: tall, strong, gallant, jovial – a veritable seducer – and only four years my senior. Maria, imagine the contrast between Francis and the ancient Emanuel. I was indeed eager enough to have the French king for my husband, and Bourbon was very quickly forgotten. But my brother made us wait almost five years. I travelled to France and to a bridal bed that Francis and I had hungered for the moment we met and exchanged kisses. But everything had changed. Too much had happened. King Francis did fulfil his part of the contract; he came to my bed, consummated the marriage and left my apartments. He never returned. He never sought to hide from me his hatred of all things Spanish and that included me, his bride. Nor was I able to seek solace in the French Court, the best I could hope for from anyone was indifference. How naive of me to ever have thought that my marriage could have been anything other than doomed from the outset. And then how stupid I was to hope that I could ever have my daughter join me in France as a prospective bride for one of Francis's sons. Why, the very thought of it was anathema to the French. I lived a life of isolation for seventeen years, brother, until released by my husband's death. Seventeen years and I never complained. Seventeen years my daughter had to live alone, without a mother."

"Dear God, she was not alone. Let me remind you she was brought up by our sister Catalina, who I will have you know is decent, God-fearing, unlike some ..."

"Why was she being raised in a royal court?" Leonor was bitter and resentful. "To what end? To be overlooked every time an eligible husband appeared?"

Carlos put his head in his hands and groaned, "We are going over this for the umpteenth time. You exasperate me. But go ahead, have your say. Then perhaps I can have some peace."

"On that first occasion she was not even given the courtesy of consideration. She was a nobody. It was her cousin who was chosen for your son."

Carlos interrupted happy to be on safe ground, "We have agreed that the cousin took precedence being the daughter of King John."

217

"So you say. But let us turn to this latest decision which was downright insulting. My daughter was to be the second wife of your son. Everything was arranged, the contracts had been signed. She was overjoyed. She would be the future Queen of Spain. Then you tore up the contracts! You broke my daughter's heart. And for some reason she holds me partly to blame," her tears overwhelmed her.

Maria gave her a comforting pat on the knee, "You have all my sympathy. I tell you Carlos I am truly concerned about this meeting we are to have with Leonor's daughter. She is not of a mind to be easily placated. Good Lord it took long enough to get her to come at all. At one point she vowed she would only come if she was en route to marry our widowed brother or ..."

Carlos snapped back impatiently, "God, but it infuriates me that this young woman should presume that she has any right to decide what she will or will not do. Let me tell you this, you should think yourselves damned fortunate that Catalina and I have finally arranged this visit after a great deal of correspondence regarding your daughter's insufferable truculence. We have at long last got her to realise that her marriage to Felipe had to be sacrificed for the good of our Catholic Faith. We finally persuaded her to see that Felipe marrying Mary Tudor and bringing the English heretics back to the True Faith was rather more important than a mere maiden's desire for a husband."

He was well versed in his arguments for his son's betrothal to Mary and the sudden breaking of the contract with Portugal. He had gone over them so many times with Gaztelu and Quijada using convenient half-truths, and sometimes blatant lies, to justify his actions.

"Come now, brother, you were impatient to have Felipe made King of England," retorted Maria.

"And you set about it with such haste," Leonor added, her voice trembling, "never considering the hurt and embarrassment it caused, discarding my child like some unwanted piece of clothing. All Europe was gossiping, laughing, mocking, ridiculing her ..."

Maria interrupted, fearful that Leonor was heading towards hysteria, "Perhaps, Carlos, had you immediately sought some other prince for her it may just have softened the blow? It must

218

have been devastating for the girl and an affront never to be forgotten." She took her sister's hand, "But we are encouraged now that she has decided, after all, to come to see her mother."

"And you never know, she might have a change of heart, might wish to stay in Spain," Carlos feigned optimism. "Perhaps the jewels will help after all." He knew he shouldn't have said that, he should have held his tongue.

"I always thought you cold and scheming, yet I obeyed your every decision; as my sister says, always bending to your will. But I tell you; if you have ruined my chances of spending the remainder of my days with my daughter I swear to God I shall never forgive you, never speak to you again. Sister let us go; I cannot bear to remain in this room a moment longer."

They kissed their brother's hand as a matter of form, without affection, and turned to go. Quijada and Gaztelu followed, Quijada carrying the all-important jewellery box.

So there you have it, a most awkward situation for the mother and daughter.

Poor Leonor, all she ever wanted from life was to love and to be loved, and for the majority of her fifty-nine years she has had little of either. Count Frederik was the first to stir her heart to thoughts of love, then she and Prince John of Portugal shared those years of clandestine passion. There; I have let you into Leonor's secret.

Her hopes were raised once more when King Francis paid court. She was overwhelmed the moment she saw him. This was her promised husband: he was tall, handsome, strong, and elegant. When they met for the marriage blessing he put aside her hand, drew her to him and kissed her on her lips. The king's kiss stirred Leonor's passionate heart. She was as desirous as he to retire to the bridal bed once the feasting and dancing were at an end. But Carlos would have none of it, insisting that the marriage would only be consummated once all conditions of the peace treaty had been met.

So Francis had to return to France alone to have the treaty ratified, his two young sons sent to Spain to be held hostage as a guarantee. These two little boys, only seven and eight, passed from the dazzling French Court into a bewildering life of imprisonment in a foreign land, shuttled from one fortress to another. They were placed under armed guard in ill-lit rooms and always in the most inaccessible parts of the buildings. Their only clothing was the poorest of plain black tunics and breeches.

At the end of five years, and after a hefty ransom had been paid – most of which Carlos needed to pay off a debt – they returned to France accompanied by Leonor who was now allowed, finally, to go to her husband.

Not one Frenchman forgave Carlos for the crime of imprisoning those two little innocents. When Francis came to meet them on their return to their homeland, he went straight to their room to waken them from their slumbers. Wave upon wave of unstoppable painful memories burst from them to outrage their father's ears; his two dear boys had been deprived of their childhood and would carry the scars of those brutal years forever.

As you heard, the marriage was consummated. Leonor was crowned queen of France, and then promptly ignored. Her husband cruelly told her that to gain the freedom of his children he would have married a mule. In any case he was already deeply involved with his latest mistress. Leonor found herself completely alone, despised by all around her. Could Carlos

have expected anything other for his sister? I
doubt it. And she would not be freed from
that 'prison' as she said, for seventeen years.

Carlos looked up as Gaztelu and Quijada returned, "They have
gone then? Good. Glad to have got that out of the way. Silly,
sentimental old fools. I need the comfort of some music; yes,
some singing to accompany me while I have my lunch will
wash away all memory of this morning."

A Matter of Luck

I

Carlos sat in isolated splendour at his table squelching and belching his way through the meal set before him. A small group of musicians played and sang intent on filling the room with delicate melodies.

Partridge in brandy, rabbit in white wine, chicken in almond sauce, cod in wine and parsley sauce, were all being noisily despatched with a swilling of red wine a barbarous challenge to the musicians' tender refrains of young maids captivating the hearts of young men, other young swains wracked by love's never-ending pain, regrets for heroic deeds neglected.

"These songs are all blasted copies! Heard the very same things years ago. Barefaced robbery, blasted plagiarism," spluttered Carlos, throwing down his knife.

"Not so, my lord," replied his master of music, "simply fresh arrangements, variations or transpositions."

"Not true! You cannot fool me so easily."

Male, Dr. Mathys, Brother Regla and Torriano stood nearby idly chatting. The cook waited at the serving table not once allowing his gaze to shift from Carlos hoping for the merest recognition of today's culinary masterpieces.

At the far end of the room by the door the two chair lads stole some time to gossip.

Samuel whispered, "That was a right old carry on about that Portuguese princess then, eh?"

José nodded, "I don't fancy Queen Leonor's chances much, trying to get 'er daughter to forgive her and all that."

"Me neither. Now me, you could easy get me to change me mind on anything for a box of jewels."

"Maybes, but then for these folk what has so many already a few more's not going to change anything. And as for hopin' she'll come and live with 'er, why, that's as good as saying she doesn't stand a cat in Hell's chance now of ever gettin' wed, that she's going to die an old maid. That plan will go down a right treat, see if I'm not mistaken. What you got to understand is that for rich folk gettin' wed, and to the right person, is more important than anything else in the world. Believe me." José impressed Samuel with his knowledge of all such matters.

"And what was all that about throwing stones? What you reckon Queen Maria meant by that?" Samuel was eager to learn more from his mentor.

José stretched up tall accommodating his vast wisdom and understanding, "Well, she meant that Carlos shouldn't say anything about his sister fooling around when he has been doing the same thing, God knows how often."

"Right, got yer; like the pan calling the kettle black. And he's been at it a few times, eh?"

"Except 'e was worse, 'e got the women into trouble, if you know what I mean. Here's a few f'rinstances; remember how he's often talking about the number of times he was hoppin' into bed with the French woman in Valladolid when he came to Spain the very first time, when he was but a lad? She was queen somebody or other, his grandfather's widow. Anyway, seems she had a kid, a girl; and, and, *and*, this is the best part, when Carlos got married this kid gets brought up by his wife; not as her daughter exactly, but like a proper little princess."

"Heard that one; and no one batted an eyelid! Nice for 'er though ending up living in a royal palace."

"And then he had a right old time when he was in Flanders; one woman after another, couldn't get enough."

Samuel's eyes grew wider, "Is that right?"

"As God's me witness! Now I don't know the exact order but it makes no difference. There was an Italian beauty, but that got covered up pretty nicely, probably 'cause she scarpered off to Italy quick as a wink to get married, and the feller brought the kid up as his own."

"So that kid done alright as well. And no one making no fuss nor nothin' that time neither, amazin'."

"You know why? 'Cause both mothers was pretty important. But here's one that'll really surprise you. Talk about luck!" José waited as some of the dishes were taken away, eyeing and enjoying the smell of the remaining wreckage of chicken legs and pieces of rabbit strewn in disorder on the salvers.

José's information is fairly accurate. The first child, Isabel, born to Queen Germaine, did eventually find herself in the court of the Empress Isabel. Most forbearing and Christian of Isabel to attend to the welfare of her husband's bastard child.

The second, a little girl called Tadea, fared almost as well in the home of an Italian count. Her brothers never treated her very kindly, but she survived, unlike her mother, who was poisoned. The Italians have this penchant for poisoning, stabbing or running through with a sword anyone who offends in any way. Yes, Tadea is still alive and well; and in a few years time she will be pestering King Felipe to recognise her as his half-sister. Naturally he will have none of it. Can you imagine what would happen if he did? He would have everyone writing to him, begging for status and the money that goes with it!

The doors were closed, Samuel could barely wait, "You were saying, José, about luck?"

"This other woman he gets into bed with ain't royal nor nothing like. She's a lady in waiting to some baroness or other. Strange thing is, it wasn't a secret; everybody knew. Anyways, this woman has a kid, mind you Carlos is long gone by now, and it's given to a ordinary family to look after."

"Doesn't sound lucky to me, not after the other two."

"The luck is when Carlos hears about this little girl. He insists his aunt, living in a great big palace, takes her in and looks after her. And then, *and then*, our very own Dowager Queen Maria, when she takes over as governor, also takes over looking after the girl until she gets married – to an Italian prince, no less!"

"So Maria has had first hand experience of one of the results of Carlos's you-know-what, right there in front of her eyes. But you're right about the kid; some folk are just damned lucky. I guess if Carlos was the father you always would be."

"Not always, Sam. What about the one at that convent in Madrigal?"

Samuel's face lit up. "So there's one in there! You know I said to meself at the time it was a right queer place for us to stop. I mean, all them nuns."

"Alonso 'as told me as 'ow the king has a daughter in there, maybes the mother as well. See, she was another of his playthings, one what wasn't rich, nor noble. So when Carlos knows there's a kid on the way he brings her back to Spain with him and has her locked away in that convent. Now, there's luck; bleedin' bad luck!"

"I see what you mean; the others get to live like little princesses and this one gets to live like a nun. Talk about picking the marked chickpea out of the hat." Samuel shook his head and pursed his lips. "Isn't it bloody amazin' though, you've just mentioned three extra kids belonging to the king and there's probably more."

"Yeah, and how about that one we heard about earlier, the one what drowned in the barrel? That kid might've been his an' all."

"And to look at him you wouldn't think it possible, would yer? Can you just picture him with some lady and saying stuff like, 'I lu your sarkling eyes, your rose ud outh and ru i lis', and them just looking at him all puzzled, saying back at him, 'You what? What the heck you talking about?'"

José couldn't resist joining in, "No, the way I sees it he would be straight under their nightshifts and heading direct for the honey pot with his honey stick, and spluttering, 'No 'ooling around, let's 'uck.'"

A snort thundered down Samuel's nostrils, which he valiantly strove to disguise with a fit of feigned sneezing and coughing, his fist earnestly thumping at his chest.

225

We will ignore those last few remarks and turn our thoughts to the convent for a moment, where Carlos briefly halted on his journey here to Yuste.

José is right, Madrigal does guard one of the king's secrets. When he was staying with the Conde de Nassau a certain beauty amongst the ladies caught his eye. A child was the result of the liaison, a girl. Because the lady was of relatively lowly birth he decided that no one should know of the affair, so mother and child were brought secretly to Spain and placed in the convent, a home for illegitimate babies with noble connections, under the watchful eye of the Mother Superior, herself a bastard daughter of King Ferdinand. Carlos never replied to any of the letters the Mother Superior wrote telling how, with the passing of every day, the little girl began to look more and more like her beautiful mother; how she was learning to walk on her own, her little reins trailing behind; how all the nuns loved her and her endearing ways; how she herself found her such a comfort in her waning years.

No, he never replied. Mother and daughter were ignored and forgotten; they had simply ceased to exist. Now both are dead and gone. The little girl passed away when only three years old.

Why do you suppose Carlos decided to visit the convent after so many years?

"What a dreadful cough, young man, and it came on so suddenly! You must take more care," Quijada gave Samuel a stony glare as he closed the door behind himself and Gaztelu.

"Yes sir," Sam mumbled, feeling sick at the thought of what Quijada might have heard had he arrived a moment earlier; how narrowly he had escaped losing his job. He must remember to take much more care in future. He dared not look

226

at anything save a crack in one of the floor tiles and he focussed on it, studying it with every ounce of concentration he could muster, following its every direction, to prevent his thoughts straying back to Carlos in his role of lover. José simply stood as he had throughout, a picture of sublime innocence.

II

Carlos wiped his face and hands on his napkin, turning towards his major-domo and his secretary, "You have eaten? Good. Time for us all to return to the small salon. Lavatory first. Lads, here."

Male went ahead to prepare everything, Carlos followed in his noisy chariot, while Quijada and Gaztelu sauntered behind slowly making their way to the end of the corridor to wait.

"That fellow Bourbon. Been bothering me since this morning," shouted Carlos from the other side of the lavatory door. "That affair was a messy business."

"Indeed it was, at the very least," Quijada agreed.

"And I was damned fortunate to get out of it, would you say?" The reappearing Carlos growled over the grinding din of the chair wheels. "Or, alternatively, I was a supreme master, shaping events to suit my cause."

He looked at Quijada seeking a hint of flattery.

"Decidedly the former, without doubt, you most certainly were lucky, my lord"

"Bourbon was unpopular."

"Turncoats tend to be, added to which he created additional ill feeling."

"Did he, by God?" his gnarled fingers traced along the deep furrows on his brow. "There must have been some misunderstanding somewhere."

"And you pretend not to remember?"

"Tell me instead of being so damned self-righteous. We are not here to play guessing games," Carlos spluttered petulantly, "It will all come back to me. I just require a little reminding."

Bourbon had royal blood but was exiled from France, and had come to Carlos for

227

support. Carlos felt this might be his opportunity to gain control of France. He and Bourbon would capture the French throne, Bourbon would marry Leonor, and voila! Well it gradually became obvious to Carlos that it was far more sensible for him to give his sister to the man who already wore the crown and sat on the throne of France rather than to the pretender Bourbon.

Shall we follow them into the small salon?

"Where shall we start, my lord?" Quijada resumed once they were all seated.

"Wherever you think best, it is your blasted story," grumbled Carlos.

"In that case I propose we begin with the capture of King Francis. Not long afterwards Bourbon arrived on the scene, his sword still dripping with the blood of Frenchmen, the blood of his own countrymen I might add, demanding to see the king. He was told that Francis was your prisoner and was well on his way to Spain. Bourbon was furious. Now can you remember what happened next?"

"Of course I can; I sent a ship for Bourbon," he was beginning to feel uncomfortable.

"Yes; you actually sent a ship for him! You had the renegade Frenchman rushed to Spain to be at your side, even sending a special ship."

Carlos growled, "It was important to keep on friendly terms with Bourbon. A strong tie with a French collaborator was vital."

"You say collaborator, there are many who say traitor. When you welcomed him at the gates of Toledo with such a show of affection, it offended some of the noblest and most influential gentlemen in our land."

"Dammit! That man Villena," Carlos fussed at tucking his quilt about his knees remembering only too vividly the message the old marqués had sent him. "That pompous old bugger. What did he know or understand about the larger issues at stake? Not a thing. Far too many people are too narrow minded, cannot see beyond the immediate."

Gaztelu felt badly let down; here was more gossip he had somehow missed. He mustn't allow the moment to escape without discovering more. "What was that all about, then?"

"When his majesty commanded Villena to accept Bourbon as his guest he sent the messenger back with a blunt reply," Quijada replied then addressed Carlos. "He said that while he was in no position to refuse you anything, he wanted to assure you that the moment this unwanted guest had left he would burn his palace to the ground; he would rid his home of the pollution of a traitor. He, Villena, was a man of honour and would not have that honour defiled!"

Gaztelu's hands reached to adjust his spectacles that weren't there, "Ah, well, goodness me, so that was the reason. I did hear about the palace burning down. Do you know I had always thought that the fire had been a dreadful accident."

"He should consider himself damned lucky he went unpunished for such insolence."

"Everyone was furious that you had befriended Bourbon, and worse, that you should have offered your sister in marriage to someone so unworthy; a traitor."

"I had given him my word. I would remind you that I am also a man of honour. It was a part of our bargain." Carlos squirmed at the hollowness of his words. "And I insist I had to keep Bourbon on our side. It was necessary if I wanted a foothold in France."

"And yet remarkably that all changed quickly enough, the moment Francis offered himself as husband." Quijada shook his head tut-tutting. "You were left wondering how, as a man of honour, as you put it, you could possibly renege on your promise to your friend Bourbon."

"Damned good piece of luck! No, more like divine intervention," Carlos was now smiling; his relief was almost tangible, remembering how fortune had helped extricate him from a most embarrassing situation. "Yes, God always provides."

Quijada spoke sharply, "My lord, I protest. But, of course, you are right; you were able to offer Bourbon the Dukedom of Milan."

"Yes, with the proviso he gave up all claim to my sister's hand, that was the all important stipulation. He nearly snatched my hand off when he came to receive the documents. See, Quijada, I remember some things quite well! You have to admit it was a clever move, a very clever move of mine."

"Which brings us to the coup de grace; the sacking of Rome."

Carlos shifted about in his chair, most unhappy to be reminded of the sordid episode about to unfold. "There can never be any doubt about my innocence when it comes to that affair. It is impossible to implicate me in any way."

"Absolutely no doubt whatsoever; it was Bourbon who was to blame, it was he, defying orders, who chose to take Rome. He wanted to add Rome to the so recently received gift of Milan. That would compensate most adequately the position of power and privilege he had lost in France. But it was not to be, Rome turned out to be his nemesis. Had he not been leading his men from the front he would not have been fatally wounded. Unfortunately his men, left leaderless, went on to …"

"Never mind the rest of the story, no need to go further." Carlos leaned towards Quijada, hushing him; he would not be reminded of the brutality and bestiality of it all. "If he had followed orders I would have been saved a lot of embarrassment. God, it caused me no end of trouble."

"But that is the whole point, my lord. All along you had encouraged Bourbon to consider himself beyond orders. You had formed an unwise alliance with him."

"But in the event everything worked out for the best; I was once told that I should not expect God to be at my side forever performing miracles on my behalf. Well, believe me, He has been most of the time, and He certainly was then. At least He understands that everything I do is for the Catholic Faith and the Empire. He knows my conscience is clear. So I was nicely rid of Bourbon. I got through a very difficult period without ever altering my course. I never allowed myself to be influenced by those with doubts or with minds too small to encompass the greater good. I shouldered the criticisms without buckling or bending."

"You mean you had the power to ignore anything not to your liking. And you were lucky, circumstances played into your hands."

Carlos chided, "Not true, not true."

"I never speak less than the truth, my lord."

Carlos sighed, "Well then, you must agree, in all honesty, that the whole business was resolved perfectly. And by me! There is nothing I cannot deal with!"

His eyes closed, his chin dropped to his chest, his mouth fell open and the snores of a man at peace with himself and the world tumbled forth.

1558

January

Dreams and Illusions

I

Greetings; and a Happy New Year to you, no doubt this year will bring the same share of joys and sorrows as have other years.

Ah, here is Quijada returned from Villagarcía, no doubt still cocooned in the warmth of happy memories of Christmas at home with his family.

Christmas time, a time for celebrating the birth of Christ, a time for special religious devotion; Magdalena would insist on that, being robust in her duties as a good Catholic. I am not implying that Quijada's faith is not as strong as Magdalena's, but he often loses patience with men of the cloth (his lack of tolerance being the fruit of many years of experience of the priesthood). It is easy to understand why he has been loath to steer the young Juan towards the church, as was the father's intention, and taken delight instead in his developing skills with the sword and the lance.

Quijada dismounted, slapped his horse's hindquarters, calling to Alonso, "Happy new year to you! See that my saddle bags are taken to my room."

235

He strode across the courtyard. There were flurries of snow in the ice-cold air. He looked briefly to the heavy grey skies wondering if this was the beginning of a bleak winter or, hopefully, nothing more than an isolated storm. He prayed for the latter, Yuste being already dreary enough without the inconvenience of deep snow, drifts, ice covered wells, frozen springs, struggling food caravans fighting their way through blizzards; and worse, further delays to the building of the family home in Cuacos. Memories of his Christmas in Villagarcía stole back to cheer him.

Regla, the confessor, stepped out from the main door, one hand holding his hood tight at his chin, the other securing his cloak close about him. "Quijada!" he blinked at him through snow flakes determined to close his eyes, "How good it is to see you."

"Good to see you too. But why outdoors in this weather?"

"I needed the fresh air and an opportunity to stretch my legs; far too much sitting, you know," he answered walking down the ramp his cloak and habit tugging and flapping.

A sudden blast of cold air with swirling snow sent Quijada's gloved hand to the broad brim of his hat. "Better to walk in the arcade, it will offer some protection. I hope this comes to nothing."

"Probably not, we have had one or two days like this. And how were the festivities at home? I have almost forgotten the ones of my childhood; vague recollections nothing more."

"They were wonderful, Regla, all quite wonderful; the crackling logs in the hearth; a table groaning with sweet and savoury delights for the family and all the servants. Then later, the table cleared, everyone together making merry music." He laughed, "You know I lack talent when it comes to music, both with an instrument and my voice, so I was often relegated to playing the tambour."

"Ah, yes. I learned to play the lute alongside my young master; happy days."

"And the festivities here? Dare I hope there has not been any overindulgence on someone's part?"

Regla's face was inscrutable, "You have reminded me that I must return to the king, it must be time for prayers."

236

"Your silence speaks volumes, Regla," Quijada shook his head. He continued on his way to his room next to the new cloister, climbing the stairs from the arcade to the gallery, leaving most of the winter outside, special moments spent with his family still accompanying him, holding at bay the problems that he would be facing soon enough.

CR   SO

Magdalena had been persuaded to join them in the courtyard of their castle in Villagarcía to watch the young Juan practising his tilting. And he was every inch a proud little knight as he rode his pony with such purpose across the heavily sanded flagstones towards the board, his lance at the ready, striking the target every time and never once losing his balance or becoming unseated.

Magdalena applauded and smiled up into Quijada's eyes, "Now do you see why I decided he should be called Juan? In all honesty, could you imagine anyone called Jerome being so brave?"

Quijada was immensely proud. He congratulated his squire Galarza on his success with the young Juan.

"My lord, the boy is a quick learner," he replied, "he always does as he is told and takes it all very seriously; two great advantages for any tutor."

Back indoors how overjoyed Juan had been when he removed the linen cover wrapping to the gift from his father. It was a sword, his very own sword, and every bit as good as the one he remembered belonging to Prince Carlos. It was a fine Toledo sword with hilt and scabbard exquisitely damascened.

It was not Quijada's nature to be indulgent, except to his superiors, but the boy was deserving. Juan had worked hard, had changed remarkably from that rascal who had arrived here a few years since; he was now a little gentleman. Quijada and Magdalena had discussed the progress he had made and she had agreed to the gift. Had she not, then there would have been no sword.

And Juan's behaviour had been exemplary when helping Magdalena with her Christmas works of charity, patiently accompanying her to every home in the village where she gave a silver *medio real* to each and every one, from youngest to oldest, in every household; listened attentively to her words of comfort to them, no doubt conscious of her earlier instructions: to always follow her example for as long as he lived, to always remember those less fortunate, those who lived in want.

CS　　　　BO

"Yes, I have a perfect little family," Quijada announced to the oak-beamed ceiling of the gallery. "I have been blessed. If only I could have them here soon, instead of only dreaming of that day. The work is going too damnably slow!"

He removed his gloves slapping them impatiently one against the other.

In his room a servant had prepared a fire. He took Quijada's gloves, hat, and cloak then pulled off his boots.

Quijada turned his chair to face the merry flames to toast his cold toes before slipping on his shoes and making his way to the king's apartments to catch up on events.

The king is quite ill and in very poor humour. It comes as no surprise for recently his gluttony has discovered new frontiers: Christmas, New Year, Epiphany and San Blas presenting the excuses for his excesses. If only he had accepted the priests' invitations to join them at their table. However, their miserable fare offended him; it was no way to celebrate, certainly not his way!

Doctor Mathys is most concerned, this is the worst attack of gout he has ever witnessed, and he is frustrated beyond all patience at the king's refusal to heed his warnings.

However, instead of accompanying Quijada, I want us to go directly to the courtyard. If we hurry we should have just about enough time to get there.

II

Four horses appeared suddenly, as if from nowhere, thundering furiously across the cobbles, powdery snow scattering from beneath their hooves. The riders' cloaks, bearing the arms of the Duque de Oropesa, billowed at their backs. Reins were pulled taut, the horses stopping to wheel and slither and throw back their heads, nostrils flared and snorting, spume lathering their mouths and necks. They stamped and shuffled, their sweating and bloodstained flanks steaming.

Alonso ran from the stables followed quickly by others. "Now then my beauty. Whoa. Whoa, there," he grabbed at a halter then patted and comforted the horse's hot, wet neck, its veins standing proud, glistening. "You still wanting to race? Steady, steady."

One of the riders leapt down, calling to Alonso over his shoulder as he hurried across to the ramp, his bloodied spurs ringing out an urgency, "You; see to it that my horse is cooled down and dried properly. Get that saddle off quick. See she's put in a comfortable stable. Attend to any wounds ..."

"You bloody-well do your job, mate, and I'll do mine," Alonso hissed under his breath, and he spat, the defiant glob disappearing into the nearest of the small scattered islands of snow. "I've had plenty of experience, I have. I've been at Mühlberg, mate, and Metz, and looked after 'orses in worse states than this. Don't you try teaching your grandma how to suck eggs! You know, people like you just think you're God Almighty; your masters 'ave more civil tongues in their heads. It's just 'cause you have fancy bleedin' cloaks."

He began to unbuckle the harness, furious, so many thoughts racing, tormenting: how he had had to listen to Maria go on and on about these blokes after every damned visit and it was all about nothing, she'd never even spoken to them nor them to her, or so she said; or how she wouldn't shut up, making him feel a right nobody, and he'd been the one to get her the job – the ungrateful bitch. And another thing, it was for the feller to ditch the woman, not the other way around. Nor was it helping his temper any being told what to do by a

239

would-be rival. Anyway she'd get her comeuppance, see if she didn't.

He decided that only horses could be relied on. "We'll soon have you all comfy, like. Steady there, you be patient with Alonso now, he knows what's best." He took a blanket from his young helper. He patted the horse again, clicked his tongue and picked up the reins, "Let's go for a nice walk then, shall we? Then a nice rub down. Your friend's here to look after you."

"Hey, I say," Manuel came alongside him leading a second horse, "somethin' deadly serious must be up for this lot to be riding post."

"I bet they've come from that place where they took the two old ladies, wherever it was."

"I can't remember neither. What you reckon then, good news or bad news Alonso?"

"Don't know, but listen to this," he dragged himself free of his ill humour, "if we plays our cards right, we can get a couple of free days out of this. I mean, someone has to take these horses back. Bet yer!"

"Great. Fingers crossed then."

The riders cannot possibly be the bearers of good tidings. We should follow them.

The four men stepped indoors to be met by Quijada, the servant girl Maria, and a wall of heat.

Maria rising from her curtsey was overwhelmed, her gaze one of complete wonderment: thigh boots, then breeches, jerkins (with those oh so glorious coats of arms high on the left breast) were revealed as cloaks were hurriedly discarded. The un-gloved hands were strong, manly, and without the scars and sores carried by all the men she knew. Finally, when riding hats were removed and scarves unwound, she marvelled that she should have the fortune to be in such close proximity to not one, not two, not three, but four handsome faces, here, together, at the same time. She closed her eyes; and the image was sealed and set forever.

"Sir, we bring a letter for his majesty from the Dowager Queen Maria. We were commanded to deliver it post-haste and to return with his majesty's instructions."

"Give it here, my man, I shall attend to it," Quijada took the folded paper. "Maria, have somebody see to their clothes, while you take these gentlemen to your mistress. Tell her that nothing but the best is acceptable for them."

When she didn't move he spoke more sharply than he intended, but he was already seething over what he had just been told about the king's infirmities, and now this more than likely unwelcome news had arrived to make matters even worse. "Maria, did you hear my orders?"

"Oh, yes sir. I beg your pardon, sir. This way, if you please," and she led the way her mind a tumult of blissful thoughts of a betrothal with one, any one, of them. No more for her the vulgar romping in the hay with a lowly stable lad. She had already improved her looks, her posture; there was every chance.

Her idle dreams will bring her no harm. For a while she can indulge herself and in days to come she will have the memories to cherish. So often I have seen folk either enfold themselves in dreams to escape from their unhappiness or rely so heavily on fanciful illusions that they are led by them headlong into despair. However, Maria will survive.

III

In the large salon Gaztelu, spectacles precariously perched on the tip of his nose, was writing, he and his pen industriously working on yet another document. Neat, perfectly formed letters followed one after the other in groups of varying length and all arranged in the straightest of lines, organised like soldiers on parade.

"Gaztelu, good to see you again; I hope I am not interrupting, but this has just arrived, and must be attended to immediately," Quijada crossed the room tearing at the seal, already convinced of the contents. "Dear God, what next?"

241

"Ah, good friend, welcome back. As usual you have been sorely missed," Gaztelu lay down his pen and pushed his spectacles back onto the bridge of his nose. "Something to add to our present woes?" He quickly scanned the letter, "But this is a sorry business. I knew all along no good would come of it. This illness sounds serious; not at all what he needs to hear right now."

"I tell you Gaztelu, I am furious. Every time I go away from this infernal place the king is allowed to do what he pleases; and then, of course, he suffers the consequences. And now this. We are going to have to sound as positive as we can about the news. Shall we go? If only it could have happened at some other time. And I do so hate seeing him looking such an ancient wreck of a man. It is disheartening to see him so determined to destroy himself. How bad is it this time?" Quijada ushered his friend before him, out of the room and down the corridor towards the king's bedchamber.

"Bad, my friend, very bad. You will be shocked."

The festivities of the Twelve Days of Christmas followed by the feast of San Blas had indeed taken their toll on Carlos. He sat uncomfortably on a newly designed chair, its seat drilled with holes in several places so that a sponge soaked with boiled potions could drain into a bowl underneath. It was thought that the medication would be more effective if applied directly to his piles. The king nonetheless still had to suffer the indignity of having his nightshift raised up around his waist. Once again his arms and legs were enveloped in layers of bandages reeking of vinegar.

He looked up as the two men entered, his face drawn and heavily lined with pain, his eyes tired and red. He started to raise an arm in greeting but then grunted something at the chair lads. He was lifted, carried to his rumbling little chariot and trundled to his lavatory.

"Quickly before his majesty returns," Doctor Mathys almost ran to Quijada's side. "Thank God you are here. You left your family well, I hope. Please, do speak severely to the king. Yes, I beg you to admonish him. This is no way for him to behave; he is killing himself by continually ignoring my warnings. This is now his second attack this winter. If only he had sat at the priests' table, as the prior requested, all this pain and misery would have been avoided."

"The king refused?"

"No, but within minutes he left abruptly to go to his own dining table where, according to him, he could enjoy some decent food and drink. Promise me you will say something."

The room filled with groans of exertion issuing from the lavatory followed by howls of pain as haemorrhoids were left torn and bleeding.

"You see, something must be done," the doctor pleaded.

"Quite so, quite so, but not today, I cannot discuss the follies of his indulgence when I am to tell him of the grave illness of his sister Leonor."

"God have mercy."

Carlos was returned to the room and laid gently on his bed. The curtains were drawn around as the apothecary cleaned his wounds and applied a soothing ointment of celandine before wrapping the area in a large napkin. A fresh nightshift was slipped over his head then he was sat up to lean amongst his generous pillows, ready to meet his friends.

"Th – th – schl – th …"

"What the devil?" Quijada demanded of the doctor.

"His majesty's mouth is horribly inflamed, his tongue is very swollen, his gums are bleeding …"

"Dear Lord, what a mess. If only I could have been here to prevent at least some of this. However, doctor, it means you are now at last able to control his majesty's diet so we should soon see some signs of improvement. We will discuss all this later." He clapped his hands, "You may all leave us now. Regla, please stay."

Carlos looked questioningly at him but Quijada waited until the others were gone.

"Sire, you have done yourself great mischief. Hopefully this attack has been severe enough to have taught you the folly of your ways." He hesitated, "Would that I could wait until you were in better health to receive this news; however this letter has arrived from your sister Maria."

Quijada paused again, uncertain how to begin. "Now, although it may sound serious Gaztelu and I are of a mind that it sounds so because of Queen Maria's sadness at the outcome of events."

Carlos grunted his impatience to hear the news then made as if to grasp the piece of paper, but Quijada moved it out of reach.

"Allow me to read you the relevant parts. They will suffice.

The meeting with Leonor's daughter was a complete failure, save for the longed-for embrace. Despite all Leonor's pleas, promises, and of course the jewels, my niece announced her decision to return immediately to Portugal. We should have realised that a rich Portuguese princess would never wish to surrender her wealth and position to become a spinster companion to her ageing mother. Leonor has been left distraught. She hoped that if she were to go on pilgrimage to Guadalupe, she would find support from Our Lady. However we had not travelled far when she became ill."

Carlos cried out his panic, his eyes searched Quijada's face seeking reassurance that the illness would definitely be of a temporary nature remembering Leonor's last words threatening never to forgive him, never to speak to him again should her daughter not come to live with her. He was wretchedly uncomfortable with the idea of that particular finger of guilt pointing in his direction.

"My lord, it is as I said. So many heady expectations followed by such a dashing of all those hopes. I know I am no doctor, but I am convinced that highly charged emotions are the cause of Queen Leonor's illness. To continue with the letter,

Her fever started a few days ago, but sadly her cheery spirit and fortitude that have helped her bear so much over the years have deserted her. She has also had an asthma attach.

My lord this next part is important and we should focus on this.

Brother, if you could send her some words of encouragement I am sure they would be enough to rally her strength during these difficult days.

244

Indeed, my lord, encouragement on your part, patience on theirs; and in a day or so when the fevers have run their course …?"

Carlos wept, he sobbed. He pointed at his confessor then put his hands together as if in prayer.

Regla bowed, "I shall order the priests to say prayers for Queen Leonor's speedy recovery. The prayers will be said hourly, both day and night," and he strode off to attend to his mission.

Gaztelu bent towards the king, "Your majesty, I propose that I write a letter to your sister Leonor, telling her of your love and prayers. Perhaps an invitation for your two sisters to stay here while Leonor recuperates? I can say that their rooms are already being prepared." He paused for a moment. "Perhaps it would mean even more to her if I were to deliver the letter myself as your most special representative. It would emphasise your love for her, give her more heart? It would be an honour for me to serve you both in this way."

Carlos looked up at him, his bandaged arms slowly, painfully, reaching out towards him, tears of gratitude welling up and streaming down his face.

"My lord you can rest assured that we, your servants and friends, will do everything in our power to help. I cannot ride post, but I will go as swift as God allows."

Quijada put his hand on his shoulder, "You are most charitable, dear friend. I will ensure that Oropesa's men do everything to make your journey trouble free. Lads, here, you have errands to run. Be quick for I want you back immediately. You, Samuel, find the riders and tell them they will not be needed for some time. Tell them they must rest. You may also inform them they will not be riding post, but instead will be escorting his majesty's secretary. José, go to the stables and tell them to have the five best horses to be ready for saddling up."

Samuel and José ran down the corridor, José proudly congratulating himself, "What'd I tell you, Sam? I knew there wasn't a cat in Hell's chance of that princess coming to live with 'er mother. Was I right, or was I right, eh?" He punched Samuel on the shoulder.

"Yeh, but what a bleedin' shame that it's making the poor old lady all sick, like. Makes you kind of sorry for her, doesn't it? I hope as how she gets better, she's 'ad some rum deals. Sorry Father," he apologised, almost colliding with Regla who was rushing back to comfort Carlos.

It is such a tragedy that Leonor did not accept the invitation to go to live in Portugal. Oh yes, her daughter brought the offer from Queen Catalina. I am sure she could have found some happiness there, and she would be near her beloved daughter. That long-cherished dream is now completely beyond her grasp.

Carlos is taking the news very badly. Leonor was always his favourite. He always called her 'my best sister'. She has certainly always been the most amenable to his every whim.

When they were children she was a little mother to him. She took him by the hand as he learned to walk, and she was always there to pick him up when he stumbled. They played their childhood games together. In fact she was always there when he needed her, all her life.

Now we should follow Quijada and Gaztelu to the large salon, where we will find? Ah yes, Male.

"You have heard the news Male?"

"Sadly, yes. But, Quijada, these have just arrived."

He looked at the seals concerned that one might be from Maria. "Ah, they are all from Valladolid. I expect the regent is sending her thoughts and best wishes, she must surely have heard." He put the larger package on the table and tore open the seal on the letter. "Great God in His mercy, Calais has fallen. At all costs the king must not hear of this, not yet awhile. He is in no state to cope with more bad news."

Gaztelu shrugged his shoulders, "I am not in the least surprised at this. It was a disaster just waiting to happen. King

Felipe was concerned about Calais, but the stupid English had no intention of heeding his warnings. So there you are."

"It was ridiculous to believe that they would accept Spanish advice or learn from wisdom gained from our vast political and military experience. No, their vision is too clouded by suspicion."

"Exactly so, Quijada. Felipe warned Mary well over a year ago that the garrison at Calais was left grossly undermanned throughout the winter, and he told her of the rumours of shady deals apparently going on with the French. The problem is Carlos will see this as only the beginning of something far more serious, perhaps a French invasion of the Netherlands."

"I think it would be best if the old campaigner ZuZiga came to explain everything to Carlos. What do you say?" Quijada asked of the others. "Then, yes, I shall send for him. He will choose the right words to describe a very sorry situation. He can tell it as an entirely English defeat, which it is, with Felipe as the lone, but ignored, voice of reason, which he is. Provided he portrays Felipe as the astute commander, a man of vision and foresight, it should soften the blow and lessen the king's fears of attacks against the Netherlands. Yes, it would be best to delay the news until I have informed Zuñiga."

He opened more letters. "As I thought Gaztelu; I shall go through these state papers on my own."

"If you would be so kind; an excellent idea, for I must write the letter for the king and then prepare for my journey."

"God speed you on your way."

Male shook his head, "It never rains but it pours, is the common saying I believe. First the king's sister, and now this debacle in Calais; hopefully bad fortune will stop at these two; I would hate to think of there being a third."

"Just so, Male. Now if you will put these state papers in order while I write a brief note to ZuZiga."

What was I saying to you about dreams and illusions? It never pays to set much store by them.

I am sure Quijada is right about inviting Zuñiga. Have no fear; we will be here when

247

he talks to Carlos. I will let you know the moment I hear of his arrival.

It is time, now, for a quick visit to the servants' quarters.

IV

José had just arrived at the kitchen door when Samuel emerged grinning from ear to ear, "I say, José, our Maria's puttin' on some airs and graces these days. You should've seen 'er just now."

"So, did I miss somethin' good then?"

"Nah, not really, it was just the way she was struttin' about like she owned the bleedin' place."

"She makes you laugh she does, the way she carries on these days."

"Bless 'er, she must think one of them rider chaps is going to fall for her and whisk 'er off on his charger to a place where she'll live happily ever after."

"With servants doin' the work while she sits about, doin' nowt."

"And her dressed in somebody's hand-me-downs."

They laughed at the images they had created.

"Never mind, we'll leave her be with her silly ideas, except when we gets the chance to make fun of her. Anyway, let's get back, we might be missing something. Heck, there's one of them drafts again, right down me back." Samuel looked down the corridor.

My fault again. But it is no more than a slight inconvenience. Some feel it more than others.

This, then, is the kitchen, and here is our Maria.

"I can just picture it, there's a farm not far from here exactly like that." Maria was standing between the huge open hearth with its cheery fire, the flames licking the blackened pots of bubbling soups and stews, and the end of a long trestle table.

248

The riders sat tearing off chunks of bread to accompany the steaming salt-cod soup they were hungrily spooning up into their mouths.

"So, what's your name, young miss?" said one blowing on a large spoonful of hot greasy soup with its chunk of fish.

"Maria, sir."

"A pretty name for a pretty lass," commented the one who had been talking of his home. He pushed his bowl to one side and leaned forward, elbows on the table. "And are you from a farm, too, Maria?"

"Um, yes; but not as grand as yours," she couldn't, wouldn't say more. He had spoken of a gentleman's farm, where labourers did most of the work, a farm with a high wall set all around it, a farm with all kinds of buildings for animals and implements. It actually belonged freehold to his family! And it would be his one day! In the meantime it was an honour for the family to have him in the service of Oropesa.

Madame Male, returning from the dairy bearing an enormous cheese, rescued her from having to reveal or lie about her humble family and their hovel where everyone, including the animals, shared the one room; saved her from having to disclose or deny anything about her former life from which she had been so fortunate to escape.

"Maria, see to it that the gentlemen they are having enough of the food and the drink. You are not here for to make the gossip."

The men pulled faces behind Madame Male's back and Maria almost laughed, "Yes ma'am. What can I get you, sirs?"

"More soup, please, and some of that cheese."

"Water for me."

Maria attended to their every wish. She impressed herself with her much-practised new style of walking with shorter steps, her way of keeping a discreet distance from the men's bodies as she placed food and drink before them. Her dress was neat and tidy, even if old, and her freshly laundered apron positively gleamed its whiteness; its status! Yes, she felt justly proud and stood tall.

She had just finished serving them when one of them announced, "I tell you what, Maria; I think I shall come to

249

Cuacos for the *noche de San Juan*. I would like you to be my partner."

Madame Male's eyebrows shot up and disappeared under the brim of her cap, "Young lady persons should not be doing this dancing late on a summer night. It makes to sinning and babies left upon the steps of church. This is my belief."

Knowing smiles, winks and nudges passed amongst the men.

"Miguel at your service, ma'am, I can assure you there is no harm in it whatsoever. I will have the lady home before midnight. You have my word of honour," said Miguel this time winking at Maria, both of them knowing full well that the fun didn't begin until midnight.

This was too good to be true. Maria was overjoyed, could barely contain herself, "Oh, thank you sir."

Her heart raced at the prospect. She would be going on the arm of this handsome man with such beautiful unscarred hands; a man who might, one day, just like his friend sat across from him, inherit a farm! Everyone in Cuacos would be gawping, unable to believe their eyes that she, the Maria they'd grown up with, had got herself a proper farmer, a man of property. Oh, she would show them, right enough, that she was going places.

And Alonso, yes, Alonso; she must tell Alonso; and he would be jealous, or angry, or pretend he didn't care. Perhaps, after all, she wouldn't tell him, perhaps it would be best to say nothing, at least for a little while. She would savour her precious secret until she was good and ready to make the most of it.

But, dear Lord, what was she going to wear? That was going to be a bit of a worry over the next few months.

250

February

Pride or Prejudices

I

ZuZiga wafted a sheaf of papers before running his hand over his balding head, "How did his majesty react to this Calais business?"

Male, sitting some distance away, set down his quill, "Badly, very badly, indeed." He adjusted his broad red sash of the Companion of the Bedchamber then leaned back, resting his elbows on the chair arms. He studied the knuckles of his interlocked fingers. "Do you know, since the beginning of the year everything has gone from bad to worse. The king has had the worst attack of gout I have ever witnessed, then the infection in his mouth started, the haemorrhoids became inflamed and swollen, then the arthritis in his neck and the joints in his arms and legs flared up, the ulcers on his legs are weeping, then there's his migraines, his vomiting …"

"Good God, man; are you going to recite the whole of a doctors' manual? You'll excuse me the details of the pills, potions, and ointments I hope."

"Forgive me. Added to all this he was tormented for weeks by doubts about the outcome of Leonor's reunion with her daughter." He sighed, "As most of us feared it was a complete disaster; the daughter never had any intention of leaving Portugal and Leonor could not bear to leave Spain. Next came the news that Leonor was ill, seriously ill, and you know how deep his feelings run for her. And now we have this Calais blow."

"Fortunately this blow can only be to his pride, nothing more." ZuZiga moved towards the fire stretching his hands to its welcoming warmth. "We have nothing to fear from the French. They are merely flexing their muscles after their humiliating defeats in France and Italy." He turned to face Male, taking the opportunity to raise his short gown enough to warm his comfortably wide and round backside in front of the flames. "The king would not be so affected if his son were not married to the English queen. What is Calais to us after all?"

"Aye, you are probably right, but I cannot stop thinking how different it would all have been, in many ways, if Felipe had married his Portuguese cousin. Leonor would not now be estranged from her daughter and this French disaster, which I am sure Spain will be blamed for, might not have come to pass, not yet awhile at least."

"If only we could rewrite history, eh? But, no good can be gained in crying over what is past and done, Male. Let us see if I can persuade Carlos to take a more dispassionate, more objective, view of the events."

"Amen to that. If you will bear with me for one moment while I finish this, we shall go to the king."

Carlos had cherished such grand designs. He wanted England for his son, hoping to see even more power in the hands of the Hapsburgs. Felipe, sadly, was only too eager to fall in with his father's plans. Carlos's desires unfortunately blinded him to the unthinkable; failure.

Let us go on ahead of the others. The king is still not well enough to leave his bedchamber, a very sorry state of affairs. At least he has Quijada for company to help him through these black days.

II

Carlos nodded at the letter in Quijada's hands, "So how is Barbara doing?" He sat uncomfortably hunched in a well-cushioned chair a small book of hours, looking

252

ridiculously small, smothered by his swollen misshapen fingers.

Ah, you remember the tale of the little boy drowning in the barrel and Quijada saying that the chaperone would not retire but would certainly remain with Barbara to comfort her? Well, in fact, Carlos thought that that was not enough, that more should be done for Barbara; leaving all the details, naturally, to Quijada.

"Barbara is quite well, my lord," Quijada answered scanning Barbara's letter.

Regla looked up from his Psalter to listen.

"And her new home; is it to her liking?"

"It is indeed, sire, and she is seemingly overwhelmed with gratitude that you should be so sensitive. She says the move has helped her overcome her distress caused by the loss of her son; to have remained in the same house would have been a constant intolerable reminder."

Regla's eyes returned to the page of his Psalter but without seeing a single word, unable to concentrate, curious as to why the king had more concern for the suffering of this Barbara person than for his ailing sister who might well be in mortal danger; and more than a little perplexed by the omission of her name from every prayer or confession of Carlos.

"Is it a goodly size?" Carlos asked.

Regla raised his head and Carlos turned from him as if to deprive the priest of his innermost thoughts.

"Larger than the last; and she has a steward, housekeeper, chaplain, two pages, six ladies and four other servants."

"Good, good. Is that the same as before?"

"No, her household has been increased as you suggested."

"Ah, yes, of course. She deserves it." He opened his book awkwardly turning over the calendar pages and giving only fleeting glances at the pastoral scenes, the red letter days; his mind wandering, his thoughts drifting ... "Aye ..."

Barbara deserved every *ducado* he could afford and more, if only for that one evening, that extra special evening. He closed his eyes remembering that whisper.

CR   ɞɔ

"I came when you called," Barbara's whisper floated towards him through the intimate darkness. A solitary flickering candle with its swaying pool of light guided her to his bed. Carlos was lying, as he had been lying for hours, feeling sorry for himself, complaining bitterly about aches and pains that refused to go away.

The bedcovers were raised and she slipped her naked body between the sheets, leaned over to kiss him, and lay down beside him, an arm resting across his chest. Her lips, as they brushed his cheeks and mouth, and the silk-like skin of her arm had begun their magic. His hand caressed and traced its way from her shoulder down to her hand and her beautiful slender fingers.

"What will you sing for me tonight, my darling nightingale?"

"I thought that you should have two songs. The first is *How much more must I suffer.*"

Carlos laughed away his discomfort, "Good Lord, a song about arthritis and migraines; musical medicine indeed!"

"Silly, don't tease; you know full well it speaks of the pain a mistress would suffer if she were not allowed to be with her lover when she loves him so much. It tells of my pain if I could no longer see you."

"There can be no danger of that happening, dear heart. Sing for me."

And she began; it was the voice of an angel filling his heart with love, compassion, yearning, fondness, and tenderness that was almost unbearable.

> *"How much more pain can there be*
> *When you refuse even my sighs,*
> *Though you forever deny me*
> *You will remain my one desire ..."*

The song was ended. There was no time for a second one. He reached for her, finding her young breasts, her belly, seeking further, lower, between her thighs. She raised his nightshift, whispering, "My Carlos is stirred by my song of love."

He heaved himself onto her. She helped him, holding him gently. They moved as one, slowly, carefully. With a howl of passion he flooded into her.

"My dearest and sweetest Barbara; that was the best song you ever brought to my bed."

ଔ   ଯ

Carlos sighed into his beard, "That was the best song ... Aye, dear me." He rubbed his eyes and looked about him blinking away his reverie.

Quijada asked, "You spoke, my lord; something about 'Aye dear me'?"

"Only remembering some wonderful moments, and God knows I need any I can lay my hands on these days. It was too bad that Barbara's visits had to be kept secret."

Regla, who had finally got back to his reading, looked up again, by now more intrigued than ever as to why he had never heard of this woman before in any of the king's confessions.

Quijada shrugged. "It was your decision not to allow anyone to know of your lady musician."

"What else was to be done? Good God, she was a nobody. One should never stray beyond rank and position, you know, and she lacked both. No, it was never done before so far as I know; unacceptable, quite unacceptable. So her presence had to be kept quiet, even if she was nothing more than my musician. A certain distance has to be maintained; think of the gossip. Can you imagine the sport that could be made of her family?"

"There was no shame to her father being a belt maker."

"If that was what her father truly was. We never did know, did we? Do you remember how every time she and her mother came to court they were in borrowed clothes? Not one decent dress between them! If they borrowed clothes they probably borrowed identities as well. And neither of them had money until I opened my purse."

"And, by God, it has been open ever since," the words had been there, ready, on the tip of Quijada's tongue, "as if you

255

were pouring its contents into the river and watching it flow away and out to sea."

Carlos growled, "I draw the line at that sort of criticism, Quijada!"

"I apologise for speaking out of turn, although my observation is perfectly justified. Still, we shall put an end to the subject." He folded the letter and tucked it inside his jerkin marvelling once again at the ease with which Barbara received anything she wanted, and often without having to ask!

Regla returned to his book, extremely interested in the hiding of the letter, extremely disappointed in not hearing more about considerable amounts of money being poured into rivers.

There was a polite knock at the door and Male and ZuZiga entered. Quijada greeted his old army friend then begged his leave of Carlos pleading urgent matters in Cuacos. He wanted ZuZiga to have the floor to himself; he knew he would inevitably interrupt if he stayed.

Regla had left his seat too, "My lord, now that ZuZiga is here, perhaps it would be best for me to leave?"

Carlos gave him a piercing look, "You sit still. I will tell you when you are to leave. Welcome, ZuZiga, Quijada told me he had sent for you."

The king's old friend and comrade-in-arms bowed, "I made every effort to get here as soon as I received the letter. The news of your sister Leonor is most disturbing, have you heard anything further?"

Carlos snapped, "No, I have not!"

"And you, my lord, I understand that your own health is improving."

"You did not come here to discuss my sister's health; nor are we going to waste time talking about mine. I know well enough that you have heard about Calais."

"A sorry business."

"Sorry business be damned! Dangerous business. God knows what the consequences will be. And was Felipe there? No, he never is there when he should be. The damned fool is forever studying documents, thinking, holding conferences, writing letters to all and sundry, but never ever doing anything. Fat lot of good that does anyone. He is hopeless I tell you."

"To be fair, he warned Mary of the situation. He wrote as soon as he inspected Calais and saw how weak it was."

"There you have it. He wrote! He should have done more than write, for God's sake. If only he were like me; when a job has to be done I set to it immediately, no dithering. Which reminds me, do you have the letter for my daughter?"

"Here, my lord," Male handed it to Carlos.

"You know as well as any, ZuZiga, that things will not stop with the fall of Calais. This heralds the damned French marching straight on into the Netherlands. And what about Burgundy, eh? Felipe will need money if we are to stop all this. Read my letter. This is the kind of letter that needs to be written, one of authority, none of this damned consensus of opinion rubbish."

ZuZiga read of Carlos's insistence that the Cortes despatch funds to maintain a standing army of sufficient strength to protect the Netherlands, urging his daughter Juana to remind them how he had warned the Cortes in the past of the dire consequences of underfunding the army.

"I am being more diplomatic with her this time," he smiled his benevolence. "I am letting her see that I trust her."

ZuZiga applauded the final words, reading them aloud,

"'... J will have no peace until J have heard that my demands have been complied with.

Excellent, sire. It gladdens my heart to know that you are still issuing commands. I salute you."

Carlos nodded his acknowledgement.

ZuZiga returned the letter to Male. "So, shall we look at Calais, as experienced campaigners; they say old soldiers ..."

"You had best not be patronising me. I am in no mood for it."

"My lord!"

"Why did Quijada go? I wanted him to stay," Carlos pouted.

"He is overseeing the work being done on his house," Male offered. "He has lost patience with everybody; the carpenters, the plasterers, in fact everyone involved. He is infuriated by the delays."

"Me too, this blasted business is going on for ever; not good enough," growled Carlos. "The sooner he has his wife by his side the better for all of us. And I am still waiting to see that boy of his. Quijada promised I would see him soon and that was months ago."

"Ah, the young Juan. How is the lad doing?"

Carlos brightened, "The boy is doing well. And I am told he is quite a lad, at that. Going to be a soldier, too, no priest's frock for him. Quijada says he is damned good with the sword, and a skilled horseman. Just as well, the country needs young soldiers. Spain needs someone to take our place, eh, ZuZiga?"

"How right you are. How old is he?"

Carlos scratched at his forehead, "Not sure; about the same age as my grandson; eleven, twelve, thereabouts, I really have no idea. Good God, some soldier my grandson would make. Spanish troops' lives would be more at risk from him than from the enemy. His temper always gets the better of him. He loses all control; crazy."

"Shall we talk about Calais?" ZuZiga would prefer not to hear anything about the young Prince Carlos. He'd heard more than enough over the last few years. Much better to discuss the loss of English territory.

"Now there were several enemies, all waiting to strike."

"Exactly! You saw it friend. I saw it. Why, in God's name did Felipe not see it?" Carlos ranted.

"Sire, calm and cool is the order of the day. Remember, we are seasoned soldiers. To continue, looking first at enemy number one, the Protestants in Calais, there were too many of them and they were certain to go over to the French sooner or later."

"Blasted heretics! Why was Mary so stupid as to allow Calais to be governed by heretics? Should have seen to it that there were more Catholics."

"You are right, that was rather short-sighted of the queen, my lord. Moving onto enemy number two; there were traitors aplenty."

"Felipe must have known all that, too. That is what is so damned annoying. He could have prevented ..."

"Later, my lord. Now to enemy number three, the French; the Duke of Guise to be precise."

"That blasted name again! God, how long am I to be haunted by that *hijo de puta*?"

258

"With permission, Guise was determined to find a way to salvage his own pride and that of France at the same time. So there you have it, simple as that, Calais provided the perfect stage for his victory with not the remotest chance of failure. Calais was doomed."

"Humph! By God, but it would have been a different tale altogether if I had been there."

"Without question, my lord; but you chose retirement instead, much to the regret of many of us. Your son has been left to shoulder the heavy burden of the English. Now, had you wed Queen Mary yourself ..."

"Impossible. A young stud was needed." He snorted. "It seems Felipe has failed me there as well. If he were here I would give him a piece of my mind, I can tell you. How could he let me down so badly? Am I to sit here and watch my empire crumble away because of his incompetence? He is a great disappointment. I tell you, this has caused me more pain and anguish than any of my gout attacks."

"My lord, we must not exaggerate; we are, after all, speaking of Calais, an English possession in no way connected to Spanish or Austrian lands. Now, if you will allow me to speak on behalf of King Felipe. He did everything humanly possible, but the English refused his advice and assistance. There is no blame to be apportioned to him; the bungling English have been the problem all along."

Carlos uttered a reluctant, "So you say. But I doubt if it helps matters; I can still see us losing ..."

ZuZiga interrupted, "Let us consider what Felipe is doing now. He has his troops at the ready in their winter quarters in the Netherlands; excellent forward planning. He is also doing everything in his power to put a stop to any designs the French may have on the English throne."

"Impossible for him to get anywhere without me. My God, I have had years of experience keeping the thrones of Europe within our family. He should be asking me; seeking my advice. Nor would England be in such a mess if he had sired a child."

"Now that is a worry. It would appear that Queen Mary is not going to provide an heir, but I cannot think the fault is Felipe's, he has a son, after all"

"Dear God, that idiot!"

"Queen Mary is old and ill. If she dies without issue, which she surely will, her sister Elizabeth is next in line, and after her?"

"I have no damned idea, I lose track, and I have no wish to play guessing games."

"Mary Stuart of Scotland. At the moment she is in France, being raised as a little French princess and about to marry the heir to the French throne. If Elizabeth also dies without an heir, the throne of England goes to the French."

"Dear God in Heaven!"

"Felipe's close friend is doing everything he can to persuade Mary to insist upon Elizabeth marrying Savoy; of your family and obviously a good Catholic. England could yet be saved from heretics and the French."

"Clutching at straws."

"Perhaps so, but I insist you acknowledge that Felipe is doing all he can. He is acting with all honour towards England to protect her; while furthering the cause of your family and the True Faith. You should give credit where credit is due; to your son Felipe."

"Perhaps so." It was half-hearted and begrudging. "But he should have asked my advice in the first place. I would have found other and better ways around these problems. I know so much more than he will ever know. Male, give me the letter to sign. Must get the money for him. So, Zuñiga, something to eat and drink before you go?"

Carlos has not lost his usefulness. He is still a political force to be reckoned with. The letter he is sending to the Regent Juana will persuade the Cortes to provide more than ample funding for Felipe to maintain a standing army in the Netherlands. Perhaps Felipe will excuse his father's unsolicited support or interference on this occasion.

Diplomacy

I

We have received sad news; such sad news, very sad. Admittedly everyone had expected it but it still came as a shock. The king has been devastated, sinking into black depths of melancholy.

The death of his sister Leonor has reminded him of his own mortality. He is continually dwelling on the morbid assumption that the eighteen months difference in their age will be exactly that which separates them from the grave. Such maudlin thoughts are most upsetting for those around him.

But, good news, his sister Maria has arrived, and Gaztelu is back with us, and once condolences have been exchanged I am sure we will see quite a change in the atmosphere.

Do you recall Carlos offering his two sisters lodging here for a while that Leonor might recuperate? Maria has decided to accept the invitation. She has one of the apartments on the lower floor. Personally, if I were Maria, I would find the honour of staying in close proximity to a dear brother quickly offset by the discomfort of such miserable accommodation. Those rooms are bad enough in summer, but in the heart of winter they must be intolerable. They are dark, dank, and more reminiscent of cellars than bedchambers and retiring rooms. She could not be offered one of the guest rooms adjacent to the new cloister as that area is

261

strictly the domain of gentlemen. Perhaps as compensation, and in a rare show of generosity, Carlos has given his sister the most beautiful quilt I have ever seen. It might just fend off the bitter night air, and she could wear it around her shoulders throughout the day should she find herself having to spend any time in those apartments.

Have you noticed that everyone is dressed in black? Carlos insisted the whole household, from the highest to the lowest in his service, should be in deepest mourning. To many it may not be their favourite choice of colour but, consider this, the clothes are new and not hand-me-downs; a rare experience for most.

The door to the king's bedchamber opened and a priest flew out as if propelled by the bellowing voice from within.

"And you can tell them all, every blasted one of them, to get on with their own business, for I will have none of it!" Carlos picked up the precious crucifix that was once his wife's, the one she had held to her breast at the time of her passing. He contemplated it for a moment before returning it to its place on the table at his side, barely controlling his fury. He fumbled with a pair of glasses, settled them on his nose then opened his Book of Hours, turning the pages until he got to the hours of the Virgin. The page showed the Holy Mother with the Christ child standing on Her lap, leaning against Her breast. This picture more than any other in the book could stir him to tender thoughts and reminiscences. He sighed and followed the words of the prayer, reciting, "*Orato beate Maria Virginus …*" then suddenly snapped it shut. "Regla, when will those damn priests learn, once and for all, that I want nothing to do with their blasted affairs? First they pester me to become one of them. Can you imagine it, me a monk? Ridiculous. Now they try to insist I decide who is to be their new prior. Now, I feel as sorry as the next man that poor old Prior Tofino is dead, God rest his soul, but I could not give a damn one way or the other who

262

takes his place. They give me no peace. The whole affair has completely ruined my prayers this morning; put me in a bloody bad temper!"

Regla winced at the intemperance, "My lord, because of your sorrows you have misjudged the priests. Given time for reflection I think you will come to understand that they extended this invitation out of respect for any preference you may hold. After all, the duties of the prior do bring him into your presence a great deal. They realise it would be far more convenient for you to have someone to your liking rather than someone who perhaps you may not feel comfortable with."

"And I say I will not be bothered by such matters. I have heavier burdens on my mind."

"Perhaps, too, they sought to occupy your mind in this matter to ease your grief?"

"There is no more to be said!" Carlos warned his confessor.

Gaztelu entered, "You sent for me, my lord?"

"Of course I sent for you. I want to hear about my sister. You should know better than to keep me waiting," Carlos growled without offering one word of welcome.

"I ask your pardon. I came as soon as I could. The weather was so ... My clothing was wet and I was thoroughly chilled ... I took a few moments to change into something dry and warm ... At my age my old bones ..."

"I suppose if you had to, you had to. You may sit. Now tell me how it went. Get straight to the point."

Gaztelu sank into a cushioned chair allowing himself a second or so to enjoy its luxury.

"My lord, I arrived in time to speak with your sister, the Dowager Queen Leonor. Ah, the sweet, dear, gentle lady," he sighed. "Although weary of this world and tired of her own suffering she waited with patience and forbearance, as a true Christian, for her time to come and her gentle spirit to be released." He paused, remembering. "She spoke of her great love for you, made me promise I would emphasise its warmth and depth. She told me of the many joyous times she had spent with you when you were children. She recalled her increasing admiration for you as she grew into adulthood. Before she died she humbly begged that you would do one last favour for her;

and that is to protect her daughter, who is her sole inheritor. Yes, the young lady will receive considerable estates here in Spain and in France."

"Ah, so my sister still had trust in me?"

"Implicit, my lord."

"She said nothing about the bitterness she felt in her heart towards me when she was last here?" Carlos had been nursing the dread of some final, cold accusation from his dying sister's lips.

"There was never an unkind thought spoken, my lord."

With that resolved Carlos could address another important issue. "And did she confess those gross moral sins she committed in Portugal; cuckolding her husband, behaving like a whore?"

Regla swallowed hard, crossed himself and reached for his rosary.

"My lord all words spoken in confession are secret; your sister died a good Catholic, she went in peace to her Maker."

"Good, good. Hopefully our Lord God will look kindly upon her sinful lapses. But why did she die before I could see her once more?" he complained. "Why was I not allowed to be of comfort to her? There were so many things I wanted to say to her." Carlos sobbed inconsolable tears for his departed sister, and for the lost opportunity to play the role of sympathetic brother listening to her tale of grievous disappointment; something he had promised himself he would do rather well.

Gaztelu sat patiently and in silence with his master for a moment or two before suggesting he receive his sister Maria. "Sire, she wishes desperately to be with you, to share your grief. Indeed she has spoken of little else since Leonor died."

Regla leaned towards Carlos, "And I am here, my lord to offer comfort and support to you both. I shall gladly remain at your side." Hopefully there would be further information regarding Leonor's past.

Carlos nodded, "Yes, stay." He sniffed and wiped away the remaining tears, "I need to be dressed. Gaztelu, organise everything. No point in delaying the inevitable. I just hope she will be gentle with me."

The king will be some time before he is ready
to meet his sister Maria. I suggest we follow
Gaztelu to the Grand Salon where we will
find Quijada.

II

Quijada looked up from the papers he was studying and he
smiled. He pushed himself from his chair and came to greet his
friend.

"Gaztelu; welcome home! It is so good for this
much-harassed victualler to have his dear friend back again
and, I am glad to see, none the worse for enduring such a
journey in this dreadful weather. These incessant rains are
intolerable, every time I look out of the window all I see is
either a wet grey shroud or a curtain of slanting icy arrows. I
should not be complaining, you are the one who has had to ride
for hours in it. But what a relief it is that after days of my being
nothing more than a fishmonger I have you to enlarge the
world far beyond the boundaries of cod and herrings."

"It is good to see you too, my friend. Dear Lord but I have
been too much in the company of women recently."

"I had every sympathy for you and your undertaking. You
are a very selfless man, Gaztelu. How bad was it?"

"At times it was desperately sad. Poor Leonor's spirit was
quite crushed. The daughter, so dearly loved, had cruelly taken
her mother's hopes and dreams and trodden them under her
dainty little feet, before turning on her heel and rushing back to
Portugal. I had not thought to see Leonor looking so old, so
injured, so frail. It was almost as if life had already deserted
her. The doctors maintained that it was an attack of asthma that
killed her, but I would swear she died of a broken heart."

"And the king, what did you tell his majesty?"

"I made it sound as positive as I could, all peace and
tranquillity; her continued love for Carlos, and a dignified
departure from this world for the next. He received my report
with tears and a certain satisfaction."

"Nothing contentious, then?"

Gaztelu shook his head, "No. He tried to draw me on those
disagreements when Leonor was last here, about her marriages,

about that liaison she had in Portugal; but I would have none of it. However he is to meet Maria in a little while and she will not be so diplomatic. On our journey here she certainly made no secret of her feelings."

"She is still angry despite her mourning?"

"Angry? I would say furious and frustrated that she had never had the opportunity to support Leonor at those times in her life when she was most in need of a strong sister's help."

"Then she is the very medicine that Carlos requires. He has been weeping at the least provocation. He has been wallowing in tales of himself as a child, of 'little mother' Leonor, always there to straighten his little gold chain with its tiny gold lamb; ever at his side to ensure his little cap sat just right on his golden curls. As for that dreadful episode when he decided to abduct Catalina, taking her and leaving their mother alone and distraught beyond words; well can you believe he has rewritten that as a romantic tale with Leonor and her heart of gold in the role of some selfless benefactress setting the child free from a wicked and cruel parent. With the passing of each day he has likened her more and more to a saint, that Portuguese love affair quite forgotten. And he speaks of God calling him to join this blessed saint of a sister!" Quijada realised he had raised his voice. "I beg your pardon. But it really is getting out of hand. He will not be diverted from bleak despondency. Dear Dowager Queen Maria please succeed in doing what I have so patently failed to do."

"Cheer up," Gaztelu grasped him by the arms. "If I know Maria she will very quickly remind him of how he so mercilessly used his beautiful and gracious sister Leonor. She has repeated it often enough over recent days. She has fumed over Leonor's long and lonely life; the two appalling marriages, being forced to abandon the beloved daughter to return to do Carlos's bidding. I tell you, Quijada, Maria has ranted unceasingly about the senselessness of it all. She has even raised the tragic life of their other sister Isabel to reinforce her argument of how meaningless some lives are." A wry chuckle escaped him, "Regla said he would stay by the king's side. I think neither he nor the king will be overly pleased to hear some of her observations."

"Dear Lord, I had quite forgotten that sister; it must be all of thirty years ago. ZuZiga had a few dealings with her husband; he swore the man was crazy."

"All of Denmark knew he was crazy! More to the point, so did Carlos. Maria has been telling me many a tale. Fortunately, after many years of suffering, Isabel and her children at last found refuge from their tormentor with Maria in the old family home in Mechelin. Now," he looked about them to ensure they were alone, "Maria's big questions are: why was her sister Isabel made to marry someone crazy, and why did she then die so soon after her release from his physical and mental abuse?"

"That will certainly shatter his majesty's self-indulgent sorrows. My goodness me, the poor man will be torn between defending himself against her accusations of having used those two sisters' marriages to further his own interests, and terrifying himself over the safety of Maria's soul and thereby his own. He may well fear she is putting it in jeopardy for even hinting at questions such as why did God allow such things to happen, the more so if she is espousing such ideas in Regla's presence. We all know of his intolerance of the merest hint of freedom of thought, even amongst fellow priests. Did you know he actually accused one of them of being cunning enough to be a Lutheran. Too bad we cannot be with them to watch the performance."

Gaztelu waved his hands to dismiss the very idea, "Not for me, thank you, I have heard enough. I might find more interest in your fish."

He walked towards the window, where the rain lashed angrily against the glass. "Do join me over here. Listen to this," he whispered. "Maria told me this little anecdote about Isabel's daughter Christina."

"Hopefully she is not going to harangue Carlos about that arranged marriage, too, when Christina was, what, just twelve, to that doddering duke in his dotage?"

"No, nor about when she was offered to Henry VIII and she told him that she would only consider it had she been blessed with two heads, but as she only had the one, and she wished to keep it, she would decline."

267

"I believe that more than a little of Maria rubbed off on Christina while she was growing up under her protective wing."

Gaztelu whispered, "Evidently she has grown into an exceptional lady; beautiful, highly intelligent and, what is more, a very popular person in Felipe's court in Brussels."

Quijada leaned towards him, "So Ruy Gomez mentioned when he was here, he also said that Felipe had sent her to England as an ambassador to persuade Mary to insist that Elizabeth marry his cousin Savoy. Mary was not disposed to follow Felipe's suggestions, and a disappointed Christina returned to Brussels."

"And?" queried Gaztelu.

"And nothing except that now the Duque de Feria is continuing where she left off still trying to have the Princess Elizabeth wed Savoy."

"Ah, but, there is more." Gaztelu lowered his voice still further, his words almost inaudible, "Christina's other duty was to hand over a portrait of Felipe to Queen Mary. Would you believe that Mary destroyed it in a fit of jealous rage?"

"My word, Gaztelu. Are you suggesting that she suspects some romance between her husband and the fair Christina? Well, well, well, and here was I assuming it was a platonic relationship."

"It is said that he shows her rather more affection than a cousin should, and in public too."

"Poor Queen Mary, one does have to feel sorry for her. Life can be very cruel. Having lost any looks she may have had, she has been brought face to face with a beautiful young woman, who as ambassador is in regular close contact with Felipe; it is all too sad. I think we should stop there. We will allow Carlos and Maria a few more minutes then we can enquire if the king requires our presence. I can also inform their majesties of today's exciting Lenten menu; fish, then fish, followed by pickled sardines."

"Is that truly what we are reduced to these days, Quijada?"

Carlos need not fear for his son leading a dull life in the Low Countries. Christina is one of the many secrets that Gomez guards.

268

Maria has raised Christina to be a strong willed lady like herself. And so she remains a young widow with no wish to marry. She is quite a merry widow, too.

As for her and Felipe? They make no secret of delighting in each other's company. You might wonder, inasmuch as Christina is family, why Carlos did not consider Christina a suitable match for Felipe? The answer is quite simply because she does not possess a crown and Denmark is lost and gone. Such a marriage would bring neither wealth nor lands; so no wedding bells there.

I wonder if Carlos is surviving Maria's onslaught.

April

Tears

I

The halberds standing in the corner were naked, robbed of their tassels and looped ribbons of yellow, white, and red which now lay in dejected satin heaps. Escutcheons which until today had looked proudly down from their positions over doorways and fireplaces leaned against each other disorganised, undignified. Painted wooden two-headed eagles, castles, lions, all lay haphazard on the floor. Silver and gold plates, tankards, goblets, and cups with their splendid imperial insignia were piled high on the table while ever more pieces were brought from dressers and chests to join them.

"Remember to bring everything bearing his majesty's coat of arms," Male ordered the servant.

At that very moment Madame Male strode into the salon with Maria close on her heels. She halted in disbelief at the devastation before her.

Male turned to his wife to mutter under his breath, "It is preposterous that the king should want it all melted down."

"His majesty is to be persuaded by someone in this house, I think, not to do this dreadful thing. To destroy such work is a very bad action," she gave her husband a fierce look accusing him of neglecting this very duty.

"We can only hope, my dear. Perhaps when he has had more time to reflect? I hope so. So very sad; not only is it the destruction of the artisan's craft, it is the fact that his majesty wants his coat of arms wiped out, obliterated, as though they, he, are no more; no longer exist."

Madame Male dismissed the idea with impatience. "Maria, come here girl. Take his majesty's colours to my room, and please to give them the respect. Someone who allowed their putting on the floor did not give the respect," she glared once more in her husband's direction.

Maria gathered the tangled nests of ribbons carefully one by one into her white apron, hoping that this was showing enough 'respect' to the pretty bows and tassels that until a few moments ago had decorated those fierce weapons.

Ideas began to race as to how she might become the owner of some of the shiny red and yellow satin lengths that wanted to slide so delightfully through her fingers. If she worked extra hard, was more than obedient, Madame Male would surely give her some? On the other hand might she not simply borrow one or two for a while and no harm done? They could be put to good use on the hem of a skirt for the fiesta of the *noche de San Juan*. If the rider Miguel kept his promise to take her to Cuacos, a bit of bright yellow or red trim would make a dress look perfect for the occasion; she wanted to look her best. Madame Male had taught her to make oh so very tiny stitches with the finest of threads and smallest of needles to repair the linens – so different from the large, rusty, squeaky needles of those days in the past – and this skill she could so easily put to a better personal use.

Of more immediate concern was why the house was in such dreadful turmoil. It was disturbing. She closed the door behind her, running quickly to José and Samuel clutching her precious cargo.

"What's going on?" she demanded.

"Nothing, really." José opted for his 'years of experience and wisdom' voice. "His majesty's upset that's all. By tomorrow everything will be different, just you wait and see."

"Upset about what?"

"Seems it's all done and dusted, like. Made all proper."

"What's done and dusted?"

"I always 'as to explain everything; it's like this, you see, his brother is the emperor now. But seeing as 'ow he has been for ages it's not going to make one scrap of difference to no one. So you don't need to look so worried. It's just that it's finally hit him, his brother gettin' crowned and all that, and

271

he's takin' it a bit hard. He's like a big kid really if you wants to know the truth, gone right over the top, he has, bleatin' about being a nobody. Says that now he's no different and no better'n any of us."

Samuel leaned towards her, "So you see anything to do with him being an emperor has to be got rid of. Plain and simple."

Maria was angry. "That's just stupid that is! His majesty can't be anything different from the royal person he was yesterday, and taking these ribbons and things off everything doesn't change anything either. Just like the rest of us! Whatever next?" She stopped, her face blanching, stinging tears threatening her eyes. She bit her lip to stop it trembling. "Dear Mother of God, I hope all this isn't really because he, they, think he's going to die? He has been ill all winter, he has, and what with his sister up and dying, well you never know." She glanced down at the ribbons in her apron and thought how that would definitely put a cruel end to her dreams of the *noche de San Juan*.

José was about to offer something wise, but Maria's fear had changed to resolution. She was not prepared to allow anyone, not even the king, to spoil her arrangements. "José, someone should tell the king to snap out of this mood before things get really bad and it's too late." On no account could she allow that to happen. Something had to be done.

"I tell you what, Maria, you knock on his door right now."

He stood aside, pretending to usher her into the room, "Go in and give him a bit of your mind. That should sort him out, good and proper."

"Don't be so bloomin' cheeky. You know what I'm on about. The whole house has changed, gone cold, like, well not cold exactly, not with all the fires and all; but it's like it doesn't have a heart no more. It's just like someone has actually died and everything is piled up ready to be taken away; things that once was somebody's home. It's queer and scary, 'cause this is our home too, until ..." but she didn't want to contemplate anything so drastic as an end to her new life.

Yes, you find us a very sombre group today. Carlos once more is wallowing in self-pity;

nursing his hurt, grieving over his younger brother's lack of fraternal love. Goodness knows why he should have expected any; their relationship has always been strained to say the least.

It goes back many years to 1516 when Ferdinand's very existence posed a threat to Carlos inheriting the Spanish Crown. Basically Spain wanted a king who was Spanish born and bred, and that was Ferdinand, born when Queen Juana was in Spain to be sworn in as heir to the throne in 1503. The Spanish were also highly suspicious of Carlos, a foreigner. Carlos, not unnaturally, was deeply distrustful of his brother so, when he arrived in Spain, he wasted no time in despatching Ferdinand to Flanders to a new life far removed from Spanish politics.

And today's turmoil and disruption? News has recently arrived that on March 12th Ferdinand was crowned Holy Roman Emperor. It comes as no surprise, as young José was saying, we all know he had been de facto emperor for years; but it has opened up old wounds.

Shall we go to the small salon? I see Male is already on his way there.

II

Carlos, Van Male, Doctor Mathys, Quijada and Gaztelu were already there: Quijada reading over some papers; Doctor Mathys absorbed in a recently acquired book; Gaztelu fussing at the table checking the contents of the ink pot, inspecting his quills, the quality of his writing paper; Van Male simply waiting should he be needed for further acts of vandalism, as his wife would have it. The only sounds came from the ticking of one of Carlos's favourite clocks, the turning of pages and the shuffling of papers.

273

"Are you still not ready, Gaztelu? It takes you forever to get a few bits of paper and a couple of pens organised," Carlos grumbled at him from his gout chair.

"Almost ready, my lord, I apologise."

"None of this my lord nonsense! I am Don Carlos from now on, just as you are Don Martín and Quijada is Don Luis."

"Yes, as you say my lord. But at last I am ready."

"Good. The first letter is to my daughter. She is to make certain that all despatches to me in future will be addressed to Don Carlos, for I am nothing more, Carlos the emperor and Carlos the king no longer exist. The next letter is to order two new seals to be made bearing only the arms of Spain quartered with the arms of Burgundy. The eagle and the crown are to be removed."

Gaztelu settled his spectacles on the tip of his nose, dipped his quill in the ink and began his faultless calligraphy.

Carlos shuffled uncomfortably in his seat, his fingers tapping agitatedly on his knees. "What a damn miserable mess the whole affair has become. My brother, who should have had only love for me for all the favours I granted him, has always stabbed me in the back whenever he could. Because of my brother's scheming my poor son has been forced to watch me throw away so much of his inheritance and now makes no secret of blaming me. Dear God, but I have been sorely misjudged all my life. I have never received an ounce of gratitude for the countless ways I have helped our empire, our country, our family. I have devoted years to serving our people and the Faith. And all the while there have been those in my family sitting and waiting, like goddamn vultures, eager to snatch any scrap they could. I have been unable to do anything but stand by helplessly watching as my family tears itself asunder," he looked at Male for confirmation of this truth.

"Perhaps, my lord, you might wish to add these observations to your Commentaries?"

Male is assisting Carlos with his autobiography, or rather a book relating all his great deeds and acts during his reign as the Holy Roman Emperor, possibly as a

274

model for lesser mortals. This is something
else for Felipe to have destroyed.

He made as if to get pen and paper, but Carlos called him back.
"Not now man! And call me Don Carlos! Doctor Mathys, be a
good man and bring me some slices of ham, and some beer."

"Your majesty, if I may suggest, after all those weeks of
suffering, and now that you are finally recovering, you should
not allow yourself to ..."

"Doctor Mathys," Carlos snarled, "I am unsure which to be
the most bloody annoyed about, you calling me majesty or
your trying to give me advice. Let me tell you this, my man,
you are not permitted to suggest anything. You may be a
doctor, but you are of inferior quality. I chose you so that I
could give you my instructions and not vice versa. I want you
to remember that. Now get me some ham. Some people think
that just because I am no longer the emperor I cannot give a
simple command without its being questioned. If I can
remember my status, then so should the rest of you, for God's
sake!"

Quijada's voice cut across the scratching of Gaztelu's pen
and the ticking of the clock. "I truly fail to see the point of your
behaviour today! Good gracious, if this is the way you intend
to go on it is as well that you are no longer the emperor. You
are acting like a spoilt child who having had his favourite toy
taken from him retaliates with petulance."

Only the clock continued its steady tread, Gaztelu's pen
remained frozen above the paper, even Carlos's hand with its
cargo of ham stopped halfway to his mouth.

"My lord," continued Quijada, "someone must tell you,
and I am the best one to do so. The rooms, no doubt, by the end
of the day will show no traces of the plate, escutcheons,
halberds, canopies and flags, the symbols of your glorious
years as emperor; but it will be far more difficult to erase from
the minds of your servants the fears that their removal will
have caused. Some had thought you dying or even dead. I have
tried to explain the situation to them but there is still unease
and disquiet. And now you are behaving as a tyrannical ruler
towards those about you who seek nothing more than to be
your faithful and devoted servants earnestly desiring what is

best for you. Your words and actions offend or hurt those who love you most. My lord, this simply will not do!"

"How in God's name am I supposed to behave? And what about my feelings, how do you think I feel? My brother is emperor and he hates me, has hated me for years, even sided with my enemies. I dare you to deny it! No, you damn well dare not! You know as well as I he refused to send me help that time I desperately needed it." Carlos began to weep.

"Granted, my lord. We are all aware that there have been some very difficult times for you. But face the facts, sire; the size, the nature, the diversity of your vast domains had to bring about a natural division. It was too unwieldy to rule on your own. You had to enlist your brother's help years ago. And you must concede that the Germans have always been wary of Spanish power. If you are honest with yourself you will admit that it is only because of your brother's support that the empire has remained united for as long as it has."

"And he has taken advantage of everything! Not just for himself but for his son. My son has been left out in the cold." Tears of abject misery rolled down his cheeks.

"My lord, you know I always speak the truth, so hear me out. Your brother is favoured by the Germans. He is one of them, he speaks their language; correct? His son Maximilian was born there, they know him, they like him; is that not also correct? The very fact that they are German has kept the empire in the hands of the family, and the Imperial Crown far removed from a French monarch's head; true? By the way you do remember that it is an elected title and not inherited?"

Carlos glowered at him then sniffed, "I did everything for the empire, and when I asked Ferdinand to look after that side of things it was only supposed to be until he died when it should be handed on to my son Felipe."

"Heavens above, you did not listen to me!" Quijada threw up his hands despairing. "It is not the Hapsburg family's right to hand the crown to anyone."

Gaztelu pushed his spectacles up onto the bridge of his nose, blinking hard. Doctor Mathys clutched his book to his breast.

But Carlos still wasn't listening, "And my brother turned the Germans against my son. I heard their feeble complaints:

that Felipe cannot speak German, that he is distant and cold; whereas the wonderful Maximilian is perfection itself. I am convinced that Ferdinand bought their votes," he dabbed a handkerchief at his wet eyes and nose.

"Not an uncommon practice." Quijada retorted. "Need I remind you how once you, too, bought the German princes' votes?"

"They were damned lucky to have me as their emperor!" Carlos wagged his finger angrily.

"No one can dispute that. Why, you opened up new horizons to them. You made it possible for them to fight in the Netherlands, Italy, North Africa; and France."

"You are so damned sarcastic. All those wars were in a good cause, and you know it. How else could we have kept the damned Turk at bay? An impossibility without the reserves of the whole empire. And I still say my poor Felipe has been left with only Spain."

"Only Spain? You surely jest. Have we forgotten her vast domains, her wealth from the New World?"

Carlos burst into spluttering laughter, "And that blasted Pope Paul, doing me a favour at long last! Would you believe it? I never thought to see such a day. He refused to crown my brother! I like it, I like it very much! It went against his principles to put the Imperial Crown on the head of an emperor chosen by damned German Protestants. Oh, the satisfaction that gives me. Yes, I would like to remind my dear brother Ferdinand that I was crowned by a pope."

Quijada smiled, shaking his head. Carlos would never change. He thought that a little reminiscing might continue his master's lightened mood. "A pageant passed into history never to be forgotten; robes, cloaks and crowns encrusted with jewels, the heavens raining gold coins on the crowds. Such glorious days."

"Forget all that; too long ago." Carlos, determined not to be cheered, slipped back into despair. "I have allowed my brother to make a fool of me. Dear God, how I grovelled; I swallowed my pride and offered him the Netherlands if he would only return the empire to my son. I pleaded, promising him Italy in its stead. I made myself look ridiculous, and he turned a deaf ear. How he must have gloated."

277

Quijada sought to comfort, "Be more positive. Felipe has Spain as we have mentioned, and it must have slipped your mind that your daughter Maria is married to Maximilian, and one day will be empress and eventually, no doubt, her son will become emperor, then her grandson. These emperors are of your blood, my lord."

"Quijada, bless you, what would I do without you? My family! My grandchildren! Of course! And as you say Felipe does have enough to contend with. He will soon realise that he could not cope with the empire as well. Years ago, as usual, I saw beyond the short term, had the foresight to plan our family's future; a balance of Austrian Hapsburgs and Spanish Hapsburgs. We should celebrate; ham and beer!"

Quijada shook his head.

And there you have it; everything is in perfect order after all. And all due to Carlos's foresight!

Gaztelu, glasses back on the tip of his nose, dipped his pen in the ink, scanned what he had already written and resumed where he had left off. Doctor Mathys returned to his book. Quijada asked Male to have the servants gather in the large salon in readiness for the king who would join them in a few moments as proof that nothing had changed, and that they could rest assured that walls and fireplaces would soon have new shields and flags while some of the originals would be restored to their rightful places.

"I think you might also want all your servants to prepare for something, perhaps just a little out of the ordinary, my lord."

"I might, might I, Quijada? And what would that be? For God's sake, no guessing games."

"I have news to cheer you. DoZa Magdalena and the young Juan have arrived in Cuacos and will soon be coming to visit, if you so wish."

Carlos began to weep anew, but these were sweet tears of joy.

There is no doubting it, Felipe is furious. He wanted to inherit everything from his father. But from what you heard Ferdinand is decidedly the best choice, with the likelihood of Maximilian to inherit, or should I say be elected? And my goodness that is a far better option than Felipe followed by his son Prince Carlos. Unimaginable; that Prince Carlos should have any power anywhere is simply too frightening to contemplate!

For good or ill from this time on there will be the Spanish Hapsburg House, and the Austrian Hapsburg House.

July

Captive Audiences

José and Samuel stood either side of the door in the large salon. The room had never been so crowded, so lively. Everyone had come: the doctor, the clockmaker, the masters of the king's wardrobe and jewels, Regla the confessor, and the new prior along with a few favoured Brothers. Gaztelu and Male were also present with ZuZiga and Oropesa who had ridden over from their homes that morning that they, too, could participate in the afternoon's events.

A small group of musicians entertained them all as they stood in their small groups, buzzing with gossip; and waiting.

Along the entire length of the room ran a table heavily laden with savoury pastries, cream desserts, fruit pies and many other mouth-watering delights.

Carlos sat straight-backed in his chair; no hunched shoulders today. He had deliberated long and hard over which diamond and ruby brooches should be pinned to his bonnet and jerkin, determined to look his best; and of course there was his huge gold chain with the Golden Fleece laid over his shoulders. There was a jovial sparkle to his rheumy eyes, and a smile lifted the lines around his mouth as he listened to the music, music which he had taken such painstaking care in choosing; nostalgic music recalling those exciting years fighting for Christianity, for the empire, for Spain, for his pride. These were the songs of trampling the miserable enemy underfoot, triumphal marching and vengeful punishments, and finally those of the celebratory feasting as soldiers made war on bottles of wine and demolished sides of beef and whole hams.

José whispered across the space that separated them, "I tell you what Sam, we're in for a really interestin' afternoon."

"You're right an' all there José. What a change, eh? We finally get to see the two folk as what we've 'eard of for months. It's cheered the old king up no end. I mean, look at him. It must be ages since he looked this good."

"Aye, since Don Luis Quijada said as how he was definitely bringin' his wife and his lad the old feller's never looked back, 'as he?"

"Although, I'll tell you something," José checked that no one was within earshot, "this lad what Quijada's taken on has got me thinking, you know; whose kid do you reckon he is? He might be Felipe's, they say as he's always 'aving a bit on the side, like. What do you think?"

Samuel grinned, "You're askin' me? You're the one with all the brains. You're supposed to be comin' up with all the answers."

"He might be his and I'll tell you for why. This person what we're going to see was just a village lad like you and me, right, till the day he goes to live with Quijada and he changes, all of a sudden like, into a little gentleman. Now does that sound like he's a ordinary kind of kid? Smacks more of royalty to me."

"Heck, by that reckoning he could be," Samuel's eyes grew large with wonder, "José; you don't think the old king himself is the …?"

"Now that's just plain stupid. You get worse, have you learned nowt from me? The king wouldn't have dumped him in a village, all his kids got settled somewhere rich, well, except for that one what got put away in that convent, and that would take a bit of paying for. Now, let's put our thinking caps on; we has to remember that this kid was born in Germany. Who was there at the time?"

"He might well be Felipe's, then, 'cause he was over there somewhere so Alonso says. Hell's teeth! I've just had a thought! He is probably Quijada's kid and Quijada's just pretending to look after him for someone else, and it's a lie he's doin' somebody a favour. He was there, José."

281

"Sam you never cease to amaze me. Now honestly, can you just see Don Luis fooling around? He's just not that kind of chap."

"What kind d'you have to be then? I thought all chaps, given a chance … Still don't answer the question as how come the kid ended up living with them peasants."

"They wasn't peasants, Sam, the kid was living with a musician feller and his wife."

"Beats me, it does. Hey up, there's somebody comin', I can hear their voices. It's them, José. Here we go."

We are all going to be treated to a very different afternoon, not only José and Samuel, but the guests too; but most of all Carlos.

The music ceased. All conversations stopped, all attention was centred on the small group who had entered. Quijada, proudly wearing new lace cuffs and collar, made entirely by his wife, led his little family into the room. Madame Male followed enjoying her role for the afternoon of official attendant to the beautiful guest of honour, Doña Magdalena.

Quijada approached Carlos and bowed, "Sire, DoZa Magdalena de Ulloa and the child Don Juan await the pleasure of your granting them an audience."

Carlos knitted his brow then laughed, "You are so damned formal! I am too old, too impatient for such games. Bring your good lady wife over here to me."

Every eye was upon her, the dark haired DoZa Magdalena in her mulberry coloured brocade dress, tall and slender, possessing loveliness never before witnessed within these walls of Yuste. No one was left untouched by her natural elegance, the dignity in her step, the grace and ease of her three deep curtsies.

"Your majesty I am deeply honoured," her voice fell on their ears like divine music.

"Dear lady the honour is all mine. Quijada, I see now why you always wanted to be up and away from here. I would too. DoZa Magdalena de Ulloa, if you will excuse an old gentleman's boldness, may I tell you that you are the most beautiful lady I have seen in many a year; and you, Quijada, keeping her out of our sight, holding this charming secret from us all! But at last we have you here with us. I thank God that he managed to arrange everything so that you could live in Cuacos. I hope everything is to your liking."

"We are gradually making it our home, although I do admit to missing the castle in Villagarcía where there was so much space and light. To be with my husband, however, is far more important than where we live."

Carlos studied Magdalena, a lady descended from the most powerful of families, the Ulloas, Osorios, and Toledos, who was prepared to make such a huge sacrifice. "Excellent sentiments, ma'am; how lucky of Quijada to have someone like you to care so much. And let me tell you, he is a changed man ever since you arrived. He was often grumpy and sour, even unkind to me on occasions; a bully, ma'am."

DoZa Magdalena's brown eyes widened amazed that her husband should dare.

"I tease you dear lady, you were not to know that your husband and I are like brothers. But come closer for I want a quiet word. Come, sit by me." He pointed to a chair at his side then motioned to the musicians, "More music, please."

A recorder, harp and viola de gamba accompanied a small group of singers as they sang first of new dawns and new loves, then of a heart's longing to be taken captive, then for a soul to be governed, and another of the joy of a kiss that seals a vow. They were all Barbara's songs; today Carlos was intent on fully indulging himself.

Carlos leaned towards Magdalena, "How do you feel about the boy; his being brought into your life?"

"Your majesty I love him dearly. He is everything I could ever have wished for, prayed for. Perhaps it is difficult for men to understand the desperate longing of a childless mother, the deep emptiness hungry to be filled. My heart aches for the lady in the village who had to part with him, but I thank God that He gave him to me; and he is a good child."

"A good child. Tell me more."

"He is a clever child and learns easily, although, like many a boy he is not always eager to go to his studies," she smiled. "His reading and writing are progressing well, due mostly to the writings of Don Luis de Zuñiga y Avila and not to his primer; war stories are far more inspirational than prayers or texts. His Latin continues at a comparatively slower pace as a consequence although my chaplain is more than satisfied. I have noticed a marked improvement in his French and also his lute and vihuela playing." Now she laughed nervously, "Forgive me, that was not what I had intended saying. I sound like one of his tutors making his report. Your majesty everyone in our home loves the boy for his gentle manners, his consideration, for his constant openness and honesty. As for the rest, I am sure my husband has kept you informed of Juan's delight in riding, fencing, hunting ..." Magdalena stopped; everything had tumbled out so quickly; had she been fair to the boy, had she omitted anything, had she said too much, had she been too eager to impress?

"And you, what of you Doña Magdalena? Tell me, might it not prove too heavy a charge on your feelings, not knowing the boy's background, his parentage? Be honest with me."

She swallowed hard, "My lord, I must admit to you that I have had moments of suspicion, and yes, of jealousy. May God forgive me."

"Ah, I wondered."

"For some time it was difficult for me to accept the boy given no explanation other than that he was the son of an eminent man, a dear friend of my husband, and that I was to care for the child as though he were my own. I have always known my husband to be honest in everything he does. There is none to better him, and I do have every trust in him, and yet I am ashamed to confess to being overcome by doubts and fears, suspecting there was some truth he was hiding from me, something too dreadful for me to bear. And then there was the fire ..."

"Good God in Heaven!"

She smiled to dispel his alarm, "It was a few years ago and Juan had not been long with us. It was not as serious as the servants first supposed; a minor incident as it turned out, but the alarm had been raised. My husband burst into my bed chamber, snatched up Juan from his truckle bed and rushed with him from the building. It was not until he had him safely in his squire's keeping that he returned for me. What was I to think? Why was the child more important than me? That prompted me to remember his fury regarding the child's circumstances with the musician's family, to remember some letters he concealed and would never discuss. Was the child really his? I had to tell my confessor of my fears."

Immediate regret at what she had just said consumed her. If only she could take back the words. Why had she laid her soul bare? What had possessed her to divulge her innermost thoughts? Carlos was neither her husband nor her confessor. He was, however, the king and must be told even if he was the one with the most influence over the child's real father. What must he think of her, what would he do now?

"I can assure you that Quijada is not the father of the child; you must have every faith and trust in him and everything he is doing."

"That is what my confessor said. He advised me to set aside all unworthy and unseemly notions, declaring that God would determine the right time for my husband to disclose the child's identity."

"Exactly. And that spiritual advice will be enough?"

"Oh yes, my lord; and I have begged my husband's forgiveness for my weakness. I think now on all the good that God has granted me. The boy fills the void I once had in my breast. My days are filled with a joy I would not otherwise have known. I am a most fortunate lady; at last I am a mother. My lord, I am the happiest of women."

She hoped she had vindicated herself by being completely frank, would still be seen as the only possible mother for Juan. But she was plagued by doubts, and waited for the king's verdict. If Juan were to be taken away from them it wouldn't only be the pain of separation it would mean shame and ignominy for her husband. She, who was always so confident, so self-assured, had shown herself as a weak and miserable failure. This day, meant to be so wonderful, had gone entirely wrong. She wanted to weep. She waited.

Carlos reached for her hands, clasping them into his, "The lad is fortunate to have found such a mother, while you and Quijada have the blessing of a son that God could not give you in another manner."

Doña Magdalena sighed her relief. She should have remained quiet but instead went on, "But I must admit to something else which may disappoint the father; we have failed in not ensuring that the boy will enter the priesthood. It is a life of soldiering that awaits Juan."

Carlos drew her hands closer to his chest, chuckling, "So I have heard, but looking at the lad I cannot believe for one moment his true father would or could have any reservations whatsoever about the way you are raising the boy. And let me tell you there is a lot to be said for soldiering, and if he grows up to be anything near as good as Quijada, he will be one of the best. Now I think I should meet this young Don Juan."

Magdalena rose, curtsied and moved aside.

Quijada clasped Juan by the shoulders giving him some last minute encouragement for what could prove an ordeal, reminding him that he would have to concentrate as he had never concentrated before in order to understand the king. He smiled down at him; this little knight of his was still after all just a little boy, and he wished he could have found some excuse not to bring him, to avoid putting him through this. It was some consolation that Carlos would prefer to listen rather than speak, only too keenly aware of his lispings and slurrings. With a final pat to Juan's shoulders and a whisper that he would be close by should he need assistance Quijada nudged him forward then went to his wife's side to watch him, their son, approach Carlos.

Juan made three deep bows, sweeping his bonnet wide to the side then down to the floor and up across his chest. He then knelt before Carlos who had inspected every inch of him as he approached. He had scrutinised the dark blue velvet jerkin and padded breeches, the dark blue bonnet with its solitary silver brooch, the fine show of linen at his neck and wrists and he silently congratulated Magdalena. He had noted the proud bearing in Juan's stride, recognising Quijada's influence, and now with the young man at his feet his thoughts centred on the handsome face with the honest blue eyes, the high forehead, the blond hair curling about his temples.

"Stand up, let me look at you. Come closer. Good God, what the devil is that, there on your cheek?"

286

Doña Magdalena's hand searched for Quijada's. Everyone's gaze centred on Juan. Juan stood shamefaced, his fingers moving quickly to hide the wound. He didn't wish to cause trouble for his parents, but he also knew that he had no option but to tell. Hesitantly he began, "Your majesty, I got myself involved in some trouble in the village." He swallowed hard then dashed headlong into his explanation wanting to get it over and done with as quickly as possible. "I hate to say it, but the truth is I climbed over a wall into someone's orchard where I helped myself to an orange, the owner saw me and I fled under a hail of stones. One of them hit me," his fingers returned to his cheek, to the scar. The stream of words finished, he hung his head.

DoZa Magdalena and Quijada held their breaths. Were all Magdalena's dreams and aspirations of winning the king's approval still to be dashed because of their boy's regrettable lapse? They had known when he first came to them that, along with the other village children, fruit stealing had been one of his sports, that and the use of catapults to kill small birds. He had been told that such behaviour was unacceptable, and he had never repeated the crimes all the time he was in Villagarcía; yet the other day in Cuacos, it had happened again.

The whole room was listening, had heard every word.

Gaztelu, who knew beyond question that the voice always revealed the true soul, nodded his unwavering approval of the boy despite this disclosure.

The other gentlemen struggled to remain serious remembering their own errant ways when young.

Madame Male folded her arms tight across her flat chest, not doubting for a moment this child's good character; she was an excellent judge and had never been wrong. She muttered, "The good behaviour she is still there beneath what is only a little wandering away from that good. Boys they are like this and require only a clip of the ear."

However, it all depended on Carlos, whatever his opinion they would all naturally concur.

Carlos looked at Juan sternly, "And what did you do then?"

"Sire, I went to the man's house to apologise. Then I returned home knowing I had to tell my mother. She was mightily angry with me, but not as angry as my father, Don

287

Luis. Sire, believe me, I have promised them both I will never ever do such a thing again, and I really do mean it."

"Come here," Carlos whispered and Juan drew closer to the mouth with the saliva gathering in the corners. "Boys will be boys. I expect your father did the self-same thing when he was a lad. I certainly did, even if they were my own apples that I climbed over walls to steal. However," he raised his voice for everyone to hear, "this is not good enough, we never want to hear of such behaviour again, you understand?" He turned to Quijada. "We all know it would be a sorry sort of lad who never got into such a scrape, and I know what kind of rascal he was when he came to you. He tells me he has promised it will never happen again so we shall say no more." He smiled at Magdalena, "No more worries of that sort for you, my lady. I can see he is a good lad at heart."

As expected, everyone was in total agreement and the matter was closed. More importantly Magdalena's silent prayers had been answered.

Carlos shuffled about in his chair. "Where is Regla, I want him."

Regla emerged from the small group of gossiping priests and Carlos sent him off on an urgent errand.

"ZuZiga, over here quickly; would you believe it, he prefers learning to read using your books. Now then boy, since you read this gentleman's books in preference to your primer, perhaps you would like to tell him what it is that makes you like them so much."

Juan looked at the author of his favourite tales, the retired cavalry man who still had traces of military about him despite his being, well, so old. "Sir, I never in my wildest dreams expected to meet the writer who stirs me so." Grinning from ear to ear he turned to his parents, "Father, you never mentioned I would actually see ...this is unbelievable!"

"While I never expected to find so young a reader of my works," ZuZiga drew up his slightly stooping shoulders. "Tell me more."

"Oh, sir, the accounts are so vivid, so real. I get impatient to turn the pages to see what happens next even when I already know. There is so much information that I am able ... Sir, I have made my own battle ground for the lifting of the siege at Pavia."

Carlos was overjoyed and called out, "Well I never! I want everyone to listen to this. Carry on lad."

For a moment Juan couldn't go on, he was embarrassed, but then remembered his beloved game; no, it was more than any game. "My armies are small blocks of wood, and I have marked out a piece of old linen to show the city, the park, the rivers and the roads. I start with the undercover breaching of the wall and night march into the park, drum sticks clicking to guide and encourage the men, and continue from there following your text word for word."

ZuZiga was more than intrigued, "And how do you keep track of your commanders?"

"Sir, my mother's sewing basket was the answer. I found all the colours I needed to make tiny banners: red for Lannoy, gold and white for Avalos, white for Bourbon, Vasto blue and gold, black for Alarcón ..." he went on, his excitement never allowing for any hesitation. He was a man amongst men, a boy amongst boys.

Carlos joined in, "What about your numbers, and which are horse and which foot?"

"Sire, I learned those by heart: Lannoy, two hundred lances, one hundred foot; Bourbon, three hundred lances; Pescara six hundred foot; then Quesada with his arquebuses ..."

ZuZiga shouted his joy, "What a student!"

Carlos slapped his thighs, "It is as if we were there, by Jove. I tell you ZuZiga he will be as good as you at telling the story. Well I never! But here comes the big test. Do you know Pescara's speech to his starving, unpaid men?"

"Sire, I recite it to my men every time we give battle to the French."

They all laughed at his youthful enthusiasm, wishing they had been invited just once to join him on his linen battleground, lying stretched out on their fronts, chins cupped in hands awaiting the call to mobilise their 'men'.

ZuZiga silenced them then bowed to Juan, "Sir, we are your soldiers awaiting your rallying call."

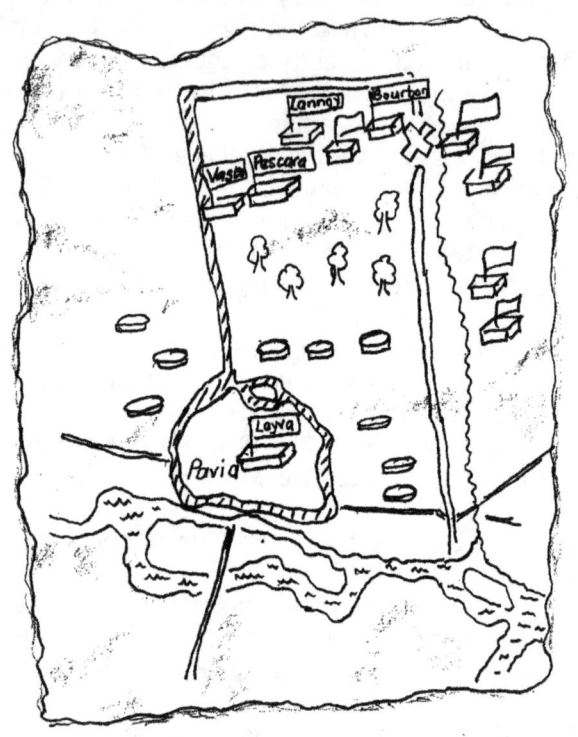

Juan's Plan of Pavia

🏳 Imperialist troops
🔵 French troops
✖ Breach in the wall

Magdalena smiled at the one—time urchin who had grown into the self-assured eleven-year-old at ease in the company of these illustrious men, speaking knowledgably, yet with deference. She felt her heart might burst with love and pride. For Juan this was nothing short of a miracle; before him stood a real army of men instead of the linen sheet with its wooden blocks of make-believe troops. He placed his feet slightly apart and put his hands on his hips. His blond head was held high, his eyes were afire, "*Of all the earth, only that which is beneath your feet can you consider your friend, all else is against us ...*" and so he continued, not one word omitted from the famous speech, "*... there is no bread for tomorrow, except in the French camp over there. Some of us saw what they had when we went there to spy ... such an abundance: bread, wine, meat, fish ... In effect, my brothers if we wish to eat tomorrow, then that is where we must go ... Is that the way it appears to you? Tell me for I must know your will.*"

"Bravo, bravo," applauded Carlos. This was immediately taken up by everyone, accompanied by several hurrahs. Juan blushed scarlet and his cheeks burned.

Carlos beckoned to Male. "We must show him the original battle plan. Let him see how it compares with his linen sheet. Set it out in the other room ready for the lad. In the meantime he should see the tapestries. Quijada, I wonder how much Juan knows of that battle." He sat back in his chair and closed his eyes relishing again the young lad's performance.

Father and son walked over to the magnificent wall hangings made at the Dowager Queen Maria's request by the very best of artisans in Brussels.

Quijada put his arm around Juan's shoulders. "You did remarkably well, Juan. You certainly impressed your troops. Now, these tapestries commemorate the battle of Tunis. You remember our talking about it? There you see the fleet under the command of the High Admiral Doria. This part here shows our troops attacking the city, over there the Turk are fleeing into the desert, and those are the thousands of Christian slaves set free by his majesty."

"Sir, how splendid to have beaten them so soundly. How I hope to follow in your footsteps one day to fight off the warring hordes of heathen Turk." Juan pointed at a soldier lying wounded but still clinging to his sword, his horse fallen at his side, "Could that be you? And, over here, this dying man, is that your brother?"

Quijada smiled down at him, "I doubt that the artist ever considered any particular individuals when designing his work; but it is nevertheless an interesting thought, to be immortalised in such a way."

Juan looked a while longer then turned to find the king's eyes were upon him, "Your majesty I wish more than ever to be grown up so I can join the Spanish army."

"And what do you think of my portrait over there?" Carlos beamed with anticipated pride at the boy's reaction to the Titian painting.

Juan looked across the room at the enormous painting on the far wall, "Sire, I am sure I recognise it from the story my father told me. This must be the painting to celebrate Mühlberg. May I take a closer look?"

"Of course. Chair lads, over here. Take me to Mühlberg." Carlos chuckled, "My steed has changed to one with four wheels, but my heart is as young as that fellow's on the charger."

Samuel and José pushed the rattling chair across the tiles.

"So, my young man, what do you see?" Carlos waited impatiently for Juan's verdict on this painting of him in his prime.

"Sire, I see you on your black stallion ready to lead your troops into battle, your lance pointing the way. You have crossed the Elbe under cover of fog. The grey mists have lifted and you are face to face with a startled enemy. The Elector of Saxony and his army will soon flee your gallant men. Their losses will be many whereas yours will number no more than fifty. Sire, if only I could have been there; I would have moved Heaven and earth to follow such a fearless commander."

Carlos had never felt so well in months. "Aye, you know my battles well enough. Did you all hear what this young man said; moving Heaven and earth to be under my command?"

José whispered to Samuel once back at their place by the door, "Moving Heaven and earth, and knowing all about his battles! I tell you what; I bet Carlos is not goin' to allow any talk of

Metz. He didn't do such a good job commandin' there, did he? Mind you, in this Mühlberg picture he does look a pretty fierce soldier."

"Yeah, but Alonso said Metz was completely different, said he was hopeless there. Kept his men hanging around for months in the middle of winter, half of them dying of sickness and starvation; Alonso said they lost thousands and thousands."

"He also said it was cos the king had no flaming idea what was going on outside his tent; too busy having tantrums and playing with clocks."

Quijada, hearing the name Metz threw a severe, reproving glance in their direction then walked briskly towards them. "Did I hear you mention Metz?" He was angry but he kept his voice low to avoid attracting anyone's attention.

"God, he heard." Samuel choked.

José, rarely at a loss for words, gambled on the ploy that Quijada had obviously misheard. "No sir, we were talking about a dress, Maria's dress for the *noche de San Juan*, about how she'd fretted about not getting any of them bright ribbons, the king's colours what were going to be thrown away, to pretty it up like, and how it didn't make no difference anyway 'cause the rider from Jarandilla never showed up to take her. We'd been teasin' her something rotten and now we feels badly."

"I am sure I heard you mention Alonso and Metz."

"No, sir, we was just saying as how Alonso told us that the rider feller had left Jarandilla; gone home 'cause his father had got sick and died." José looked as wide-eyed with innocence as he possibly could.

Quijada shook his head, swallowing his wrath, deciding to ignore the lad's lies. Those dreadful tales of the Metz disaster were certainly tales best forgotten. "This is not the first time I have caught you gossiping. Fortunately for you I will do nothing more than remind you to hold your tongues, I do not intend to spoil the day for anyone."

Carlos called out, radiating delight, "I have never had such a day. Doctor Mathys this young man has given me medicine far better than any of yours. I think I shall be going riding with this

293

young man before too long. But perhaps that is enough for today, best not to overdo things. I am tired."

Regla came to his side, "You asked for this, your majesty."

"Ah, just so. Come here, young man. I know that you have learned to read and write well using ZuZiga's books, but that is not good enough. I insist you pay more attention to your Latin. To help you here is a new primer for you."

The book had a worn, green velvet cover trimmed with delicate gold embroidery. It was fastened with thinning yellow satin ribbons. Juan set it down on a table to untie the bows then fold back the faded and crushed velvet.

"That Book of Hours is over fifty years old. It once belonged to my mother, Queen Juana. Her likeness is in the Hours of the Virgin; yes, it shows her kneeling next to her patron saint, San Juan. A devout lady, my mother, very devout," he shot a guilty glance in Quijada's direction who nodded his understanding. "You must promise me you will be more determined in your studies, and that you will treasure this book."

"Your majesty, how can I thank you enough? This is too great an honour." Juan knelt before him, "I solemnly swear that I shall apply myself more and I shall keep this book safely by my bedside next to my other special gift; my partly burnt crucifix, my Christ of the Battles. Sire, the Turk had thrown it onto a fire but my father, Don Luis Quijada, rescued it."

Tears welled in the king's eyes, "I remember it well. Quijada, we have a Christian soldier here in our midst. By God, yes! Make sure you bring Juan to see me again very soon."

"My lord, I am pleased that you are content with the lad."

"Refreshments for everyone! Quijada, a private word." He turned to Juan chuckling mischievously, "How would you like a bowl of cherries, and without having to climb a wall to pick them? There are cherries and lots more on the table. Help yourself. Off you go."

Such a day! You remember my mentioning celebrating the birthday of another person on the same day as Carlos, someone rather special? Perhaps you do not; it was more than a year ago. I will tell you now that it is

294

this young man, Juan, who shares that day;
and I think you must agree he is rather
special.

August

Making Decisions

I

Samuel and José waited on the covered terrace sitting on the flagstones and leaning idly against the wall, gentle splashings of crystal droplets in the newly installed fountain, the latest of Torriano's innovations, adding to the air of general indolence. The king's chair stood nearby, empty. There would be nothing for them to do other than talk and laze in the shade, deliciously whiling away the afternoon; today Carlos was finally fulfilling his desire to go riding with the young Juan.

After dispensing with more general gossip, Samuel finally introduced his most important question. It was a query he had been guarding for the right moment for it deserved time and opportunity to be explored fully and at leisure instead of via the usual snatched furtive whisperings. Today, now, was the moment.

"So, José, have you made your mind up whose kid he is then?"

A short while ago Samuel had been standing quite close to Juan and had given him as thorough a scrutiny as he dared as he watched him mount his mule to ride out with Carlos. What he would have given to be either Alonso or Manuel who were accompanying them! He would have so much time to study him close up. The boy stood tall; looked strong; was handsome with blond curly hair; he spoke proper, looked every inch like he properly belonged to a rich family.

"I don't know, Sam, I just can't fathom it. I mean, if he is royal, where's the family chin? They all have it, more or less:

296

Carlos more, Felipe less, and the Prince Carlos somewhere in between. No, let's face it, this lad's too bleedin' good looking to belong to the king's family. I'm still working on what you said, like his being Quijada's. But no, I can't see him having it off, he's not the sort, and then deciding a few years later to look after him, not when he'd just got married, an' all, and to such a beauty. Nah; but then, if not him, who?"

"Well I changed me mind on that. He's nowt like Quijada. And don't forget this kid's a foreigner, a German. So the way I sees it now is, the king knew somebody important over there who had this kid what shouldn't have had and decided to do him or her this favour, and keep it really hushed up, like, in a place no one would suspect. That's why they chose a little village what no one knew even existed. How about his sister, Queen Maria?"

"Nah, Sam, she's a bit long in the tooth for that sort of carryings on; in fact so's just about everyone we can think of."

"Well maybe that Princess Christina; I heard as how she was, you know, with Felipe a lot, she sounds a bit of a ..." he stopped short and leapt up, "Hey up. What the heck! They're coming back already, just when we was getting started. What's gone wrong now? I'd better shout for someone to get Quijada and the others."

He rushed to the door, pushed it open, and called to unseen servants to prepare for the king's unexpected return. He straightened his black tunic then brushed the dusty seat of his breeches with his hands. José did likewise and then they checked each other.

Manuel was walking alongside the king's mule, a steadying hand on the bridle. The moment Carlos had growled in pain he had leapt down from his own mount to guide the faithful one-eyed creature. He led it slowly up the slope where he, Samuel, and José freed the royal feet from the stirrups and gently levered the king up and out of the saddle. Despite their care every move was proving an agony to Carlos. Stabbing pains, worse than any enemy's dagger, plunged and twisted in every part of his body. He was under a fearsome attack from everything that plagued him: haemorrhoids, the arthritis in his neck, arms and legs.

"Damn and blast these pains! Not even able to bloody ride any more. Godammit!" He muttered and cursed at his agony and frustration. "Sorry young Juan, but if you want to be a soldier you may as well get used to soldiers' language; just never go repeating it to your father, or I will be in serious trouble," he put a finger to his lips.

With the help of Samuel and José he hobbled the few paces to his chair to rest against it for a while offering some respite to his burning backside. He apologised to Juan who had dismounted and come to join him. "I have let you down badly. What can we do to make up for it?"

Male and Doctor Mathys arrived, breathless, to discover much to their relief that their master had not been taken seriously ill as had been suggested by the calls of alarm.

Carlos growled, "Before you start, I want no fuss from you two. There is no problem except the old one; pains everywhere. Blasted nuisance, means I cannot ride, and now the boy will be disappointed."

Juan felt relief rather than disappointment. A ride on a mule was only a ride on a mule after all, and in any case he preferred palfreys or at the very least ponies. Now, with a couple of hours to spare and goodness knows what discoveries to be made in the small salon, this would be infinitely better.

It would have been preferable had bad weather been the cause of their interrupted ride rather than the king's ill health. First it had been a shock and then he was scared by the king's distress. Never had he known an adult cry out so, nor seen a grown man crumble under the weight of pain. As he watched Carlos recovering he wanted to tell him that it was of no great importance that their outing had been curtailed, but he didn't know how without possibly embarrassing someone as important as a king, so he mumbled a few words that he hoped would suffice.

"Perfectly alright sire, another time if you would allow."

The king shook the supporting shoulders of Samuel and José, suddenly laughing. "I know what we can do. Male, bring me the parrot." He winked at Juan, "You will enjoy this."

The hooded cage was quickly found and placed on a table on the terrace. Carlos was helped into his chair and trundled

298

towards it. He removed the cover to reveal the parrot in its full glory of red, orange and green.

Samuel and José whistled with delight.

"Did you ever see such colours? They's so much brighter out here, aren't they Sam."

Juan's blue eyes grew larger and rounder in wonder. "Sire, what a beauty; I have never seen anything like it."

"And not only is he a pretty bird, he is very clever. Gather round, as close as you can." Carlos waited till they were settled then told his parrot, "This young man here, Juan, knows all about King Francis, especially at Pavia. Now I want you to tell him what you think of Francis. Let me get you started; Francis, Francis ..."

The black, hooked beak opened, the head bobbed up and down, the scaly claws danced and sidestepped along the perch, squawking, "Francis is froth and feathers; Francis is froth and feathers. Blasted liar, blasted liar, awwh ... froth and feathers ..."

"What do you think of that then?" Carlos beamed.

"Holy Moses!" Samuel cried out, he and the rest of the small audience were impatient for more.

"This is even better. There was this priest called Luther who was a thorn in my side for many a year, inciting God-fearing people to break from the Catholic Church. Have you innocent lads ever heard of him? You can be assured that he was evil. Now then, my pretty one, tell us what you think about Luther and his followers; Luther, Luther ..." he pushed his face close to the bars of the cage.

The parrot squawked, danced another bobbing dance, "Awwh Luther, Luther, awwh burn all heretics, burn all heretics ... incestuous bastard, incestuous bastard ... married a nun, married a nun ..."

Juan slapped his thighs and giggled. The chair boys nudged each other amazed, fascinated, cries of, "Yeah; gawd almighty!" exploding from both of them.

Carlos revelled in their delight. "This is my favourite. Right, my pretty one, tell us, what do you think of Pope Paul?"

Samuel and José exchanged glances of disbelief. Juan clapped his hands over his mouth.

First a rustling then a furious flapping of wings; next, a raising of one leg followed by a noise for all the world like the parrot was farting and then an enormous dropping splattered onto the floor of the cage. To hilarious guffaws the bird squealed, "Pope Paul is a duplicitous bastard, Pope Paul is a duplicitous bastard ..."

"My lord, I must protest," Quijada admonished, throwing the cover over the cage to stifle any further blasphemies.

Gaztelu and Regla hovered nearby, glaring their disapproval.

The fun was over. Samuel and José shuffled their feet, rearranged their tunics; waiting. Juan felt he had been caught doing something he shouldn't.

Carlos growled, "Quijada you are a killjoy every time. It was all good sport. And what harm is there in hearing the truth, you know well enough that the man is not to be trusted; a cheat and a liar; and, after all, if Juan is going to be a soldier?"

"There is more than enough to amuse Juan indoors. Male, go with Juan, have Torriano join you. The two of you will find countless items to interest him; the pocket clocks, maps, charts, astrolabes, compasses, books, mechanical toys. Anything; everything."

Juan disappeared into the house with Male, disappointed that the crude and vulgar entertainment had come to such an abrupt end, holding dear the images of the extraordinary bird. How he would have loved to have seen and heard more.

The chair boys retired some distance away.

Samuel scratched his head, "Bleedin' unbelievable, eh? A bird what can talk. What a bit of luck us being there, eh? And the little bugger can talk as good as the king. I bet if Quijada hadn't come along we could have heard some real choice words."

"And them stories, and that fart! A pity it was all cut short." José sighed. "Never thought about the king being ordinary neither; you know, making fun of important people. Bleedin' clever all them tricks."

When I asked you to arrive at this hour I did not intend your witnessing the outbursts of an uncouth bird; shame on Carlos for

300

teaching it such outrageous remarks. However, as I said, it was important that you were here for what is about to happen. News has arrived from Valladolid. Regla will explain, and believe me he is just the fellow to do it. The reactions of Carlos I am sure will be of equal interest to you.

As soon as Juan and the chair boys were out of earshot Quijada began and he was in a sour mood.

"My lord, Regla has been impatient to talk to you about recent events in Valladolid. The information he has will no doubt anger you, but I do urge caution. Regla, I beg you, do not allow your zeal to colour your report. Again, my lord, I ask you to consider carefully before taking any decisions."

Carlos, still smarting from Quijada's rebukes brusquely waved him aside. He joined Gaztelu who had shared his anxiety from the moment the confessor had spoken to them earlier, employing all the fervour of an inquisitor, about action which must be taken, and taken immediately.

"My lord," Regla began eagerly, "I have had some of my Brothers keeping a watchful eye and reporting regularly on events in Valladolid. I am afraid it is my painful duty to inform you that the seeds of Lutheranism have been firmly planted there. Yes, even under the very noses of the Regent Princess Juana and the Cortes. These seeds have taken root, and heresy has not only grown, it has blossomed!" He relished his bad tidings. "After all those years fighting the heretic wherever we found him hiding like a sneak thief, after our attempts to crush the Reformation where it dared to raise its ugly head, we find that our efforts have not been enough. It is my belief that from the beginning the punishments have been woefully weak, totally lacking in the necessary severity, and so have proved ineffectual, my lord. Our Christian tolerance has been our undoing, has become nothing less than an affront to God. He must be avenged. These men must be plucked from our midst and burned like pestilential weeds …"

Quijada broke in barely disguising his anger, "The truth of the matter is, my lord, a very small group of reformers has been discovered in Valladolid. Regla, I begged you to show some restraint, to avoid exaggeration."

Carlos fumed, "Blasted heretics, the lot of them! That blasted Luther, how could anyone have any credence in him or his words. A man not fit to mouth one word of God; he renounced his Holy Orders, persuaded a nun to throw off her veil and marry him. Incest, and yet people listen to the ranting of a man who commits incest."

"Perhaps profanity would be more ..." Quijada ventured a weary sally in a lost battle.

"If I say incest, then it is damned incest. I thank God we have discovered what is going on in Valladolid. I want the Inquisition to be ready to take action immediately. Gaztelu, you will write to my daughter. Tell her she is to follow my orders to the letter. I want all heretics who do not repent to be burnt alive; those who do repent will be beheaded. Every damned one of them is to be sought out and brought to justice! There will be no favour, no mercy granted to anyone. No trials, only judgements."

Quijada tried the voice of reason, "My lord, I beg you to consider further before demanding such harsh measures. Do you not see there will be those who find this an ideal excuse to be vengeful on those who may have offended them, or for others a way to rid themselves of people who stand in their way?"

Carlos ignored him, "Gaztelu, say that I want the axe taken to this root of evil before it has time to spread further. Write that if she does well she will have my blessing, and the Lord will look kindly on all she does hereafter. She had best see to it that my demands are carried out to the letter or I shall have to leave Yuste and attend to it myself. Dear God in Heaven, did I spend all those years fighting blasted reformists only to have the bastards turn up here in Spain? A black day, a very black day."

"Exactly, my lord; may I be the first to congratulate you on taking up the sword to champion the cause." Regla raised eyes filled with joyful tears to his God in Heaven, his hands clasped together in praise and gratitude for making this task, his mission, so straightforward.

Carlos was fired by a newly found enthusiasm, "I will not tolerate the True Faith being insulted by anyone. There will be no straying from the rulings of the Church, because they are not to be questioned. Anyone deviating from its doctrines, in whatever manner, is to be sought out and destroyed. I will not suffer any part of Spain to be contaminated by those not fit to be in our midst, to tread on the same earth, to breathe the same air. Make a copy of the letter to send to Felipe, it should encourage him to take similar action in the Netherlands. By God, but we will rid ourselves of them all. Get to it now. Regla will assist with any wording necessary for the duties of the Inquisitor General, Valdes."

Quijada begged once more for reason, "My lord, this is overreacting. You are promoting intolerance, encouraging bigotry. Again I say you are appealing to those who bear personal grudges and would find this a perfect opportunity to strike. You also alarm me greatly when you order that there is to be no defence. You must give this matter more consideration."

"Must? Regla is right, we have been too bloody lenient for too bloody long, and they have taken advantage, seen us as weak. I tell you, if we do not show strength now we are doomed. I say that from this moment no quarter shall be given!"

Gaztelu and Regla left together in silence; one deeply saddened by the task Carlos had given him, the other elated, euphoric.

Fanaticism is such a dangerous path to tread. People become blinded to all common sense in their desire to reach their goal.

Sadly this will prove counterproductive. The Inquisition and then the fierce bloodletting in the Netherlands will drive many thousands away from our Church, and a heavy shadow will hang over the True Faith forever.

303

II

Quijada handed Carlos a letter, "This arrived earlier, my lord."

It was quickly scanned then returned, "Good. It pleases me my sister Maria intends to go to the Netherlands to act as governor once more. This means that Felipe can visit us at long last. My eyes and heart long to see him." He paused for a moment. "You know if she changes her mind then Margaret de Parma will continue; she is a very clever woman, thinks for herself, a damn good Catholic. Lord knows I have been at the mercy of her temper a few times."

"And every time you were the cause," Quijada snapped welcoming the opportunity to stand once more on the side of reason and justice. His judgements on this matter were as sound as those he held regarding the Inquisition; this time, however, he had the comfort of knowing he had a better chance of winning his argument. "Remember, when she was still but a child of twelve, you had her marry that vicious, immoral reprobate Medici. And why? Because he was related to the pope and you thought that would be of use to you. The poor girl had to flee for her life. And then, after Medici was assassinated you married her off to a boy, no more than a child, who just happened to be yet another relative of the pope."

"The young madam had the insolence to write to me complaining about him. I told her she had to be quiet and learn to respect her new husband. Some women do not know their place and other women who do dare to challenge it."

"And it was only a few months ago that you tried her patience yet again, when you insisted on her young son marrying Leonor's daughter, who is well into her thirties and he only thirteen or thereabouts, almost the same age as Juan I might remind you. She had no intention of having him sacrificed to ease the problems between mother and estranged daughter!" Quijada applauded Margaret, another of the women in the king's family who had nerve, passion and resolution, able to stand their ground against Carlos when he was so obviously in the wrong and they so patently in the right.

Margaret's refusal to allow her son to marry Leonor's daughter had infuriated Carlos, and he had no desire to be reminded of the rebuff. "She never learned to have respect; for her husbands and more importantly for me, her father. It is all very well you criticising, but where would she be if it were not for me?"

"In the first place she would not exist; but having sired the child you felt it incumbent upon you to give the daughter of a respected Netherlands lady a home that befitted her station."

"And I recognised her as my child."

"Because your aunt gave you no peace until you rid the girl of the stigma of being a bastard. It was a young lady she was going to raise in her home, not some …"

"Get me some beer, Quijada."

Quijada laughed, "I always know when you realise you are about to lose an argument, my lord, you always request beer."

The Margaret they are referring to is a love child. She was the result of a short affair Carlos had in Flanders with a lady-in-waiting, one of the Van der Gheenst family.

Maria will not be going to the Netherlands as governor. No, sadly she will soon be joining her sister Leonor in Heavenly repose, God rest their souls. So the task will indeed remain with Margaret, and she will find herself thrust into the boiling cauldron of religious discontent and nationalism under which Carlos and Felipe, as you have just witnessed, are at this very moment stoking the fires and fanning the flames.

Carlos wiped his mouth, belched loudly and settled back in his chair. "Aye, I am a fortunate man."

"Fortunate in possessing the gift of moving from one topic of conversation to another with the ease and grace of a knife sliding over butter?"

"Quijada, one of these days, so help me I … No, I was thinking of Barbara. By God, such a girl. No idea why she came into my mind."

"Perhaps because she is another member of the fairer sex not prepared to be dominated by us when the only justification for our authority is that we are men?"

"I shall pretend not to have heard that. I was put in mind of that time in Brussels when she came striding into my bedchamber as though the place belonged to her. She was furious because someone had dared to try to keep her out. A few blasts from her and the room emptied, everyone scurrying like curs with their tails between their legs."

"Or falling like corn beneath her scythe of invective?"

"True, she was not one to mince words, would have made a good trooper. She let them know without any shadow of doubt that she was my doctor and nurse and that no one else was to set foot in the room until she said so, or else. And, by God, her remedies were better than any prescribed by those damned quacks."

"Which remedies would they be?"

"What are you insinuating, you old devil! I mean the vinegar and rose water bandages, and then her special oils. And what a difference it makes when they are gently and lovingly smoothed onto the skin by a woman with her body so devastatingly close." He smiled, "That is the only time I ever had a doctor slide into bed with me."

"And you swathed in your bandages, my lord?"

"Swathed in bandages, but we managed. That kind of medicine works every time, I can tell you."

"So my insinuation was justified, as I knew it would be."

"But all good things have their end. Not long after that Barbara became pregnant and she had to go."

"Naturally, that is the way of things, but we married her off to a good man, although she had hoped for better."

"He was on a damned decent salary," Carlos insisted.

"Barbara would have liked more, for services rendered shall we say?"

"Careful, Quijada!"

"She was most fortunate, you sent her to her mother for a while, with enough money to see her through."

"She had to be kept away from the court, had to be kept secret, too delicate a matter at the time. She understood."

Quijada shook his head remembering the newly-wed commissary, "Her husband was put out, poor chap, no sooner married than the beautiful wife was whisked away."

Carlos had no interest in how the man had felt. "A purse of gold soon helped him overcome his frustration. Anyway as soon as the child was born he had his wife returned to him."

"While I had to take the infant from its mother within hours of its birth."

"No other way to deal with the situation. Barbara has been well looked after. Not once have I let her down. I still see to her every wish."

"To the point where she now lives in luxury, and is extravagant beyond words. I have difficulty at times keeping up to date with her debts. And let me tell you she likes everything settled promptly, hates to be kept waiting. I am constantly besieged by her letters."

Carlos thought of Doña Magdalena's suspicions of Quijada's secrecy over Barbara's letters; it was unfortunate, but it couldn't be helped. "Barbara is worth every penny, every gift of mine, and you know it."

"You are right, my lord, forgive me."

"Yes, well, just as important to me is the child and his home. Dear God, but it very nearly turned out to be a disaster. I thank God you found out how bad things were. Just because Massy was sworn to secrecy about the boy's origins that did not give him license to raise him as a damned peasant. Good God, he was no peasant himself, he had been one of my musicians! A damn mistake that; what a fiasco."

"It was no fault of ours, my lord, we had been misinformed. If you recall we understood his wife to have inherited a much larger property than was the case. You know, it was amazing that I should only have discovered Juan's circumstances because Massy had always thought the child was mine. He had actually told his wife that I had no intentions of allowing the child's mother to raise him as a German, and therefore I wanted them to bring him to Spain. So, after Massy's death she had someone write to me, the putative father of the child, to inform me that she would require additional financial help if she was to continue to look after the boy."

307

"God works in a mysterious way, eh? Just as well she broke her silence, even if she had sworn an oath never to reveal that the child was not theirs. But everything has been set to rights." Tears were finding their way over the king's cheeks.

Even Quijada had to swallow hard, "Your son could not have a better home, my lord, nor, I swear, a better mother than my beloved wife, DoZa Magdalena. And we have a young soldier in the making."

"God has blessed us all then, Quijada. You understand this will continue to be our secret."

"My lips are sealed." Nonetheless Quijada nursed the hope that one day Juan would be publicly recognised as Carlos's child.

Quijada's cherished hope will be granted. This love child of Carlos and Barbara Blomberg, this handsome, intelligent boy Juan will become Spain's famous and best-loved military leader, the great tactician and brave hero of the sea battle of Lepanto where he gloriously vanquishes the Turk, saving Christianity once and for all from the dreaded infidel. Yes, he will be known throughout history as the great Don Juan of Austria.

The right man for the job?

I

This weather is appalling; I do apologise for asking you to come today but there was no option. This must be the hottest September ever. Everyone and everything is suffering under this relentless sun. We have had day after day of it with no respite.

But please, do let us get into the shade on the terrace. This is where Carlos comes to spend the afternoons following his oh so very substantial lunches.

His majesty is enjoying better health now than he has in years. Since Regla's disclosure of the presence of heretics in Valladolid a fire has been rekindled in his belly the like of which he had thought never to know again. Yes, he is a man with a mission; he is on a crusade.

Of course the long wait for information is beginning to exasperate, but he remains confident that the Grand Inquisitor Valdes and his cohorts – his fellow inquisitors I should have said – are dependable. Oh yes, one can rely on them to sniff out the merest hint of dissent, of radical or reformist thought.

So, to the reason you are here. We are to hear of the fruits of their labours.

What else? Ah yes, there has been a good deal of sickness in the area, mostly malaria. It is those infernal mosquitoes wreaking their havoc; and that damnable pond, as I said once before, is of no help, positively encouraging the beasts. His

majesty was ill with malaria for two or three days, but it was nothing of any consequence, the man seems so much stronger these days.
And here he comes.

The wheels of the king's chair rattled through the doorway of the grand salon then rumbled over the flagstones of the terrace. The chair boys positioned it close to the balustrade so that Carlos would have an uninterrupted view of the gardens below, including his beloved fish pond and the new sundial Torriano had recently completed for him.

The cat that had been standing on Carlos's lap in a high state of alarm, agitated by both the noise and the movement, now allowed itself to curl up and resume its sleep.

Gaztelu, Quijada, and Regla had a few moments wait as chairs and a table were brought from indoors.

Carlos yawned and emitted an enormous belch proclaiming his feelings of general wellbeing, "Nothing like a good rest after an excellent meal. That was probably the best roast pork I have ever tasted, and the oysters were exquisite ..."

Regla had no interest whatsoever in the lunchtime menu, eager instead to discuss the news from Valladolid, frustratingly aware he couldn't do this until after the royal siesta, therefore endless talk of food would only delay matters. However, he noted with satisfaction, Gaztelu and Quijada were too preoccupied with the papers they were arranging on the table to respond or encourage Carlos to offer further details of the various dishes that had so delighted him.

Within minutes they had settled down to their tasks, the king's chin had dropped to his chest, and Regla smiled and opened his Psalter.

At the far end of the terrace Samuel and José leaned their backs against the wall seeking some coolness in the stones, longing to slide down until they sat against it; these were long, hot days.

"God, but it was never this hot last year, was it, mate?" Samuel ran his hand around the back of his wet neck.

"Nothing like."

"Thank God we didn't have to push him down to the pond today, and then have to push him all the way back up again."

310

"Tell you what I'd love to do Sam; I'd love to take off all me clothes and jump into that fish pond right this minute."

"Me too, my tunic's fair stuck to me. And there's the king with that eiderdown tucked round him, that great big cat on his knees, saying as how he's quite comfy."

"Well, Sam, didn't you notice his hands when we was helping him into his chair? Bloody freezing they were."

"I did; and his fingers looked ready to burst through their shiny skins; like bloody great purple sausages they are."

"That's as may be, Sam, but we was talkin' about him and how cold he feels when we touches him."

"Aye, and after all them hot baths he keeps on havin'; you would think they would make him warm enough."

"The only hot thing about him is his temper, really gets himself goin' about them Lutheran folks." He winked at Samuel, "Tell you what; I'd rather listen to that parrot goin' on about them. Now that was entertainin'. What a laugh! What I wouldn't give to hear them stories again!"

"Better'n all that serious stuff what's goin' to come from down there, eh?" Samuel glanced down the terrace to the four men so still and silent, "They could be one of them pictures in the grand salon."

Insects buzzed, a few birds offered short, lazy songs; occasionally Carlos snored, papers were gently shuffled. For more than an hour time stood still.

II

Doctor Mathys hovered in the doorway, not wishing to disturb the king's rest, the only advice of his that Carlos had decided to follow; to always rest with your feet up after a meal. And there was no doubting that the meal would have been a substantial one. He didn't have long to wait.

Carlos yawned and rubbed at his eyes. "God, but I have a terrible thirst; beer, quickly!"

Quijada brought a goblet and held it to the king's lips, Carlos's almost useless hands resting on his as if to help guide the vessel.

"Blasted useless fingers, Quijada, what are we to do with them?"

Doctor Mathys now approached them, "Quite simply, my lord, you should heed my instructions instead of ignoring them."

"Ah! So you are back, then, and how is my friend Oropesa?"

"Recovering well, my lord."

"And so he should. He is recovering well because I sent you to him. Malaria is the only bloody thing you are any good at!"

Quijada shook his head and tut-tutted.

Doctor Mathys ignored yet another of the king's insults. "I have a letter from the Duque de Oropesa."

"Yes, good, give it to Gaztelu, he can read it later. First I want to hear the good news from Valladolid. Get me some more beer for this thirst."

Regla clutched his Psalter to his breast. "You are so right, your majesty, I do indeed have good news for you. News to gladden your heart, your very soul. Canon Ponce has been detained by the Inquisition in Seville."

"Ponce? Ponce? But damn it man, I chose him as canon. What the devil has he been up to?"

"Reading and espousing the works of Luther and Calvin!" Regla's face contorted in pained anguish at the full horror of it all.

Quijada, ever the sceptic, asked, "The books were in his possession?"

"No; he had given them to a family friend to hide. You see the deviousness of the enemy, my lord!"

Quijada would not be deterred, "And the friend surrendered the books?"

"No; the friend did not!" Regla's smile was pure triumph. "It was her son who delivered them in person to the Inquisitor, denouncing his mother for her heresy!"

Quijada threw up his arms in despair, looking at Gaztelu and receiving his full support. He turned to Carlos, "Sire, did I not warn you that there would be those waiting for such an opportunity to further their own cause. I have no doubt the son in question was too impatient to wait for his inheritance."

"Silence, Quijada!" Carlos snapped back. "I will have none of it! Ponce, a man I trusted, has betrayed the Faith; that is

312

enough for me! He must go to the stake; an example must be made. Any other news?"

"In Valladolid an even greater catch has been landed, all arrested at a meeting called by their leader, Cazalla." His words came slowly, deliberately, as he savoured every one; he revelled in the joy of reporting the downfall of someone he had never liked and had recently grown to hate.

"Give me strength! Another of my personal choices, returning my trust with treachery! At great cost to my health I have spent my life fighting God's enemies; the infidel and the Lutherans. Finally I come here to Spain to retire in a country where God's word was sacred; and what do I find? I find that the bastards have followed me here!"

Quijada made another effort, "This all sounds so much worse than it is; a gross exaggeration of the facts. Regla is talking about a mere handful of reformers, nothing more. Moderation is called for, some time given to considering ..."

"Be quiet! I was too lenient with Luther, should have had him burnt; that was where I went wrong. But I will show the way now, by God I will. Spain will lead the world by example." He shuffled restlessly in his chair, his words degenerated to a garbled babble, his face purple with fury, "The heretics shall burn and the news will spread throughout Europe. Yes, this is more like it; nipping the damned worm in the bud before any further damage can be done!" Now he could compensate for his weakness in the past, his lack of resolve. God would be avenged. "Gaztelu, you will write to the regent and to King Felipe informing them of our good news. Valdes is proving himself an excellent and rigorous Inquisitor. Finally got the right man!"

A frantic chorus of birdsong shattered the uneasy silence. Birds wheeled and darted in frenetic flights across the garden before disappearing into the trees where, for the first time in weeks, branches began to stir and leaves trembled. A cool breeze made its way along the terrace brushing past the chair boys.

"There's that bleedin' draft again José. Now don't you go sayin' as 'ow you never noticed."

"Course I bleedin' noticed you daft beggar. There's a storm brewing. Just look up that hill. All the same the breeze is nice and welcome." He leaned forward freeing his neck from his sweaty tunic, enjoying the tingling chill across his skin.

Threatening black clouds eerily tinged with orange tumbled over the crest of the hills quickly enveloping the once blue skies. The breeze became a whirlwind. Petals and leaves scurried along the terrace, innocent vanquished victims fleeing the enemy, finding a moment's refuge beside a chair leg or pillar before racing off again in a frenzy.

Daylight was gone, the afternoon now as black as midnight. A jagged fork of lightning ripped down through the darkness plunging into the oak woods, followed by a resounding clap of thunder. Huge dark spots of coin–sized rain splattered onto the balustrade, splashing onto the terrace.

Samuel and José were behind the royal chair immediately, pushing Carlos indoors, as concerned for their own lives as much as that of the king.

"Jesus wept!" Samuel flinched and ducked to avoid a series of deafening thunder claps determined to bombard the very palace itself. With a yowl of fear the cat was gone, presumably to find sanctuary in the king's bed.

Carlos bellowed, "Good God, I am freezing; more blankets, more blankets and a hot bath."

Quijada and Gaztelu had hurriedly gathered their papers and followed the king indoors. The terrace had turned cold and wet, and Regla, last to leave, looked up to the heavens earnestly crossing himself.

The grand salon was too dark and candles had to be lit. Blankets were brought and arranged over the king's shoulders and knees.

A howl from Carlos wrested everyone's attention from the storm. "Mathys get me something for my head. God I have never had pain like this." He held his hands first to his forehead then to his temples and howled like a tormented beast.

Samuel and José at their usual place by the door were more concerned about the life-threatening events outdoors, not convinced they were out of harm's way.

"Sam, just look at that rain, you can't see through it."

"You look at it; I'd rather not thanks."

314

The room was suddenly illuminated by an intense light, followed by yet more brilliant flashes; thunder hurtled and bounced its way through the garden and Yuste seemed to be drowning under a torrential downpour.

"Shit, I'm scared, José!"

"You've every right to be Sam; I've never known God be as angry as this. Trust me somethin' pretty bad is about to happen."

September

Departures

I

I am afraid the king is ill; gravely ill. You will remember the day it started, two weeks ago, when he came out here on the terrace to sit in the benign shade following a very fine lunch.

It had been a day apparently no different from the rest until after the excitement of the Inquisition news, and then, of course, there was the thunderstorm, and suddenly he was complaining of the intense cold and unbearable headaches. Later that evening he became uncomfortably hot; and then the vomiting started. The heat of his body aggravated the sores on his arms and legs. They itched and burned so much so that he insisted on the windows in his bedchamber being left open throughout the night.

How often have I mentioned those infernal mosquitoes? Of course I could be wrong; it might possibly be a recurrence of his old malarial fevers. Whatever the cause he could find no comfort.

As the days and sleepless nights have passed so his chronic migraines have grown increasingly violent.

The old Spanish remedy was decided upon; daily bloodletting. The poor man, fourteen ounces in one day! That is a lot of blood for a fit man to lose never mind someone as weak as Carlos.

He is aware that this illness is different from the others and he insists on having a small portrait of his wife at his bedside and, more ominously, a sketch for *La Gloria*. You will remember it is the painting over the altar.

Several days ago letters were hurriedly despatched to Valladolid. Doctor Mathys wanted the regent's doctor to come to assist, realising by this time his own limitations. His meagre repertoire of purges and bleedings, the recommendation that the patient wear various rings and bracelets of gold with coloured stones or bones and even some with gall stones with their supposed healing qualities was quite exhausted and, unfortunately, found totally ineffective.

What else has happened? Quijada has written requesting that Gaztelu be made notary for the king, for there have been times when Carlos has been unable to speak, in fact there have been periods when all his faculties have completely failed him.

Quijada has moved back into his rooms here to be on hand for any situation which might arise, and Oropesa and Zuñiga are constant visitors.

The king has been in a profound sleep, lasting more than twenty-four hours, making everyone fear that the end had come. However he awoke this morning much to their relief. But you must prepare yourself. His majesty is dying, that is beyond doubt, and Death will not be kept waiting much longer.

Ah, I hear riders.

Alonso and Manuel, whose hearing had become remarkably acute over the last few days, constantly on the alert, waiting, ran from the stables.

"This'll be them two from Jarandilla again. They must be making one heck of a deep furrow between here and there with all the comings and goings."

Two mules picked their way slowly and daintily over the cobbles as if fearful of dislodging the smallest of stones and shattering the silence. They brought their riders, Oropesa and ZuZiga, to the receiving hands of the stable lads. As the two gentlemen made their studied progress from saddle to ground there was a sudden thundering of hooves. Everyone stopped and turned shocked and annoyed at the noisy, untimely intrusion.

It was a messenger bearing the coat of arms of the regent. He slung himself from his sweating horse almost before it had halted, bellowing, "Where do I go, lads?"

"Straight up that ramp, sir. There, see, someone's at the door," Manuel pointed, standing well clear of stamping hooves and thrashing flanks.

The stranger raced towards the porch, drawing off his gloves, wiping around his streaming eyes, rubbing away caked on dust.

We shall join the messenger. He is on his way to the large salon to meet Quijada and Gaztelu; as you can see our two visitors will take a little longer to get there.

"Sirs, I have messages from the regent," he said breathlessly, unbuckling his pouch and handing over three letters bearing Princess Juana's seal.

"We thank you. I suggest you find some refreshment quickly, for we need you to return to Valladolid as soon as possible." Quijada beckoned to Maria, "Show the gentleman where to go."

He opened the first letter, "What have we here? Ah, Gaztelu, we along with Regla have been appointed executors." He laughed a short, harsh laugh. "Not that the regent has left us very much to do, having taken everything out of our hands."

318

Gaztelu took the paper, read it and placed it in a folder already bulging with the myriad of directives that had been received from Princess Juana.

Quijada scanned the second letter. "You can put this somewhere, too. Anywhere, so long as it is out of my sight. This is a copy of a letter from Felipe agreeing wholeheartedly with his father's treatment of heretics. If only the whole wretched business could have been avoided; have you noticed how Regla is becoming bloated with self-righteousness? Dear, oh dear, oh dear, where will it all lead?"

Quijada dropped the offending missive onto the table, inspecting his hands to ensure nothing foul remained. "This last one," he tore the paper free from its seal, "Dear God in Heaven! Well, his majesty will most certainly not be told of this."

Gaztelu reached for it then positioned his spectacles on the tip of his nose. "This is too dreadful to contemplate."

It was a report of a bloody massacre, telling how the Governor of Oran and all his men had been hacked to pieces by the Turk. "What in the world made Juana send this? She surely never intended that her father should know? Strange lady, she does make some odd decisions at times."

He looked up as Oropesa and ZuZiga entered, set his spectacles down and refolded the despatch.

"Any change?" They asked, hoping against hope that this time they might hear something encouraging, something optimistic.

"The king has awoken from his slumbers," Quijada replied, quickly adding lest they took heart, "I have written to the regent's secretary explaining the situation. Here, please read it."

ZuZiga held Quijada's letter close squinting at the fine but feint writing,

"The doctors told me that the king's illness was worse and that every hour his pulse was growing weaker. I still cannot believe that he could be so near his end. It breaks my heart. I suppose the doctors know best. I have served my master for nearly forty years, and am now about to lose him forever. May it please God to take him

319

if he must go; but it cannot be tonight. God be with him and with us all."

Zuñiga returned the letter then clasped his shoulder, "Amen to that, Quijada. This must be more difficult for you than for the rest of us, my friend."

"It is certainly the heaviest burden I have known in many a year. But you must go to his majesty. I shall join you shortly."

Quijada folded the letter, sealed it then called for Samuel and José, "This letter is for the messenger. I want you to go to the stables, tell the lads you need a fresh horse for the messenger, a horse litter, and two mules for yourselves. You will travel with the messenger as far as Jarandilla where you will be joined by guards to protect you on your journey to Valladolid."

The chair boys shot surprised glances at each other.

"Once you have given your instructions to Pepe go for your belongings, lads." He patted them on their shoulders, struggling to maintain his dignity, struggling not to weep. "So, the time has come. Your work here is finished; there is only this last duty. When you have collected everything come back here for this revolting bird. You are to put it in the litter and ride alongside it to Valladolid to ensure its safe journey to the regent." His voice hardened, "Her orders are that everything, absolutely everything, belonging to the king is to be transferred into her ownership!"

His anger helped him overcome his desperate sadness. In fact he felt more than anger towards Princess Juana; she had even turned down her own doctor's simple request for one, just one, of the king's countless mules. As if one less would make such a difference to her stables! "If she wants everything she can have everything; it is most unfortunate that the damned cat has gone missing or it could go too! However, it is still of comfort to know that the parrot is going to a good home. And if it should say anything offensive, which we can rest assured it will, why then she can cook the blasted thing!"

Samuel and José glanced at each other again taken aback by Quijada's outburst, but then quickly turning their thoughts to that wonderful day on the terrace when the king and the bird had entertained them. Now, unbelievably, here was a glorious opportunity for more excitement, and days of it too.

320

"And if you have nothing better to do on your way there I am certain you would have no objections to lifting the cover of the cage and having a little chat yourselves. And who would blame you?" Quijada gave them a weak smile and patted their shoulders again. "Go then, lads. Take care on your journey, keep your purses safe and try not to spend all of your money. I thank you for your services to his majesty; your work here has been greatly appreciated. After Valladolid return immediately to Jarandilla; work hard for Oropesa your new master and do take care about your whisperings. God bless you both."

José cleared his throat, "Sir I know it's not me place but may we say thanks, sir, for puttin' in a good word for us, sir? We does realise how important it was, sir, you getting us this new job. And, well; thanks and, well, we'll miss you, you've been like a …"

Samuel broke in, "It's been like family it has."

Quijada nodded, "Yes, quite, now off you go." He turned and made his way to the bedchamber.

Nor should we delay any longer. Best to follow Quijada and stay as close as we can to him. There is no easy way to prepare you for what you will find in the royal bedchamber; Death, you understand, knows no etiquette, pays court to no man, defers to none.

II

The bed chamber was dark and oppressive, the black wall hangings and black velvet bed curtains looking thicker and heavier than ever. What little air there was to breathe was foul and disgusting. Crowded into the tiny space were thirty priests chanting from the Psalms. The doctors, friends and companions and his confessor were all there too. The combination of body odours, candle wax, the king's vomit and diarrhoea filled every part of the room weighing heavy, overwhelming.

Carlos opened his eyes sensing his friend Quijada had arrived and managed a weak smile of greeting. He stirred, beckoning him to his side, asking to be raised. Quijada and

Gaztelu lifted him gently while Male placed several pillows at his back.

"Better ... tell them go ... private ..."

Quijada motioned to the others to move away from the bed.

In a barely audible whisper of only partly completed words Carlos sought reassurance from his major-domo regarding his wishes for the future placements of his staff.

Quijada put his master's heart and mind at rest assuring him that everything had been dealt with: some were to return to the Netherlands; others would pass into the service of Carlos's friends, or the regent; or, like himself some would retire to the privacy of their own homes.

Images took him by surprise, the familiar sights and sounds of Villagarcía, the comfort of his own special chair, his bed; but these would be bought at such a heavy price.

Finally he was able to tell Carlos that even the lowliest of the servants had been found positions.

Carlos nodded his thanks then tugged at his friend's collar. "About my son Juan; you have the letter? Felipe to recognise him as my son, accepts him as his half-brother; but not a prince. Felipe to grant him title, His Excellency Don Juan of Austria. You and DoZa Magdalena to be the boy's parents until he is of age."

Quijada was overcome with emotion to hear once again what would soon be made public; the recognition of Juan as the king's love child.

"The letter is safe."

"Got to look after the boy's mother, too; purse in the box for Barbara. Her pension. A few hundred *ducados* a year. I give her permission to come to Spain. She would be treated well."

"Everything will be done according to your wishes, my lord." He hoped against hope that Barbara would not show the least inclination to come to Spain. He would much rather she remained where she was, in Germany, while he paid her bills when required; knowing full well she would never be able to restrict herself to this pension, generous though it was. But he didn't want to hear of these bequests; they spoke too brutally of the finality of it all.

"Bring my mother's mortal remains from Tordesillas. They should be interred here."

322

Quijada made no reply; his guilt pained him. Carlos could well be suffering qualms of conscience and all because of him. Why had he been so persistent in probing? Why had he not stuck to his philosophy of committing past events to the past? He waited, praying that Carlos would not repeat his request.

"Bury me here. Bring my Isabel, to be laid at my side."

Quijada gently shook his head, "When I said everything would be done according to your wishes, that was not included. Sire, your beautiful Empress? This place is simply not good enough for her. Granada is far more suitable and, remember, that was where you spent the happiest days together."

Carlos nodded, "You are right. You always are," he smiled at his friend. "Felipe will arrange. But these monks here will get a bloody shock if he decides not to let them keep my bones here!" He tried to laugh but could only cough; his throat was too tight and constricted. "Picture of Isabel," he held out his hand for the miniature. "I was the richest man on earth. ... You talk ... not possible ... tell me about my Isabel."

"Your beautiful Portuguese cousin Isabel, who came to Spain to become your wife. Unbelievably you kept her waiting in Seville for five whole days! She was a princess worth a fortune, a lady who was an invaluable treasure herself, outshining all her magnificent jewels. Had you only known what kind of bride awaited you, you would never have wasted those days negotiating a treaty with King Francis."

"She was God's greatest gift to me."

"And you presented yourself to her looking more like a courier than a king, dust and sweat from head to toe. But you soon dashed off to bathe and change; a flurry of embarrassment as I recall. Within hours this precious being became your wife. How fortunate you were; not only was she beautiful, she was intelligent, witty and exceedingly wise. And she had such a wealth of love for you and your children."

"I never expected to love my wife, just not done, yet I loved her as I never loved before. I never betrayed her."

"No, my lord, you never betrayed your wife. She was everything to you: your wife, the mother of your children, ruler of your country in your absence, your friend, and the love of your life."

They both wept for a truly remarkable lady so prematurely and cruelly taken from this world.

You have seen the portrait of Isabel; undeniably beautiful with her fair hair and those almond eyes. She was sensitive and tender but also strong and firm. With the frequent absences of Carlos she had to be both mother and father to her little family. Three sons were born to Isabel and Carlos, but only Felipe survived infancy. You have heard of course of the daughters, especially the Regent, Princess Juana. Three children from seven pregnancies. And then she died; within hours of an aborted still-born, the impatient midwife hurriedly tearing the babe from the mother's womb, wrenching away any hope of Isabel's recovery.

"A lady."

"So she was, my lord."

"Never allowed anyone to see how she suffered in childbirth, always covered her face with a handkerchief. Dear God how I loved her; no one like her in the world; royal through and through." He paused, exhausted.

And she loved him as dearly. Every time he left for one of his military campaigns she would say that his swift return would bring happiness to this land, but above all, to her. And during those absences, amounting to about half of their thirteen years of marriage, she proved herself an excellent regent. The Spanish people loved her, respected her, and they rejoiced because she provided them with their first Spanish heir.

"The chapel in Madrid … San Isidro … saved her life."

Quijada smudged at the tears on his cheeks, "Indeed. I remember how it seemed inevitable that both Isabel and the

324

young Felipe would die of malaria, but she had heard of the saint's miracles, especially the one about how he had saved his own two children from drowning in a well. She sent servants to fetch water from the very well; she and Felipe drank some and were immediately cured."

"A devout Catholic; made sure the children spent a good deal of time at their devotions. The world needs more like her …" Carlos gazed lovingly at the cameo portrait of his beloved wife. "Oh Isabel, I want to be with you. I am tired and lonely. Quijada tell Regla. Confess …" Carlos closed his eyes, unable to continue.

I must tell you of one of the most touching pieces she ever penned. "I kiss this sheet of paper with the same warmth and tenderness with which I would kiss your lips if I were with you."

Everyone mourned her passing, and they mourned for Carlos's great loss. There was a lament often heard being sung throughout the whole of Spain:

'Carlos, why do you weep for Isabel
And why do you still seek her?
She is not dead, she is well
She is now the bride of our Maker.'

And Carlos is soon to join her in Paradise.

Regla came to the bedside. "I am ready, my lord."

"Pray, father, bless me, for I have sinned in thought, word, and deed …"

"The Lord be in thy heart and on thy lips, that thou mayest truly and humbly confess thy sins …"

At this point we will withdraw. Confession is a private matter.
This would be an ideal opportunity to see what is happening at the stables.

325

III

Maria and Alonso were standing by the stable wall having a serious conversation.

Alonso concluded his frank observations on Maria's recent attitude towards him by tempering his comments with some indulgent words, "You see, Maria, too many good things happened to you, too quick, like. You just got your head turned. Like as not it's because you're young."

"And you still spoke up for me, in spite of everything."

"I did. It seemed only right."

"So it was lucky for me that Don Quijada has decided to take me on, then?" Maria nervously smoothed her white apron.

Quijada had taken no persuading whatsoever. In fact it was Quijada who had asked Alonso if by offering Maria a position it might create an awkward situation knowing how their relationship had changed. But Alonso saw no reason for telling Maria this, far better for him to take the credit.

He leaned protectively over her, as he had throughout their lengthy chat about Maria's expectations and disappointments, one large calloused hand resting against the rough stones the other gently on her shoulder. "Too right you're lucky, if you thinks about what I've been telling you."

"And DoZa Magdalena is lovely, isn't she? I expect she'll be really nice to work for; you know, kind and helpful."

"I expect so but, by God, she won't stand no nonsense neither; can be fearsome strict."

Maria then asked the big question that had to be asked; the main reason she was standing there, "And we'd be together again, just like before? I never did anything with that Miguel, you know. We never even touched hands."

"That's as it should be. Yeh; I reckon we probably can get back together."

He knew that at last he had got her back, she was his again, and he thanked his lucky stars; but from now on he would decide each and every step they took, she took, before he married her. He would be master.

"Well, that's alright then." But it struck her that he had only said probably, leaving a worrying doubt. "I was scared you might have found someone else."

He took his time before answering, "As a matter of fact, no, there's no one else. Now I think you'd best be getting back or you'll have Madame Male after you."

"You're right. Well, I'll be off then." She held her bonny face with its full, sensual lips up to him; but there was no kiss, only his friendly smile as he turned to go into the tack room.

Manuel looked up at Alonso as he whistled his way to join him at the table. "I'm sat sitting here still thinking of our good luck, eh, Alonso? Can't get over it; could've done a damned sight worse." He put down his cloth; resting his hand, stretching cramped fingers, gazing at the remaining lengths of leather reins and traces still awaiting his attention.

"You're right. We could've been sent to Jarandilla. Can you imagine that, with them pompous bastards that used to come galloping in here like they owned the bloody place? Mind you any job's better than none. But, like, we knows Quijada, known him years, know how to work for him, what pleases him."

"And from what we've heard his castle at Villagarcía is a damned sight better than here," he picked up the waxing rag and resumed his polishing. "And what about Maria, what she 'ave to say about goin' there? I thought as how she might be wantin' to go to Jarandilla."

"I tell you she can't be thankful enough."

"She upset still about that rider and her not getting to go with him for the *noche de San Juan*? Couldn't have come to anything, them two, could it?"

"Manuel, them lot's too fancy for her, I mean just look at the way they treated us. I'll tell you, like I told her, not being nasty nor anything but just the way I sees it, what exactly would have happened. You've seen or heard it all, mate. I said to her that if she had gone out with him that night it would've meant his havin' his way with her, and then not botherin' no more. She'll soon forget him. But, more important than her missin' out on her big night out, she was worried sick about the king probably dying an' all and her havin' no place to go; and she couldn't face the thought of goin' back to her folks, even supposin' they would want another mouth to feed. Said she could always get a job in a tavern. She has this picture of

327

herself in that bleedin' white apron of hers servin' gents like the ones she's served here. I had to put her straight on that. Them gents in the tavern, I pointed out, would be all for draggin' her out into the back yard and up against the wall in amongst the stinkin' heaps of rubbish, other fellers watchin' when they came out to piss and fart, yellin' filthy things. Am I right?"

"Yeh. Dead right. Then she'd get thrown out cos she was goin' to have a kid."

"Anyway this job at Villagarcía came up, and when I told her about it I laid it on a bit thick as 'ow I'd got her the job."

"You beggar!"

"You got to know the best way to play this game, Manuel. Anyway, it's turning out just right. She sees I'm her best chance for a husband. Mind you, she's lucky I'll still have her; I was fair put out with the way she was carrying on there for a while. So, as I say, I guess we'll end up at the church door." He picked up a halter he had been working on and walked down the room.

"I hope as 'ow you ask me to be a witness. Hey, you'll have to get her some bonny ribbons for her dress, like the ones she fancied for the *noche de San Juan!*"

"Won't hear no more of that, right?" Alonso called sharply over his shoulder. "What's past is past and best forgotten, unless it's me what's doing the rememberin'. Anyway, more to the point as they say, I wonder 'ow long it'll be before we goes to our new place? Sam and José says as they've never known the king be so sick. They've had nowt to do for days and days; just hanging about," he continued, hanging up the halter at the end of a steadily growing row of newly burnished harnesses. "All smart and tidy like soldiers you lot are." He scanned the ranks of collars, halters, cruppers, all arranged with military precision, wondering how many more times he would be doing this job in these stables.

"I think it's the first time he's been in his bed all the time, so he must be pretty bad. And then, what about all them visitors? Aye, it probably is the beginning of the end. And 'im so chirpy after that young Juan came. A bleedin' shame."

"What I says is, Manuel, you never knows when your time's up," Alonso reached for a crupper and slowly wiped it with a fresh cloth. "See, who's to say this isn't the last time we does this?"

José and Samuel ran in as if being chased by the devil. "Where's Pepe?" José panted. "Quijada wants mules and horses and the litter!"

Pepe bustled proudly into the tack room. He had been overseeing the work in the stall where the messenger's horse was soon to be tethered. It was his responsibility that everything was perfect for a horse belonging to the regent who would, before too long, be his new mistress. He wanted his reputation to go before him. "What can we do for you lads? I take it this is not a social visit?"

"We need a horse litter, a fresh horse for the messenger and a couple of mules for Sam and me."

"Don't tell me you're going already?" Alonso asked for all of them. But they all knew the answer and the reason. The reality, the finality of it all, engulfed them.

"I guess it's just about all over for the king. We're off to Valladolid with the parrot and then to Jarandilla."

Alonso, Manuel and Pepe accompanied the chair boys out to the courtyard.

"Well, best of luck mates!" They exchanged hugs and claps on the shoulders.

"Enough of that now, there's work to be done. Horses? Remember? Come on, let's be havin' you." Pepe turned quickly and walked off to secretly wipe away the tears.

Saying farewell is difficult enough without there being a sad reason for it such as this. Shall we return to the bed chamber?

IV

Confession over, Regla told Quijada he would return in a few moments with the consecrated bread.

"My lord, I strongly advise you not to do this," Quijada whispered to Carlos.

Carlos wheezed, "Good provision for my long journey."

"Your throat, my lord. You may be unable to swallow."

"I shall be able, I know."

329

As the confessor left the room via the short flight of steps up into the church, the door to the bedchamber was opened to admit another priest who rushed to the king's side, knelt, and kissed his hand.

This will put some cheer into the king's heart. This is the Dominican Carranza, The Black Friar of London; the recently appointed Archbishop of Toledo, Primate of Spain. King Felipe has rewarded him with this appointment because of his many years of devoted service.

"Your majesty I have only just returned from Brussels, from King Felipe, who is in good health. I was on my way to Toledo when I heard you were ill."

Carlos smiled his welcome. He knew of the archbishop's tireless efforts to save the souls of the English heretics. "Welcome, welcome, archbishop. Read to me; read, *Out of the depths to Thee I have cried ...*"

Carranza read Psalm 130,
> "*... Let Isreal hope in the Lord:*
> *For with the Lord there is mercy,*
> *And with him is plenteous redemption.*
> *And he shall redeem Israel*
> *From all his iniquities.*"

Then holding up his crucifix he announced clearly and firmly, "Behold Him who answers for all. There is no more sin. All is forgiven."

Regla, who had returned with the consecrated bread stood at the top of the steps in disbelief, consumed with loathing. He forced his feet to bring him down the steps and across the room to Carranza's side to hiss in his ear, "Our master, King Carlos, has spent his whole life fighting for the True Faith; yet you dare come here, into this room!" The hiss became a snarl, "Valdes has told me of you and Ortiz and Cazalla; daring to discuss Purgatory; suggesting that through Christ's death man might be cleansed of venial sin. Whatever you may have done to rid England of heretics I say you offend our Church with your scandalous writings. Get away from here and take your stinking ideas with you. It is the likes of you that will destroy our Church. Let me remind you that contrary to what you think the world *is* full of sin and it behoves us, each and every one, to make atonement before we come to meet our God. Go! Get out of here!"

Zuñiga, who along with others whose curiosity had drawn them to Regla's side, ventured supportive mumblings.

Quijada held his hands over his face; this was neither the time nor the place for this; his beloved king and friend was dying, for pity's sake!

Archbishop Carranza spoke quietly, "I did not come here to argue the scriptures or doctrine or anything else. I came here because of my concerns for the king's health." He retired into the shadows, but would not leave.

Moans from Carlos reminded Regla of the reason for his being at the royal bedside. Regla summoned Mathys, "Doctor, ensure that the king's throat is clear."

Doctor Mathys opened the king's mouth, and inserting a finger cleared away the phlegm that threatened to obstruct.

They all bowed their heads as Carlos received the Body of Christ. "Lord God of Truth, our Redeemer, into Thy hands I commit my spirit."

After a few moments Quijada checked to see that no bread remained. To his great relief his fears were unfounded. He crossed himself, thanking God.

Fouled linens were carefully removed from the bed and replaced with fresh ones. Carlos was gently bathed and dressed in a clean nightshift.

The hours passed slowly, heavily. The priests continued their doleful chanting of the Psalms; others in the room found themselves doing what most do when in the presence of someone they know is dying, whispering remembered tales of long ago, when they were all in their prime.

At some time after midnight the king held his left wrist, tugged at Quijada's sleeve, "The pulse, weaker. Candles."

The large candles, brought specifically for this moment from the Monastery of Our Lady of Montserrat, were lit and placed at the four corners of the king's bed.

Regla held the crucifix close to Carlos, "Your majesty came into the world on San Matías' day and will leave on San

Mateo's day. With these two intercessors, you will have nothing to fear." He hoped Carranza was taking note heeding the fact that all men are sinners and that the help of these two saints would assist Carlos during the time that God would allot for his cleansing and preparation to become pure and holy enough to see Him. "Let your heart turn with confidence to God, who will this day take you to Himself."

Carlos checked his pulse once more and shook his head. He signed to Quijada that he wished the taper to be lighted. For a moment he held his crucifix next to his heart. It was Isabel's crucifix, the crucifix she had held in her final moments. He motioned for Regla to take it from him. Quijada supported his master and placed the taper in his hands.

"Now it is time," whispered Carlos. The flickering taper was removed. Carlos leaned towards the crucifix to kiss the feet of Christ. "Ah, Jesus." With a sigh he dropped back into the arms of Quijada who gently lowered him onto his pillows.

Quijada fell forward sobbing on the bosom of his king, his friend, his 'brother', who was gone from him forever.

The king is dead.

The man who for many was generous, was regarded by others as selfish. The man who was loved, was also reviled. The man who was hailed as the mightiest and noblest Christian emperor since Charlemagne, was detested by some as the greediest, most vainglorious of tyrants. The man who loved so passionately and generously, hated many and was the author of despicable acts of brutality. The man who considered himself as a man of high ideals, was judged by others a shameless schemer. The man who saw himself as fair and open-minded, was regarded by others as a bigot whose heart and mind were filled with ignorant prejudices. The man who considered himself a mighty ruler, was judged by others as incompetent.

332

What motivated Carlos; was it pride in country, empire, the True Faith, himself, the Hapsburg Dynasty?
I will leave you with that question.

A Return to Yuste

Welcome to Yuste once more. It is quite unbelievable that it is more than four hundred years since I greeted you with those very same words.

What a beautiful October day. I do enjoy the freshness of the early morning.

Ah, I see you find it quite amazing that everything appears unchanged after four centuries.

That is the reason for my invitation. Despite what your eyes seem to be telling you this is not the Yuste of old but an exceptional and faithful restoration that strictly adhered to the plans lodged in the National Archives in Simancas. The work began in 1941 and took fully seventeen years to complete. It might not have taken quite so long had there been some decent roads in the area; however there were none which meant that all materials and equipment had to be brought here using horses and mules over roadways little better than those travelled by our friends in the past. And money was scarce, too; remember Spain was in the process of recovering from the Civil War.

As I was saying, despite all obstacles and inconveniences the restoration was completed by 1958.

The best way to approach Yuste without doubt is on foot from Cuacos, sauntering up the winding road, as so many have done before; perhaps pausing to pick wild oregano, or to pass the time of day with an elderly local on his mule as he leisurely rides back down to the village.

Yes, indeed you are right, one must first get to Cuacos, but that is no problem these days as it is only twenty-eight miles from Plasencia; less than an hour by car.

But I digress. Shall we go up the ramp and sit on the wall where Quijada and Gaztelu once rested and chatted?

May I draw your attention to the plaque on the wall;

His majesty the emperor, Don Carlos V, our lord, was sitting in this place when he was taken ill on August 31st at four in the afternoon. He died on September 21st at half past two in the morning in the year of our Lord 1558.

The first date is incorrect; no doubt Quijada would have smiled a wry smile at the monks' inaccuracy.

I mentioned the restoration, but my story must have a beginning. I shall start with King Felipe's visit here not long after the death of Carlos. The first thing he did was order the removal of the Titian painting that hung over the high alter; do you remember it?

The monks were very cross to say the least, but that was nothing compared to how they felt sixteen years later when the remains of Carlos were taken to El Escorial. Their removal meant that the monks had lost status. Felipe tried to make amends by giving the monastery the title of the Royal Monastery of Yuste and presenting them with a copy of Titian's painting of *La Gloria* to hang over the altar, but there is no doubting they were deeply hurt by what they considered a humiliation.

And why did Felipe make such a decision? Do you recall his letter after the Spanish victory at the battle of Saint-Quentin? In it he promised to build a church and dedicate it to San Lorenzo, since it was on his day that the battle was won. I can tell you that he built something rather more than a church. He built a huge monastery and palace providing what he considered a worthy tomb for his father. Over the years it became the family vault.

The small mountain town of El Escorial is within a reasonable distance of Madrid, close enough that Felipe could watch the monastery's progress through his telescope from the royal palace.

It seemed an ideal site having fresh, clean and fast-flowing streams, and a plentiful supply of all the necessary building materials. I should point out that it is a rather bleak and windswept place and that it owes its name to the 'scoria', the slag from the smelting process at the long worked out iron mines.

Having said that, I do recommend a visit to the Royal Monastery of San Lorenzo at El Escorial.

Did you know that San Lorenzo was a third century martyr? Oh yes, he was a Spanish deacon in Rome, who, having refused to hand over the treasures of the church to Valerian when Pope Sixtus was taken prisoner was then himself taken prisoner, placed on a gridiron and burnt to death. It is said that the monastery/palace is based on the shape of a gridiron.

Legend has it that San Lorenzo said that as soon as he had turned golden brown then he was thoroughly cooked!

But as usual I digress; there seems to be no cure for it.

Getting back to Yuste; the monastery here continued under royal patronage, the palace unused but well guarded, and life went on uninterrupted with only the rarest of visits from anyone. I suppose one might say it slipped into obscurity.

And then it happened! In August 1809. You know of the Peninsular Wars, of Napoleon's invasion of Spain? I will confine myself to but a small part of that whole despicable period, only that part which involved Yuste.

Some French dragoons fleeing the battlefield at Talavera, about twenty or so miles from here, broke into the monastery and palace. They brutalised the monks, committed sacrileges and profaned the church. It is all too appalling to contemplate.

They remained here, unwanted guests wining and dining, their numbers gradually increasing until finally their commander arrived. Then they left, except for a few who were far too drunk to move. Some locals were not long in seizing the opportunity. They set about the soldiers who were too far gone in their drunken stupor to retaliate. Not one Frenchman survived.

Shortly thereafter a small detachment of French cavalry arrived to round up their lazy, malingering compatriots and of course discovered their bodies.

What did they do? They ransacked everything: church, cloisters, monks' cells, palace; having done that they set fire to it all. For eight days the fires raged.

Over the years nature completed the devastation. Where charred beams and roofs had collapsed weeds and shrubs

337

flourished. Ivy strangled the broken pillars whose capitals lay scattered like fallen warriors, a growing blanket of wild flowers intent upon concealing the tragedy. The waters that Torriano had channelled to feed the fountains raced freely and randomly on their ways undermining any structures in their path. The ornamental patio gardens with their trimmed box hedges became forests. Flora and fauna held a free rein.

By 1941 you would not have recognised the heaps of overgrown rubble as what I had described, those many years ago, as a 'veritable jewel nestling in an emerald sea of evergreen oaks and chestnuts', that idyllic gem of monastery and palace of 1557.

But cheer up, for as you can see, all was not lost! For a start the palace had not been completely destroyed, although it grieves me to tell you the purposes to which it was put. Some of the rooms on the first floor were used for drying tobacco leaves and storing grain and the Grand Salon served as a kitchen and living area. Although I always thought the rooms on the ground floor were far from commodious, it still offends one's sensitivity to know that they had become pigsties and cattle pens.

However, following years of unshakeable devotion, a sense of national pride and duty, dedicated workers brought forth this Phoenix from the ashes.

The monks then came back to the monastery.

And so it is with the greatest of joy I repeat, welcome to Yuste.

The interior has also been restored to its former glory in every detail. The archives of Simancas and the Jerónimos along with the bills of sale for items sold at the time of

Carlos's death all helped to ensure the return of the furniture, the tapestries, the paintings. The jewel is indeed shining once more in all its glory and splendour.

Shall we go inside and take a look around?

After you; our friends may no longer be there going about their duties, but with a little imagination ...

www.ingramcontent.com/pod-product-compliance
Lightning Source LLC
Chambersburg PA
CBHW061929170626
46813CB00006B/2346